Praise for Safe Houses

Gerda is a phenomenal character – pure life force. In spite of its grim theme, the book is funny and rich in imagery.

Clare Boylan

This is, in the best sense, a subversive achievement . . . It is hard to think of recent novels on this modest scale which contrive to entertain with such a bewitching diversity of resource.

Jonathan Keates, *The Observer*

Its extravagant language, clever word-play and balancing act between humour and the grotesque mark it out from other recent fiction on the theme of the Holocaust and emulate the masters of fantasy Gunter Grass and Gabriel Garcia Marquez.

Deborah Steiner, *TLS*

The extravagance and richness of Lynne Alexander's language find their fullest expression in transforming Brooklyn itself into a nightmarish fairyland, where gingergread ovens wait for innocent little girls, and the wicket flourish and fatten on *Windtorte*.

Elaine Feinstein

Safe Houses is a brilliant and disturbing novel . . .

Julian Alexander, *Literary Review*

There is nothing safe about this audacious first novel . . .

Washington Post Book World

Alexander has fashioned a work that is layered in its moral complexity, sensitive and humorous in its treatment.

San Francisco Chronical

Praise for Adolf's Revenge

Lynne Alexander's exhilaration with words carries her and the reader along . . . Angela Carter with a kinder heart plus jokes. And good ones at that.

Fay Weldon

Wonderfully fanged and fetid.   *The Independent*

Alexander's toxic narrative, full of pseudo-biblical curses, lends a rich comic patina to the proceedings.

The Sunday Times

A tale of power and manipulation that deals in raw enotions and pokes run at predictable happy endings.

The Times Weekend Saturday

Praise for Resonating Bodies

Skilfully and in the most entrancing prose, she makes the reader accept the instrument as a voluptuous woman of unfading beauty.

Miranda Seymour

Lynne Alexander, who once earned her living as a professional harpsichordist, has written a persuasive and erotic love story about a superior fiddle.

Philip Howard, *The Times*

Alexander raises questions about changing fashions in sex roles, musical style and how far art justifies the sacrifice of personal and political commitments.

Jane O'Grady, *The Sunday Times*

Part of Alexander's achievement is to show us the need for 'irrelevant' comforts in a 'hell-bent century' and to convince us that at least one half of life is fantasy.

Anna Vaux, *The TLS*

Praise for Intimate Cartographies

Lynne Alexander has chosen the most difficult of subjects, the death of a child. She has treated it with sensitivity and wit, manic levity and the utmost respect, and has created something quite haunting.

Carol Birch, Independent on Saturday

The core of this lively, dense and at times infuriating novel is Magda's relationship to her dead child, and this I found very moving indeed.

Paul Binding, The Independent on Sunday

Loved Intimate Cartographies . . . The map of grief was utterly compelling . . . the glimpses of Molly were perfect . . . Most of all, I liked the tone of the writing – sharp, witty, clever and requiring absolute attention so as not to miss a single nuance.

Margaret Forster

Also by Lynne Alexander

Fiction

Safe Houses
Resonating Bodies
Taking Heart
Adolf's Revenge
Intimate Cartographies

Poetry from hospices

Now I Can Tell
Throwaway Lines

Non-fiction
Staying Vegetarian

THE SISTER

A novel based on the life of Alice James

Lynne Alexander

SANDSTONEPRESS
HIGHLAND | SCOTLAND

First published in Great Britain 2012
Sandstone Press Ltd
PO Box 5725
One High Street
Dingwall
Ross-shire
IV15 9WJ

www.sandstonepress.com

Editor: Robert Davidson

The publisher acknowledges subsidy from
Creative Scotland towards publication of this volume.

ISBN: 978-1-905207-80-0
ISBN (e): 978-1-905207-81-7

Cover by Rebecca Pickard, Zebedee Design, Edinburgh
Typeset by Iolaire Typesetting, Newtonmore.
Printed and bound by TOTEM, Poland

'What could justify a life for Alice –
and perhaps for all the Jameses –
was not so much the living of it as the writing about it.'

Linda Anderson,
Introduction: Alice James, Her Life in Letters

'. . . her tragic health was in a manner the only solution for
her of the practical problem of life.'

Henry James, in a letter to William

'Delight becomes pictorial
When viewed through pain, – '
Emily Dickinson

I. BOSTON, USA

(1878–1884)

One

My father's curse went something like this: "I fear, my dear Alice, it is the natural inheritance of everyone capable of a spiritual life to wander alone in an unsubdued forest where the wolf howls and the birds of night chatter." Sometimes 'the unsubdued forest' became 'a clanging rookery of hell', but either way his meaning was clear. *Well thank you for that benediction, pater.*

The year is 1878 and I am about to be thirty years old. I sit at the small corner writing table with my eyes facing forward as if mesmerized. On the desk before me lies an assortment of papers which I have divided into three: (1): engraved wedding and engagement announcements from Sara Sedgwick and Annie Ashburner – the last of my single allies to desert me for the enemy; (2) a letter on onionskin from the Society to Encourage Studies at Home (signed by Katharine P. Loring); (3) a draft of an essay by my brother William entitled 'The Hidden Self'. Tucked inside it I have discovered another engraved wedding announcement: his own. I freed it from the essay and placed it among the others in pile one. My other brother Henry's newly published *nouvelle*, Daisy Miller, occupies a space of its own.

My father, meanwhile, sat at the desk in the middle of the library facing the garden. He would be thinking hard or pondering his Swedenborg, the philosopher who claimed, among other crackpot notions, that *the great toe communicates with the genitals.* Blake, who was also a follower, had done a self-portrait showing his body flung back while a flaming

3

star descends towards his left foot. I could not resist swiveling round to observe my father's foot. It waggled beneath his desk. But I must not snigger or he would ask me to recount the reason for my amusement.

"Did you speak, Alice?" he asked, without turning to look at me.

"I did not intend to," I replied, my words snapping like sticks around the hilarity that threatened to burst out.

Then I remembered William's announcement.

In my bureau upstairs was a pile of letters from William tied up with a blue ribbon: blue for clarity and hopefulness. The letters had been addressed to: *'You Lovely babe', 'Charmante Jeune Fille . . .'.*; inside they told me I was *'sweet lovely delicious'* but *'must be locked up'*. To my face he'd told me he *'longed to kiss and slap those celestial cheeks'*. What had he meant, that I should be made love to or punished, or both?

The wall before me was papered in brown with splodges like gravy spills through which he appeared smiling with his handsome face: William, brother; his voice crooning and melodious: *'Dearest little sweetlington, beloved beautlet . . . my grey-eyed doe . . . Now, can you guess what I have to tell you?'*

"What is it, William, what?" The pulse pounds in my temples quick and hot reminding me how wicked I am and deserve to be smacked and locked up &etc. 'Guess,' he says, dangling his metaphorical ball of string.

"Please, William . . .". Must I *meow*? reach out my paw?

"Kiss my hand, my little beauty."

I do as I am told.

"Now then, I have decided to do the usual thing."

I drop the kissed hand. "The usual . . .?"

"I am to be married, Alice . . . and to another Alice!" Someone it seems is slapping him on the back forcing the air out of him along with the hearty words. I'd always had a weakness for having my friends married, but my brother was a different matter. "But you promised to marry *me*,

William. You vowed, you threatened – I have the letter – if you couldn't marry me you would kill yourself." I have the evidence; I am quite rational. I go on: "You even wrote a 'sonnate' in honor of me. You sang it in the parlor, Willie, you sang:

> *Since I may not have thee,*
> *My Alice sweet, to be my wife,*
> *I'll drown me in the sea, love,*
> *I'll drown   me in   the sea!"*

"Were you serious, Willy, or simply trying to turn me into a scrambled egg?" But he does not reply. He has retreated back into the gravy spills with his intended.

Alice meet Alice.

My mother came running. "What on earth is going on in here?"

My father saw in my shaking body the proof of his prediction. He rose to announce, "I fear she has inherited my affliction: 'Tis the obscene bird of night. It has begun its chattering."

"*Chatterchatter,*" said I.

My mother held her temper. "It is not night," she told my father tightly. "It is neither a wolf nor a bat, it is your daughter Alice. She is in trouble." He shrank before her, and who should blame him. Meanwhile I had crashed to the floor dragging down books and papers, yet part of me could still make out what was going on around me. William, you see, had written about this phenomenon: The only difference between me and the insane was that while I suffered the horrors and suffering & etc. the other part of me played doctor, nurse and straight-jacket. It was very tiring.

But William's letter had contained another message:

"Let your soul grow wings, Alice," he'd written. Yes, that.

grow wings   grow wings

My poor heart feasted. And there was more:

5

"Let your voice be musical and full of caressing . . . let every movement be full of grace . . . my Alice, you have no idea how lovely you will become . . .".

Even as my teeth knocked within my silly head I felt his words rising me up. I would not need a hot-air machine however as I would soon grow wings to fly . . .

"But . . ." he'd added. I pictured him finger-in-air.

" 'But' what, William?"

"But only very short ones!"

Short wings! haha!

The ball of string had been cruelly retracted. I reached up. My nails gripped paper and tore, my arm struck out. Fury ripped through me: I will make his head roll like a ball of string! But he was not there to receive his punishment so I turned my wrath against the benignant pater with his silver locks, nearly knocking his innocent block off; and when that was foiled I tried flinging myself from the window. I panted like an animal for breath then tried to hold it until I was no more. I could not tell if I was dry or drowned but that I was sinking, my limbs making swimming motions, while over my flailing body my parents argued about what to do with me. My father was convinced it was the wolves come to get me, *wooo-hooowoh*. Well, I thought with my 'observing' brain, at least it's a change from the chattering birds of night!

There would be a struggle, Father predicted, but I would be victorious.

"And if she is not?" Mother inquired icily.

Later, my father knelt at my bedside. Clunk, came the sound of his peg-leg hitting the floor as it bent. Perhaps he will pray for me, I thought.

Suffering brings love, tenderness, forgiveness . . .

Sometime in the night I dreamed of my father as a boy heating a balloon to make it fly. Up he rises lifted by the heat of the turpentine soaked ball of tow . . . but the fire soon spreads simltaneously down to his leg and up to the silk canopy, rising above him like a great flaming sky-rose. Then, in the way of dreams, my father transforms into me with wings shrunk down to wagging stumps (*grow wings! but only short ones!*). And so I fall to earth, my head divided from my neck, my arms and legs all in a heap.

Poo-wor Alice.

William and Henry came to see me. They leant over me like a pair of bearded bookends. "I am not a book," I said, pushing them gently apart. I had no book inside me, I had been emptied out. It felt quite restful, especially in my brain; it meant I did not have to think. Besides, I'd managed to control my muscles and their murderous twitches; otherwise I might have been tempted to crack the two balding heads together like a pair of coconuts.

But Henry was saying something. "You have heard that William is to be married?" he asked gently. William looked away. I nodded, trying not to snarl like a wolf and bite his neck. *You were going to marry me.* But there was Henry saying in his smoothing-iron voice: "The future bride, we gather, is also called Alice: Alice Howe Gibbens." At this, William The Sinner bows his head. "I have been ill," he wails: "a spoilt child, an errant soul – but she will be my cure." *Oh, for goodness sake*! I long to squeeze him until all the disgusting syrup of figs runs dry and all the maudlin furniture coated in it falls out, *clunk*. Henry meanwhile wisely attends to a hangnail. William, having no idea he is being absurd, raises his head.

"She is an angel if ever there was one." *Amen.*

"Alice," I tried. *Alice meet Alice.*

But now it was Henry's turn. Henry, 'playing it' lightly, chose his moment. "What on earth," he asked, "will we call you for distinction's sake?" I was no help at all, so then he began entertaining the various possibilities himself: "William's wife could be 'Mrs William' or 'William's Alice', or even 'Mrs Alice'; while you could be 'sister Alice', or 'our Alice'." It was the only time I had known him before or since to have been less than exquisitely sensitive. But then he redeemed himself by adding warmly: "Of course you will always be 'my Alice'." Dear Henry. My mouth arranged itself, my chest rose and fell. There were more-or-less even beats within. I observed these things with interest but felt nothing. My mother came up behind Henry, ever her favorite, and laying a hand lightly on his shoulder peered down at me. Then I heard her say – having somehow managed to wipe from her mind all of the previous scene: "Is she not the sweetest invalid in the world?"

*

On the day of William and Alice's wedding I lay in my bed where the wolves came to join me. By this time we'd become quite companionable. I had tried to get up to attend the ceremony but the wolves wouldn't have it. Jealousy is a terrible thing. But really it wouldn't have done to take a pair of howling wolves to a brother's nuptial. My beasts turned circles and plopped down beside me, snuggling and snarling contentedly. I might have told William about them, and he might have been interested, but he was otherwise engaged.

Left alone in my bedroom I made a desk of my legs. My story would be called 'The Wedding'. It began, 'He had put her off with all his sweetly argued reasonableness." It featured a man and two women; really it would be about a decision and its consequences. It began with the sound of church bells, the effect of distance on the bells' pitch, how the air currents seemed to bend and twist them into a terrible out-of-tuneness, tumbling one tone upon another in a dreadful cacophany. I tried noting the sound – *bronggonggg-goinbbwrung* – but decided the uncontrolled spray of letters on the page failed to conjure the actual blare of sound; and anyway, I concluded, best to leave such things to the reader's imagination.

The bells could be ringing for only one reason. The man – I

called him Billy – must have decided. The bride's name is Anna Arbuckle. The rejected one is also called, coincidentally, Anna. They are distinguished as 'One' and 'Two'.

Now what? I rested my pencil as I recalled the biblical Judith decking herself out to go and slay Holofernes, how she'd washed her body, anointed herself, plaited her hair, added bracelets and lilies and earlets and rings & etc. But Anna Two must get dressed and in a hurry if she's to attend the wedding. What's she to wear? *Black*, comes her reply: *Let me wear black* . . . It's her voice, as if she were real and had the power of speech and a view on what she should wear to an imaginary wedding: *Like the deepest of deep-water lakes: lapping, lazy, luxurious black.* I shivered in my bed with a mixture of excitement and dread as Anna Two effected her transformation:

"Anna Two (so I wrote) lights a candle and places it on her dressing table so that the flame illuminates her face from below, throwing dramatic shadows into the hollows beneath her cheeks, her eye sockets, her throat. Now she darkens her brows which are shaped like gannets' wings. She rings her eyes in kohl, rouges her high cheekbones, outlines and paints her lips. Out of a secret box handed down by her grandmother she pulls yards of jet: necklaces, earrings, bracelets. This is no mere bedizenment. She is protected by her glittering black chains and ropes like plates of armor. 'I am a walking blackness,' she hisses. 'I am gravity and I will drag them down with me. I am spite and venom.' Her black dress is so dark it is almost invisible. 'I am dressed in the night.'"

Anna Two was now ready; but for what? I did not know. I was exhausted by my efforts, limp with despair on her behalf. Her power was an illusion. There she stood 'all decked out', magnificent arms akimbo but helpless, helpless. As was I. As for the story, it was transparently obvious. 'That accurst autobiographic form,' as Henry called it: 'the loose, the improvised, the cheap and the easy.' All my pathetic inadequacy flooded back in. Then one of the wolves came and curled up on the very page I was scribbling upon. So that was the end of that.

Sometime later Henry came to my room to tell me about the real wedding. I held out my hand to receive him, my head cradled by a bank of pillows. I imagined the scene as a painting, 'Visit to an Invalid' by one of those 'impressionists' Henry had told me about; perhaps the woman-artist called Mary Cassatt. We are enclosed in an envelope of light and air. Except that my bedroom is quite small and dark and stuffy with coaldust (an unseasonal fire smoldered in the grate) and my own fetid breath. Still to a certain eye the room and I with its busy patterns of quilt and wallpaper and carpets and curtains and invalid and visitor might have blended into one. The moment caught in pretty paint, only without the pain that kept me there.

June, the correct month for a wedding.

Henry began: "William nearly brought the whole thing down around our heads saying he could not go through with it after all, his vision had become blurred and he was having a nosebleed – he was sure he was suffering a cerebral hemorrhage. Once he was reassured to the contrary," Henry continued, "he merely fussed and flapped about with rings and was his collar straight and who would say what at the breakfast; that occasion, when it transpired, was very sumptuous and agreeable and the whole affair pleasant." He went on to describe the various dresses, one particular yellow satin with a yellow veil which he thought would have suited me. I disagreed, saying yellow, with my boardinghouse-pie complexion, was hardly my color – but he poo-pooh'd that. He described my friend Sara Darwin's new husband as 'a gentle, kindly, reasonable, liberal, bald-headed, dull-eyed British-featured, sandy-haired little *insulaire*.' Which made me convulse with laughter in spite of the pain pinning me to my mattress.

"And William's Alice?" I asked. "She looked very pretty,"

he replied simply. He would spare me the details, I saw, because once he'd 'painted' her for me in all her bridal finery, her true garments of gladness, I would never get the picture out of my head. It would be there forever:

Alice meet Alice.

But there was pain in Henry's eyes too, though of a different kind from mine. Or perhaps not. It had taken William nearly two years to make up his mind – but he had finally done it.

"He has divorced us," I said: "He does not love us as much as he loves Alice." Henry winced. I'd dared to say what he was feeling. Poor Henry. He'd been following William around like an orphaned gosling ever since I could remember but could never, ever, keep up.

As he was leaving he placed the bride's bouquet on the shallow mound of my body. "For you, Alice, from Alice" – as if she'd thrown it and I had caught it. "How generous," I muttered ungratefully, privately thinking: oh I *will* be next . . . But my furry companions disabused me of the notion. *You are the last lorn spinster on earth. A-woooo*, they concluded, raising their snouts to heaven. The gardenias soon began to turn brown and their rotting odor gave me a headache.

Two months later Henry sent me a story called *Confidence* in which a marriage separates two intimate friends. They do not remain separated forever, however, as the 'groom' ends up murdering his wife. Henry's accompanying note read, "The violence of the denouement does not I think disqualify it."

Two

The next day I was visited by Clover Hooper – well her real name was Marian but everyone called her Clover. She had been to the wedding and had been distressed to find me absent. "Actually," she confided, "I was rather intrigued. It occurred to me it might be a gesture of principle."

"Principle?"

"Against marriage."

"I see." What I saw was that she had overestimated me; that she had taken me for a blue, an 'intentional' spinster opposed to spending her life as an appendage. An imposture of course; I was no Katharine Loring. I had failed to attend William's wedding not because I was *against* marriage but because I was so much *for it* it made me ill to think it was not for me. As for saying *But he was meant to marry me* – that would have exposed me as cracked – childish. But Clover was perceptive, and knew me well, perhaps too well: "Of course you and William have always been very close," she commented. "It must be hard to lose him," she went on, "oh, and to another Alice."

"Yes," I agreed, relieved, as if the thoughts that had been going round in my head, of a world in which my name and everything else had been taken from me, was not merely the product of a sick imagination. On the other hand Clover had been, like me, one of the 'odd' ones. She'd studied languages; meant to travel; was clever. Henry had once called her 'Voltaire in petticoats.' But she had also spent time 'inside'. "There, now," she'd announced after her release from Somerville Hospital: "I have done my duty. That was the smelliest and most hideous of all the bins." 'Doing her duty' in a punishing asylum seemed to have salved her conscience, for aside from bandage-making and fund-raising – we're talking War-time here – what were we to do? "We work so hard," she'd complained, "but it is all for ourselves."

She took my hand; it was as cold as a corpse's. Then she dropped it, 'framing' me as an artist would a portion of landscape.

"May I take your picture, dear?"

"Clover," I replied, "I am not a waterfall."

She scowled. "I know that perfectly well. I have little interest in the picturesque."

"Go on then."

"Good," she said. Then she turned her back, distracted by one of her old photographs of The Bee hanging on the wall above the fireplace.

"I see you aren't there, Alice," she observed, scanning it with her finger.

"No, I must have been unwell that day. Katharine isn't either."

She laughed. "Katharine was too academic for sewing."

"Still is," I said. "Nor are you," I added, "in the picture."

"That's because I was behind the camera, silly. Anyway," she added, "I was too skittish for quilting and such, I might have poked someone with my needle."

I said I thought it might have enlivened proceedings immeasurably, picturing some of our stodgier friends leaping about like stuck pigs.

But she'd begun rootling in her camera bag, reminded of her purpose. As she worked setting up her equipment I was reminded of the 'old' Clover. How she'd come to me one day with such excitement to tell me about her language studies; and then her plan. I'd always had a weakness for hearing of my friends' plans, even if I couldn't share in them. "Yes, Alice, to go abroad, visit . . . all sorts of places . . . with my camera of course . . ." she was almost twirling with excitement. And then in a conspiratorial whisper, "Even battle zones." Battle zones? I had a sudden fear for her. If she was to carry out her plan, I'd thought, she would have to be more circumspect. I had advised her not to tell anyone. "Best not advertise it too loudly, dear. Make your preparations as you must; then, when you are ready, and only then, announce your departure." She had regarded me with surprise. "You speak as one who has had such plans herself, Alice; have you?" But I would not, could not, say.

Clover, ten years later, was now quieter as well as sturdier, yet somehow smaller with it. "I'm sorry," she said then. "For what?" I asked, but at that she became flustered and went about poking at things as if trying to set up a more tractable still life. Sorry; for what? For her good fortune and my less good? For all the weddings in the world not my own?

"That you are ill, Alice," is what she finally said.

But it was time to be 'shot'. I doubted that I had the strength to pose, but she said I was to stay right where I was; she preferred her pictures 'naturalistic'. She did however place an extra pillow behind my head. "We don't want you looking half-dead," she said. And then she ducked out of view beneath her black curtain as if sneaking a sniff or peering into a forbidden room, or even into some Williamish 'beyond'. It seemed to me she was enacting her own disappearance even as she was 'appearing' me; yet no more so, I reminded myself, than Henry hiding behind his characters, and his words. Then came explosion after explosion.

Before she left she took my hands. Hers had warmed with her efforts while mine were chillier than ever. I tried to smile but found I was fatigued to the very muscles in my jaw: well, you would be too had you been 'shot' as many times as I had. Finally I dared to ask:

"Did you photograph William and Alice?"

She looked quite wolfish. "Absolutely not. Wedding pictures do not interest me."

"Do they not?" I was pleased, I admit it. I could have

petted her. Then I recalled one of our outings. Her sister Ellen had invited me to their place at Beverly Farms, and the three of us had gone for a walk along the coast – Ellen – Clover – me – and as the sun was setting Clover grabbed both our hands – she was between us – and made a solemn promise that she would never marry. But she'd lied of course. A year later she did. And to a Henry. She was now Clover Adams, *nee* Hooper.

I thought: Why, there are so many '*nees*' in my life, I could open a horse stables. Not that I could blame her for that.

The resulting photograph had an eerie glow. It was shocking really: an old person in a young body, or do I mean a young person in an old body? Anyway, hardly what you would call lively or attractive. In it I appear to be saying something but with an anxious, almost querulous expression on my face. The light streams in from the window, lighting my forehead so it looks pale and sweaty. It also highlights, in an old masterish way, the folds and puffs of my sleeves as well as the neck-ribbon on my bed-jacket. But it is a ghastly, unaesthetic light. My nose and chin are too sharp, my forehead too high, my upswept hair too severe. I do not look well; but then I am not. I stare out from my sick-bed, fixed forever. It's quite horrible, really.

*

Sometime later Clover's sister Ellen came to see me, preceded by her exquisite Boston *parfum*. Here is a lady, I thought. "I see you are in a state, poor thing," she informed me, "so I will not stay long." She had brought a bunch of perfect roses, at odds with my own wilted state. But then, weirdly, she contratulated me on 'the wedding'. "Why," I pointed out, "William and Alice did not marry me, merely one another." She registered alarm in the manner of very superior Arabian horse. I thought to put her out of her misery by asking instead about her own marriage.

"Oh, Whitman, Whitman," she fairly coo'd: the breathy whistle of a bird calling to its mate. "Why, the things people tell you when you're married, Alice, you would not credit it." She went on, "Some even intimate that the matrimonial state is rather a complicated one and subject to more or less rubs of one sort or another." She drew herself up. "Can you conceive of such a thing?" And then she burst out, "I can't, I'm sure!"

Well, there was not much I could say to that, though I thought *What gush.* But then my father came to mind, that soft-headed old turnip who believed in goodness and marriage, so I told myself to be pleased for her, to allow her pleasure to 'spill over' – if such a thing were possible – into my lap too. Yet her certainty, her denial of any 'rubs' struck me as rather brittle, not to mention unrealistic.

"I'm pleased," I responded, "you're finding wedded bliss with your beloved Whitman. But," I cautioned, "it would be well not to take yours as a sample of marriage generally, especially as you have only been married under a year."

"Oh, Alice!" she cried, "don't be such a killjoy, your own time will come and then you will find out for yourself how absolutely divine . . .".

But my time I suspected would not come and I would not find out for myself. After she left I fell into a deep sleep. In my dream there were two sisters named Ellen and Clover. They could not be more different, yet I woke fearing for them both.

Three

I had a chamber pot: a shapely, ladylike thing resembling a giant cup with a fluted handle. In the dark I felt my way round its embossed rim as if reading phrenological bumps on a skull. I could not in the dark make out its sprigs of blue roses though I knew exactly where they were; and that there were thorns painted with the flick of a single-haired brush along the stem. The pot's roundness felt comforting: like a globe, like the earth. A joke of course. It was nothing but a hollow receptacle absurdly decorated and inconsistent with its true purpose: to fill with my body's wastes. That splashing sound in the night. When it was full I would slide it back under my bed, stuff my nightgown between my legs and curl into a tight hard ball.

I guess I lived in my bed with the chamber pot lurking coyly in its commode for the next year and more. My 'monthlies', even less ladylike to mention, came like rivers in spate and clotted with gore. I counted sixteen in one year. But the wolves were happy: they lapped greedily while I held my cramping belly with one hand and buried the other in their thick matted fur.

My nurse Milly rolled me from side to side like a sausage. There were bowls of warm water and boiled rags. After I and my bed-linen were made clean again my father would come clunking in to read to me from one of his theological tomes, but I failed to distinguish his words from the chattering birds who'd returned during the night disguised as bats spangling the ceiling with their wings and staring down at me with their red glass-bead eyes. They adored blood of course.

I had my share of visitors. Well, visiting is what one did: young and not-so-young ladies hoping to exchange toothsome gossip. However they came bearing offerings as to an effigy, smiling pityingly/encouragingly &etc, while I lay with my arms stuck outside the quilt and a planted expression upon my face. In some of their smiles I divined a barely suppressed impatience *Oh, do get up. . . .* But mostly they accepted my horizontality. They had no choice of course. As for me, my body ruled: *Movement comes to stillness*, it once instructed, ludically – which I was able to interpret as: Visitors may come and go; I must be still as a pudding. At some point William accused me of ruling over the family like the sun in the heavens. Wildly inaccurate of course. I was merely a pathetic, sick spinster. "But what do you *do*?" Fanny and Annie and Sarah would ask, and I would say, "I do not *do*, I simply *am*. I exist in the way of a mushroom." And they would look me up and down trying to decide whether or not I was poisonous.

One day William's Alice presented me with a soft boiled egg. "Why," I cried, "you have brought me the sun!" Only I couldn't swallow it, having noticed a perfect pearl about to fall from one of her nostrils and land upon the egg's head. I had a sickening vision of William kissing that viscid nostril but just then she pulled her handkerchief from her sleeve and staunched the drip. She was recovering, she explained, from influenza assuring me however that she was no longer contagious. I said I was glad of that adding, "I hope it will go lightly with you and not lead to suicide." Her hand flew to her throat. "Suicide," she yelped, "whatever can you mean?" I explained the papers had been full of stories of 'the exaggerated American response to the disease' culminating in a 'rash' of suicides – had she not heard of it? "No I have not," she replied allowing the hand to unclaw itself but her angel's eyes grew darker and she did not visit me for a long while after that. Nor did William for that matter, though he wrote largely of his 'imbedment in the soft domestic bosom'. His Alice had saved him: 'I was a diseased boy,' I read, 'whom she has lifted from the dust and transformed into a man'. Well, I thought, picturing her raising him up and dusting him down, You cannot do better than that, Willy. I also understood that his 'marriage-cure' depended on his keeping his distance from the 'neurotic' unhappiness of his bedridden sister Alice. 'Give my love to Alice,' I wrote, 'but don't let her know you address me as Dearest Alice,' I advised, 'or it may complicate our relations.'

Doctors rumbled and mumbled over me: *nervous paralysis . . . prostration . . . female hysteria . . .* prescribing rest and more rest and custard and rest. "But surely, Doctor, I may be allowed to read and write?" "*Write?* certainly not!" Writing was bound to excite the imagination in morbid ways, though letters might be permitted. I was of course being managed and defined, yet I gave myself up to their inferior wisdom letting them believe I played into their hands. Was I not after all the sweetest invalid in the world?

Only Henry's letters continued to amuse me with their talk of London life with its 'inscrutable entrees' and 'feeble tinkles of conversation': *chatterchatter*. Yet I preferred 'horrible' London over 'aesthetic' London: low neighborhoods at night with numerous poor wretches reeling home to squalid dens or rolling across the roadway and cutting themselves till the blood flowed. I lapped up such descriptions along with bulletins detailing the state of his bowels, back and stomach – which Aunt Kate thought should really be marked private.

Time passed. Picture a Rumpulstiltskin-like figure stomping along my prone body with his little leaden boots, marking the seconds. Nor could I spin straw into gold. In other words, it passed slowly, painfully and reproachfully.

At some point Henry (who could make time pass in his stories by sheer sleight-of-hand) appeared in the flesh (and quite *meaty* he looked too). He'd returned from Paris to see

his publisher and friend Dean Howells. Mere pretexts, he
insisted, to see me. Dear Henry. He held my hand and asked
after my health. "My health?" I was beginning to think
communication by letter was far easier. "I do not have such
a thing: I am as you see me." His cheeks wobbled like a
dog's. I patted his hand *therethere*, my dry skin touching his
moistness, his solidity. I am holding Henry, I thought: a
handful of Henry. "Tell me about you," I encouraged. He
complained about Dean who'd insisted on delaying the
complete edition of The American until all the serialized
copies had been sold out. "But it is selling well?" He nodded.
I said how pleased I was, which was true. Then he announced his plan to settle in London. I said it sounded damp.
He patted my hand again, turned it over, stared into it and
was gone.

*

After Henry left I took up my writing things and began a
story about a chamber pot. But a word, before I go any
further, about my writing – or rather scribbling. Henry
wrote, I scribbled; that was how it was. And yet. The
question that occupied my mind – assuming I was to continue – was what to write *upon*? Paper was the obvious thing.
But what sort? The local stationers' had provided a list that
went on for several pages describing various weights and
qualities of papers. I was tempted by onionskin – thin,
slippery and transparent as skin itself – but far too noisy.
And then, paper of any sort was problematical in that it
proclaimed its right as the correct material to be written
upon thus making it far too official, too professional a
medium for a nobody like me. I would have to be certain
that what I had written was worthy of the stuff
it was written upon. Which I would doubt. At first I

didn't doubt. At first I thought my efforts rather good. But when I read them I decided they'd 'gone off' like sour stews.

Yet if not on proper paper, what then?

On one occasion I asked Aunt Kate to collect an assortment of leaves for me. "What sort of leaves?" she wanted to know. "Large, soft ones," I replied, "not too brittle yet not too soft: large-leaved limes, sweet chestnuts, maples." Then she wanted to know what they were for so I explained I had decided to study the pattern of their veins. "I see," said she suspiciously.

But the pen tore through the leaves.

There could be a notebook, of course, one of those cheap, roughly-sewn school notebooks with lines or even without lines. Each tale would be self-contained. Having completed one, I could begin another. But what if I could not complete a tale? There would be the evidence, clear as an account book showing I had failed to pay my debts. Failure after failure; lined or unlined; stamped or unstamped.

There could of course be a *large* blank book: thick and leather-bound, which could easily be disguised as a diary; indeed, could *actually be* a diary with a lock and key to ensure its privacy. Filled it would contain a collection of my tales; in other words it would then have become *a book*. Which must not happen, I saw, for it would amount to announcing myself as a writer which I could not do. I dared not *author* a book even if I was capable of *filling* one. The distinction must be made.

There was only one solution left. I would write on scraps: the backs of discarded envelopes, shopping lists, bills of sale, the reverse sides of letters. When I had completed a tale, I would simply gather up the pieces and 'file' them in a large manila envelope which I would slip under my mattress. When it became overful and lumpy, I would start another manila envelope. The solution pleased me.

But about the chamber pot. My preoccupation with such a thing must have seemed to the New England snowdrop souls round about somewhat Rabelasian. It would not do, therefore to make it the subject of a tale. I mean, imagine Henry writing about a chamber pot. I could not. But then came this owlish message: *Do not mock chamber pots, Alice, they speak truth.*

Four

One day in late winter my old friend Sara Sedgwick came to see me. She had gone over to England in '77 to visit with relatives in Yarmouth and had caught herself a husband. "I hear the herring are plentiful again this year," I said spitefully: "perhaps I will go and fish myself one." Her eyes popped. "Alice, William Erasmus Darwin is a banker not a herring." "No, of course not." I did not repeat Henry's description of him as 'gentle, kindly, reasonable, liberal, bald-headed, prosaic' & etc.

"So, Sara Darwin, *nee* Sedgwick."

She scooped like a swan. What must it be like, I thought, to cast off one's original name and slip into a new one like some off-the-peg garment? What if it pulled under the arms and across the back? Or was so loose and baggy that you felt lost inside it? Of course alterations could always be made but . . . was not marriage the occupation of occupations? It was, if nothing else, as Henry called it, 'the usual thing'. But she was looking droopy and miserable.

"Well?" I asked.

"Well *what*, Alice?" Her attempt at defiance.

"You know very well," I replied, adding, "And how is it being *a wife*?"

"Ah, that." She made a sour little face: "The Darwins are thick as thieves, as you can imagine."

"Can I?" I supposed I could: the men with their cigars huddled around the fire while the wives stabbed at their canvases like great spotted woodpeckers at dead branches. But William Erasmus, the new husband, would not abandon

23

his Sara for long. What would it be like to be allied with another against the rest of the world? Once I thought I knew of such a thing but now I could hardly imagine it.

She was showing me a photograph her father-in-law had given her: not the usual cameo of a human head but a frog leaping off a leaf. "It's a Coki Tree Frog," she explained: "Mr Darwin says according to Indian folklore the sound of this frog is the voice of springtime. It was regarded as a symbol of good fortune and – she paused meaningfully while touching her barely-swelled stomach – "*fertility*." Ah. I allowed the news to register before pronouncing with some sincerity: "Well congratulations, Sara Darwin." She blushed a deep rose madder then perversely looked annoyed: "For what?" she asked, opening wide her doll ribbon blue eyes. I thought her disingenuous or dim, or possibly both, but then it dawned she was quite right to be provoked. That one should be congratulated merely for one's biology: which would in any case leave her helpless as a pudding. Or a frog.

Something of herself, she was trying to tell me, had been given up in marriage, and would be lost further through childbirth. Of course there would be the blessing of a child – that first cry piercing the membrane of the world; and perhaps another, and another. And it would be exciting, true, but also rather alarming, to have produced a *family*; indeed, to have enlarged the world with several more human creatures; whereas I was as I was: plain and ill, yet whole, entire, un-pierced, un-reproduced. So that I thought to myself: the next time you are tempted to feel sorry for yourself, Alice: do not. You may be the last spinster on earth, but here you *are*. Now she was appealing to *me*: "You think men should be mastered, Alice?" I laughed. What did I know about men? But I owed it to her to be serious. "I think loyalty to oneself is the thing; husband, children, friends and country are as nothing to that." I sounded, as ever, more sure of myself, more snappish, than I really was. And it shocked her, so I retreated.

"Is it not sweet," I asked, "having someone to comfort you in moments of distress?" I was thinking of the nights of course.

She laughed. "But Alice, as you must know, it is the other way round: it is our role as wives to comfort our husbands."

The other way round, I thought. Even so, I said, "Please remember it is only my book I press to my heart at night."

This annoyed her: "A book can be a great comfort, Alice, do not disparage its benefits."

"No, I do not." But still. I wanted to shake her, shout at her: *You are married! How dare you be sour, you complacent little vole!? You are married! married!* Instead I coo'd, "Your husband is delightful, everyone says so." I felt a shiver go through her but she would not be drawn.

"I'm sure he is," she replied.

So much for your Boston enthusiasm. I tried to put myself into her shoes (which had pretty straps with covered buttons). I could hardly blame her for finding fault. Marriage, I knew, was not the perfect solution to happiness. But it was a refuge, a privileged club to which I was denied access; and therefore to me, precious. Which is why I could not forgive her for taking it so for granted.

She was all done up in her braids and collar and cuffs, and muff . . . which she suddenly flung off: "Let us do something naughty, Alice" – showing her pointy white teeth – "like we used to do as girls." "What do you suggest?" I asked coolly. She put her finger in her mouth: "I have a longing to commit a sin." "A sin . . .?" Now my curiosity was piqued. I was instructed to wait while she went down to the kitchen to consult Aunt Kate who in turn gave the order to our servant.

An hour later, a box was delivered from MacElroy's in Harvard Square and brought up to my room. Sara held it on her lap as if it might contain something dangerous, explosives perhaps. "Go on, Sara," I prompted, "or do you propose staring at it like a clairvoyant for the rest of the afternoon?" She gave a little shiver and, in time, began teasing open the lid, peering in, then sliding it closed again as if what she'd seen and sniffed at inside the dark box was just too impossible to reveal; then, again, raising the lid another crack, and another, until finally it was flung back and all was revealed. At which a low growl erupted from deep within her throat. And I thought: ah, so this is what happens when our miserable sex has an urge towards vice and wildness – why, we send out for eclairs! Which is what the box – which had come from our snooty Boston bakeshop – contained.

As we squeezed the pastries the cream squirted out the sides and down our wrists where it dripped off our elbows: the leakage was quite astonishing. Together we licked cream and chocolate from our fingers but it soon spread to our chins and cheeks as far as our ears. Later, the quilt and my night-dress had to be laundered and I bathed because the chocolate had somehow slithered between the buttons and onto my chest and stomach; and Sara's muff had to be abandoned. There was even a smudge on the wallpaper like dried blood that had to be wiped immediately. And I was sick and regretted it. But I can still taste the sweetness, see our two faces lathered with cream-beards and chocolate moustaches grinning with pleasure like two five year-olds. And I do not blame her for her limitation of choice. Nor myself for mine.

Five

Katharine Loring Peabody peers round my bedroom door like a coy Dutch angel of the annunciation with her finger to her lips. Except that she's neither coy nor an angel: "What, still in bed, Alice?"

Katharine Loring was another 'left on the shelf' spinster like me, yet unlike me she was thoroughly transatlantic, stretchable and modern. And her perch had been self-chosen: a solid, safe place from which to step out into the world. She was no Sara Darwin, *nee* Sedgwick; she was *nee* nothing but that with which she was born. As she entered my room that day in early spring her name slipped between my lips, silky as a slice of ribbon. *Katharine.* I feasted on it until I was full: full of Katharine, and no need for eclairs. I breathed it out and the room was cleared of howling wolves and chattering birds and bats.

The facts. Katharine Loring Peabody: full of health and vitality; one year my junior. Fine features, elephantine ears. Eyes pale as blue smoke. Heroic bones yet of a willowy form, delicate as a tulip – bright and waxy to the eye and smelling of lemons with pointed petals arching like a royal collar or a pair of praying hands; with a long hollow stem which after some days in water 'gives', curving into balletic shapes. Oh, but she was no more a tulip than a slice of moon or melon. She was none other than my dear friend, my companion Katharine. Henry said he thought she combined "the wisdom of the serpent with the gentleness of the dove." I told him I thought it had the makings of a good title for a novel.

"Move over, Alice." She sat beside me on the bed. "How

27

are you?" she asked in her plain-speaking way. I said I was much improved and suddenly I was, though it may have been the effect of her rolling her thumb round the bone at my wrist as if polishing a pearl, and entreating me in her liquid voice to get better . . . to *be* better. After that she began pacing round the room talking of the 'blanks' in our lives. Which reminded me of my own situation.

"In a hundred years from now," I began – my voice was rather swoopy – "when the reader of that era opens one of Henry's novels, they will come first upon a brief biography of its author in which they will be informed, following upon the basic facts of his birth, that his father was a prominent theologian, and his elder brother William was a famous philosopher. There will be no mention of a sister, however, or if there is, she will be described as a useless invalid."

"Allowing it should be true," granted Katharine, "your brothers have had advantages which you have not. We are living, as you know, in a man's world. So you must not blame yourself for not accomplishing what they have."

We'd been introduced at Ellen Tappan's engagement party. "Alice, I'd like you to meet Katharine Loring". But no sooner had we stuck out our hands than we'd both been swept on to 'widen our circle of acquaintances.' I'd looked for her later on but she'd gone. After that I watched my brother's friends drooping wetly over their intendeds, half-strangling them, and felt quite queasy. Love affairs were so much less appealing, I thought, in real life than in novels. And yet, as I moved about the party trying to avoid them I kept being drawn to them. Those flirting couples, the desire to be close, to absorb something of their heat; at the same time to get as far away as possible, to laugh at them, condemn them as absurd. And yet there was something deeply desirable about such a state of possibility, of things dark and hidden, even dangerous. William would soon know of it. Aunt Kate, who'd been married, though briefly and tragically, would certainly have known of it. Even

Henry, who entertained *pantings* and *spasms* and *convulsions* in his stories, must surely have been touched by it. It was obvious of course what 'it' was all about: *sex*. There, I have said it.

Sometime later Katharine Loring interviewed me to teach history on her Home Studies Program. The date was marked on my calendar for that year: *friendship*, it said. Friendship, the very word sounds cool. It was not.

"Alice," she now announced, "I believe you are in need of a holiday."

"Me?"

"You."

I laughed: "But I am an invalid."

"That is not *all* you are, Alice. In any case, your Aunt Kate and the evidence of my own eyes tell me you are much improved." I admitted I was somewhat better but in no way well enough to do such a thing as travel: why, I could barely get out of bed without falling over, not to mention bleeding all over the carpet. She flung back the quilt. "Now stand," she ordered. I stood. "Now walk." I walked. "How do you feel?" "I feel . . .". I barely knew how to express my condition. "Nothing," I said at last, flapping like a new bird.

"Well," she declared, "in summer, there are two possibilities: to go abroad or lose oneself in the mountains." I immediately replied that I would certainly choose the former. She smiled ruefully. "Ah, and I would choose the latter." Then she did a surprising thing. In spite of my avowed preference for 'going abroad', she invited me to go with her to the Adirondacks. And I did an even more surprising thing: I agreed.

According to William I was a good deal tougher than I'd been. I was still stupidly wobbly with snarlings behind my eyes, in the pit of my stomach, up through the soles of my feet and the palms of my hands. But Katharine was there helping me at every turn. 'Miss Loring is a real savior to her,' as William had written to Henry. Which left me feeling quite smug, thinking: So Willy has his savior, and I have mine. Once my wasted muscles had recovered – it took several more weeks – off we went to the Adirondacks.

*

It wasn't until she actually pushed open the cabin door and guided me in that I realized we were occupying the very shanty that William and Alice had occupied during their honeymoon. I sagged down onto one of the wooden chairs while Katharine came and knelt before me.

"Do you mind very much, dear?" she asked.

"Of course not," I lied.

I woke during the night and there they were, William and Alice: rumpled, blushing, blissful. He was rough and bristly and full of growly pent-up passion while she was shy and demure. I recalled wrestling matches with William and saw that this was rather similar. The wolves returned and joined in with their mating yowls. Meanwhile Katharine held me in her arms, rough nightgown to rough nightgown. I whispered deep into her ear, "We are not alone," – but she would have none of it. "That was the past, Alice. *We* are here now, together, and they are not." She was wrong of course: we were *all* there crowding that creaky cabin bed. The place reeked of them. But we'd travelled a long way and Katharine was determined to have her holiday, and I did not have the heart to deprive her of it.

Out on Lake Placid I watched her swim as if she were flying on her back while I plopped about in the shallows stumbling over slippery stones, my wet skirts threatening to drag me down. "Undress!" she cried: "There's no one about." She herself had a penchant for nudity. But all I could do was hold my arms across my papery body and shiver in the heat. I could not trust Nature or myself not to do me in. Kath loved it; revelled in its rocky, mossy, animal'd, tree'd, flower'd, largely unpeople'd wildness. The peaks, imposing, threatening, hulked around us. I cowered as from an attack of giants; she invited their benign gaze.

Most days she would take off on long solitary hikes. "Beware of bears," I'd warn. One day she proposed I come along saying the exercise and air would do me good. I cared not a bear's toenail for the exercise but welcomed the excuse to get away from the cabin's resident ghosts.

As we tramped through the woods however I felt only fear and discomfort: from the branches scratching our skin and the spiders spreading their sticky webs which I tried to pull off but could not. I heard myself scream. "It is nothing," Katharine soothed. I knew she was right, of course, but that very nothingness disturbed me even more than the positively biting fleas, the vicious red ants, the sportive midges, the humming mosquitos and giant hairy spiders; for beyond these things, there *was* nothing: nothing to call one out of oneself. No paintings or buildings or people but only a great tangle of confusion – stems, twigs, leaves – intertwinings mossy, damp, dank. After that the rock-strewn blankness. And always the droning biting insects.

"Please, can we stop?"

"Of course." She pulled a rubber mat from her rucksack and placed it on a patch of bare earth so that I'd be protected, while she sat, unconcerned, directly upon a fissured rotting log. She handed me a cup of sweetened coffee from her thermos. "Drink that, it will give you oomph." "*Oomph . . .?*" I scoffed.

That night she made a bonfire. We sat around it hugging our mugs of cocoa, the creamy stars above and no one else within a mile – or so we thought. "It's quite romantic," said the normally prosaic Katharine. Burnt marshmallows coated my teeth and tongue. An owl hooted. Down on the Lake the loon rose up and cackled hysterically.

The next day she persuaded me to go with her again but after an hour of climbing I came to a halt. "I cannot go on," I declared. I felt as if all the blood coursing round my body had been drained out and substituted with mercury. She looked around. "Then wait here," she said, "I'll just go to the ridge: I won't be long, I promise." Sunlight streamed down through the trees. I leant against a bank crisscrossed with tree roots, determined to make the most of the peaceful silence. But the longer I waited the less silent, or empty . . . or peaceful it became. The scents of pineapples . . . dry, hot combustible pine needles. As I swivelled my new boots nervously back and forth, the needles were displaced revealing the dry earth beneath and the ants making their way here and there.

I guess I was trying to distract myself from the lurking fear, or boredom, that had crept up like a spider, by focusing my attention on the ants. It seemed logical; after all ants were known to be quite fascinating creatures. And it worked. A whole army had been revealed, lines of them marching to and fro hauling bits of wood heavier than themselves, some of them joining forces to share a load. As I stared down at them, the minutely articulated parts of their bodies became more evident. What did I know about the parts of ants? Nothing. Anyway, there was a limit to my curiosity. I got up and plucked a blueberry from its branch. I carried it back to my perch against the bank and held it up to the light. It was a deep blue-black overlaid with a bloom of white through which small streaks of red appeared like veins. I rubbed it tenderly against my skirt to bring up its shine; noted how its 'flower' end gaped like the mouth of a baby bird; let it roll around in my palm.

But how long could I hold the perfect berry without crushing it? It was surprisingly hard work not to squash the life out of it. Not that it *is* alive, I reminded myself . . . not like an ant. Still, some voice, some impulse, warned me against damaging it, so I held my hand artificially still, the berry dead center. I stared down at it. Why was I doing this? Why, having torn my attention away from the industrious ants, was I concentrating on an unremarkable if 'blooming' blueberry? Surely, I told myself, you have not picked it for an aesthetic experience but because you're *hungry*. And so I raised my palm to my mouth. But just as was about to pop the berry in, I sensed the danger. What danger? "You are being silly and superstitious," I said out loud. Yet there it was palpable in the berry's blue-black fatness, its promise of sweetness, its tiny seeds, the sharp mineral tang that would, if I allowed it past my lips, burst inside my mouth. But I must not or else . . . what? Some nameless dread. No . . . it had a name, only I was reluctant to voice it. *Bear . . . Ursus horribilis*. I sensed it lurking nearby, rising on its hind legs . . . sniffing, its big wet nose like a shiny black marshmallow with its cavernous holes growing wetter and wetter and dripping with . . . appetite. Warily, it draws closer and closer until . . .

Was I mauled by the bear? Did Katharine come back to find a bloodied mangled corpse? Or did the bear wait and – greedy guts! – gobble up both of us? I began to laugh; it was too ridiculous, there was of course no bear. But there *was* something in my hand, wet, crushed. Ah, I told myself, so *that* is what this is about: not the bear itself but the *possibility* of it, the prickle at the back of the neck, the fear that causes the skin to be coated in a particularly pungent type of perspiration. Which might or might not, after all, summon a keen-nosed bear . . .

I stared down at the berry now crushed and oozing its juice between my fingers. All I knew was that there was something, or not a thing but a sense of a thing lurking, and that that something had somehow been contained in the blueberry. But it was over. I stood. What now? I thought of Henry who liked to cause a twist in his tales: would a surprising thing occur? Or would it be something more subtle, a feeling, an understanding, a failure to see what had been there or not been there, an opportunity lost, or even . . . a mistake in the original scenario? For by now the 'import' of the bear had become still clearer to me. The bear in the wood (or 'The Bear in the Wood'as I'd begun to think of it) was an idea, an idea that lurked *like* a bear or a beast crouching in a jungle; so that it signified little whether it was 'real' or not, or indeed whether I was destined to be slain by it or not.

Katharine apologized for having taken longer than she'd anticipated. She waved towards the horizon. "The path kept leading me upwards. I came to a clearing where most of the trees had been uprooted by storms, burnt by forest fires. In their place young pines have sprung up in the gaps, thin as eyelashes." I pictured her, another 'eyelash' among them. "Wheren't you afraid?" "Afraid?" she echoed as if the meaning of the word escaped her. She reached down for my hand to pull me up but dropped it in disgust. "It was only a blueberry," I said.

The next morning Dr. Charles Putnam, who turned out to be occupying another shanty a small distance away, came stumbling over to introduce himself. Katharine, not liking to be encroached upon, held out her hand but did not extend her hospitality to breakfast. "No need," he made a dismissive, wavelike motion, "I have brought my gentleman-cook." We managed to restrain ourselves until he'd gone at which point we collapsed giggling. Fighting for breath, Katharine speechified, "You see . . . just goes to show . . . the same inequality between the sexes exists in the wilderness as that which disgraces the effete civilizations to which most of us cling." "Hear hear," said I, still spluttering. At some point he crept up on us again, this time to offer his 'protection' if we should need it. "I doubt that we shall," affirmed Katharine, pale with the effort to remain straight-faced, "but thank you anyway."

One night, after we'd gone to bed, there arose a great tumult outside the cabin. It sounded as if someone were trying to batter down the walls. I hid under the blanket, nightmare-ridden, but Katharine jumped out of bed, threw a shawl around her shoulders, grabbed her revolver (!), and slammed outside. I pulled the blankets over my head.

"Away" Shoo! Boo!" I heard her yell. The sound of hoofs; mooing.

"Cows," she reported on her return.

"Just as well it wasn't bears," I said, peeking out from my coward's nest.

"That's what the pistol was for," she added matter-of-factly.

I stared: was there anything she could not do? I could think of nothing. She who possessed all the brute superiority which distinguished man from woman combined with all the distinctively feminine virtues. I recalled a passage from *The Minister's Wooing*, by our friend Harriet Beecher Stowe: 'Katy could harness a chaise, or row a boat; she could saddle and ride any horse in the neighborhood; she could cut any garment that ever was seen or thought of, make cake, jelly and wine . . . all without seeming to derange a sort of trim, well-kept air of ladyhood that sat jauntily on her' . . . and I knew for certain that 'Katy' had been based on my Katharine.

As for Dr. Putnam, our 'protector', why, he was not to be seen during the entire episode. Still, it amused us to think of our friends gossiping about the two virgins of thirty summers living alone in the woods with a bachelor. It amused us still more to take turns imitating his pious expression with the virtuous spectacles sitting far down his nose, his general maiden-aunt-like turn of figure and limp-wristed, sashaying walk. It was the most fun I'd had the entire time.

At the end of our stay I made my confession: "I wish I loved Nature more, dear Kath, but I do not. The truth is I prefer a tub any old day to a slimy pool with weeds grabbing at my legs." I did not say how they'd reminded me of all the dark forces in my life, of all the dreads past and to come that would if they could ensnare. "I'm sorry," I snivelled: "I've spoiled your vacation." "Don't be silly, Alice," she soothed, endlessly patient and reasonable. "It is perfectly defensible to favor a tub over a pool: merely a difference in temperament and preference. Do not turn it into something more than it is. Let's face it, you have never really been one for nature, that is all." And so we returned to the City where I found my mother dangerously ill.

Six

My mother's voice rasped and wheezed: "Henry . . . where is . . . Henry?" "Henry is visiting friends in Washington, Mother, he's very well." "Tell him . . . there is . . . no . . . cause . . . for anxiety." Then there was father to worry over: "Your father . . . do not . . . forget . . . your father's . . . bedtime . . . cordial." While puffing out the recipe – *half a lemon slice, three whole cloves, a jigger of whiskey* – she gulped air like a caught fish for water. But she was not a fish, I reminded myself, shamed, she was my mother. How much is a jigger, Mother? Would I make my father drunk? But then the cordial went out of my head as the tiny air-carrying vessels in her lungs closed up and her breath grew even more ragged and constricted. I reminded myself I was in charge and felt the fresh air fly into my own chest and my heart grew steady as the grandfather clock on the landing.

Her death came quietly. All four of my brothers – William, Henry, Wilky, Robertson – carried her body to the cemetery in Cambridge. It was a splendid day, the weather having no regard for our small human loss. Clear cold crisp: I coughed until my shoulders shook but refused to cry. Our father managed to embarrass us by invoking the Divine Nature throughout his funeral oration, and afterwards by producing small mewling noises as if an abandoned rodent was hidden in his patriarch's beard. Aunt Kate stood beside him like a wife-in-waiting. Would she look after him now or would I? What, I considered, was to be her place in our family? Mother/ Father/ Aunt Kate: the three of them had stood solid as a milking stool. But one of its legs – my mother,

Kate's own sister – had been lopped off; so how would the stool now stand?

Later, Aunt Kate said she thought mother would be proud of me: "I see her looking down from heaven rejoicing that her death has given you renewed spiritual life." I said I would rather not be spied on from above, if she didn't mind.

I had many letters of commiseration from my old friends Sara Darwin (nee Sedgwick), Annie Richards (nee Ashburner), Ellen Gurney (nee Hooper), etc., implying insultingly that the loss was heavier for me because of my single 'condition'. There was also one from Italy from Henry's 'friend' Constance Fenimore Woolson: 'A daughter feels it more than a son of course because her life is so limited.' I would not deign to reply to that one either.

Back home we stood about like store dummies being fussed over by mother's relations and family friends while Aunt Kate and the servants scurried around us. The parlor had been cleared to make room for the food and flowers, their rotting, sweet smells combining not unlike the sentiments being served up. *A truly exemplary life . . . such selflessness.* Black bombazine shapes glided and swirled or stood like silhouettes of gloom. Two women reached greedily for the same smoked salmon *hors d'oeuvre.* Father's cheeks above his white whiskers were violently red as he made his way towards me. I dived for a cheese canape but there he was at my ear: "Alice!" so that the square of cheese flew off its cracker-bed and landed on the white tablecloth which mother had *selflessly* crocheted.

"Father . . .?"

"Alice," he repeated removing me from the fray. "There is something I wish to present to you." He fiddled about in his vest pocket to retrieve a small, tissue-wrapped parcel. "What is it, Father?" He waved, "Open it, open it." I un-bowed the ribbon and parted the tissue. "Oh," said I; and again *oh . . . .* No doubt my mouth stood open in a parody of surprise, tho' whether pleasurable or horrified he was not to know. The ghastly thing – a hairwork and jet brooch – consisted of loops of intricately woven strands cinched in the middle by a gold clasp and engraved with the word 'Mother'. Three worked tassels made from my mother's mousy, obedient hair dangled from the center. "Let it be a reminder," he pronounced, "of your mother's goodness." His hand shook as he pinned it to my chest, while my own hands clenched and unclenched.

"Thank you, Father," I managed as three large females pounced, oohing and cooing *"How very charming!"* . . . *"I'm sure you will never want to take it off!"* I had to restrain myself from ripping the thing from me and despatching all of them with the pin, but instead I felt my brooched heart shrivel like a salted slug. I longed for Henry to rescue me but he'd hooked his thumb into his waistcoat pocket, and there it hung along with the rest of his hand like some newly shot game-bird.

But it was William who steered me into a corner, for my own safety or everyone else's it was not clear. "I see you are still a hyena, my little grey-eyed Alice." "Am I, Willie?" Had he read my mind, word for word, seen me as 'The Mad Brooch Stabber'? "The hyena," I informed him, "is not a very attractive animal, you know. Aside from its ungainly body and mangy fur, it is known for its pusillanimous behavior. Is that what you think of me?" "Now, now, Alice," he smirked.

A story came to me about a girl and her two older brothers. 'Every year,' I began in my head, 'they grew in stature and reputation.' *The author and the philosopher*, I whispered to myself. 'Both were clever and kind,' I continued in my head, 'and both fond and protective of their younger sister.' But I rejected that for so much pabulum; instead came this: 'As their beards grew longer from their chins so the hair retreated from their heads, leaving them exposed to the elements like two half-domes of Yosemite.' It was wicked but it warmed me like medicine; like the truth, harsh and real.

The brooch had come with a card containing, in my father's own hand, a quotation from Lady Godey's Book:

Hair is at once the most delicate and lasting of our materials, and survives us, like love. It is so light, so gentle, so escaping from the idea of death, that with a lock of hair . . . may almost say, 'I have a piece of thee here . . .'

I ran to my room and spewed up into the sprigged, ladylike chamber pot. When I'd recovered I began a tale about a young woman who is given her dead mother's brooch as a keepsake. Instead of being grateful, however, the creature is possessed by some malign force so that she begins using it as a weapon against all those who counsel her to be good. She aims for the neck and so does a deal of damage especially among her frailer relatives . . . . But a picture of my Mother cold and alone in her new grave intruded and I flung my pen away and screwed up the card I'd been writing upon.

*

Some weeks later I rode out towards the coast around Beverley Farms. I made my stumbly way onto one of the narrow lanes. It gradually dwindled until it disappeared altogether and there was only the cliff path and the bay before me. As I walked William's words sounded in my head: "You walk like a goose! Like a *girl!*" I thought of Katharine in britches: *she* would never get tangled up in her own skirts, never trip over her own feet like some dumb cluck. But on I went. Once past the last of the houses I stopped above a deserted cove where I swung my arm round clockwise three times as I'd seen William and Rob do while playing baseball, then let fly the brooch. It rode a wave like some tiny, whiskery mollusc before it turned, winked its gold clasp in the sun, and sank from sight. I thought, it has pierced the sea; yet the sea will barely know of it. After that I felt chilled to the bone, limp and womanish, as if the throw had unwound me.

It was after that that I saw the For Sale sign swinging to and fro in the wind, its painted letters faded, the chain upon which it swung crooked and rusted. The property had obviously been on the market for some time. It overlooked the ocean separated by a sloping overgrown field and a barbed-wire fence. I considered the money my mother had left me. I could buy it, I thought: *I* could *buy* it! And so, after a deal of negotiation overseen by William, I did: nearly an acre and a half plot of land on that Point of Rocks. And a mere two miles up the coast past Prides Crossing . . . and Katharine.

I paid $4000 for the land with rights to the pier and a common beach just to the south and west. It looked out past several little bay-bound islands towards the open sea. My property, mine. After the signing of the deeds I stood out on 'my' pier thinking *I am well and have been well since my Mother's death everyone says so and I will continue to be well . . . and Katharine will be close by . . .*

The snake-oil words dripped inside my head trickling down my arms and legs until I was coated in wellness. I saw myself hovering kestrel-like above the house and its grounds, my own establishment to which others would come for refuge. The trouble with hovering, however, is that when the magic fails and the sun sets and it's too dark to see where you're going and the person who has abandoned you has disappeared under the waves – you drop down from the sky with an almighty thump. You are not a kestrel, you are a calamity. But I am getting ahead of myself.

There was honest work to be done, a cottage to be built on the rocky earth. My dear Katharine arrived at Quincy Street with her books of photographs. ''There you are, Alice.'' We sat together on my bed on the tree-of-life quilt – which I'd made years before at The Bee, spending countless hours poking my needle up and down until my youth was largely spent – with the raw materials spread around us.

"What are all these?" I asked.

"Houses . . . churches . . . cottages: all built by women." Katharine turned the pages of her photograph album. She pointed to a church with a 'rotunda' at one end: Italian, I presumed. Katharine laughed. "Almost as far from Italy as we are from it. That particular church was built in the North of England by Sarah Losh. She sent her workmen over so they could see how it was done. The stone carvings are unique."

"You have seen it?"

"I took the photograph."

She flipped two pages further on. "Those are workers' cottages designed by Harriet Martineau: different of course, but equally radical in their way. So you see, Alice, if you put your mind to it you can . . .".

"But they were Englishwomen," I pointed out, as if that somehow made them of another species and beyond me.

"True," admitted Katharine, "but you are an *American*." Clearly the greater pedigree.

So to work. She'd also brought a blank sketchbook, graph paper, ruler, compass and sharpened pencils. I did not know where to begin but practical Katharine, teacher Katharine, began by asking: How many stories would I need, two or three? How many rooms facing which way? Did I prefer a modern design or a more conservative one? Did I value light over warmth . . . a view of the sea from the major rooms?

She produced a compendium of architectural styles, such as the 'Stick' house on Cape May with its pitched roofs, weird staring dormers and shadowy arcaded piazza over-hung by a low brooding roof-brow. "Can't you imagine it on a bleak winter's day inhabited by ghosts and goblins . . .?" Oh I could, I could. I turned the page to a monstrous edifice resembling a tightly corseted lady with flaring hoop and bulging bustle. But the most hilarious of all was a house from

Wellsville, NY with more fringes and tassels and lambrequins than an interior decorator's lampshade. The designs went on: Richardsonian Romanesque, French Mansard, Queen Anne, Italian Villa, Carpenter's Gothic, Eastlake . . . fussy scrollwork, ornate weathervanes, widows' walks, turrets, keystones, cornices, finials, dentils, consoles, pedestals, pediments . . . . until I could bear to look no more. I took up one of the needle-sharp pencils and drew the simplest, most blocklike house imaginable: cleancut porch posts, simple lattice railings, plain horizontal moldings and chimneys.

"I want a seaside cottage," I declared, "not a giant lampshade."

By the end of a week we had a design of two stories; roomy enough for all the boys and their families plus Aunt Kate, Katharine herself, and Father of course: eight rooms in all with their elevations and wide-awake windows to let in as much light as possible. But then I thought: Where will we stand to watch the sea and the islands, where swing on warm summer evenings? Katharine guided me in adding broad porches with low balustrades running in two directions off a central pavilion, the walls straight with no roof slope visible.

"It's very reserved, Alice," she said wrily. "Precisely," I replied. But in the end I gave way to fancy, adding a few twiddly cutout patterns connecting the porch supports and again under the eaves.

It took a year to be built and was still not quite finished, but I was determined to move in that spring of '82. And so I did. And a month later I was able to stand out on the very porch I'd sketched leaning on a balustrade looking down on my future garden. The smell of bayberries, a rowboat waiting at the pier, even a horse and carriage for taking Father into town.

Look, I thought, look what I have made: oh, not a house of fiction or philosophical theories but a real house made of wood and stone and plaster and tiles and pipes connecting and pumping like a vibrant thing with windows that look out reflecting the living bundling sea and sky. My own design, my own. Mother, you *will* be proud of me.

*

Henry, having stopped off on his way back to England, was sidling towards me in his aesthetic toggery, with his growing paunch and 'alabaster brow' – oh, stuff that – dear balding pate. As he approached, I felt an urge to place my hands upon that naked patch of skull: to warm it, protect it. I saw him, twelve years old again being shouted at by William: '*I* only play with boys who curse and swear!' Which had left him pushed aside, a boy who did not curse and swear but who always hung back: seeing, watching, applauding, envying, desiring, pitying, making up stories inside a head covered in a boy's own sweet lank hair. But he was all grown up now, and famous, and did not need my protection. We locked forearms sliding them gradually forward forcing me up onto my toes, Henry surveying the house over my shoulder: "I suppose you call it Carpenter's Gothick, with a 'k'?"

"Henry," I replied, "I call it my own design."

He smiled a crack. "I do admire your piazzas."

I released myself. "I call them plain old porches."

He sighed, "I suppose I cannot get it right today."

Yet he was pleased, I could see: my snappish reply told him what he needed to know: that I was vastly improved, was in fact better than I'd been for a long while. We continued to circle the house clambering over piles of timber and slates, pipes and gutterings. When we'd come full tour Henry said, "This might certainly be called pleasure under difficulties." It was a remark I'd heard before; but where? when? I recalled a long-ago drive from Paris to Boulogne-sur-Mer . . . a dusty road full of potholes that had seemed to go on forever; and Henry . . . was he eight? ten? calling it 'pleasure under difficulties' . . . and me feeling poached like an egg, in love. My brother, that is to say, had a way of putting his finger on the exact perfect description; for living in the unfinished cottage was, as it had been during that drive from Paris, precisely a situation of pleasure under difficulties.

"Or is it perhaps," he now began refining his position, "pleasure *because of* difficulties?" "You may be right," I admitted, ignoring the implied if gentle 'dig'. But what did I care so long as I continued to be well? The air brushed at me but did not hurt. I was tough as a toddler. My limbs were not aware of themselves. That is what it meant to be well, I realized. You walk and run and skip, and feel nothing but a puppyish tiredness. Wellness is next to numbness. Long live numbness.

Later that day I watched as Henry, dressed in his English tweeds in spite of the warm weather, leant upon one of the new porch railings. He in his turn was observing the builders who were stripped to the waist. Hot work digging new drains. He continued to watch them on their lunch break: one sprawled full length leaning on an elbow, the other two sitting up. *"Le Dejeuner sur l'herbe,"* he remarked dabbing at his forehead with his handkerchief. He'd recently seen Manet's 'scandalous' painting in Paris, whereas I'd only seen cartoons of it in the papers; but I knew, as everyone did, that Manet had dared to depict two dressed gentlemen and a nude female. But was that what Henry saw? Or did his own version perhaps feature two naked lolling workmen and a single modestly attired author; or – even more titillatingly – two modestly lolling workmen and a single naked author? I put the disturbing possibility out of my mind but it would not stay put. Henry and I may have thought with the same mind, even shared the same soul – whatever that was – but I guess we had our particular tastes: his, for instance, unaccountably, for raw steak.

But there was Henry turning to me, smiling, pleased to

report on the workers' progress. They had finished their *dejeuner* and were connecting the pipework; soon it could be covered up, a garden planted. I thought of writing a story about manly love; after all, hadn't the poet Whitman unashamedly sung the praises of the male body? But then I remembered William (who almost certainly had not *read* him) calling him disgraceful, or possibly disgusting . . . No, I would not write about such a man. His confusion (attraction – temptation – retreat: always retreat) would joggle my mind until I became ill again. In any case, hadn't I been warned off writing stories? Not that it mattered. Who said it's the writing down that counts? So long as the stories wind on and on, I thought, I know I am alive; and even if no one else knows it, even if my words are poor and I am forced to write in disappearing ink, in the hand of a ghost, I hereby declare: *I am a writer*. Do you hear me?

Just then Katharine burst from the house, the new screen-door screeching on its hinges before banging to behind her.

Henry straightened, taking in the small cataclysm of what was about to happen: "You are leaving?" he said, giving voice to the obvious. "I'm afraid so," said Katharine. It was one of those moments which Henry might have called 'prodigious', when it appears that nothing is happening yet everything is. Three people stand about in a kind of temporary suspension. We do nothing because once one of us 'acts' something will be destroyed forever. We are, just as we are, complete, and equal in our tension. It is Katharine of course who breaks up our balanced configuration. And once she goes, I thought – for it was too late to stop her with her battered-looking haversack already hitched onto one shoulder so that neither Henry nor anyone else could help her – everything will change; and Henry and I will be left like twins again with no room for her.

She held out her hand to my brother. "Please do not take my timing as in any way significant: it's just that I must get back to my sister Louisa, she's not well."

Thus rubbing in the snub of her departure on the very day of his arrival.

By now the workmen had resumed digging, filling in the drainage ditches with new compost and topsoil. As I watched, a butterfly landed on my breast. I went still as glass, forced my heart to calm so as not to disturb the delicate creature with its noticeable rise and fall. Then, for no apparent reason, something shifted in me causing that same organ to contract, turning pebbly and hard. Perhaps it was Katharine's rudeness to Henry, not to mention her walking out on me. Not that either of those could excuse my disgraceful act: how the creature's dusky wings smeared like powdered ink across my white dress.

Seven

My brother watches over me. I am The Spirit of the Dead. "Henry," I whispered, "I have been hearing strange creakings and groanings during the night. Have we a ghost already?" Ever a willing entertainer of immaterial things, he did not however think it likely on this occasion: how would it have divined the new house prior to taking up residency? "No," he concluded, "it is only your house's growing pains." Witty Henry. Still, I thought, pains of any sort could be worrisome. I pushed myself further up in bed:

"Where is everyone?"

"Katharine, you remember . . ."

"Yes, Henry: gone. What of the others?"

"Aunt Kate is down in the diningroom with Father. They're weighing the War and its legacy: *Are such catastrophic bellicosities necessary for regeneration to take place? Was or was not Ben Franklin a true radical?* Meanwhile Rob's little girl is attempting to dig up the new drainage ditches . . . and I believe Mary is down the hallway packing up."

"Packing up . . .?"

"Indeed, I heard the clicking of her valise . . .".

"But why, Henry?"

"Why?"

"Why, I was fast losing patience, is she packing up?"

"Ah, that's because our brother, having been sent a sermon by our father on the subject of commitment and family devotion, arrived late last night from London to take Mary and the children home." He paused; then: "Do you wish to see him . . . shall I bring him up?" The idea of seeing Rob made my chest hurt. He has messed up his marriage, I thought, shaking my head.

"No . . . tell him I am too ill . . . but do send him my love."

Henry nodded. We might have stopped there but I carried on:

"What is wrong with their marriage, Henry?"

He wagged his head. "I am hardly one to pronounce on that subject." Yet *imagine* it he could, brilliantly, vividly: Rob's disturbed state of mind after our mother's death, the claustrophobia of their small Milwaukee dwelling, their childrens' scraps, Mary waiting for him to do something, but what is he to do . . .? "He has shooting pains in his kidneys sending spasms up his spine . . . his digestion is sour and he hasn't emptied his bowels in weeks." On he went narrating Rob's situation until I began to feel his growing desperation, almost as if I were Rob: wanting to get away, become unattached again, feel the desire to drink, to forget. *Without the burden of a family, I might become well again . . .?*

He continued with his remembrancing of Rob: his reluctant service in the War and its attendant guilt . . . his memories of Kitty, who haunts him still, whom perhaps he should have married in spite of her illness, who was to say . . .? He rose from his chair and stood at the window. "Ah, Kitty," he sighed, as if the subject of our cousin was all too much for him; then he returned to his chair and made a girdle with his fingers over his stomach. "Yes," he was coming to a beautifully rounded out summation of Rob's motivation: "And so the resolution, the intention forms that he cannot stay a minute longer. Where he will go he has no idea, Egypt perhaps, but that he must go is certain or he will do something he will later regret."

I observed my brother. He has been telling me a story about Rob, I surmised, in order to deflect attention from himself. A story about our brother Robertson and the causes of his 'weaknesses'. He has no experience of marriage, yet he feels how it makes Rob feel, and so we believe him, and we listen. Everyone listens to Henry, that is his gift. But is it true?

"There is also his early history to consider," he added, "about which you might or might not be aware: that Rob, as a small boy, was 'shoved off' onto Aunt Kate the day you were born."

"But I was also 'shoved off'!" I cried with a pummel to the mattress.

"Ah." He did not know of it, but now that I had brought it to his attention he supposed Aunt Kate had picked up many pieces – "and you, Alice, were alas the last James 'piece'."

"The puzzle piece that wouldn't fit," I grumped unattractively.

"But Henry – to return to the subject of Rob's marriage – everything you have been telling me about Rob is entirely from his point of view. Imagine what it must have been like for poor Mary, abandoned and left alone with a child."

"Ah Mary . . . indeed," he allowed.

"I mean, poor *Wob!*" I lisped, my voice like one of Macbeth's witches sweetened with blackstrap molasses. Surely – I was convinced of it – *he* was the problem, *he* was the selfish, restless, irresponsible one. How else could he go galivanting off to Egypt, leaving Mary with the children; and before that, checking into an asylum, for goodness sake, where he might rest and be taken care of? Selfish selfish Rob!

Henry recoiled, which shocked and frightened me. Suddenly I saw myself through his eyes, how merciless I seemed, how unforgiving. I heard my father's words from long ago: "How hard you are, Alice!" Of all people *I* should understand about nervous illness. But I was like an animal who, catching sight of itself in the mirror, springs to the attack because it loathes what it sees. I shivered, aware of Henry pulling away from me, fearing an awful gap opening between us to swallow up our 'perfect mutual understanding'.

I hugged my knees to my chest. "Mother is dead," I said in a small, sawdusted voice. "Yes," agreed Henry placing a restraining hand on my knees and another on my shoulder. I'd begun rattling all over like a pane of glass. "Are you cold, Alice?" I could not reply. He closed the window but the rattling did not stop. *Dope*. What had I been thinking? The truth was I could never live up to my mother's example: such shine does not transfer. I'd supposed myself managing the house, the servants, the meals, the workmen, the visitors *just as my mother had*. But she had gone about her domestic business so efficiently we were hardly aware of her; whereas I, Alice, had had to point here and there, saying *I did this and I did that*, like a small girl fishing for a pat on the head. I began making a drilling noise through my teeth while poking a hole with my finger through the bedclothes.

"Alice . . .?"

Something was driving me on in my wretched pursuit of what Henry would have called 'the whole picture'; only in this case I risked losing Henry himself. I did not care. Oh, let the gap widen, I thought, let him never speak to me again.

"Henry," I imparted, "our Mother was not perfect, you know it. She was also meddlesome and controlling." A laugh erupted, painful as a bark. "She wanted you to stay close, she was always intruding: were you eating well, getting sufficient sleep, spending too much money, or not enough? And what of the 'life of the affections'? On and on it went, Henry. Don't you see," I pursued, "we have been damaged. Can you not feel the vibration of her selflessness and devotion, on all of us, like a dentist's drill?"

Henry threw out his lip, pale as the jug beside us. My brother, I understood, who claimed to indulge in 'fictional verities', feared the unstoried, unembroidered. Call it the bald truth, if you dare. Off he trotted to fetch me a hot water bottle. The heat was comforting but my Mother's presence pressed in upon me. Give all but ask nothing, that was her message; or was it command?

"But I do ask, Henry," I cried urgently, as if she'd actually spoken: "I *do.*"

"For what do you ask, Alice?" he asked.

I could not explain. I feared I wanted too much, which made it even more sickeningly impossible. Finally I blurted out:

"I can never hope to be like her."

"No," he agreed," smiling benignly: "You are yourself, Alice," he pronounced, "that is more than enough."

After another pause he announced, *domage*, he must return to England. He had already written to his friend Lord Rosebery saying he was 'desperately homesick'.

"*Home*-sick? But Henry," I objected, "our home is here, across the ocean. As for London, you recently described it as 'a mighty-flesh-eating ogress'."

"Ah, but the poor ogress is only human."

"But doesn't the heart harden in her company?"

"On the contrary: she teaches people their places, breaks reputations, tears out their hearts."

I leant forward: "And that is a good thing?"

He believed it was.

"Henry," I dared ask, "do you remember that letter you once showed me?" He nodded. It had been from our mother: *'It seems to me, darling, you must need this succulent, fattening element,'* she'd written, urging him to return to the bosom of the family. But the 'succulent, fattening element' would have trapped him like a pig in a vat of its own lard. He'd had to get away, escape into the arms of his ogress-mistress, across an ocean at least.

Now, I thought, I must let him go.

As he bent towards me I observed his lips, so like my own, bowed in the middle and downturned at the corners, but just that bit fuller and less pursed-up. They brushed my forehead: "Alice, you will keep me informed about Father. And take care of yourself, of course." He did not look back, quickening his pace down the creaky new stairway as if fearing I and my illness would come crawling after him, enormous and engulfing; while I lay there thinking how some of us must hold on for dear life while others must let go or perish.

After he was gone I wrote a story about a daughter who nurses her ailing mother. One day the daughter goes to the market and purchases a pig's head which she carries home tenderly in its slippery white beribboned parcel as if it were a newborn baby. Back in the kitchen she dismisses the servants: she must make the stew herself. It will be her masterpiece. As she chops up the various bits – snout, ears, eyes, cheeks – she tells herself, 'Mother will just die for a good rich pork stew.' And she does. Die. It was not Art, it was illness. I destroyed it, of course. The doctors were right: I must not *write*.

Eight

"Here comes another death scene," I hissed outside father's door. "Hush, Alice," scolded Aunt Kate, "do not disgrace yourself with irreverence." She was carrying a washing bowl filled with some disgusting liquid. "But I am the *reverent* one," I objected. It was my father who was claiming to be dead before his time, and that was surely a crime against Life. Our father who art not yet in heaven yet not quite on this earth, warm in his bed but yearning to go, reaching with his pajama'd arms towards his vision of paradise; an ecstatic aged child anticipating his finest Christmas present ever: *Take me.*

By this time we'd returned to Cambridge. My father had had enough of rocks and sea, he said; not to mention the gulls wheeling about ululating outside his window. "Mary! Mary!" he'd begun wailing, convinced the seagulls were his dead wife. Time to go, I announced miserably, starting to close up the cottage. The slam of shutters and doors, sheets ballooning over beds. And the new house's promise? Spilled like paint. All that clean glass, those waiting drains. Had I called it 'my creation'? *Fool.*

He refused all doctors but the homeopathic Dr. Ahlborn, who could find nothing organically wrong. Father hooted like an owl invoking The Unknowable Reality Behind Phenomena. Ahlborn coughed, lamely prescribed rest of body, stomach and brain. Aunt Kate tried tempting him with thin gruel, but he would not be tempted. "Mary, Mary," he wailed again while I silently supplied the *quite contrary.*

"He talks only of joining her," said Aunt Kate: "I fear it won't be long."

I let myself into his sickroom. "Shall I close the curtains, Father? The sun was directly in his eyes, but he would stare it down. In it he saw the fiery gaze of his opponent and friend, *M. le diable* – for without him there would be no chance of transformation. My father, fierce yet soft-headed as ever. 'The age of the severe and remote patriarch is over,' he'd once written: 'a more appropriate symbol of divinity is the maternal, the benevolent.' Perhaps, Father, I thought, you should have been born a woman?

"But what exactly does your Father do, Alice?" our cousin Minny had once asked. To which I'd replied, "He doesn't *do*, he thinks." "About what?" I reeled off, "Philosophy, theology, morality" – the words flying out detached from meaning. I selected one of Father's books to show her – *Substance and Shadow; or Morality and Religion* – but when she opened to the title page there was Henry's woodcut of a man beating a dead horse. "Oh dear," she'd cried, shutting the book and putting it from her. Years later William, less gruesome but equally cruel, would summarize Father's life's work as: *The monotonous elaboration of a single truth.*

Poor Pater, I now thought: to have had two such brilliant sons!

But there were practicalities to attend to. "What should you like done about your funeral, Father?" I asked. He sat up, shocked into lucidity. "Tell the vicar to say only this: 'Here lies a man who has thought all his life that the ceremonies attending birth, marriage and death are all damned nonsense'. And don't let him say a word more. Promise me, Alice."

"I promise, Father."

His eyes shadowed over.

"What is it, dear?"

"Henry," he began muttering: "HenHenHen . . . ."

"It's allright," I soothed. "I've telegraphed him. He's

boarding ship as we speak. He plans to bring William with him."

My father was clearly agitated: "What is it, Father?"

"No Woom."

"No . . .?" I put my ear closer to his mouth.

"No *Wi-wm*."

"No William?" I guessed correctly, to his relief. So that was it: William was not to be summoned. William the Sensitive must not be made to witness the pater's confusions, his arms waving about like twigs in a gale. William the Susceptible must be spared his father's descent towards death. It smelled. It was not nice.

"And Henry . . .?" I asked. He blinked. Yes, Henry may come. And Rob and Wilkie? Let them all come. "I am dead, Alice, I am in Glory," he intoned. He made a noise like a valveless trumpet trying to play a passage from Bach or Handel. Suddenly he took my hand and pulled me closer: "An urgent message before I depart this world," he whispered. I put my ear to his dry chapped lips, my heart unfolding ready to receive the gift. "I have such good boys," he announced, clear as anything: " – *such* good boys!"

I tried to stifle the whimper but it would out, along with the barely audible cry, "What about me, Father? What about *me*?"

I am in my father's study. I am eight years old. The boys are away at school. I, a girl, am being treated to a different kind of lesson. "My darling girl," Father calls me. The smell of books – paper, ink, leather – of the roses my mother has placed on the table beside him; dust motes in a sunbeam. I am alone with him, so I must be special. "You are goodness personified, my Alice," he tells me: "Do not ever forget it. It is a gift, natural goodness, a virtue that does not have to be learned." He places his hand on my head as if personally passing his blessing onto or into me. I feel the heat of his cupped palm, then its hot pressure forcing me down: *You are goodgoodgood*. "But I want to *learnlearnlearn*!" I cry: "I *like* to learn!" I jackknife so that his own hand – the hand that has been holding me down – flies back slapping his face and knocking his spectacles off. A bead of blood appears at his brow, a cut from his own heavy gold ring. I must not find it funny, or think *serves you right*. I have caused it to happen.

I run to my mother who sprinkles a damp cloth with rosemary oil; I grab it and run back to my Father and dab at the wound. When it's free of blood – it was only a scratch, after all – I paste a tiny plaster over it. After that I scrabble for his glasses, which I find under the table unbroken, and place them back upon his wise old nose. It takes a moment for him to focus, as if he's forgotten who I am; then, remembering, looks pleased, for his point has been proved: "You see, you are another ministering angel." He holds me by the waist and jiggles me from side to side. *Goodgoodgood*.

No I am not, I want to crow, biting my tongue.

Instead I employ a rational argument. "But I have heard you telling the boys that *evil* leads to goodness since it is the *struggle* that marks the path to divinity.' Therefore do I not have to be *bad* first before I can arrive at true salvation and goodness? If we, I, do not struggle, then we, I, account for nothing."

My father places me squarely between his legs. "Ah," he sighs, "My little heiress of the paternal wit." I find I am dismissed. Later as I lie awake in bed, I try reasoning to myself: 'I have hurt him. I have been bad. But then I made it better so I am *good* and saved.' But that only confuses me more, for it leads to the conclusion that I will grow up to be a *man*.

I left him to search out my sister-in-law Alice. "He is adamant," I reported, "that William not be summoned back: should we obey?" She thought that we should. "It is no doubt best for your Father. As for William," she added without a touch of irony, "he prefers to be out of the country in moments of stress." She hugged her stomach. Strange to say, my brother had been called away 'on professional business' a week before the birth of their second son Billy only a month before. Which left me musing to myself, Where do you hide, Willie, while your Alice is laboring with child and your Father with death? Is there a secret place where their pleadings cannot get at you, the blood not seep into the cracks of your flesh? Is that how you know so much about the split-off self? How we all know, whether or not we smell the smells and suffer the visions?

"Where is he now?" I inquired.

"Oh, he's on sabbatical in Oxford, working on a theory of the emotions." *A theory of the emotions?* Ah, I thought, an Oxford college, perfect: the life of a cosseted student. "It's for the best that he stays put to complete the writing otherwise he will be impossible. Besides, it will distress him too much, he's been having episodes of blurred eyesight." Aunt Kate concurred. Having William fussing around would only make things worse. "We'd have to nurse him as well. It would not do." We struggled to keep our faces on straight.

Nine

A trickle of embalming fluid had escaped my father's lips. As I plucked my handkerchief from my sleeve and reached towards him I felt Aunt Kate's hand close firmly around my arm. "What on earth do you think you're doing, Alice?" "Cleaning him up," I replied, pointing: "He's . . . leaking." She snatched the handkerchief. "You did not see that." She peered in. "Besides, it has stopped."

The third day of his death. Floor lamps had been placed at either end of the coffin in which he lay like a life-sized bewhiskered doll. Beneath the myriad of flowery and perfumed scents you could detect wax and chloroform, and death of course. Yet he himself appeared more peaceful than in life. He has escaped, I thought, just as someone remarked, "I guess if Abraham Lincoln could be embalmed, so could Henry James Senior." And another: "Well, after all, he is one of Boston's famous sons."

The affair would have suited Prince Albert himself with its coffin photographs, memorial cards, door wreaths, drapes – all in black of course; not to mention the black-bordered front-page obituary in the Boston Globe. (My mother, by contrast, had stipulated her funeral and its aftermath should be as simple and unfussy as possible, causing the family the least amount of bother.)

Eventually he was removed and taken to the family plot where, in due course, a modest mausoleum would be erected. My only fear, which grew as they began lowering the coffin, was that his demons – bats, albatrosses, raptors, wolves of course – would escape and latch onto me, circling my throat like some fantastical zoological necklace. *We are a gift from your father so you can struggle too and achieve goodness. . . .*

A cold, snow-infested January day. We held onto our hats. According to my father's dying wish, that he be spared the usual Unitarian 'claptrap', the minister read from one of my father's own theosophical tracts laced with mad Sweden-borgian notions. But then we got the 'damned Unitarian claptrap' too. I tried not to picture him spitting with fury in his coffin, as he surely would be, or I would lose my composure. Aunt Kate and William's Alice were gripping me, one each side, to stop me throttling the minister – which I was sorely tempted to do. "The bare trees are busy applauding bony death," muttered I.

William's letter from Oxford – to be read out to father on his deathbed – had arrived too late. I'd been tempted to send him a telegram saying TOO LATE WILLIE BAD LUCK – but he might have thought it somewhat tasteless.

Henry did not arrive in time either. I'd left a note for him at the shipping office: *The funeral is today, we have gone ahead, there seemed no use in waiting for you as the uncertainty was so great.* As we stood beside the grave I kept thinking his cab would come rattling through the gates of the Cambridge Cemetery and he'd appear like the hero in a mushy story out of Girl's Own. He did not. He arrived late that night. "All over," I sang. He tilted against me as if he might collapse and I felt the vibration of a groan pass through his chest and into mine.

"Where are the others?" he managed, righting himself.

"Rob has gone back to Wisconsin. Wilky is too ill. William, as you know . . . ." Henry mopped his brow, his poor head all a-sweat. He was exhausted. I pictured him trapped on that sluggish ship for days and days pacing the deck, urging it forward. Finally, he consults the Captain, who explains they are having engine trouble. "Is there nothing to be done? I am due at a . . ." Here he hesitates: would 'a professional engagement' carry more weight than 'my father's funeral'? He decides upon the former. The Captain shakes his head, he is very sorry but there is nothing for it. Henry stands gripping the railing, staring into the sea. "I am going to miss my father's funeral," he confesses. The waves cannot care less: *laplap*, they sing.

Henry took to his attic bed, I to mine. Aunt Kate looked after us both, bringing us cups of tea and bowls of weak broth. Up and down she went. In between, she began sorting through some letters which she'd found in father's chest of drawers. I slept on, dreaming of papers being burnt.

When we were well enough Henry and I returned together to the Cemetery. I watched from a distance, ankle-deep in snow as he stood at our father's newly-cut grave with William's letter flapping at his thigh. It was late in the day; above him the western sky had turned into a deadly polar pink behind the bare branches of the winter woods. Henry removed his hat tucking it under his arm to protect it from the wind, and as he did so the moon came up, white and young, and was reflected in the white face of the empty Stadium which framed one of the boundaries of Soldiers' Field across the Charles. He stood on the little hillock by the group of graves that made up our family. As he read, I saw that he was moved by everything he had once known, and with it came a recognition of the stillness, the strangeness, the American-ness. And the words. Written words are like injections, I thought, they pass directly into the bloodstream. Our bodies get in the way, whereas words are life. He began: *Darling old father* . . .

How odd, I thought, for Henry to be reading William's words. But he was used, after all, to erasing himself, to becoming phantom-like. His was a gift for not getting in the way. Indeed, he soon became so transparent I could see William standing there hunched over his own letter. William, ever the responsible one, promises to look after the literary remains. He also promises that the brothers will

61

stand by one another, and also stand by their sister Alice. He is full of tender memories and feelings in his heart but "you, Father" he finishes in Henry's voice, "will always be for me the central figure. *Good night, my sacred old father. Your William.*"

Now Henry must fish for his handkerchief: an awkward manoeuvre what with having to keep hold of his hat and the letter. Eventually he manages to wipe his nose. When he is sufficiently composed he places his hat back upon his head, gives it a one-fingered tap, pockets William's letter and backs away. It is a signal that I am to come forward, which I do, only my lips are rolled in upon themselves. If I open my mouth a howl will emerge. I shake my head. I have nothing to offer. I am frozen in time and space. I cannot feel my feet. Henry places a hand at my back and leads me away as if I were a very old person.

Ten

The recently opened and conveniently located Adams Nervine Asylum had been endowed specifically for the treatment of 'nervous people who are not insane.'

"I trust I am not insane," I told the interviewing panel, "merely dilapidated." Dr. Mitchell looked away; the others harumphed.

My mother and father were dead; my dear friend Katharine was swanning about the country 'selling' her Home Studies Course to other female educationists; Henry was in London working on a novel set in Boston; William was teaching at Harvard; Wilky was down in Florida recuperating and Rob was 'drying out'. And, yes, I'd done precisely what I'd once blamed *him* for doing: *asylum*, a place of refuge or sanctuary.

I admitted myself in the spring of 1883.

I was given a tour of the house and grounds. "Adams House is built in the Queen Anne style of architecture," the manageress helpfully informed me. "I guess Queen Anne had a sense of humor," I rejoined. Frankly, I thought it a disproportionate abortion with its excrescenses of cupola and turret, its girdling porch ("an especially *American* feature"), its claustrophobic restraining posts and struts. Had one of its inmates, I inquired, designed it in one of her more lurid nightmares? No reply. It had chillingly weedless lawns and "sixteen acres of mature woodland." I saw that it would do as a setting for one of Henry's gothic tales. Or mine, should I ever write again.

"You are quite relaxed, Miss James?" Dr. Mitchell inquired. I was all too relaxed having survived a steam and massage treatment. "I feel like a fat pink shrimp," I reported, tongue protruding. "Good good," he responded, up-ending his pen upon its vulnerable nib. Now, if I was ready, he would present me with a list of words. "It is a newly concocted method for tapping into an unusual or, shall we say, pre-conscious state of mind." "Yes, I know," I said, "my brother has spoken of it: based on an association of ideas." "Your brother?" He blinked. "William." "William James?" "The same." "I see. Well." He shifted about in his leather chair in an attempt to reassert his authority. "If you are ready we can begin. Simply say the first word," he instructed, "that comes into your head." I announced I was ready, and he began:

"Egg?"	"William."
"Feather?"	"God."
"Wedding?"	"Death."

"Did you say 'dress', Alice?"
"No, Dr. Mitchell, I said 'death'."
"Ah." He continued:

"Death?"	"Father."
"Father?"	"Silly."

He cleared his throat:

"Pen?"	"Henry."
"Marriage?"	"Mistake."
"Marriage?" he repeated.	"Aunt Kate."

He sat back in his chair. "Fine, excellent." He'd flipped the pen over so that it now stood on its holder end: *taptap*.
"Tell me about your Aunt Kate," he said.
"She lived with us."
"And why was that?"

"She was useful about the house. She helped my mother to look after us."

"But she was married . . .?"

"Yes, but it was not the usual thing . . ." Here I slid forward across his desk until I was close enough to make out a scar over his right eyebrow. "As a matter of fact," I told him with relish, "it was scandalously brief."

Aunt Kate and I had been staying at Clifton House near Cambridge, just along from Marble Head. I was nineteen years old and needing to be 'socially aired,' having been isolated during my recurring illnesses. One day she led me out along the cliff path. At some point we stopped to gaze down at the churning waves hitting the rocks below. We stood close together; suddenly I turned to face her. "What about you?" I began. "What about me, Alice?" The other decrepit spinster-bitches and I had already compared notes. Marriage was their theme-song: *Louise Wilkinson is now married, have you heard? . . . And Mary McKim has just landed a Mr Richard Church . . . And Serena Mason is promised to somebody else . . . and Ned Lowell's engaged to a Miss Goodrich. Oh, and Kitty Temple's friend Mary Hane has also done the deed and . . . marriagemarriagemarriage, until the world had begun to feel like a giant mating pen with only us, the sorry inmates of Clifton House, locked out.*

Aunt Kate took my arm as my feet seemed to be going in different directions. "So am I to be trotted out like a bitch in heat?" I taunted her. "Concentrate on where you are going," she admonished, obviously trying to distract me from 'the subject'; but I would not be deflected from my purpose. What purpose, you well might ask, for it was obvious no good could come of it.

"Your so-called *marriage*," I pursued.

"Never mind about that," she waived dismissively. She'd warned us off the subject before, but I was determined not to be put off this time. "After all," I insisted, "you know all about marriage: describe to me the joys of marriage." I'd learned teasing from William: William who'd once made up an Ode To Aunt Kate, ending with:

O the gallant Captain perished for the love of Kate . . .

"That's cruel, Willie," I'd objected: "how could you?" Our Aunt's marriage had by then been annulled after only a year, though no one knew why. Something, we guessed, that her 'husband' Captain Marshall had done, or not done; but that he'd been anything but gallant was certain. Once, riffling through Aunt Kate's jewelry box I'd come across a secret compartment containing a yellowed newspaper cutting from an 'Obituaries' page. My eye picked out the following: *'Like many men, who have from early life been engaged in nautical pursuits, and accustomed to command . . . Captain Marshall had an air of sternness about him that was somewhat repulsive to strangers . . .'* After that I re-folded it and stowed it away, but the phrase *somewhat repulsive to strangers* stuck in my mind.

But there was Aunt Kate at my elbow with her innocent fat sausage curls and her *never mind that.* "Oh, I do mind," I complained insisting: "and I will know." For marriage, I think at this stage, must be like rain: it blurs things yet it is right because without it we die. (Would I die unwatered?) Being married, in spite of all the whispers about what happened to you afterwards – the disappointments, the failures, the unmentionables – had come to seem a necessary outcome. Perhaps it's like flying, I thought, dangerous yet still somehow desirable. I pictured myself being pushed off a cliff and being caught and borne aloft by some gravity-immune hero called 'a husband'. Music accompanies this ridiculous scene, Aunt Kate rippling through a Chopin waltz.

"But you were *married*," I cried, as if that were a better cure-all than Mrs Emerson's homeopathy or William's sea-baths or mesmerism or anything.

"Oh," said my Aunt, as if the very thought of it wearied her, "it all happened so long ago, Alice . . .". But then, as if she'd seen into the heart of a breaking wave: "And, as you know, it did not last long."

"How long?" I demanded.

Her face hardened: "Just short of a year." She prodded me on with one finger. "Best to let sleeping dogs lie, Alice."

"Was he a dog? Did he turn vicious?" And then, recalling the obituary: "Was he as 'repulsive' to you as he was to strangers?"

"Alice! Enough! Suffice it to say it was a mistake." After a pause, she shivered, then added in a barely audible whisper:

"A frightful mistake."

The next day I was more determined than ever: I must, would, know more. Over breakfast I nagged and nagged until my Aunt got so fed up she blurted it all out. "Now see what you've done," she cried, adding ominously: "You will regret it."

I stumbled off down the cliff towards the shore. The air was clear as anything, the October leaves turned to gold: perfect treasures, I thought giddily. The rocks awaited me below: some pointed, some smooth and banked like the backs of whales, fully as bold as the rocks at home, only without any surf. I kept up my descent until I reached a path then poured myself down gaining more and more speed until I couldn't stop even if I'd wanted to because the rocks were loose and I was not used to running with my clumsy, weak legs, and with the speed and the slippage returned the secret I'd pulled out of my Aunt, the truth of her frightful mistake of a marriage. And she was right, I did regret it.

The good doctor's mouth watered with curiosity as to the nature of *the frightful mistake*. "It's the title of my tale," was all I would reveal. He frowned, "Do you mean to say what you just told me was *a fiction*?" As if that was the same as 'lie'. Well I would not reply to that. He threw down his pen.

"I think that's enough for today, Miss James, we don't want to tire you out." "I'm not in the least tired," I objected. "And I enjoy telling stories – like my brother," I added. At that he stretched forward again across his blotter, which was green and covered in inky doodles in the shape of bats with human heads: "That was *not* a game," he said. It sounded like a threat. But if it was not a game, what was it? He was beginning to irritate me, to remind me of my father, and that made me want to knock his block off. But I controlled myself. I was by this time close enough to read the scribbles on his notepad: *hysteria neurasthenia melancholia*. The words were so used-up, so meaningless, he might have written *dog cat pig* with as much effect. I wanted to bang the desk with my fists, make the bats fly, then run round and pull his ears: But it *is* a game, don't you see? A game of words containing clues to my distress which any nincompoop would guess! I almost felt sorry for him sitting there scratching his head. But then another part of me wanted to spit, You should not employ a new technique without knowing how to apply it, doctor!

On my way out, he stopped me: "One more thing, Alice," he said. My hand gripped the doorknob. "I have recommended a daily encounter with the Holtz Electrical Machine."

*

I lay on the rubber sheet which was warm and wet with my own sweat. They are trying to turn us all into swollen pink sea creatures, I thought, staring up at a huge purple glass ball. I was instructed to press my temples into the two 'bows' which were there to facilitate the passage of electricity from the great glass ball. My arms were strapped to my sides, the sharp points of the 'bows' dug into my temples as I waited for the surge of electricity. I'd once seen an engraving depicting a young woman standing on the platform of just such an electrical machine while a man turned a crank. The caption under the print read:

'The electrical kiss provides a very special thrill.'

The shrimp feeling was fading; now I was being turned into a baked apple, my brain going to mush.

August, 1869. It's my twenty-first birthday and we are all gathered in the back garden of an old farmhouse my parents have rented out in Pomfret, Connecticut. My health is much improved so that I am feeling quite lively and never think of having to lie down during the day. William is basking in a hammock which he's strung up between two pines. My friend Lizzie Boott – she and her father have a house nearby – is at her easel painting the pine trees that surround us. Father is walking about with his arms behind his back muttering to himself.

At three o'clock my mother, who has been baking, excuses herself. Moments later she appears with Aunt Kate leading a train of servants carrying the tea things and a birthday cake bombarded on top with fat cherries. "Devil's food," she explains smiling. At which, appropriately, the sky begins to darken. Father stops muttering. William stops swinging. "Look everyone!" cries Lizzie. William peers out from under the arm that's been protecting him from the sun. The darkening increases moment by moment as the moon creeps across the sun. We look as if we've been playing 'Grandmother's Footsteps'. I have fallen into a lightless cave. Father is ecstatic: "Today we are blessed to witness further proof of the Divine Nature." "Oh, damn the Divine Nature!" I cry, kicking out. "What extraordinary timing," comments William. Only Mother lays her hand gently on my arm; but she cannot stop me seeing it, *imbibing* it, as a portent: the promise of my future eclipsed.

The electrical 'kiss' came with a fierce jolt.

I thought of a story by one of the new female writers in which noises were written into the text: 'clackety clack' for a sewing machine; 'clickety click' for knitting needles. Henry, I

thought, would never succumb to such crudity. But I liked it. It brought the world and its sounds to life, like music.
Jolt jolt jolt . . . kiss kiss kiss.

"Tell me about your father, Alice."
"But I'd much prefer to hear about *your* father, Doctor."
"Oh but it is *you* who are here to be helped, not I."
"And you think my father will 'help' . . .?"
"Don't you?" he returned maddeningly.

I did not reply; I did not need to as my legs had begun trembling so hard they caused the floor to vibrate beneath us. It was as if Father himself had taken up occupancy in my body.

"You are trembling," observed the sharp-eyed Doctor.
"It is true," I confessed, "my father sometimes shook."
"*Shook*, Alice?"
"Yes, shook," I snarled, "as in 'had the tremors'."
"Do you imply he drank spirits?"
"Oh, *please*."

We had only just finished dinner when it began. The boys had shoved off and Mother and Aunt Kate were busy in the kitchen. That left me alone with my father. It was then that the shaking started up. *Judderjudder* went his head and limbs and then the rest of his body joined in. His wooden knee repeatedly hit the underside of the table sending the leftover plates and glasses skittering about. William should be here, I thought: he would interpret it as the dead come to rearrange our tableware. Or perhaps we were having an earthquake? But the quake was all in our father's brain and bones; he had begun to gesticulate at the fireplace where 'some damned shape' had begun to form itself into a troupe of squat green-eyed monsters having a knees-up, cackling and hissing and spitting, until he was forced to fling his elbow across his face to avoid being the target of their 'slime'. The word 'fetid' escaped his foam-laced lips. I watched fascinated, furious: "That's what you get for eating too much cream," I told him.

Aunt Kate put him to bed, soothing and petting. But there it was in his mind's eye, the evil thing he could not get out. *Have you tried an ice-pick, pater?* The doctor prescribed a calming visit to the countryside; but lurking in every tree were more green-eyed fiends. *Leaves, father, they are called leaves.*

Later he would find an explanation for what he'd experienced in the work of Swedenborg. 'Vastation,' he called it. Evil, he would sermonize, was necessary, yea, essential to God's plan. God in his infinite love allows the possibility of salvation. If man was not free to be selfish and sinful, he was not free to choose good and God.

"Down is up," as I told Dr Mitchell. "Mad is sane," I went on babbling. "Welcome to the Divine Natural Humanity. *Yes, Father, of course, Father. Bad is good. Selfishness is benevolence. Lying is truth. Evil is salvation* . . . Would that the author of my being had been a stevedore, a bank clerk, an anything rather than what he was: 'a seeker after Truth'. Whatever that was . . .".

Mitchell led me away and had me sedated.

Then there was lunch: a mashed potato ring circling the plate like a funerary wreath decorated with a few soggy spinach leaves. I shared a table with three other women on the same disgusting diet. We stared drowsily into our bowls. "What d'you guess we're being fattened up for?" one of them asked, scooping the remains of her crusted potato into her napkin for later disposal. Another, winking, said, "I guess so's the old witch can eat us for her supper!" Dessert was a bowl of milky gruel over which maple syrup had been liberally sloshed.

Alone in my room I plotted a story about a group of women imprisoned in a beautiful but dark old Boston mansion, set in extensive grounds patrolled by dogs trained to catch escapees. The women are being fattened up for some malign purpose. It would not be clear in the story what the purpose was, but a sense of menace would pervade the tale as the women went waddling about the halls and grounds, barely able to move or think.

*

"Tell me about your brothers," encouraged Mitchell.

"My brothers? But I have four."

"Choose one."

I closed my eyes. I saw Willie slipping naked from the bathroom up to his room. Somehow he'd managed to forget his towel. But I did not tell him about that. Instead, I told him about our wrestling games, how he would pin me to different surfaces as if testing for the best one. One day he began in the garden but I screamed because it was wet and would make me ill, which frightened him, so he pulled me up and pushed me into the garden room instead whereupon he threw me to the floor, which was gratefully carpeted, and there he pushed and pummelled and would not desist, flattening my arms out and pressing himself hard into me while grinding his teeth; then of a sudden wrenching himself off and shoving me away from him so that I rolled like a despised thing, as if what had occurred had been my fault.

The telling tired me out.

"But," Dr Mitchell leaned forward, "had anything actually occurred?"

"Occurred . . .?" My voice, in its innocence, rose higher in pitch. "How exactly do you mean?"

"Anything of a violent physical nature, that is . . .?"

I'd had enough 'soft soaping' to last me a lifetime. I accused him of cowardice. "You're afraid to say it," I taunted, "aren't you?" And then I dared him to say it. And so he did.

"Allright then: did any sexual impropriety take place between your brother and yourself?"

"Of course not," I said disgustedly: "what a vulgar suggestion. It was all perfectly innocent."

*

William found me occupying a bench under a sprawling beech. It was late summer and the tree had flung out its fullest, frilliest leaf-petticoat. He followed my gaze up the substantial trunk. "The mother goddess," he named it, keen as he was on mythic figures. "Yes, Willie: do sit," I said patting the seat beside me. There was of course too much to talk about: Father's death; Wilky's growing illness; his own year in Oxford and London; my 'incarceration'. He fixed me with his cross-eyed stare. "It's wonderful to see you . . . my little grey-eyed doe." He patted my hand: "You're not suffering?"

"Hardly. As you see, it's more like a country retreat than a madhouse."

"And the accommodation?"

"Entirely satisfactory. Our rooms are currently painted a clinical white but they are threatening to re-do them in consoling pink tints with moldings and wallpapers. They are worried the glaring whiteness might nudge us – I demonstrated with a precariously positioned pebble – over the edge into madness. We are highly suggestible, you see."

"Sensitive might be a more accurate word." He paused: "And you are eating?"

"Like a goose being prepared for slaughter."

"Slaughter, Alice?"

"I am being Fletchered to death. Stuffed to the gills on a high-starch diet of potato-rice-blancmange-bread-spaghetti. I chew every stodgy mouthful for at least 15 minutes: first one way, then the other." I demonstrated puffing out my cheeks, as if they needed any further puffing. "Then I swish milk around in my mouth before finally swallowing, thus rendering any identifiable foodstuffs total mush."

He groaned. "Don't tell Henry or he'll be violently ill."

"I wouldn't dream of it. They say he is able to cycle two hundred miles a day on his own dietary regime – Fletcher that is."

William tsk'd. "Sheer quackery. Anyway, do you intend to cycle two hundred miles a day, Alice?"

"My ambitions are rather more modest: merely to get up the stairs to my attic room: I can barely manage it."

"That's because carbohydrates make you fat and lethargic."

"They like us that way; we do not cause trouble."

"What you want to give you energy is a high fat, low carbohydrate diet. Beef, raw or cooked – that's what I recommend."

I snarled: "Mmn, red meat . . . then I shall be even more of a hyena, Willie, and you might not like that."

"It would be better than . . .".

"A stuffed goose?" I sighed. "Actually, Katharine would agree with you, she thinks they're turning us all into brain-less idiots."

There was a pause. "How is Katharine, by the way?"

"Boringly well, as ever. Writes at least twice a week. Travelling suits her. But she hates me being here."

He looked around. "I'm not sure I like it either," he said.

"What is there not to like? The grounds, as you see, are quite magnificent . . . ."

"However disguised it's still an institution for the . . .".

"Neurotic, hysterical, neurasthenic, hypochondriacal, etc etc etc?" I supplied.

"Is that Mitchell's diagnosis?"

I nodded. He refuted it. I was not hysterical, merely ill. "In any case, however defined, I don't like you being secluded with a bunch of . . . mentally and emotionally unstable females."

"But Willie, that is precisely what I am!"

"I don't care," he repeated. "I see it leading to either an unnatural demureness . . .".

"You mean it will break my spirit? Turn me into a sugary cringing little Dame Durden?"

"Just so. Alternatively . . ."

"Yes?"

". . . to open revolution."

"Ah. That's more like it, Willie. You see me as Liberty leading the rabble across the lawns, as in the Delacroix, with Fletcher's head on a pike?"

But then I realized he'd used 'open revolution' to stand in for madness; that after awhile I would 'graduate' from mere dilapidation into stark raving lunacy.

"Don't worry, Willie," I soothed, "I won't let them turn me into the mad Mrs. Rochester." I looked up towards my own top floor turret room. "Though the idea of fire had occurred to me."

"That's my Alice," he grinned broadly, adding: "Obviously they have not destroyed that part of your brain where the imagination resides."

"Not for want of trying," I told him: "they have jolted me out of my wits. But which part of the brain is it exactly?"

He took my cranium between his two hands and drew upon it with his finger – somewhere near my left ear – a shape the size of a soda biscuit.

I said, "I will request they stay away from that area in future."

We sat silently for a time.

"And how is Alice?" I asked. "And your little Billy?"

"Ah, the domestic catastrophe is nearly eighteen months old. He has a rich orange complexion, a black shock of hair and is of a musical disposition – though not too musical. I find I have affection for the little animal."

"And little Henry?"

He smiled. "Thriving." Alice, he added, was soon to have another: "It's only just been confirmed."

"That's splendid news, Willy: congratulations."

He shot his fingers through his hair leaving it spiked like

an artichoke. "She is my earth, Alice. What would I do without her?"

"Don't fuss, Willie," I said: "She'll be fine: she's like Katharine, hideously healthy. Anyway, it's mostly the poor that die in childbirth."

He'd begun tapping his foot. "She's always there, when I have my nervous attacks . . . you understand, Alice." He was breathing noisily. "She knows exactly how to calm me down with her . . . mellowness." He turned to face me. "She is not like us, Alice . . . not an ounce of morbidity in her body. And the house," he went on, "she creates such a sense of order and calm, yes more calm . . . even when the children cry, she manages to silence them, or take them away somewhere because you see I find it . . . disturbing, but she protects me from . . . oh, everything." He blinked; he was having trouble with his eyes again. I wanted to say *As our mother did our father* but instead I took his hand, "I'm glad you found her . . . Alice, I mean. I'm happy for you, truly." And I was – to know that she would keep him safe. But who would keep me safe? Katherine, of course. Yet could I say, *What would I do without my Katharine?* The two statements did not appear to carry equal weight. Even in my own mind 'Alice's Katharine' and 'William's Alice' seemed to belong in separate compartments.

William twirled one end of his moustache, then the other before reaching round to my other side where there lay the latest Cornhill Magazine. "What's this you're reading?" I explained it contained a reprint of Henry's *nouvelle* Daisy Miller: the story of an all-American girl – brash, even vulgar, yet somehow appealing – who refuses to conform to the code of behavior in Roman society and is therefore punished. She flirts in the Colosseum by moonlight, catches malaria, and dies.

"Have you read it?" I asked.

By way of reply he muttered, "An echo of Newport, indeed."

"And why not," said I, "as a way of portraying a New England 'type'?"

But he had no rational response: the whole enterprise seemed to annoy him:

"What a way to make a living!" he burst out.

I allowed the unguarded exclamation to die away. "Practicing an art, as Henry does," I said at last, "is not so much a way of making a living as a way to make life more bearable . . . to make your soul grow, for heaven's sake."

His eyes widened. "And for whom does this 'Daisy Miller' make life more bearable?"

"Henry, for one," I said. "She is his creation, she and the rest of her 'vulgar' American family. Part of him, I believe, is devoted to her; is one with little Randolph when he asserts, 'American candy is the best . . . American girls are the best.'"

"Do you mean to say you think it was a mistake for Father to drag us off to Europe when we were children?"

"A mistake?" I repeated. I read out a sentence I had earmarked: "'Winterbourne wondered if he himself had been like this in his infancy, for he had been brought to Europe at about this age.'" I looked up. "It is his paean to all that – candy, girls, not being 'stiff as an umbrella'. His regret at its loss."

"Regret . . .? But he took it upon himself to leave!"

"True enough, but acting never stops one regretting. As for Daisy herself," I went on, "Winterbourne is drawn to her, of course, but he also wishes to *be* her."

"And exactly who or what is this Daisy Miller?"

I held out my palms, as if testing for rain. "I guess," I said, mimicking Daisy's favorite speech pattern, "all this." My fingers clutched at the empty air as if to draw something meaningful out of its dry sedated mildness, except that Henry's world was divided and divided, viewed from so many different angles and points of view it seemed impossible, ridiculous, to try and reduce it to some comprehensible shorthand. But I saw no other way.

"I *guess*," I said, "it's about confusion, temptation . . . attraction and repulsion towards this 'Americanness', this 'innocence' he has left behind."

"But he has chosen it: the *other*," he almost sneered.

I turned to fact him square-on: "*That* is the whole point. Daisy is sacrificed to Europe."

We said nothing for a few moments. "It is also of course," I added, "about sex." He stiffened. Clearly we should not be discussing such things – *I* should not be discussing such things – but was it not the privilege of madness, after all? I had found the passage where Winterbourne stands at the bottom of the hotel's great staircase watching Daisy as she trips down towards him and senses 'something romantic going forward'. I read out: " 'He could have believed he was going to elope with her.' There," I exclaimed, feeling mildly triumphant: "What else is that but a barely veiled way of saying, *He undressed her with his eyes . . . he imagined running away with her and throwing her down on the bed and ravishing her . . .* Am I not right, Willie?"

He gave a great puff of disapproval while running his fingers repeatedly through his hair. "You are getting over-excited, Alice: I think we had better get you back in the house." I reached up to pat down the rather mad-looking tufts. I guess I felt quite calm.

After William had gone I made my way down the central corridor, narrowly avoiding collision with a nurse carrying a steaming pile of linen. Then on the narrow stairway up to my room I met the so-called decorator. I was beginning to feel encroached upon. "Must my room be painted *pink*?" I spat the word, as if someone had stuffed my mouth with over-sweetened marzipan. "Do I not have a say in the matter?" He began to back off, poor man, trapped as he was in that confined space with an inmate. He was merely following orders, he explained. "Well, then," I pursued, "*my* order is – if it must be painted at all – for blue, the palest of blues." The color of French cupboards, of Katharine's eyes; the clear, unsentimental hopefulness of blue. But he had gone before I could explain all that. And meanwhile my room was still white.

Before leaving William had presented me with a copy of his 'What Is An Emotion?' It was his year's work which had been published in the philosophy journal, 'Mind.' "I do not suppose," he'd said with that familiar tinge of competitive bitterness, "it will water your soul as Daisy Miller did, but it is . . . what it is." Having had enough of soothing him, I'd had to bite my tongue from agreeing. "Goodbye, Willie," I eventually managed. "Love to Alice and the children."

I curled up in the window and read. I did not find its turgid academic style easy, but I persisted. *Do we run from a bear because we are afraid, or are we afraid because we run?*

His theory, in the end, appeared simple: a refutation of the natural assumption that we feel first and act later. According to this theory, upon catching sight of the bear, we experience complex *bodily* responses: racing heart, tight stomach, sweaty palms, tense muscles, etc. – which causes us to flee. As we do so, the body goes through further physiological upheaval (blood pressure rises, heart rate increases, pupils dilate, etc etc.) At some stage (when we are halfway up a tree observing the bear climbing after us?) we translate these responses into an emotion: in this case, *I am afraid*. In other words, the mental aspect of emotion, the feeling, is a slave to the physiology, not vice versa.

We do not tremble because we are afraid; we do not cry because we are sad. No, we are afraid because *we tremble. And we are sad because we cry.*

The year is 1862. Winter. William announces his intention to walk the Appalachian Trail come spring. "But there will be bears," objects Henry. We can all see he's afraid, but it's part of his 'new regime'. He will battle his demons. He will take his rifle. He is not a sissy like Henry. He will not be beaten. Later I lie in bed thinking of him tromping along in terror yet forcing himself not to fear. How like a bear he is, I think.

I stopped reading and gazed about me. The walls of my attic room, I realized, were like enormous empty pages. "Never touch paper with pen, brush or pencil as long as you live," Mitchell had advised.

Well then I won't.

I began my story on the south-facing wall working my way round with a crayon I'd found in the games room. The story was called 'Billy's Bear'. It featured a young woman called Angelica, and a rather older man called Professor William Beard. He is a philosophy teacher and Angelica is his student. He is very attracted to her and she is naturally flattered. "Call me Billy," he instructs. In due course he seduces her. She experiences certain bodily sensations (rapid heartbeat, sweating, etc.). I am in love, she now feels.

Thus proving William's theory.

Angelica soon discovers she's with child. "I do not believe it can be mine," protests the philosophy teacher called Billy. "But it is yours, it cannot be otherwise," cries Angelica, helplessly.

Two years later we meet her again. She has had to drop out of college in order to look after her child. Each night as she tucks him in he calls for his bear: "Billy, I want Billy." The bear is much loved but sightless because of an 'accident' quite early on in its life. It occurred one night after the child had fallen asleep. As Angelica looked down upon him holding the bear, she announced confidently: "I am angry." She confirmed the sensation before slipping the bear out of her child's arms with the sleight-of-hand of a magician before tearing its eyes from its head. Only then did she begin to tremble.

Thus refuting William's theory.

*

"Your walls . . .," Dr Mitchell began: "Can you explain . . .?"

"It just came upon me," I said sweetly: "rather urgently . . . the need to write it down . . . And since I'd been disallowed paper . . . In any case, I'd been told the room was about to be painted . . . *pink.*"

"I do not see that that has any bearing upon the . . ."

"Personally," I interrupted, "I think it looks rather artful: like one of the new wallpapers."

"Well, that is not the opinion of the staff, I'm afraid."

"And is it yours?"

He ran his fingers through his hair, just as William had done earlier in the day. "I haven't actually seen it, Alice, but I have been told . . .".

"Would you like to . . . see it?" I imagined him twirling round, enchanted with my creation. But he only shook his head, scratching his scalp with the end of his pen, his helplessness palpable. Yet it made us more equal, so I valued it. But then I began to feel sorry for him. His 'games', he admitted, had done nothing to alleviate my physical or emotional symptoms. Beyond that, all he could offer was 'complete rest and freedom from responsibility', a regimen that proved helpful for a majority of the asylum's over-burdened inmates, but obviously did nothing for me except fatten me up and slow me down.

He did not try to dissuade me from leaving. "I fear we have failed you, Alice. We are not equipped to deal with the more . . . subtle psychological confusions and pressures." He shook my hand and wished me luck. I thanked him for . . . everything. Then he did an amazing thing: he called me 'extraordinary'.

Eleven

I returned to the narrow-shouldered Cambridge house at the end of summer but longed for my cottage. How I missed its moss-clad rocks, its sand-choked grass and ocean. And Katharine, above all Katharine. "I intend to return to Beverly," I announced to Aunt Kate. "You will do no such thing," she rejoined: "you will never manage on your own." "Of course I will," I asserted, already undermined by her certainty. What if she was right? By bedtime I'd gone limp as a paper doll. I held up my arms as she slipped the nightdress over my head.

Next morning there was a letter from William announcing, in the same paragraph, the joyful birth of their baby Herman and the sad death of our brother Wilky. Sad . . . joyful? a birth . . . a death? *Hip, ho, hip ho,* I began swinging my arms wildly high and low as if conducting a chorus of sopranos and basses, listening with relief to how they cancelled one another out. *What news, Alice? Oh, nothing much to speak of . . .* But gradually the voices separated and there it was:

(1) a birth: a boy called Herman.

(2) a death: my brother Wilky

The birth of a child even I understood as good news. But Wilky . . . dead? Surely not! I appealed to Aunt Kate, who nodded her assent.

"You mean you knew of it?"

"I did," she confessed.

"Then why . . .?"

"I didn't want to distress you."

"But he was my *brother*!" I howled. "I should have been told . . . I should have known!"

"Well," she said drily, "now you do."

I sank to my knees, defeated. It was too late: for tears, for the funeral, for anything.

"So what killed him?"

"Bright's disease," she explained: "it affected his heart."

I scribbled notes for a story about a brother and sister, close in age but separated by distance, circumstance and interests. The sister has been told of her brother's illness but not of its seriousness as she is judged too ill and frail herself to bear the news with equanimity. The family are 'together' in their deception, leaving her to imagine her brother haloed and spangled like an angel as if *Bright's Disease* were a blessing, the result of having fought and been wounded in the war. She pictures an angel covered in scales like shiny medals.

But she has been deceived. Instead of getting better, her brother dies. She has been stupid, gullible. However, the reader is begged not to hold her entirely responsible for her childish blindness; after all, has she not been kept deliberately in the dark through the family's deception? In any case, their 'strategy' is soon shown to have been an ill-conceived 'bungle' as the sister, overcome with remorse and guilt, is tipped into irretrievable madness.

"But *why* may I not return to Beverly Farms?" I took up my plea. Aunt Kate shook her head. I simply would not cope. The responsibilities involved in managing the seaside property and its acreage, its outbuildings and stables, would be too great for me. Would they? Oh, they would. There would be storms along the coast, the wind would howl down the chimneys and the wolves would join in.

I pictured Henry's 'house of fiction' beside my house of failure. Each time I closed my eyes I saw it staring back at me out of its uncurtained, abandoned windows; while outside the horses and the sea both bucked and foamed at the mouth, rolled and retreated and returned again, pawing the ground before lying down glossy and peaceful to lick each others' backs.

It no longer belongs to me, I thought; nothing does, not even my own body.

William's letter ended with the following: 'Well, Alice, you will now face your freedom and your nakedness'.

*

"Can you describe the pain, Alice?" asked Dr Beach assuming an unctuous familiarity.

"No, *Dr Beach*," I told him pointedly, "I cannot describe the pain; my brother Henry is the describing one." But that left me feeling as if I'd been emptied out. So, desperate to 'refill' myself, I decided since it was *my* pain I *would* describe it, however lamely and inadequately.

Where to begin?

"Anywhere you like," encouraged Beach perusing his fingernails.

I considered describing the multiple clamorings in my head as of a dozen hungry children banging on empty metal plates with metal spoons. But it would not be helpful. I must try and isolate one of the sources of distress. Immediately my hands flew to my stomach, which had been hugely swollen and hard as a new rubber ball. He brushed my hands away and palpated the area. "Tumors, assuming that's what you're worried about, do not come and go," he twinkled, obviously amused. Furious tears leaked out from under my lids. Pain. The problem was I could only speak about it when I was *not* experiencing it. Pain drove the words away rendering it, literally, unspeakable. But without words, what could he do for me?

I felt a sharp jab in my buttocks: something to 'relax' me., he explained.

"Now," he moued, "if you don't tell me, Alice, how can I help you, hmmm?"

I moued back. The pain had begun to abate so that I was able to describe the pressure towards a gripping center, the pelvic muscles threatening to break apart; the digestive convulsions that now left me weakened.

"You are 'out of the woods,'" said Beach.

But woods had nothing to do with it.

"I feel nothing," I reported, gratefully content. It struck me then as a possible definition of health: *to feel nothing*.

But the memory of *it*, of course, was not the same as *it*. Given my euphoric pain-free state, the words came tripping out, light and cheerful, belying the pain; for once pain is gone, I realized, it cannot be re-experienced in the same way. A mercy. The body is clever in that way. We can reel off, after the fact, a list of adjectives to describe pain (mild, soaring, intense, unbearable), or employ metaphors (it pinched like a crab . . . pummelled like a boxer's fists) but there is no way to convey the actual, lived experience. A problem in logic. I saw no way out. William would understand; Beach had no idea. He hoped, by the way, I would come to his concert next Saturday evening.

"Ah, a musical doctor," I commented; then: "Have you ever observed a piano being tuned, Doctor?" I was thinking of Aunt Kate's upright that had been moved into our parlor when she returned to live with us. Her preference had been for Chopin. Our father had wanted her to play Bach which he found more 'cerebral', but Aunt Kate ignored him and went on playing Chopin, dreaming of who knew what. Her marriage, remember, had lasted less than two years. I appealed to Beach: "What kind of marriage is that?" I asked. Unfortunately, he explained, that was not his field of expertise. "About the pain," he reminded me: "something about a piano?" "Oh, yes," I recalled: "The way to tune a piano is to place a special wrench-like contraption over the head of the tuning pin, and then to lower the pitch, slacken

85

the string counterclockwise; to raise the pitch, turn the peg clockwise. Tighter. Tighter still until the string is so taut you can feel its vibration. There is a point just before it breaks, literally at breaking point, when it can almost sing to itself, and then it sets all the others singing." I paused.

"That is how it feels inside of me."

"Quite the Hallelujah Chorus in there," Beach quipped, pleased with himself. I stared. Soon he would tell me I would be skipping about in no time. I had blundered again. There was too much energy in my description of pain recollected in, if not tranquillity, relative wellness. I had failed to convince him. He thought I was enjoying myself too much, and perhaps I was. *In love with her own illness . . . painting her symptoms in metaphorical terms . . . a literary family, don't you know.* I began to think a pair of scythes tearing at me might have made a more accurate description. And the piano had been wrong; a symphony orchestra made up of blind, deaf musicians would have better represented the rumble and smash of instruments all playing out of tune and time, more like an army turning against itself. But I had been afraid of over-dramatizing. Yet how was I to know? As soon as the pain was no longer with me, the telling of it, about it, became another fiction. You have to make it up, I thought, once it's gone. That is what Henry is so good at, and I am not. Yet how could Beach help me if I could not make him understand? So if Beach failed to diagnose the problem, it was my fault, not his. *Stoopid stoopid stoopid.*

"Well, Miss James." He stood tall, a handsome man with wide shoulders and a shock of prematurely white hair. He examined my heart, pronouncing it, unlike poor Wilky's, a 'vivacious' organ. "You mean I am alive?" I asked. "Evidently," he replied. Then he gave his summation: "I hold out strong hope that in eighteen months or two years time, at the outside, you shall be strong enough to have some special treatment for those poor spindles. But we shall see, it does not do to hope for extravagant results. As for the digestive problem, keep away from fatty foodstuffs and get out and enjoy yourself. I believe you spend too much time indoors with your books. I will bring you some charcoal next time," he concluding, patting my stomach as if I were his pet dog.

Twelve

I walked the ten blocks to Dr Neftel's office on East 48th Street. It was late February by now, cold and slushy, but I felt warm inside my coat and fur-lined galoshes. My brother Wilky was dead, but I was not. Or was I? Neftel's building, an elegant East side brownstone, was sandwiched between two tall, ugly brick buildings. I was admitted by a nurse who took my coat and led me to Neftel's 'inner sanctum' – it occupied the entire first floor – where the 'great man' was waiting, fingers a-twiddle. What would he *do* to me? Would he sit and 'Mitchell' me about my family? I prayed not.

"So, Miss James, sit, sit, tell me, you have a problem, take your time we have all day." At $100 a visit, I thought, he can afford to take all day. While I described my symptoms (headache, indigestion, back pain, stiffness, heaviness and sometimes paralysis in the legs), Neftel scanned the notes I'd had sent from the asylum. "Wrong!" he burst out, "all wrong! What are they doing to you? Rest? Rest? Any more rest and you will fall asleep for the rest of your life!" He was standing now, pummeling his desk. He swung one leg up and let it hang there while he outlined his treatment: "Your symptoms, Miss James – hysterical neuralgias, spinal irritations causing pseudo-paralysis, etc. etc. etc – are the result of electrical currents that have gone wrong in the body but which can be redirected, while those that are dormant can by the same token be electrically stimulated. "Are you with me, Miss James? Good, we will start immediately." When I inquired what else the treatment would involve he slapped his thigh, "Exercise! exercise and more exercise!" "But," I remonstrated, "Dr Mitchell prescribed total rest."

"Mitchell? *Weir* Mitchell??" Neftel came close enough for me to smell his garlicky breath. "Weir Mitchell is an old-fashioned fuddy-duddy. He tells old ladies what they like to hear: *rest and food*. Hah, you like to spend your days stretched out on a *chaise longue* dropping *bon-bons* down your throat? Fine by me, but you will not get better. If anything, worse. Nervous disorders affect the body's tissues and the accumulated products of tissue-metamorphosis act in a deleterious manner upon all the vital processes producing a depressing effect upon the muscular and nervous system and a feeling of exhaustion. Rest exacerbates this by deactivating the sensitive electromotor system of the muscles. Exercise, on the other hand, brings fresh blood and lymph to the affected muscles, removes the effete substances so that the organs can resume normal function. Simple."

He snapped his fingers.

"However," he added, "Rome was not built in a day."

"No," I agreed. I began to relax enjoying the way his Slavic tongue lapped at the English language. He was small and dainty with golden hair on the backs of his hands. He hopped about the room, barely able to contain himself, as if he were on some youth drug. But what was I to do, run a marathon, climb the Matterhorn, swim the East River? "Yes, of course, why not?!" He could not be serious. He was. Neftel belonged to something called The Penguin Club. He and a handful of others went early every morning for a plunge from Rockaway Beach.

"Even in winter?" I asked incredulously.

"Especially in winter!" Neftel replied.

"But surely not . . .?"

Neftel laughed. "Come come, we are not lunatics, no, we wear special insulated suits. But only until maybe March and then, yes, we go in starkers. Most exhilarating!"

Starkers? That night I had a dream in which I swam alone

with Neftel, my hair loose and streaming. I am laughing. 'My mermaid,' he calls me, which makes me laugh even more, delighted by our exotic intercourse. But then I feel my legs becoming trapped inside my mermaid's tail so that I cannot kick and begin to drown . . .

"You read too many tales!" he said when I told him about it. "Come, time for another electrical treatment."

I allowed myself to be led over to the machine which enfolded me in its sinister-looking arms. He hooked me up. "Are you ready?" I nodded, bracing myself for the jolts which I remembered from The Holtz Machine. This one was even more vicious, like being attacked by swarms of bees, then hammers, then . . . .

"So!" cried Neftel. "Now you walk!"

"Walk . . .?" I could barely stand. Still, if I walked I did not have to think about Wilky, or about Katharine who hadn't written in weeks. Each day I forced myself to walk further, uptown to downtown and back, crisscrossing East side to West side. The neighborhoods changed, the sidewalks filled and emptied with clutter, the fashionable women came and went, but I kept moving. Perhaps, I thought, this is what William meant by my 'freedom'. So long as I kept moving the funk could not get me. I wrote to Aunt Kate and friends Sara and Fanny and Ellen telling them it was doing me a deal of good. Only to Katharine did I express my doubts. But it was true that I had more energy than I'd had in a long while. I felt light. Best of all, I slept well and was free, ever since the mermaid dream, from nightmares. I was alone yet did not feel lonely. I even attended the gala opening night of the Metropolitan Opera, a performance of Handel's Jephtha, sung in Latin. Afterwards, I walked home fueled by anti-biblical fury. To sacrifice a daughter? And then, that she should spend two months running about the mountains *bewailing her virginity*? As if chastity were some social lotion for the extermination of evil? But then I turned my ire on the daughter: enough bewailing, you nincompoop, go and *lose it*!

But who was I to talk?

A month passed. "Walk!" ordered Neftel. "I cannot," I said. I was walked out. The electricity had left me feeling starched. My shoes were worn to onionskins, my feet blistered; and then the nightmares and palpitations returned. I was afraid to go out, could not face the squalid, alien, odious City, with its brick-faced houses, its ash-barrels and vendors, its bleak treeless sidewalks, its screaming fish-wives. Its smells. Give me back my blessed humble Boston, I prayed. Besides, I'd begun to feel degraded by the treatment, by being yelled at and worked like a slave. 'Neftel,' I wrote Katharine, 'is a quack with the moral substance of an avian.' I paid him his exorbitant fee. Even then he squawked: "Walkwalk!" squawked the parrot, and I obeyed: I walked out of his office.

Thirteen

I returned once again to Cambridge only this time I was alone, Aunt Kate having moved into her own small house further down the hill. "How will you manage, Alice?" she asked. "Perfectly well," I replied, "with Nurse's help." I'd had enough of her fussing over me.

I allowed myself to be dressed and combed, took the air and meals at regular intervals. Letters arrived. Henry was mildly alarmed by Neftel's 'cure'; Katharine was outraged. 'How dare he!' she wrote. William unsurprisingly thought it sounded quite sensible.

'*Dear William,* I began; then the pen slipped from my fingers and my whole frame began to jiggle and then go rigid. I stumbled over to the doorframe and held on to stop myself from breaking into pie and flying out the window. My head was a tangle of terrors, full of traps. The pit of my stomach, the palms of my hands, the soles of my feet, my very heart: how to keep them *intact*? Something must be done with me, I thought. The idea of self-disposal occurred in the way of a sack of rubbish.

It got worse. I had to watch my step, avoid bumping into the 'undesirables': doctor-ghosts breathing through the walls, medical presences rustling down the stairs. It was like All Hallows Eve when the divide between this world and the next, according to William, was at its thinnest. I imagined a sheet that had been washed and patched to the point of meshwork so that they could tear at it with their disgusting yellow nails and teeth and step straight through. *"Get out!"* I ordered. But they only laughed. *"Hysteric!"* they squealed, flapping like crows round a run-over rabbit.

I objected to their diagnosis: "But you said I was a *neurasthenic!"*

"Ignorant female!" they roared: "One must distinguish: the *neurasthenic* is rather . . . genteel. The *hysteric*, on the other hand, is emotionally volatile, violent even . . . she suffers hallucinations, trance states and fits. So you see: you have 'graduated' from civilized debility to wild lunacy!" They whooped with glee.

"You know nothing of female maladies," I charged. "I refuse all your useless medical cures and claptrap, mere catch-pails for the ills of the world. I have read about it all in William's medical textbooks."

"Books?" they cried in unison. "Books give you ideas! Who might you not become," they sneered, "Joan of Arc . . . Jane Austen . . .?"

' "And why not?"

My father, racketed with his wooden leg like one of his own demons crying: *"Rebellion! Disobedience!"*

My mother: "Our perfect sunbeam!"

Aunt Kate: "It does not do to hope too much, Alice."

William: "Have you tried Motorpathic therapy? mechanical orthopedics? Physical exercise is what you want, Alice. The ice-treatment? You must! It's a real shocker. I suggested it to Henry but he has not kept up with it . . ."

"Where was he meant to apply the ice?" I entreated, but he did not reply. Then in an owlish voice: *"Your freedom and your nakedness."*

Dr. Taylor: "Bend your toes . . . now bend the ankle and flex the knee . . ."

"But it hurts!"

Here Dr Beach poked Dr Taylor in the ribs. "Look here,

Taylor, this is not some malingering female – she's suffering from gout, rheumatic gout!"

Neftel: "Ignore any pain! Bend those toes!"

"I cannot . . . . I will not!"

"Enfeebled female . . . exposed to too much intellectual stimulation . . . nervous system perverted from tissue-making . . . the body is literally starved while the mind. . . . romps away with itself!"

"*Romps?*" I tittered. They ignored me.

"What is to be done?"

"Reverse the energy flow!"

"Balderdash! Arrogant phantoms and ghouls!"

On they went squabbling amongst themselves:

"Have you considered writing down your thoughts and observations, Alice?"

"*Writing?*" came the interruption, "Writing encourages morbidity: counter-indicated!"

"Agreed: writing, thinking in general, causes mental strain in women!"

"*Dis*-agree . . . far too simplistic. It's not just thinking but excess emotion that drains the body of energy."

"Look here, I only meant a journal to record everyday events, domestic details. It might soothe her, you know . . . like knitting."

"I say leave it to her brothers!"

"The *knitting*?"

"No no, you fool, the writing . . .".

"Hear hear!"

I clapped to get their attention: "You're not healers, you're ignoramuses! None of you has any idea what is wrong with me!" I covered my ears so I wouldn't hear their guffaws. "And I don't need your permission to put pen to paper . . . I will not have it, GO AWAY!" But I was surrounded by all the doctors who'd attended me since I was a child: George M. Beard, James Jackson Putnam, William Henry Prince,

Charles Fayette Taylor, Silas Weir Mitchell, Henry Harris Aubrey Beach, and finally Neftel, all telling me I was *irascible and nervous and morbid and*

I cannot breathe, help me . . .

"It's allright," Katharine soothed, manifesting like the heroine she was and taking me in her strong capable arms. "You're safe now, you can come back to England with me; I will look after you, you will not be alone. There will be English doctors who will know what's wrong with you and prescribe a cure."

"And I will not be an invalid forever?"

"Don't be silly, Alice, you are resilient."

"You mean like a lump of dough?"

"Oh, do shut up, dear."

II. LONDON

(1884–1886)

Fourteen

"You're quite safe now," said Henry, propped like a sand-bag beside me on the bed.

"That's precisely what I'm afraid of," I said. For however solid, he could not be my bulwark against England.

"Of being safe?" he pursued.

"Of coming to you," I replied. He'd had me transported from Liverpool to London to rooms he'd rented for me on Clarges Street, around the corner from his own flat on Bolton Street. But whereas my brother had *chosen* the Old World as his need, his life, his inestimable blessing, I was merely *there* in that alien world. In short, it was Henry's 'patch'.

"I have crossed the ocean and suspended myself around your neck like an old woman of the sea."

He understood my meaning at once: my fear of depen-dency, of constraining him – but he would not hear of it. "You have not come in any special sense 'to me': you have simply come to Europe and I happen to have been here when you arrived." Leave it to Henry and his gift for verbal legerdemain to swiz my words into a kindness.

"I do not intend to be ill the whole time, Henry . . . to impinge." I wriggled my way into a sitting position. He took my hands in his. His beard, I noted, closely barbered to a dapper little point, had a slimming effect.

"But where is Katharine?" I demanded. Without her I knew I would not get well.

"She has taken her sister to the south coast," Henry explained. "Bournemouth, I gather: weak lungs."

"Please telegraph. Tell her I need her."

"I already have, and she has replied. Apparently the sister is in rather a fragile state."

I made a rude noise.

"You may not get her undivided attention, Alice," he warned. His own, he needn't add, was of course entirely undivided.

"But Henry," I said urgently, "it gives me much joy to be cared for by her, and as soon as she has returned you shall be liberated from responsibility for me." I'd already given him endless care and anxiety. But once again he denied it. He spread his fingers wide upon his chest. "My dear Alice," he objected, "you cling no more than a bowsprit. Even putting your possible failure to improve at the worst, it will be very unlikely to tinge or modify my existence."

I considered the metaphor of the bowsprit which I understood to be the prow of a ship. "Henry," I ventured, "allowing for the fact that I am a nautical ignoramus, would not a bowsprit be *attached* to a mast?"

He burst out laughing – a rare event, and the last thing I heard before falling into a long, drug-clogged sleep.

*

The ocean crossing had not been easy; nor had the leaving. *To depart, to say goodbye*. It was hard to tear myself away from Cambridge, from William, even Aunt Kate. *Home*: already the word had been loosed from its moorings. As we were boarding I'd quailed, "I'm not going, I cannot." "Well, then, stay," Katharine had replied with such maddening reasonableness I'd flung my hat at her. "What if I get marooned forever on the other side of the ocean?" I'd cried pathetically; but my words were drowned in the melee.

All was confusion as the ship pulled out of the harbor: shouts and halloo-ings and wails of lost children mingling with nautical clankings and thumpings and foghorn blasts while bustling, purposeful passengers had to weave their way round those who stood fixed to the spot as if they could not remember why they had ever got it into their heads to leave such a place as The United States of America and board a ship bound for little old Europe.

Another thing. I'd been led to believe that Katharine had returned from her English research tour for *my* sake, that her mission had been to escort me *personally*, so that we – *she and I* – could be together. Why, she has returned to fetch *me*, I'd repeated to myself, flushing with pleasure, all swelled up like an important little personage, that I should be the object of such devotion. Only the truth, it turned out, was that she'd returned to America for her sister *Louisa*: to accompany *her* to Bournemouth for her 'weak lungs'. I, Alice, was the tailpiece.

Katharine of course denied it. "I have come back to accompany you *both*," she insisted in the way of a mother reassuring her children they are equally loved. "Both? To hell with both!" What I required was to be unique, singularly beloved, a flaming Blakean angel, an exploding comet that would fill the skies blotting out all other celestial matter. Me and only me. *Dunderhead.*

Louisa and I retreated to the odorous gloom of our separate cabins; Katharine therefore spent her time running back and forth between us. (Unusually we were travelling servant-less since no American servant of our acquaintance was willing to accompany us for such an extended stay in England.) Once I caught her looking panic-stricken, as if trying to weigh up which one of her invalids might need her more; and the thought as plain as the KEEP GANGWAY CLEAR sign: *How am I to live my life saddled with two such demanding nervous wrecks?*

I lay in a feverish heap, the engine's vibration running through my hands, up into my arms into my chest, throat and belly. I could feel the sea flapping against the side of the ship and in my delirium I saw riding the waves my friends and acquaintances, fresh and gay, preparing to tumble one after the other like young dolphins into matrimony: Jenny

Watson on the arm of old Newland Perkins . . . Nina Mason on the arm of Mr John Gray . . . Lila Cabot and Sargy . . . Clover Adams and her Henry. One after the other they succumbed. Or had they escaped out of their single state into the only really successful occupation a woman could undertake? At some point I managed to stagger up to the main deck where I hung gasping over the rails. Katharine came up behind me:

"Alice, what d'you think you're doing?"

"I'm watching for a merman, or Poseidon come to snatch me down to the other realm." I went on spitefully imagining myself as Persephone married at last: "Even if it is to the King of the Dead, even if for only half the year."

"And would you make such a deal, Alice?" she asked mildly.

"Of course I would," I said.

"Well *I*," she said firmly, "would as soon jump overboard as marry anyone, dead or alive."

At which I was sick over the side and had to return to our cabin where I lay limp as a leek. The days wore on. At some point I began to panic: what would become of me alone in London? Where would I fit in, what be my contribution? How would I present myself other than as Henry's sister? Making witty conversation was not an occupation. I pictured a cozy cell of women, with Katharine as their leader, discussing 'the woman question', plotting like wasps. Oh, the woman question! Should they be spiky or soft and yielding to the touch as if they were artichokes or melons? Women's education, the slave trade . . . of course such things mattered only . . . Katharine had the spirit for it, and I did not.

I managed to grab a piece of ship's paper from a cubbyhole. *'My darling Kath . . .'* I wrote, my letters sprawling this way and that – *'I have you for a friend & I have you haven't I notwithstanding my foolishness my sins my . . .?'*

Katharine, returning from Louisa – she'd had one of her nervous prostrations – found me down on my knees.

"Forgive me," I begged.

"For what, for heaven's sake?"

"For . . . for . . . ," I flapped and babbled unintelligibly.

"Are you trying to make yourself ill, Alice?" she accused, her patience understandably at an end.

I handed her my note. She tore it into bits:

"Alice," she scolded: "you have done nothing wrong – *nothing*."

But I knew I had. By escaping to England I had not freed myself but 'turned tail.' Going abroad to live indeed: how ridiculous can you get? I was nothing but a middle-aged spinster running for cover, a sour rag of a body, a . . .

After that I began to shake so violently the ship's doctor had to be called in. He diagnosed 'rigor', prescribing cold compresses to bring down the fever. Nevertheless, by the time the S.S. Pavonia docked at Liverpool on the morning of November 11th, I was unable to move my limbs or speak; and although I could perfectly well understand the questions being put to me ("Can you hear me, Alice? Are you in pain?"), I could not make any comprehensible noises since my jaw remained rigid and quaking. Eventually I was carried off the ship by two staggering sailors. As they bumped me down the gangway I raised my eyes to a sky so low and thick I felt sure I could reach up and bunch it into my arms like a vast grey blanket.

Katharine ran alongside the litter. She was wearing her spectacles to stop her crashing into things. Louisa trailed behind making annoying keening noises. When we stopped Katharine pressed my arm: "We are in England, Alice," her voice weary, tentative, hopeful. And though my legs would not work and I could not trust my heart not to fly out of my chest and burst like a shot albatross, I felt calmer and even relieved as I stared up into the Liverpudlian sky with the wintry sea behind us.

"I have been here . . . before," I managed to stammer. It was my first European Tour and our family had landed then as now at Liverpool before going on to Paris. "Hush, I know," said Katharine gazing down at me, and there it was, the blue of memory: Paris, the hotel where we'd stayed, a balcony high above the Street of Peace; and there, a lady wearing a blue shawl – so blue! – and her eyes, I was sure they matched it; and there it was again inside the French cupboard, that very same blue, as the governess, Mlle Godfroi, flung it open to get my walking shoes . . . ; and all around us the sound of the beautiful strange language which I and Henry, in spite of having chills and fevers, picked up faster than the others. The mystery and the pain . . . the anticipated delights . . . the hopefulness . . . . So that now it came to me again, that blue Paris cupboard, as if I had been carrying it inside me all this time and could open it whenever I pleased. My body might wither away, I told myself, but my mind could go on expanding forever, yes, like the sky. I would live for a time in this Old World with its long history and grey skies, but for me it would be new, new, and brilliantly blue. And there, further along the dock, as if to prove it, was Henry – all grown up – waiting to take delivery of me.

Fifteen

Imagine one of my father's specimen cases mounted on the wall of his study filled with toucans, great horned owls and pelicans. Now imagine the creatures, with their silly beaks and talons, inside *me* – alive and about to break me open – my body, glass – and burst out. My nightdress was soaked, I could barely breathe. My heart, a flock of hummingbirds, had flown up into my head and was beating at hundreds of times its normal rate behind my eyes in an iridescent blur. My body – joints, muscles, stomach, throat – was being attacked from within. The sharp shooting pains felt like metal spiders – should there be such things – creeping about, each slow tentacled movement causing a splintering of bone and stripping of muscle. Then came the snakes writhing about trying to tear their way out. My throat was closed stopping me from crying out. Eventually I managed to swallow two more hemp pills from beside the bed before passing out again.

At some point I was examined by a doctor. Henry arrived as the old quack was leaving. I was still in bed, floppy as anything. I watched my brother hesitate: should he pull up the captain's chair or perch awkwardly beside me on the sweat-soaked bed? He chose the latter which pleased but also frightened me: was it an indication of the gravity of my condition?

"You are out of danger," said Henry, adding reassuringly: "You shan't die, you know."

I turned my face to the pillow.

"He thinks you've probably struck a nerve, something to

do with galvanism. He claimed you applied some contraption to the back of your neck to relieve a headache thus inducing something like a paralytic stroke."

I blinked twice, slowly. True; in desperation I'd applied a vinegar-soaked pad connected to a high-voltage battery. *Clever Alice.*

"He said you were suffering mild shock following a bad attack but nothing life threatening. Do try and relax." He stroked my cheek with a finger that reeked of coal-tar and India ink. "My own diagnosis – for what it's worth," he added, "is that you are suffering from a protracted adjustment to living in this new/old world."

I shook my head. It could hardly be said that I had *adjusted* to anything or anywhere, new or old; or indeed to be living at all. I had simply woken up in England, having been picked up by Katharine and deposited over here. Which freed me of any responsibility. Piffle – of course I was responsible. I had agreed. I had allowed myself to be taken.

"Can you speak, Alice?" He would not panic: "Tell me what you think is wrong."

How should I know? There were so many symptoms it exhausted me to think of them. I hissed into his ear, "I'm thinking of having a small pamphlet printed describing them." He grinned broadly. Beneath the ink and soap, a pungent nervous sweat.

And the blood. How could I speak about that? I could not. The night before it had been so copious I'd imagined it soaking through the bedclothes and mattress onto the floor and from there – it would not stop – filling the rooms below and beyond. I'd thought of a tale, in the manner of Mr Poe, in which an invalid's blood gathers force until the city's streets are awash with it. The rats are thrilled, as are the wolves and, of course, the bats. Eventually the city and all its inhabitants drown in her blood. I'd considered describing it to Henry, asking him to write it down for me; but wisely had thought better of it.

He bent to retrieve the vial of pills that had fallen to the floor during the night.

"*Cannabis sativa*," I explained, "as prescribed by Garrod."

"And it has helped?"

"As you see." I could now speak, felt quite bright-eyed. I touched my stomach: "I could eat a horse."

"I recommend something lighter on the digestion," said Henry, "a fillet of sole perhaps."

I insisted on horse.

He pursed his lips. "So how was it with the good doctor?" he inquired. "Did his palpitating and stethoscoping meet with your approval?"

I winced. "The man is an eel. I'm fed up with 'great men of science'."

"But, Alice," Henry objected, "the last time you spoke of him you called him an avuncular Dutch cheese."

"Invalid's privilege."

"So the honeymoon is over?"

"Unravelled like a marriage."

He sucked in his cheeks.

I recalled Garrod's first visit. How he'd listened for a time with his open potato-face but after awhile held up his hand as if to say, enough of so many complaints at once. Having too many complaints, however, *was* the problem. He'd ordered nurse to sponge my spine with salt water – which had felt nice but had had no lasting beneficial effects. During his next visit he'd prescribed the hemp.

"Is that all?" I challenged.

He spread his sausage fingers on his thighs. "I can find nothing organically wrong. The disturbances in your legs and stomach are entirely functional. But you needn't worry," he added, "the weakness will not lead to true paralysis."

"But is it not unusual," I pursued, "for a person to be so ill yet have no organic trouble?"

"Yes, very unusual indeed."

"Well then, I should have thought you would like to do something for me."

But the great impotent could do nothing. As I now told Henry: "He slipped through my cramped and clinging grasp leaving me with no suggestion of any sort as to climate, baths or diet. The truth is he is entirely puzzled about me but does not have the manliness to say so."

Henry looked away, stricken, as if my harsh assessment must perforce include him. He, like everyone else, could only guess at this or that possibility. Gout had also been mentioned as an added complication, and 'an excessive nervous sensibility'. But what I craved was a clear diagnosis, which neither he nor any medical man could give me. I pummeled the mattress with my fist:

"What is wrong with me, Henry, what . . .?"

He could not say. He tried distracting me with snippets of gossip and flirtation but I'd already begun drifting off. At some point I opened my eyes a crack and found Henry in the act of sketching me. He held his pencil stiffly – he was no artist after all – making awkward feathery strokes. Was he trying to convey the lingering pain etched in my sleeping features? Presently I shut my eyes again. What matter excellence? I felt his concentration trained on me; sensed him tracing the contours of my face as if stroking them with a finger: cheeks, nose, lips: *my sister, my Alice.* I basked in the glow; was comforted by a medicine no medical man had yet thought to prescribe.

I awoke much revived. Nurse propped me up with a bank of flaccid English pillows and fed me some milky tea. The attack was over: spiders, snakes, toucans all flown.

"Better?" Henry guessed. At some point he'd moved to the captain's chair.

I nodded. "Am I flushed, Henry?"

"Like a glow-worm on a dark night."

"I believe I have come back," I said.

He rose.

"Before you go" – I wasn't ready to lose him yet – "I suspect you have been drawing me while I snoozed on like some dullard at the theater?" I wondered if he would use me in one of his stories, the portrait of a pathetic snoring invalid.

He'd hid the drawing pad.

"Don't be alarmed, Henry, I won't ask to see it; in fact, if you show it to me or anyone I'll wring your neck."

He bowed theatrically.

"And what did you observe as you drew?"

"Oh, a certain fluttering of the eyelids and . . ."

"And did I disgrace myself by snorting like a mad bull?"

"Aside from a few ladylike snufflings and a sudden cry of, 'Down with the Queen' – nothing remarkable."

Sixteen

Katharine. I pouted at her like a resentful infant before giving up in a whoosh of relief; let her have been carousing with warlocks on the moon for all I cared. As it happened, she had taken Louisa to Austria where she'd spent most of the time at a famous spa while Katharine immured herself among the archives. "Surely you didn't spend your entire time in Vienna shut up with great historical tomes?" She would admit only to having seen a very domestic Don Giovanni featuring a half-dressed Donna Elvira. "Some were shocked of course." "Not you?" "Not me. But you, Alice . . .?" She turned her attention on me, and I thought the wondrous thing was not why she'd left me in the first place but why she'd bothered to return at all.

"Thanks to Henry's ministrations," I informed her, "I got through the worst of my 'cataclysmic collapse'. *Thanks to Henry*," I repeated, "I am now on the mend, as the English would have it, like an old sock."

"Well praise be to Henry," said she.

It was early spring and my first 'outing'. We were headed for a stroll in The Green Park, that modest sylvan hideaway which Henry had once called a 'pendant' to the greater Park across the way – Hyde's poor sister, as it were – with its 'vulgar little railing'. But we preferred it. "It is a park of intimacy," declared Katharine. "And democracy," added I, observing some neighborhood children rampaging over the grass, as well as a number of oddbods asleep with newspapers over their faces. Henry had called it the *salon* of the slums, further infuriating Katharine: "I never know," she'd declared, "when your brother is striking a pose, or just trying to annoy me."

We were crossing Piccadilly, about to leave the 'huge, mild city', as Henry had called it, behind us. "Not that it's all that huge," Katharine now said, looking up, as if to calculate the size of London by the circle of visible sky overhead while comparing it to New York or even Boston. "And rarely," she added, "in my experience is it all that mild."

"Henry," I pointed out, "was no doubt referring to things more subtle than the weather." My brother had written of London's fogs, its smoke and dirt and darkness, its wetness and distances, its ugliness, its heavy, dreary, stupid, dull, inhuman vulgarity, not to mention the brutal size of the place – such things were hardly to be admired – yet, in spite of all that, he found it a 'mild' place to live.

"Henry," I continued, "has described it as 'an absence of intensity, a failure to insist'." I went on, determined to clarify my brother's meaning. "I guess he meant it takes a lot to grab this City's attention." "Alice" – she'd let go my arm and stood blocking out the light – "I am not interested in what Henry calls it, do you understand?"

I understood. Perfectly.

"I mean to say," she corrected, her voice softening: "I'm more interested in *your* view of things."

Yet how, over the wind and the traffic noise, to express in what way the City's mildness might 'work' for me, how it might allow me to be what I was in a way that America had not? As Henry knew, in Europe, whether idle or simply ill, I was somehow less of a burden than in America. I began picturing those pale, fine-featured, self-contained Americans – my friends who were now married and full of that determined American spirit, that get-up-and-go in spite of adversity – and I cringed at the thought of them; for it was they, paradoxically, the anaemic and the fagged, or so it seemed, who had left me feeling squashed and daunted. Whereas the robust ruddy-faced Englishwomen I'd met didn't faze me in the least. But what if it was *too* easy? I began to wonder if London with its endless indulgence for weakness and prevarication would ever allow me to escape my destiny.

In the end all I could manage was a feeble: "But Kath my view *is* his view – at least in this. The only thing that gets people's attention in this place is another turn of the Irish screw, or a divorce case that goes on for more than two days or . . ."

She marched me on impatiently.

The day was windy, the sky a woolly glower above the blossoming cherries, and shifting, always shifting. We went through the gate and into a green and pink world.

"Pink snow," she calls it, leading me diagonally across. The fallen blossoms move in swirls, many of them landing in drifts around the enclosure walls, blown by the wind. Katharine guides my elbow lest I trip or lose my balance over a tree root or slip on a cherry petal. "I am not an ancient," I mutter. At the other end, we negotiate the waves of horse-traffic round the 'carousel', with Queen Victoria watching over us, and make our way into St James's Park. Before us, the lake.

"It would not do for you to fall in," Katharine comments wryly.

"Nor for you to have to jump in and fish me out," I rejoin.

But a top hat is rolling our way. Katharine drops my elbow leaving it to dangle in mid-air as she goes sprinting off after it. I watch thinking her heroic – the word is not too strong for one with her quick response, her elasticity and grace of gesture as she scoops up the hat then jogs off to return it to its owner, who bows melodramatically sweeping the retrieved hat before him. But when she returns, cherry-cheeked and breathless, I hear myself say in the surliest, yowlingest, complainingest, most spine-grating nasal-whine: *"Am I to be left like that, for a hat?"* To which she replies lightly, "Oh, I prefer a hat to you any day, especially a man's bowler into which my entire head would fit." A smile threatens the corners of my mouth even as I despair of myself. To be envious of a hat indeed!

After lunch we settled down with our books, one each side of the fire. I'd begun reading a new story of Henry's in The Temple Bar Magazine called 'Lady Barberina', while Katharine pored over a compendium of dry educational statistics. What was the point, I asked, of all those *numbers*? She tried to convince me of their importance in revealing the educational disadvantage of females. Surely, I argued, one had no need of figures if one had eyes in one's head to conclude that it was so. True, she agreed, but such figures were not intended for 'people like us' but for those in positions of influence who needed 'proof'.

She paused, then said: "Mozart's sister."

I laughed: what had that personage – had she existed – to do with educational statistics?

"Oh, she existed alright: "the forgotten Nannerl. "She was clearly a prodigious musical talent, but there was her brother of course beside whom she could only fade into insignificance. Added to that, she was obliged to look after a cantakerous father; then she married a bullying widower with eleven children and moved to some god-forsaken rural exile. The only thing that kept her going were the letters from her brother. Then those stopped . . . she ended up blind." Katharine dropped her own spectacles, shook her head, tried to laugh: "It was too awful translating such a tragic life."

"So you went back to your statistics."

She looked away, as if I'd accused her of something unnatural.

We returned to our reading, but she was restless and kept looking over her shoulder out the window; while I was becoming increasingly disturbed by Lady Barbarina and her fate. "What is it?" asked Katharine, sensing my unease. I explained the situation in the story so far: Lady Barb, a wealthy, content Londoner, has been 'claimed' by the sour

American – wittily named Jackson Lemon – and taken back to America.

"I guess I'm anxious on her behalf."

"Well you might be: any fool could predict she's destined to be unhappy."

She was right of course, but the slur against Henry rankled. It was its very predictability, I argued, that made it so chilling. Lady Barb's fate was sealed; nothing could stop it. At which I began to feel afraid: for myself and Katharine. Now that I was 'well', I realized, she expected me to go on recovering, growing stronger and stronger like a creature with no past or history of illness; almost as if I had never been the jangling, fluttering, palpitating, paralyzed bundle of knots and crosses that I so recently had been. True, I was greatly improved; but like a book, over-printed, with the harsh black text of my illness visible through the spidery, uncertain story of my so-called recovery. No, this 'wellness' of mine could only be a temporary if pleasant interlude; it would not, could not, last.

The room was quiet except for the flickering notes of the fire. "You must not depend on me," I blurted out: "I mean, on my being well: I am unreliable."

"Alice," she said; and again – her voice a notch lower, almost failing: "*Alice.*" "Why must you look ahead at all? Why poke and prod until you end up . . .?"

"End up . . .?" I shot back.

"Oh, why not just allow yourself to be well *now*?" And with that she rose, she would go out again; on her own, without me pulling at her, she would stride through parks and boulevards covering vaster distances than Henry. She would tire herself out, and then she would eat hugely and sleep. What must it be like, I wondered, to be so ferociously *well*?

*

114

"Your brother, Miss," announced the landlady.

"You are writing," Henry observed: "I must not interrupt." He began reversing. "No, no, " I felt myself color, "stay, please . . . I have finished, it is only . . . a letter to Aunt Kate."

The truth? I'd been scribbling some nonsense about a woman who buys herself a new wine-red dress with deep ruffles. She lives unrestrainedly going to operas and theatre openings and museums (her favorite is the Victoria & Albert); she even holds a salon twice a week. Then, one day, after receiving a few too many compliments on how well she looks, she begins to feel anxious. She senses her past lurking behind her, and imagines that while she is frittering away her time 'being well' it will be scuttling ahead of her like the wolf in the fairy story who knows the shortcut to Grandmamma's house – and will inevitably one day be waiting for her, fangs out, ready to pounce.

"Do sit, Henry."

He did so. "I have just met Katharine," he waved, "at the end of the road."

I pictured him tipping his hat, shifting imperceptibly so that not so much as a scrap of fabric – Katharine having bunched up her skirts – could chum with his trouser leg. "And did she tell you about our walk in the Park and how she rescued a hat?" He waited. I described the scene, sparing nothing: the pink 'snow', the wind-roll of the hat, Katharine's magnificent sprint, the motion of her arm reaching forth to sweep up the errant hat only seconds before its inevitable dive into the Lake, the fulsome bow of the gentleman. Henry, evidently immune to Katharine's heroism, complimented me on 'the exquisite detail' of my narration.

"Katharine is not a detail," I snapped, "she is my dear friend . . . my companion."

He stood corrected. We sipped our tea. He told me about his own long perambulation around the suburbs of London and how, having returned 'weak with inanition', had taken a table at some godforsaken railway hotel . . .

"You were hungry, I take it?"

He simpered. He'd been presented with nothing more than a plate containing a trio of cold mutton, a pot of mustard and a chunk of bread.

A feast to me, it sounded. "Whatever was the problem, Henry?"

"Potatoes," he lamented, imitating the water: *We do not serve potatoes, sir, after nine p.m.*

"Poor Henry," said I scratchily.

"However," he proclaimed, "I have survived the denial, as you see."

He looked a long way from starvation, it was true. After a pause I mentioned his cruel little story.

"Which one?" asked my witty brother.

"Lady Barbarina."

"Ah, and you find it cruel that . . .?"

"That Lady Barb should have to be removed from her own environment into a strange one where she is doomed to unhappiness. To make it worse, there is the comparison with her sister, Lady Agatha, who is horribly happy in America."

"Horribly . . .?"

"I mean the contrast." I went on, "Do you really believe, Henry, that there are people who can be happy anywhere, while others are condemned . . .?"

He stroked his beard. "Lady Barb," he said, "suffers from a distinct lack of curiosity."

"You mean she would probably not have been happy back in America either?" It was the obvious conclusion, but I did not really believe it. I thought, in her limited way, she would have thrived had she been left in her original environment. But he merely shrugged and muttered something in French. He must be off, he was already late for dinner at Lord Rosebery's.

Katharine returned sometime after Henry's departure. She was looking unusually pink and excited, her wiry hair escaping from under her hat. "How would you like to spend the summer out of town, Alice?" "Where?" I asked. "Hampstead." She explained we'd been offered the rental of a cottage 'quite cheap'. My first thought was that I would be too far from Henry. But Henry, she reminded me, would soon be off to Bournemouth for the summer to visit his friend Robert Stevenson. So, with a nod to Lady Agatha, I said, "Yes, why not."

Seventeen

Our tiny cottage sat at the top of the Heath. Around us were a few other old houses with tiled roofs, as well as a modern red-brick school house and a few modern 'villas'. Down in the square was the Bull & Bush tavern with its tea-gardens, merry-go-round, shooting-galleries, penny-in-the-slot machines, &etc. Luckily our cottage was well away from all that. Besides the servants' – or in this case servant's – department, it consisted of four small rooms, two up, two down, into which we squeezed. (Before us, we learned, it had been occupied by a couple of *artistes* with five children. Did they pack them away at night in tiers, we wondered, like so many folded draperies?) But it was in a beautiful situation, and had a shallow balcony covered in creepers, a front gate that scraped, a rusted fence, a pocket-garden and half-glassed porch with roses scrambling over its roof.

We were looked after by an elderly servant called Clara, recommended by 'next-door'. "Have you heard," she began, "about the new lady down the way who brought water with her from the Broad Street Well in Soho, well the poor dear came down with cholera . . . there was a leaking cesspit near the pump . . . so I said . . ."

And so it went on. I attempted to find out what had happened to the 'lady down the way' but was distracted by the sight of Katharine, dressed in a pair of her brother's old summer trousers with knee patches, weeding the front garden. "Celandines," she addressed her complaint to Clara: "too many of the damn things."

I was parked in a bath chair beside the front path. "What

on earth is the point of weeding," I challenged, "when the cottage does not belong to us and anyway we shall only be here for the summer?"

Katharine sat back on her heels with a look that said *Can you seriously ask such a question, and on such a day*? The sun lit her from behind, and as she shook her head her hair loosened so that she resembled nothing so much as a human burning bush.

"My dear, you look like a porcupine that's just undergone an electrical treatment."

"Well, thank you for that," she said with an ironic sort of bow. "But my work in the garden, you see" – she was serious now – "has little to do with ownership. It's really very simple, Alice. It is done for the sake of the plants and *their* future."

Shamed I wriggled in my chair, making the new willow creak. Had I forgotten? Katherine's 'mission', her need, was to care for others – plants, animals, humans – any cause that arose and caught her attention. Of course I admired such selfless devotion. Yet was I nothing more than another needy plant? I warbled:

> *But do not wound the flower so fair*
> *That shelters you in sweet repose . . .*

She wanted to know the poem's author. "Charlotte Smith," I told her: "'To a green-chafer, on a white rose'." She stretched:

"Are we not like two turtles occupying one shell, dear?"

'Two imprisoned spinsters, more like,' said I incorrigibly.

She grabbed hold of a pair of secateurs and waved them at me:

"Why, for heaven's sake, *'imprisoned'*?"

"Because," I rejoined, "we are outcasts – outside society."

"Do you complain of it?" she asked, deadheading a rose and catching its head in a basket.

"And do you not?" I shot back.

"Why should I, when it means we're free?" Off with another head.

"Well, that's settled, then," I mocked: "Here reside two virtuous spinsters living in perfect freedom."

Katharine sighed. "Well, it's an improvement. Not that I – even I, the eternal optimist – believe in perfection."

What she did not know of course was that Henry had called her 'a *foolish* optimist'.

"And will the two spinsters live happily ever after?" I asked.

"Well," she paused, "I should say that's up to them, wouldn't you?"

Once again I was at a loss for words. She stared at the rose in her hand: "Are you *Gloire de Dijon*," she asked it, "or *Bouquet d'Or*?" "*Gloire de Dijon*," she decided: "*Bouquet d'Or* is a more peachy, coppery pink, with a stronger scent."

I continued to ignore her floriferous mutterings. I had other things to think about, such as the letter from Henry I'd received that morning from Bournemouth. It lay in my lap. Eventually she seemed to divine my train of thought:

"And how," she asked, decapitating another *Gloire de Dijon*, "is your brother?"

I hesitated before reading out the following: " 'There is no sudden change but a gradual & orderly recurrence of certain phenomena which betray the slow development of such soundness as may ultimately be my earthly lot'."

She gave one of her barky laughs. "May I translate that as 'my constipation has improved'?"

"You may." I went on: "It seems he's 'holed up' with Robert Stevenson. He writes about his rooms by the sea; how they drink claret together and discuss their work."

"I daresay they also do their share of gossiping."

No doubt of it, I thought. "Oh yes," I said, "I can just hear Henry tattling to Stevenson about Oliver Holmes who's 'broken loose' and is going about London flirting as desperately as ever, *ugh*, while his poor father, the good Doctor, has to put up with a wife who has absolutely lost her mind; and then there's the physical wreck John Cross who Henry says would have departed this life since the Georgian episode if not for his sister's care; and . . . ."

"Enough," she held up a hand. "What else has he written – something has upset you?"

"Nothing," I lied.

Katharine parked her basket on the window ledge. 'Nothing', as she well knew, meant 'something' either too difficult or dark to reveal.

"Out with it," she ordered.

I hesitated. "It's the strangest thing." Another pause. "He admonishes me not to be ill" – here I took up the letter to quote: " 'for in that there is a future'."

Deep breath: "Read it again, dear, I didn't quite get it."

" 'It would be wise for you not to be ill *for in that there is a future*.' "

"Surely he meant to write *'failure'* not 'future'?"

"That was my own first thought."

"Or perhaps he left out the word 'no': '. . . for in that there is *no* future.' There, that will be it."

I would have liked it to be so but my better self knew better. "My brother rarely makes mistakes, if ever. And so," I concluded, "I believe his meaning is quite exact: Illness is to be my accomplishment, my future."

Katharine burst into tears. "I'm sorry," she fell to her knees like a penitent burying her face in my lap. "It's all my fault," she wept.

"Nonsense, it's the heat." I could not bear to see her so distraught.

She shook her head. "It was obviously the move. I should have realized, like the time after the voyage: you were laid up for almost a year."

"You weren't to know . . . you're not a doctor."

She raised her eyes. "I wish I were," she said miserably.

I took her dear frizzy head between my two hands and kissed her forehead. "Don't worry," I reassured her. "It will pass . . . besides, Henry also thinks I'm resilient."

"Henry thinks a lot of contradictory nonsense."

I let that pass. In due course she returned to her weeding while I searched the sky. Two days ago – not a blue hopeful day but a murky chill one – the bath chair in which I lay had been delivered. Had it in some way brought on my un-wellness? The thought was too terrible. Still, I pronounced the chair "a sure symbol, if ever there was one, of failure, of renunciation.

"Don't be silly, Alice," came her denial: "It's a perfectly reasonable solution to a temporary condition. At the moment you cannot walk without difficulty. The bath chair was designed to help . . ."

"Invalids."

"People with all sorts of . . . mobility problems . . . Think of it as an *aide mechanique*." She retrieved her trowel and waved it: "Alice, it's only a minor setback, it will not be forever." In return, I waved Henry's letter. We must have looked like a pair of human windmills. "He predicts it," I said, the pages of his letter shaking in my hand: "Illness is to be my future." "No, Alice, he only warns against it: Henry, however brilliant, is no oracle."

Katharine will not allow Henry to spoil things, not now, not today on this rose-kissed day, this special day, June 1st, our anniversary, the day we first met back in Boston twenty years ago ("Alice James, I'd like you to meet our head of history, Katharine Loring Peabody: you'll be working with her on our new Home Studies program"); and so she snips off a branch laden with four partially opened blooms and gives the floppy unfolding cluster to me to sniff. I am defenceless against the rose's touch, a softness that would melt a Bismarck, even an Alice James. Katharine, seeing my eyes flutter and finally close, begins to 'paint' my lips with the velvety nubby buds and, with the open petals, to caress my cheeks. A moan escapes. I am buried – *born* – into scent, into softness. Defeated by a rose.

Eighteen

Next morning there came a thump on the door: "Telegram from Bournemouth." Our mouths dropped open as if we were about to sing a duet from *Cosi*. "Louisa," said Katharine. "Henry," guessed I: "he has put his back out again." I pictured him spread-eagled on the floor of Stevenson's rooms.

"I suppose we'd better answer it," said Katharine sensibly.

She opened the door, and there we stood in the way of mothers braced for news from the battlefield. The poor boy looked terrified. But we were not after all mothers and the War was long over; besides we were in Old not New England; and as for the telegram – remember the telegram? – it had arrived on a bright, dry August morning in the peacetime year of 1885. But who *was* it for?

The delivery boy read out 'Katharine Peabody Loring', pronouncing each syllable as if he'd been rehearsing it the whole way from the telegraph office. Tipping him generously she pushed him out the door following right behind; *slam* went the door in my face. A minute later – released – I followed her into the garden – she handed the telegram over – surprise surprise –

Please come dear another attack worse this time cannot manage without you stop Louisa *PS Potatoes to be dug –*

I flung the sheet away. Potatoes indeed!

Katharine removed her spectacles. "Alice, I will return as soon as I can."

"When?" I demanded.

"You know I cannot say exactly."

I reached for something to steady me – the rose as it happened – causing my palm to sprout a whole crop of tiny blood-fruits. Katharine muttered a sequence of *damns*. Then she grabbed the hand and sucked at it until her mouth came away wet and gleaming.

Clara saw to my morning toilet and dressing, my meals and washing-up. She would even take me out in the bath chair if I so wished. But I did not wish it, thank you very much – only Katharine would do for that. So although the weather went on hot and dry with the papers crying, 'London Sizzles in 80 degree temperatures!' I holed up inside where it was cool and dark.

In my mind I followed her to Bournemouth. It would be, I reasoned, not all that different from Newport with its cliffs and coves and secret shingled beaches, only more built-up with hostelries and guesthouses. In one of them would be an ailing Louisa moaning theatrically. But there's her devoted sister Katharine who slaps a damp cloth across her eyes to shut her up and reads to her from one of Stevenson's new stories until she falls asleep. Now what? Answer: she will go off for an invigorating 'blow' along the cliffs.

Henry is staying the other end of town. What will *he* do when he's had enough of Stevenson's irritating, resentful praise? Answer: he will go for a restorative walk along the coastal path.

On I went moving them about here and there in the way of characters in a story. Henry and Katharine are both staying, by chance, in a seaside resort on the south coast of England. (A coincidence too far, perhaps, I thought; on the other hand, was it not one of the commonest devices of the storyteller, e.g., used by Stevenson in his tale of Dr Jekyll and Mr Hyde?) But back to the scene before us:

Henry, dressed in a buttery summer suit (but carrying an umbrella just in case), strolls along feeling pleased with himself, with the sea, with the sun in the sky. A woman approaches from the opposite direction with purposeful, almost masculine strides. Her hair is wild, her dress dishevelled. He imagines an intolerable situation . . . an impossible choice . . . something precious unrealized . . . lost; or simply too many responsibilities. But suddenly there she is. Cries of mutual recognition burst forth ("Henry!" "Katharine!" "Can it really be?" "Such a coincidence!" "I would hardly have recognized . . ."). On goes their breathless tosh until the sky darkens and finger-shaped clouds bunch together into a fist-like formation. Rain pummels down. Henry, rarely one for 'action', manages to open his umbrella and hold it over them with one hand while steering Katharine by her elbow towards the warm, dry tea-shop . . . *Now* what?

Nothing. The whole absurd fantasy collapsed like a pack of damp playing cards. Ridiculous mush. In real life, as I reminded myself, if Henry had spied Katharine coming his way he'd have hid his face among the seaside flora having developed a sudden passion for botanizing. Katharine would have climbed down a cliff and hung by her fingernails until he'd passed by.

I banged my head against the glass. It made a dry, dead thump. I looked up. What if I changed their names so that they were no longer Henry and Katharine but merely 'two strangers'? No, Katharine had been digging potatoes and playing nursemaid; Henry was on the other side of Bournemouth with Stevenson; however I labelled them, they would not meet. But the pain remained of having glimpsed within the sad recesses of my own heart the fear of losing the two people I loved most in the world.

Katharine returned from Bournemouth a week later carrying a lumpy suitcase along with her usual rucksack. The lapels of her dress were flapped open and sweat glistened on her collarbones. Her hair looked as if it had been attacked by hornets.

It was late summer by now, the weather hot and humid; a heavy, blanketing heat, the air cumbrous and clotted, grey as gruel. The trip from Bournemouth had been several times disrupted, she explained, because of wheel and driver trouble. "At one point," she claimed, "he fell clear off his seat: drunk, you see." I waited. Still she stood holding the damn case as if it were attached to her arm. "What on earth have you got in there . . . Louisa's body?" She dropped the suitcase so that it snapped open allowing its contents to spill over the tiles. Crawling about she collected up the potatoes tossing them back into the suitcase. Back in the scullery – I helped her line them up in size-place – she described having dug them up, the childish pleasure of finding another and another when she thought there were no more, of detaching them from their growing stems. "It was also a relief" – she placed the last potato so it wouldn't roll – "from sitting with Louisa all day." Smug silence. "And how," I asked magnanimously, "*was* your sister?" Katharine put her hand to her heart, as if Louisa's 'hideous palpitations' were her own.

"Alice, they'd been treating her – some nurse employed in my absence – like some kind of loon." She was appealing to me – I had been treated like a loon myself, had I not?

". . . like a *loon*?"

Katharine nodded daring me to laugh. I did not.

"Poor Louisa," I managed truthfully: "I am sorry."

We surveyed the arrangement of potatoes with satisfaction. Then Katharine said, "Shut your eyes and choose." So I did. I stretched forth my hand and blindly chose two of the biggest for our supper. She drew me round the waist. "Come along, Alice."

Later she will head for the bathroom behind the small scullery. "I must have a cold bath," she will announce, and I will follow. "Shall I wash your back, dear?" I will offer. She will bend over to fit the plug, rise up and peel off her sweat-stained dress. She will give off a rather pungent smell, if truth be told, thin as a pipe cleaner and bony as a pipe. But altogether, to my eyes, beautiful.

Nineteen

"My turn now," I announced. Katharine protested, the water was disgustingly grey and unhygienic but I poo-pooh'd her: I liked the thought of bathing in her shed dirt, her flakes of cast-off skin; as they soaked in I might even become more like her: kinder, more compassionate, more reasonable.

"If you insist."

"I do."

As she manoevred my legs over the tub's lip I felt as if I were climbing into the body of a great bird, and flexed my own claws in return. She lowered me gently down:

"Is the water too cold, dear?"

"It could hardly be too cold," I replied.

Katharine was wearing a white muslim shift made of transparent Indian cotton and no petticoat beneath. As she moved against the light the flowing outline of her body, the spaces between her thighs, appeared and disappeared. I sank. My own body dissolved. I hardly knew myself without an aching head, a cramping griping belly, a pair of throbbing legs – where was *I*? *I am water. I am* . . . Perhaps I was dying or already dead?

"What is it, dear?"

"Nothing."

"That's good," she smiled.

I saw us painted. 'The Bathroom' it is called, a rather 'modern' picture, libidinous with naked flesh; and yet so innocently domestic with its soft pinks and greens, its sprigged paper, its square of mirror and light streaming in from the window. Notice too the rapt softness in the attendant's features with her gently folded body in its white muslin, now wet and clinging, leaning over the bather.

"Are you having one of your headachy fancies, dear?"

"A fancy, perhaps," I replied, "but for once not headachy."

She lifted my head and placed a folded towel behind it. I had become two Alices, an Alice divided: Alice, out of pain and Alice in pain. Out of pain, as I now seemed to be, was filled with feeling: for myself, for the clawfoot bath, for the very humidity that filled the air. And Katharine? There was the question – fundamental, radical, recurring – of why she'd chosen to devote so much of her time, give up so much of her life, to my care. There would be, I guessed, no single, simple answer: because she 'cared' for me; because we were involved, as Henry might have put it, in an inextricable human relationship which must take its course; or simply because we had 'an understanding'. I was of course dependent upon her, which some claimed gave her undue influence over me; but if it was so, I could only welcome it.

My body, no longer the enemy, had given up thrashing and fluttering. Kath's hands meanwhile, rough with earth-scored cracks, came alive in the water making me aware of my skin – thighs, stomach, breasts – still tight, the flesh beneath surprisingly springy. "Am I not a wrinkled old prune?" I asked, testing. "Oh, no: very much the young prune," Katharine replied. I stuck out my tongue and blew a 'raspberry'. Then I raised my right leg, slightly bent at the knee with pointed toe in the manner of the magazine mannequins. After that I gulped a mouthful of the mucky water and became William's 'spurting fountain'. Katharine ducked, laughing gaily. It was still hard to believe. Did I really have a normal working body (pumping, beating, churning, shedding, discharging, transforming & etc?) Yes and maybe . . . maybe, this time it would not betray me; or at least not too soon . . . please not too soon . . . .

Out of pain I became fulsome in my imagery, piling one

fanciful image upon another. "I feel like a . . .": first it was a poppy fruit about to burst showering its thousands of seeds upon the earth; then a roll dunked in coffee (frowned upon by Henry especially in public places); then a tomato – the kind we'd eaten in Italy – ready to burst. Out of pain I spouted nonsense and what of it? Between each more far-fetched comparison Katharine, who continued to kneel on the floor by my side, raised the loofah and let go a shower of watery sparks over my breasts. Out of pain, that is, I beamed upon the world and its creatures, and they beamed back upon me.

Katharine was looking as if she'd just solved a mathematical conundrum.

"What . . .?"

"Dear Alice," she mused, "how much nicer you would be if you were not besieged with aches and pains."

What could I say to that? I feared I would weep. But she would not allow it. Having sneaked a secretly prepared iced sponge behind my neck, she let it trickle down my spine. I yowled with pleasure or pain – truly it was hard to tell. When I'd recovered I asked:

"Now what do you suppose Henry would make of all this?"

Katharine sat back on her heels. "All what?"

"You know very well," I replied, flicking water in her direction.

She ducked, "And if I do?"

"Well, what then, if he could see us now?"

She gazed upwards, as if she might see Henry lurking like a spider on the ceiling, and shivered. Then she cried, "Oh, Alice, why bring him into this?"

I reached out for her, but she shied away. I had spoiled the day.

"Alright," she said. "In answer to your question: I presume he'd disapprove." She stood and fiddled with the towels, folding and refolding them.

I said nothing. Was she right? Would he dislike what he saw, or simply record it in the way of a camera: *Katharine and Alice alone. Katharine writing Alice's letters. Katharine playing nurse and servant. But bathing Alice?* "I admit," I finally said, "that my brother, in spite of his genius, is also a firm bourgeois."

Katharine shook out one of the newly folded towels (*snap* it went). "That is *not* the point," she said impatiently.

"The point is . . .?"

She collapsed back down and hung over the edge of the tub. "The point is" – here she hesitated – "your brother does not like me."

I sat upright in the bath. It was my turn to be unamused. "Henry," I countered, "does not like or dislike anyone. Anyway, he's extremely grateful for your devotion."

"Grateful, yes, but also suspicious."

"Of what, pray?"

"Of taking such good care of you."

"And that's a bad thing?"

"It keeps you dependent on me."

"But I *am* dependent on you! Where would I be without you?"

"You would be, perforce, more dependent on *him*."

"And you think he would prefer that?"

"Yes and no. Nothing is simple, as you well know, with your brother. I believe he would rather look after you himself but he hasn't the time or indeed the capacity or . . ."

"Katharine!" I slapped the water. "A year ago I crossed the water and suspended myself like an old woman of the sea round his neck where to all appearances I shall remain. In spite of all my morbid shenanigans he has never ever lost his temper with me. He comes at my slightest whim . . ."

"As I do not, I suppose?"

"As you do, faithfully, dependably, reliably . . .".

"Alice, enough."

"Alright, but it's different, don't you see, for Henry."

"Different . . .?

"He is my *brother*." I threw the wet washcloth at her. She caught it. "Bad shot," wringing it out as if it were my neck. It looked for all the world like play, but I saw that if we were not careful – I believe she saw it too – the gap that had opened between us would widen beyond closing or crossing.

"And this brother of yours . . .?" she pursued dangerously.

"Well, there's his writing and his friends and his life abroad and . . ."

"And he is a man," she supplied bitterly, "after all." She missed a beat. "Therefore, this arrangement suits him."

I sat up. "Pity you were not born male," I snapped, "you could have made the law your practice."

She winced.

But what of her argument? I imagined Henry's disapproval running alongside his inability to do anything about it. If he devotes his life to nursing his sister (so it went) then he is left with no time or energy to work. An impossible position. He has no other option than to leave her in Katharine's more-than-capable, more-than-willing female hands.

"So he disapproves, but he finds it convenient?"

"Exactly so."

I feared the churning inside me must make waves. "I hope," I said, "it's not as hot down in Bournemouth as it is here. Henry hates this weather, it makes him feel run-down, then he can't concentrate on his writing." I lifted my elbows like a child:

"I'd like to get out now," I said. Wrapped cosily in a towel I announced:

"I believe I am now quite hungry."

"And what is it you would like to eat, madam?"

"Cherries," I said.

In Italy, Henry had once led us a merry dance down a

narrow street and through a winding alleyway. The shop was cool and dark and he began collecting up all sorts of exotic foodstuffs for a picnic. Having been paid, the proprietor then presented each of us – Henry, Aunt Kate and myself – in lieu of small change, a *chiliegi*; or cherry, as Henry had translated unnecessarily. I held mine for the longest time, dangling it by its stem. "Go on," Henry had encouraged, "pop it in your mouth, it won't hurt."

I paused, sobered, remembering:

The trouble was it did, hurt; pleasure did.

Twenty

"Where will we meet him then?" asked Katharine. "Heath Brow, Jack Straw's Castle," I replied. The furthest point West from The Vale, we noted, on the Heath. Katharine tucked me up in the new bath chair and off we went passing a neat row of brick houses painted white with green shutters; from there we headed southwest over undulating ground, sunlight catching the leaves of the poplars and beeches.

"Why are we going South?" I grumped: "when the Castle is due West?"

"Because," Katharine replied, "I have decided upon a triangular route taking us towards the reservoir and from there northwards to the Castle. We'll return the direct way, thus completing a circuit. Does that meet with your approval?"

I humphed; what did I know about routes and distances?

She pushed hard uphill over broken ground covered by bracken and gorse. From the top we had a good view of distant hills, as well as Flagstaff Pond with its carriages and horses, children with flotillas of white sailboats, horses splashing knee-deep in the shallows. Directly South was the reservoir with its regimental flower-and-rhododendron beds. "Oh stuff it!" cried Katharine veering violently off the path away from parkland and into a rough field.

"Is this wise?" I queried. Katharine, dragging the chair backwards through a gate, muttered "Wisdom, dear, has little to do with it." A herd of cows grazed peaceably in the meadow.

"And there," I pointed, "is a *bull*."

"So I see," said she.

The bull lay hunched like an outsized cat. As we watched, it stirred, then one haunch shivered. "Flies," said Katharine, "nothing to worry about," – and off she went to pick wild-flowers in the tall grass. Swallows circled overhead and broad sweeps of gentle wind went rustling through the trees nearby. Then the bull lifted his heavy head to gaze at me, and I was overcome, *bulldazed*, with the desire to sink my hands into the rows of curls covering the bony space between the creature's horns; to be encircled by his bulk, to feel his bull-heat, the rumble of his belly against my back. But he had begun to pull himself up and paw the ground, snorting.

Katharine returned and tossing the posy of late summer flowers into my lap, began pushing as fast as she could. I admonished her to keep calm. She quickened her pace further; I ordered her to slow down. "Slow down, Alice?" she spluttered: "You are nothing if not perverse." But at the far gate I turned in my chair and gazed back. A flash of sun was illuminating the tips of the creature's horns, the ring in his nose. He had lain back down. "There," soothed Kathar-ine, "you are quite safe." I held tight to the sides of my chair. I was not so sure I wanted to be.

The Castle, perched on the highest ground, sported a continental-type outdoor garden cafe with striped awnings and window boxes full of bright red pelargoniums. Kathar-ine admired the Swiss chalet effect. As we approached, Henry rose to greet us. "Do sit," he said indicating the empty chairs. But which – I was already 'seated' – should Katharine take? Should she put herself *between* Henry and me or – removing one of the chairs – park me beside him? She hesitated only briefly; after all, she could afford to relinquish me – she grinned broadly – because she 'had' me.

Henry inquired after our 'adventure' across the Heath. Katharine chose a few botanical details to describe while I waved my posy. Neither of us mentioned the detour, or the bull.

135

"You will of course have noticed the dark brick house near the Reservoir," Henry stated.

"Actually, we did not," replied Katharine.

"Should we have?" I asked.

He swiveled round in his chair. "It is only the former Upper Flask Tavern, where Clarissa Harlowe fled in the Richardson novel."

She admitted bravely to not having read it, while I turned my attention to one of the other tables. I leaned close to my brother: "A honeymooning couple," I whispered. "But, my dear sister," Henry exclaimed, "how can you possibly know?" To which I replied: "I believe I can read the signs." Henry raised an eyebrow.

I was recalling the meeting during one of our Grand Tours with my friend Clover Hooper and her new husband Henry, at Thussis: how they seemed to be enclosed in brilliant sunshine while the rest of us – Henry, Aunt Kate and I – sat enwreathed in a vaporous cloud.

"Indeed," sighed Henry now. The subject of honeymoons, I sensed him thinking, is perhaps best avoided.

He directed our attention towards my invalid's chair which he proceeded to admire excessively. "There is no jarring," I explained, "and one can lie out in it like a bed, as you see." The foot extension had been pulled out so that I could sit with legs extended. He bent to examine one of the tires.

"I do believe those are bicycle wheels."

"How very observant," muttered Katharine.

"It was Katharine," I further explained, "who bought it for me."

"Ah, the munificent Katharine."

Henry's sarcasm shocked me, but Katharine rose above it.

"Not at all," she said. "It gives me great pleasure to take Alice about in it."

"Indeed."

Things did not improve with the introduction of the Irish

Question. I said it was distressing to hear of so much squabbling among Nationalist ranks.

"Their efforts sound more like the plots of boy's adventure stories than serious attempts to undermine British authority," said Henry.

"That is because you do not take their cause seriously," I replied.

"Then you do not believe in the Parnell letters condoning the Phoenix Park murders?"

Katharine looked to me. "No," I said, "I am sure they were forged."

"Will you be joining the Republican Brotherhood then . . .?"

Here Katharine's rapped the table with a finger. "No, but I have supported Anna Parnell in the Ladies' Box."

"Anna Parnell? The sister? They say she's an embarrassment to her brother."

"Do they?" charged Katharine. "Perhaps that is because she is too radical. While her brother plays at politics at Westminster or in prison, Anna and her Ladies' Land League have been busy fighting a land war. They have climbed fences and leaped ditches, bravely standing up against vicious and vindictive absentee English landlords in their abominable treatment of tenant farmers." She had risen half out of her seat in her excitement. I placed a hand on her arm, and she subsided.

Henry thanked her for the history lesson.

Our refreshments arrived. The waiter, at Henry's insistence, left us to do our own pouring. I watched as Katharine and Henry reached simultaneously for the pot. Their hands would have met but for Henry's catlike recoil. The thing was Katharine's; she turned to me: "Will you take coffee?"

The other was Henry's: heavy silver with a fluted spout. "Or tea?"

I could not decide. I *would* like coffee but suddenly it felt impossible to say so since coffee, as well as tea for that matter, could over-excite.

It had happened before. We'd been staying in Paris. One morning Henry put at least three buttery *brioche* on his plate, beside his cup of chocolate. Before actually eating them he pointed out a certain pattern in the tiny black seeds decorating them, admiring their 'jaunty little topknots'. Then, having consumed them one after the other, he ordered a second chocolate. When I tried to do the same, however, Aunt Kate's hand had moved to close gently but firmly around my wrist:

"Chocolate," she warned, "can be a little *too* stimulating, you know."

I had turned then to Henry, "What shall I do?" The waiter had remained standing statue-like, pencil poised, allowing the question to balloon monstrously.

"To chocolate or not to chocolate," Henry had mused. At last he had asked me *why*.

"Why what?"

"Why do you want a second cup?"

"Because," I announced: "it represents Europe to me: freedom, pleasure, indulgence . . ."

"In that case," he declared, "you have your answer."

As it turned out, I went on to eat and drink freely with no untoward consequences. But there remained the possibility of danger in indulgence.

Katharine was still awaiting my decision. "Do not think too hard, Alice," she counselled. "Say simply what you would like." The coffee pot hovered. What I would like, I thought, is *not* simple, that is the problem. Katharine's arm, meanwhile, strong as it was, had begun to quiver, forcing her to use the other one for support. I guess it took some self-control not to tip the spout into my lap – or Henry's.

"It is not," she insisted, "the momentous decision you make it out to be, Alice. The world will not fall if you make the wrong decision; indeed, there is no right or wrong in this case, merely a matter of giving pleasure, or not, to the palate." She sounded so damned reasonable, so sensible, so excessively prosaic, it was I who wanted to pour the teapot into her lap. Henry and I exchanged glances – barely a flicker – but enough for her to accuse me later of 'playing her off' against him. She and I might agree about Anna Parnell and Home Rule and such, but the fact was that my brother could understand things which she could not. In such a contest, I was forced to admit, she would always be the loser. Henry and I thought with the same mind, saw with the same imagination, vibrated with the same delicate nervous system, felt the same longings and sympathies, experienced the same kinds of confusions, and suffered similar – though to a lesser degree in Henry's case – illnesses. Two lives, two beings and one experience. So where did that leave *her*?

Henry gave one of his auctioneer's nods and I allowed myself to be poured half a cup of the black oily liquid. It was the end of summer, everything parched, the roses covered in rust and blackspot, the nights drawing in. In the next few days we would pack ourselves up and – it could not be helped, our lease was up – make another move.

Twenty-one

Mayfair. Our new rooms were located three-quarters of the way along a little flank of ten houses making up Bolton Row at the end of Curzon Street as it curves up towards Berkeley Square. The house was modest, flat-faced, of two-stories and near to Henry at the other end of Bolton Street. From our front window, if I squashed my nose up against the glass, I could just make him out as he reached for the handle of his front door before slipping away inside. At the back we looked out upon a 'sea' of mews cottages. As for the rooms themselves, they were a great improvement on Clarges Street which Katharine had described as a 'hole'; though I myself had spent most of the time there being too ill to notice much of anything.

The move, surprisingly, brought new energy. I began to take an interest. This was London and I was to be part of it, if only from my day-bed. As I told Sara Darwin when she came to call, "To be any better would be quite superfluous." Looking about her she gave one of her Boston smiles; imagine the stretching of a new rubber-band. "It is quite airy," she allowed. "Or at any rate," she then begrudged, "such that London sees fit to offer at this time of year."

How to let her get away with such meanness? I could not. True, the day was overcast but there was a thin stripe of blue showing through the cloud over the roofs.

"I have all the light vouchsafed by heaven," I affirmed.

"Indeed," said she. It was hard to match her with the young woman who'd instigated our eclair orgy back on Quincy Street. She busied herself with the tea-things and scones.

Eventually I said: "I gather you and Grace have been travelling together." Grace was the youngest sister of Charles Norton, Henry's latest publisher.

"Indeed, Grace is doing research for her book on Montaigne. It was very interesting accompanying her." She pouted, "You needn't make that sour look, Alice, I know you are quite allergic to Grace."

"It is merely her intellectual pretensions I find hard to stomach; otherwise I find her quite inoffensive."

She seemed about to defend Grace with her life but then, looking about her as if the dissolute prude herself might be hiding among the draperies, began to tattle: "Did you hear," she said, "Grace gave Mabel Quincy a copy of Montaigne as a wedding present?"

"Which Montaigne?" I inquired.

"Oh Alice, never mind that!" she cried impatiently. "The point is she gummed together the 'naughty' pages: could anything be more deliciously droll!"

"Pitiable, more like, in my opinion."

She could not resist one last indiscretion: "Grace," she confided, "cannot even bring herself to say the word," she hesitated before whispering: "*mistress*".

I imagined poor newlywed Mabel – her beloved has gone off to his place of business – tiptoeing down to the kitchen and applying the gummed pages to the spout of the teakettle and then with sticky fingers parting the pages and diving into the forbidden passages . . . But the truth of it was such prudery wearied me to death.

"Oh Lord, Sara," I burst out, "do teach old Grace to say *damn* and *blast . . . bloody . . .*" – I was beginning to enjoy myself – ". . . *breasts . . . buttocks . . .*"

"Stop!" cried the goose: I had already gone too far. The Nortons and the Darwins, I saw, would stick together in the end, yes, like 'naughty' pages.

"And how is William Erasmus the banker?" I asked.

She bridled: "You needn't refer to him as if he were a

waxworks, Alice. However," she continued tightly: "We are prosperous, he has done well and altogether we thrive."

"So I see." She had been to Paris with Grace and had put on a good many frills.

"Congratulations, Sara."

"For what?" she asked, much as she had ten years ago.

I laughed. "Back on Quincy Street you asked me if I thought men should be mastered and I replied that I was in no position to advise you on such a subject. But I gather you have succeeded."

"Succeeded?"

"In subjecting him."

She drew herself up. "And who has told you that?" Half the muscles in her face were tightening in displeasure while the other half struggled against a self-satisfied smile. "Oh, you needn't answer," she went on, " I suppose it was Charles who told Henry who naturally . . ."

I hoped my own smile was suitably enigmatic.

"Life," she announced primly, "would be a most dreary blank without a dear husband to love."

Had she said *'drear'* husband?

"But how is your beloved Katharine?" Her lips were puckered prune-wise.

"Stretchably modern as ever," I said.

"Henry told Grace," she went on, "you have established a permanency."

That Henry should tell Grace anything at all was a mystery to me; however I replied factually: "She is with me for months at a time, it is true. She also continues her work back home part of the year – as you well know."

"Apparently he sang her praises, her strength of wind and limb, to say nothing of her nobler qualities."

I held my tongue; then did not: "You know as well as I," I whispered savagely – I'd had enough hypcritical dissembling for one day – "that he finds something 'unnatural' in

142

our arrangement; however, he convinces himself it is all for the best. In any case, it is convenient for him."

She shook herself like a wet dog. "Well, he admits she is quite devoted to you. But you are beginning to look tired, Alice." Our discussion was clearly at an end. She stood, emphasizing the disparity between us and the fact that, as before, she was prosperous, stout and upright, while I was thin, plain-as-a-biscuit and although relatively well, still one who spent her days reclining on a chaise instead of working in a mill or a factory or a field or a tavern or a kitchen or a study or a studio or classroom, or for that matter a bedroom.

I said, "Well, Sara, I am like some Barnum monstrosity to whom people come to gawp and never come again."

"Nonsense, Alice. You are only tired. Do not disparage yourself. I advise fighting off your demons, wrestling them right down."

"Really, Sara," I paused, "I am not a crocodile hunter."

"Oh tut. I will come again," she threatened, "when I am next in London."

She did not.

Twenty-two

My brother William and I had been in touch by letter, but this was his first appearance since my defection, as he put it, to England.

"It is good to see you, Willy."

His hug was humid and altogether heartier than Henry's fragrantly skimming embraces.

"And you, my little grey-eyed doe."

I gazed moonily up at him. "Oh, Willikins," I lisped, "in my little grey dress (curtsy) and with my little grey face (tongue-ho), my two little grey hands and two little grey feet." Then hitching myself up on tiptoes I hissed into his ear: "But I do not possess a little grey heart."

He pulled away, the muscles in his jaw near his ears throbbing away like crickets. "So you are a lioness today; I'd better watch my step."

I growled, flicked an invisible tail.

He backed off further, moustaches a-twitch.

"And Henry . . .?" He peered about him, as if expecting his younger brother to manifest from under one of the turkey rugs.

"He's off on one of his Scottish jaunts," I supplied, "to be coo'd over by Lady Airy or Airlie in her great lighted pile of a castle."

"I believe he parties to escape us," he whispered conspiratorially.

Yes, I thought, Henry partied to escape his own ancestry – 'relations with consequences', he called us – disappearing to the Continent or the wilds of Scotland where we would not haunt him.

But I'd almost forgotten Willy and Alice's tragedy.

"Poor little Herman," I said feelingly.

"Indeed, I mourn the lost little human turtle," he said biting his lip, then going on to describe the child's blotched face, the nostrils flaring at the insufficient air, the chest pumping up and down, and then the terrible, tearing hiccoughs followed by a whooping bark . . .

"I *am* sorry, Willy. But you have made your lip bleed." I pressed the spot with my fingertip, then – it couldn't be helped – licked it.

"And Alice?" I asked after a respectful pause.

"You know of course she was sick herself?"

"Aunt Kate described it: she came down with it around the same time as the little one, I believe?"

He nodded. "She nursed him round the clock. For nine days and nights not more than three hours' sleep in the whole twenty-four, and yet every day as fresh and passionate and eager to keep him alive." His Adam's apple rose and fell along the column of his throat.

"But it wasn't to be. The poor little man contracted pneumonia. It was all over on July 9th just as dawn was breaking. We buried him at Cambridge beside our parents. He measured the size of the grave with his index fingers.

Once again I reached out. His hands felt like hot dinner rolls, the kind you break open in order to remove pellets of indigestible dough before consuming the crisp outer shell. How could we ever let go? But we must of course. William, blinking – the bear emerges from hibernation – shook himself free. He was good at that. Discipline; volition, overcoming inanition. In one of his essays – he'd sent it to me for comment – he explored the problem of how anyone ever decides to get out of bed in the morning. 'Not that volition has anything to do with it in my own case,' I'd written back. He begged to differ. Even illness, he believed, could be

overcome through pure will. He'd tested the theory personally, forcing himself out of his own sickbed and going for a
run around the block.

And the result?

Why, he felt a new man by the end!

Oh, Willy, I wanted to cry, must I bestir myself against all
inclination, rise from my sickbed and go running about
London like a loon, overruling all weakness and pain?

But he was going on – the devoted husband – about his
Alice. "The old word Motherhood," he intoned, "has been
given new meaning." Eyes heavenward. If I were Alice, I
thought, I'd have longed to throw something at him: *Stop
sanctifying me forgodsake and do something!*

"She is resilient," I offered more reasonably.

He ran his fingers through his hair, clearing the way for a
new topic of conversation. Life would go on. There were two
other children to attend to after all. "But you, Alice, tell me
about you." He was still alarmingly urgent.

"Calm yourself, Willy, I am doing perfectly well." Since my
health had improved I was able to say more or less truthfully,
"I am under a strict regimen of rest. As for my diet, my
landlady is possessed of the largest repertory of potato
manipulation imaginable." It was settling to talk of potatoes.

He scowled: "I hope she is not another follower of
Fletcher."

I laughed, "No, she is merely a Swiss."

"Too much starch," he muttered. His knee would not stay
still, nor his squinny eye. During the previous year he'd
published a collection of our father's work entitled, 'The
Literary Remains of the Late Henry James', with a long
introduction of his own. Henry and I had each received a
copy.

"Willy," I confessed. "When you sent it last year . . . it
came at a bad time." I did not tell him that I had been unable,
could not bear, that is, to hold the thing in my hand. The
truth? I'd flung it away. "But I have since read it and . . . it

gave me great pleasure, Willy, I assure you. What fun it must have been," I added, "to roll out all those adjectives."

"It's alright, Alice," he soothed, "Henry wrote me all about it. As a matter of fact, if it will not embarrass you, he said you burst into tears exclaiming, '*How beautiful it is that William should have done it! Isn't it, isn't it beautiful? And how good William is, how good, how good!*' I could hear your voice, clear as anything, and felt sufficiently rewarded."

"But William . . ."

"Enough, Alice. It was a thing I felt compelled to do, for Father's sake. But I am working on bigger things now. I am hoping, once things settle down at home" – obviously referring again to Herman's death – "The Principles will soon be finished." He'd already published several articles in The New England Journal of Psychology, which Henry had praised for their 'intellectual larking'.

"That's wonderful news, Willy. And Henry will soon finish *his* new novel; with luck," I added, "we will soon be able to read it." I'd intended to express equal pleasure in my brothers' successes, not to pit them one against the other or in any way measure the relative merits of their writing. But the mention of Henry's writing had sprung a sudden wave of anger, an eruption: ". . . *curliness . . . maddening . . . thin-blooded . . . priggish . . .*"

I'd known of course of his 'disapproval' of Henry's style but not the extent of it. "It's all too ornate, don't you think, Alice?" He went on without waiting for a reply: "I recommended more straightforward action but he ignored my advice. Really . . . I doubt that I shall read any more of his stuff," he concluded. "I have tried, Alice, believe me, but . . ." Here he leant close enough for me to feel the heat of his breath, its saltiness: "What does he think he's up to, Alice, with all that" – he twirled his wrist as if warming up for a duel – "fencing and parrying?"

To which I could only reply, "And do you think, Willy, that he does not *know* what he is doing?"

He hit the chair back. It was not the cohesive rejoinder he'd been hoping for, but I could not, would not, betray Henry for the sake of currying favor. Yet the situation must be 'corrected'. The best strategy, I saw, would be to focus on one of his, William's, accomplishments, avoiding any further mention of Henry's. So I said:

"I gather you have been to Paris for the annual Psychological Congress."

At once he brightens: " '*And now*'," he mimicks, " 'Monsieur. Weell-yam James will open the proceedings . . .'." He bows.

"Oh, and did you manage it in French, Willy?" I then ask, all innocence.

At which he erupts: "I am *not* inclined to spout in that flowery tongue in the way of my younger, shallower and vainer brother!"

"William!" I was truly taken aback, by the vehemence and vitriol of the outburst. "How could you! Nothing could be more wrong-headed as a description of Henry and you know it!" I restrained myself from crying out 'Why you're just jealous because Henry as we both know is cleverer, *more sensitive, imaginative and famous* than you, so there!'

But he was already grinning his wicked little-boy grin. "Surely you cannot deny that he is my *younger* brother?"

I threw one of my cushions at him. Catching it with one hand – but we must change the subject – he began telling me about the hiking trip he'd planned in Switzerland after the Paris congress.

"Yet here you are in London, Willy," I pointed out, "not clambering up a Swiss gully or traversing a glacier."

He admitted it was so. In truth, he was desperate to get home. "All I want is to see Alice and the boys again. I will not be satisfied until I do." He cracked the knuckles of his left hand, one by one, followed by the right.

"And Europe?" I was thinking of Henry's American, Newman, who could not get enough of Europe – but refrained from making the comparison for fear of consequences.

"To hell with Europe," he cried. "I have seen enough anyway. The only necessity is to get home. To America, Chocorua . . . Alice." He hugged the pillow until it was squashed flat against his chest.

Is that is how he embraces Alice?

Abruptly he flung the thing away. I feared he would launch into another anti-Henry diatribe, but he did not. I wanted to laugh, and weep, at the thought of my two brothers having to escape, from me, from one another, from some held notion of a country that was or wasn't their own. And there he was scowling at me, as if to say *How can you stand it here among the deadly, stupid, lazy, doughy lumps?* What he actually said was, "Do you not miss the American edge, Alice, the lucidity?" To which I thought it best not to reply that I had Henry, and Katharine, who together provided more than enough 'edge' and 'lucidity' for my requirements.

"Of course," he added, doing one of his famous voltefaces, "the English are superior in terms of culture – if you 'go in' for that sort of thing."

My brother's views on 'national characteristics' tended to be very crude. But I was growing tired so I said, "I will put you right some day, Willy, when I have the energy." He took his cue, gave me another of his bear-hugs, fussed with his hat and scarf which my new nurse Wardy had handed him, and made for the door. There he turned. "It will soon be All Hallows Eve," my thoughtful brother reminded me, "when the divide between this world and the next will be at its thinnest . . . so take care , Alice." And with that he was gone. I would not see him again for another five years.

Twenty-three

"Has he gone, then?"

"He has," said Henry: "I saw him onto the Liverpool train this morning. His only necessity, it appeared, was getting home to Alice and the surviving infants. One felt something pursuing him, some nameless – he paused – dread." He'd taken aim with the portentous word as if flinging a pebble into a lake. 'Plop', I heard it go.

"How very familiar," I said.

"Familiar . . .?"

"I was thinking of Father, that time . . . we were children. . . ."

"In Florence?"

There we were: Mother, Father, Aunt Kate, William, Henry, Wilky, Rob and me . . . a narrow back street with dusty shops and women in black going in and out regarding us suspiciously. Above us, a criss-cross of laundry waving like pennants, the houses tilting towards one another. "It's like being at the bottom of a canyon," says William. "Or inside a mouth," say I. Henry has just directed our attention towards an elegant courtyard with a fountain in the middle when Father, with no warning whatsoever, throws his free arm over his eyes and collapses like a wet sack. He's seen one of his green devils in the shop window or perhaps the chattering birds have descended thinking it already night-time.

"But, Father, it's only a pig's head!" I cry. William is looking rather wild himself. Mother grips Father's hands while Aunt Kate guides him towards a bench and urges water, which she has begged, through his livid lips. The two younger boys and I huddle together while Henry backs off to get a better view of the scene, or perhaps dissociate himself from it.

When Father is calmer we press him to go on with our Tour. But it is not to be. *Forgive me my children I have passed thro' an agony of desolation* – swaying like one who has just been saved from drowning – *and I fear I must return home.* So of course we must 'up sticks' and follow even though we have only been abroad a mere 36 hours and were meant to be gone a fortnight and have only just begun to recover from the ocean crossing.

And so our composite memory, Henry's and mine, that product of a single mind, that inexpressibly intimate journey back in time, is over; yet it will stay with us, binding us closer than ever. But then Henry goes and spoils it all by saying mildly, "But, Alice, surely it was William who cried, 'But, Father, it is only a pig's head!' " Which leads me to conclude *the product of a single mind* is an illusion and I am an idiot. However close we may come in our thoughts, Henry and I, we are not – I am forced to admit – literally *of one mind.* We carry about our own imaginings and are further separated by sex and time. There will always be a divide. Besides, I am not balding, nor do I wear my whiskers barbered to a rakish point.

"So you think," Henry pursued, "that William suffers from the same 'condition' as Father?"

"What I believe," I told him, "is that Father, the delicious infant, could not submit to the thraldom of his own whim, nor admit to being prey to the demon homesickness."

"And William?"

"Oh, William just can't stick to a thing for the sake of sticking."

Henry allowed himself to be amused; then he blinked gravely, as if his eyelids were taking a bow. William, he believed, suffered from *agora*-phobia or fear of the marketplace, the need to escape . . . dash home. "And yet," he went on, "the summons . . . an equal fear of enclosure, of being smothered . . . overwhelmed . . ."

Did he think of himself? I wondered. Had *he* suffered such a panic while abroad sending him scurrying home to his safe servanted London nest? No, I thought, Henry would not allow himself to be *pushed*; but he could be *pulled*. His writing would await him . . . *I must not lose the thread* . . . Only that 'siren', I decided, could persuade him to curtail one of his Continental gallivants. As to a 'nameless dread' – if there had been such – it would remain, perforce, unnamed.

But we must speak of other things:

"I gather you've been holding something of a salon," said Henry cautiously. His intention was clear, it was time to 'behave' ourselves, to revert to gossip and chit-chat.

It was true I had been visited that Fall by Americans and Britons, Henry's friends as well as my own: variously faithful, flighty, deafening and dripping with resinous virtue.

"A few virtuous maidens have come to nibble at me," I offered.

"And what are their views of you?"

"Oh, one that I am *so* like you, and the other than I am *so* original."

"Thus cancelling each other out," supplied my brother.

"Just so," I said. I went on to describe a visit from a Mrs Mason: "An American like a raw turnip to one's mental palate. Oh, and then a Sir Frederick, if you please, with a handkerchief the size of a tent who kept shooting forth volleys of honks into it."

Henry sat back, relieved to be out of 'dangerous territory'. "I have had a report about you," he related, "from Fanny Kemble: 'Your sister is an American lady,' says she, 'a *very different* thing from an English lady, I assure you'."

"But what is the *right* kind of lady, Henry?"

"Oh, American, she assured me."

I did not believe it for a minute. That night I asked my new nurse, Miss Ward – Wardy as I'd beegun calling her – if she thought Katharine and I were different from English ladies in any way. "Entirely different, Miss!" she exclaimed unhesitatingly. I waited, hoping to hear something of substance, preferably 'scandalous'. I was sick of all the prunes and prisms, had had enough evasions of a lifetime. But when questioned on the nature of the difference, all she could reply was, "Not so 'aughty, Miss."

That night I was restless and could not sleep.

I had not written anything in a long while, but during that long night I half-composed a tale which I called simply 'Brothers'.

Brother 1 is the younger. He is rather heavy in body but not in mind. There is a dancing light in his eyes. He is the observer, the recorder of complicated motives; fastidious without being fussy. To the world he displays a cool, mild 'social' self. Yet he has great insight into its ways. There is a softness, a sympathy, about him, for its strangenesses and complexities. He will not be pinned down, most especially on the subject of, to speak crudely, love.

Yet despite this reticence, he is sure of himself, of his own destiny. He is like a fisherman, allowing the world to flow by him while losing nothing of significance, or of himself. People say he and his sister look alike, think alike, *are* alike. Wrong. The Brother is a great writer; his sister is just The Sister.

The older brother, Brother 2, is more 'difficult'. A tortured soul, both ponderous and fussy. A hypochondriac, he must express every fluctuation of feeling, every symptom. He is interested, unaccountably, in spiritualism and clairvoyance. He has visited Mme Blavatsky. His sister fondly describes him as an interfering busybody and a know-it-all; indeed, he is frequently annoyed by those who do not behave as he thinks fit. He is prone to advise facilely: "Keep a stiff upper lip and snap your fingers." Yet he himself can seem 'nervy'.

153

During a recent visit to his sister his hands appeared to tremble as if a buzzing insect was inside him drawing him to her; yet to allow it to have its way would be dangerous: the insect would sting and she would be damaged – so he must pull back.

Like his father before him he is not without demons, but he conquers them largely through physical exertion: swimming in cold lakes, tramping up and down great bear- and glacier-infested mountains. He has an 'angelic' wife who, he believes, has saved him from himself. He is a dutiful family man, tho' he tends to disappear whenever said wife is nearing her delivery time. When they are old enough, he will teach his children right from wrong, good from bad.

Brother 1, now a successful author, sends Brother 2 a copy of his first novel, about some Europeans, which Brother 2 pronounces 'thin'.

Brother 2 sends Brother 1 a draft of his 'Principles of Psychology' which Brother 1 praises in the vaguest, coolest of terms. Brother 2 suspects he hasn't actually read it; at most he may have skimmed it at five in the morning.

Brother 1, in order to please Brother 2, writes another, more complicated, story about a young woman confronting her destiny. It also takes place in Europe. He sends it to his brother with a letter saying, 'I think you'll find this one *fatter*.'

Brother 2 writes back impatiently, "For goodness sake, why must you always write about Europe – why not write about America for a change'?

The reader realizes that the brothers will never, ever, please one another. The sister is frustrated with them both for 'playing upon the surface'.

Twenty-four

Henry held the umbrella over our heads with one hand while waving down a hansom with the other: a manoeuvre, it seemed to me, of infinite grace and accomplishment.

Henry had proposed the expedition. Was I up to it? I was, I'd assured him. A little rain could not hurt.

I am going out . . . I am going out with Henry.

Soon we were safely inside the cab but idling due to heavy traffic. As Henry observed, it might have been faster to walk. "But wetter," I pointed out. Henry, unusually impatient, thought it a wonder the horses did not fall to their knees in boredom. But I demurred, thinking how the well perceive not the tiny flowerets of restricted vision, full of perfume and color. "O," I gushed in the way of one who'd never laid eyes on a city before: "house! . . . bridge! . . . gate! . . . tower!"

Framed in the cab's window was a woman dressed like a fashion plate . . . there a child being hoiked by one arm . . . Even when it made me cringe, still it was *life*. Henry, I thought, may have a passion for actors prancing about on a stage, but give me this naturalistic show 'playing' all around me any time, complete with rain smashing on our roof and enclosing us in its streaming, glittery curtain.

We were creeping along when Henry announced the completion of his latest novel. "That's splendid, Henry." I was busy admiring the shops: shoemakers, watchmakers, tailors, wax-chandlers, tobacconists, umbrella-makers, cutlers, linen-drapers, pianoforte-makers, hatmakers, wigmakers, shirtmakers, mapmakers, lozenge manufacturers, booksellers . . .

Tap-tap, drummed Henry on his hat. I lay my gloved hand upon his arm. "And are you pleased with it, dear?" An impossible question, as I knew. He spread his fingers. There had been during the writing some pleasure and much agony and now . . . uncertainty. He admitted it had cost him much; besides, he was not sure, after all, of the 'territory'. But perhaps this time it would be a success; though he was of course used to being mauled by the critics and would not care. Oh, but as I well knew, he *would* care, he would care enormously, even if he hid his head among Fenimore's skirts or escaped to the Splugen or. . . . For what my brother secretly desired – let him deny it forever – was to write the kind of book that people would rush to buy and read: a potboiler; a novel that would above all make him *famous.*

"I am sure it will do well, Henry," I said rather inanely. What more could I say? *The critics are right, your work is bloodless, over-refined and constipated*?

But we'd reached Trafalgar Square. If we craned our necks we could just make out a bit of the National Gallery.

"The grotesque cupola itself," he pointed, "how it sits up and speaks to one," said my brother.

"Does it really, Henry?" Surely people had been committed to institutions for less. "And what does it say?"

But we'd arrived. "Shall we go in?" he suggested. I took his arm, as he explained about the new wing with its seven exhibition rooms. "One will do for me, Henry." I squeezed his arm. "Do let me know if you are tiring," he said. I inclined my head so that it made contact with his shoulder, allowing myself a daydream in which the woman behind the reception desk observes us, thinking *My, what a handsome couple.* Shame.

Suddenly he shook himself free, as if needing to repudiate such a public demonstration of affection, and went striding through the vestibule into a gallery where a fresh exhibition was being hung, numerous paintings leaning this way and that against the baseboards, on through a grand archway with marble pillars and into the very space he'd called from the outside 'grotesque'. He stopped dead with me right behind him as if we'd been playing Grandmother's Footsteps. Grotesque? I felt like spinning. A rainbowed light played upon us; rain sloshed on glass; we were the only people there. A triumph, it felt.

Henry was bent on drawing my attention to a Raising of Lazarus, but I did not take to it. "It makes me feel as if I were trapped in a crowded lift," I told him scuttling off to find something with more life in it. Two rooms away was a painting of a trio of women in white dresses on some kind of vessel. I went towards it as to a garden of fragrant white blossom. Henry soon caught me up.

Three stylish young women lean on the deckrail of a ship: the ship all angles, awry and tilting, the women all swaying swirls and frills. Before them stands a row of empty chairs, behind them the weirdly curving glass of their cabins. The dresses of the two front women are trained and flounced. The main one leans heavily on the ironwork railing fanning herself, or shielding herself from the view, or perhaps the sun. The next one leans far back so that her shape is outlined against the dark dress of the third, less prominent figure. The scene beyond the ship seems to be a chaos of docked ship masts, only in the mist they seem more like a forest of trees after a devastating fire as they lean this way and that, rather like the paintings we'd seen scattered round the floor of the gallery we'd passed through. I peered at the title:

" 'The Death of the HMS Calcutta'. What do you make of it, Henry?"

He cleared his throat. I sensed his disapproval but waited to hear the form it would take. It came in a whispered drawl. He found it vulgar and banal. Any longer with the ladies' stylish backs would be intolerably wearisome.

"Oh, come, Henry." I reminded him of Daisy Miller's dress – 'white muslin with a hundred frills and flounces and knots of pale-colored ribbons'.

"Ah, my clever sister," said he; "however, my argument is not with the dress but the hard finish of Tissot's painting. It is all fixed . . . the figures like mannequins drained of life."

I was not convinced. Stuff the high aestheticism, I thought, he fears contamination from any hint of effeminacy, of the effete.

"You do not agree?"

I did not. I found it alive with movement and possibility, the young women seeming to sway this way and that. "You can imagine the music . . . feel the heat beneath the flounces, Henry, the women's sensuality."

He stepped back to observe me as if I were one of the statues on exhibition.

I said: "Do you suspect I am not aware of such things, Henry?"

He did not reply. My brother, I reflected, who was all for treating the 'private' areas of life in his fictions (though always with discretion and the subtlest of touches), seemed distressed by my blatant 'impropriety'.

"But Henry," I argued, "is not their attire and demeanor the whole point of the painting – given the devastation around them – turning their costumes into shrouds and they into a trio of ghouls in frilly frocks?"

Of course I was right, he allowed; yet he seemed unwilling to engage in any further discussion involving the 'wider' implications of the painting. He had had enough. But what had happened? We'd begun innocently enough speaking of gowns, but the subject had somehow begun to billow out around us, dangerous, charged with significance. The 'seen' from which we may or may not guess the 'unseen'. Whereupon I remembered something Henry had written about dress as *the most personal shell of all* – which one strips away at one's peril.

"Henry," I brought him to a stop right there in the middle of the grand echoing vestibule, "have we suffered a" – I searched for the word – "*desamor*?"

He blinked, then turned and, striding towards the exit,

abandoned me. Then, as if remembering everything – my dependence, his responsibility to me, his own place – he turned back and drew me along. But something, everything had changed; we had changed. Our pleasant outing had become a trial for him and a source of distress for me. Was I in danger of losing him? "I didn't mean . . . ," I began . . . "I'm sorry, Henry." I was beginning to feel faint; an intermittent nerve pain had begun shooting down from my knees into my ankles so that my progress was now halting and awkward. I regained Henry's arm but it was as rigid as a chair's, while he muttered something about the 'unspeakable significance' of dress.

Back in my rooms I lay half-crumpled on my daybed while Henry hovered close by. At some point he roused himself:

"Do you remember, Alice, our visit to Wilton House back in '73?" He stroked his hat as if it were a lapdog.

Yes, I recalled being there with him and Aunt Kate: "The Earl of Pembroke had invited you," I said, "but we tagged along." Gradually the memory began to fill itself out. "We were staying at the White Hart . . . we drove from there to Wilton House like poor pilgrims."

He managed a rueful smile. "But do you remember a charming cloister, Alice?" That I should recall such an architectural detail seemed somehow critical, not so much to his opinion of me but to his sense of 'rightness' in the world. I said I did. "Good. Out of the cloister," he continued, "opened a series of drawing-rooms hung with family portraits, all of superlative merit. And among them" – he paused as if to catch his breath with the force of the memory – "hung a supreme Vandyck *par excellence*."

I could barely picture the painting but refrained from saying so since he was clearly devoted to it. For him, it had everything: design, color, elegance, force, finish . . . But what struck me most was how re-invigorated he seemed by the memory, as if the muscular Van Dyke had somehow restored *his* own noble dignity.

159

"Alice," I heard, felt him take my hand: "I shall be leaving tomorrow for the Continent."

"Fenimore, I presume?" My voice, thick. He is in need of comforting, I thought.

"I am in need of respite," he allowed: ". . . as well as egress from the jungle."

'Jungle' was Henry's private word for London. Not the London of the tour guide, nor the 'indispensable place' as he would call it in his next essay, but a word befitting the 'real', the secret London: a vicious, excoriating city lurking with beasts only too ready to pounce. But having taken two hemp pills I could offer no more in the way of memory or mothering. I was only vaguely aware of my brother rising to leave, a shadow on the wall.

Twenty-five

"A note from your brother, Miss. Hand delivered. Said it was urgent."

"Who said, Wardy?"

"Smith . . . Mr James's servant."

"Does he ask for a reply?"

"No, just that he will be with you shortly with some news."

As I stood at one of the front windows watching for Henry Katharine came up behind me and began walking her fingers up my spine, step by step. The feel of that 'walk', the pressure of her fingertips through the fabric of my dress and their stealthy, sneaking step only reinforced my sense of dread, so that when her fingers, gentle but firm as ever, reached my neck I flinched as if anticipating some murderous squeeze. "Alice?" she inquired. "I'm sorry," I said: "I was thinking of something else." "It's alright," she soothed, "I'm here. Nothing will hurt you." She held me against her. In the early December half-light we could just make out our reflections, the moonlike and the monkish. *Nothing will hurt you.* A foolish thing to say.

Katharine normally excused herself during Henry's visits, but today as a favor to me she would remain. I pictured us as if on stage, two stiff-backed characters, hands folded, awaiting the significant third. The news, they think, cannot be good; the atmosphere 'bristles' with tension . . . Only we were not acting. When my brother was announced Katharine and I turned as one. He stood. He seemed less stout. He was of course not used to confronting us *ensemble*. From the nose down my brother's features were as placid as ever but his eyes flared and darted as if an escaped mink had entered the room. Katharine was very still except for twiddling her ring.

We took our places together on the daybed, Henry directly opposite. We looked to the floor, to our hands or feet, anywhere but at one another. Three palpitating hearts and acrobatic stomachs.

"You have delayed your departure for Florence," I said.

He nodded gravely.

"The news . . .?"

"Not good. I have had it from William. He asked me to let you know." He withdrew the letter from his breast pocket:

Clover Hooper, our childhood friend, had died. Was dead. Clover Hooper *Adams* whom we'd met honeymooning at Thussis: she whom I'd so envied; she whom I'd observed being 'handled' by her new husband Henry as if she were made of the finest porcelain.

"How . . .?" asked the business-like Katharine. The Hoopers had been neighbors of the Lorings at Beverly Farms.

Henry paused before saying the word we feared: "suicide."

We said nothing for some seconds.

"How?" asked Katharine; relentless.

"I take it," said Henry, "you refer to the means employed? Apparently she swallowed some of the chemicals she used to develop her photographs. It was," he added, "her hobby."

Katharine glared: "It was not her *hobby*" – nasal, mocking – "it was her *passion*; she was devoted to it."

"It was Clover," I recalled, "who took the photograph of you and Louisa that John Sargent used for his painting 'Study in Greens'."

She agreed it was.

"Clover also photographed The Bee."

162

"And that portrait of you, Alice." She pointed above the mantelpiece.

I nodded.

We were silent again.

"There is of course," Henry hesitated, "the connection William makes between the creative urge and the destructive urge."

Katharine was rising up, "How dare he . . . ," but I pulled her down and shushed her. She was glaring at my brother, her eyes narrowed to slits.

"Do you rate it?" I asked.

Henry, inclining more to "a case of hereditary melancholy," cited the Hooper sisters' history of suicidal depressions, their not infrequent breakdowns and incarcerations and . . .

"Henry," I interrupted, for once not inclined to 'side' with him in Katharine's presence: "do not forget that I was also 'incarcerated', as you so politely put it. And we were not the only ones. As girls Clover and I used to swap comparisons of the hospitals that, leviathan-like, seemed to swallow up our female friends and relatives. While so many of our brothers were going off to war, we did our 'duty' with stays in various 'bins', the smellier the better, to salve our consciences. Clover was especially frustrated."

"So you suspected it?"

I shook my head. "But it doesn't altogether surprise me. Not long ago I had a letter from Ellen saying she was worried about Clover. Since their father's death she'd become so depressed she couldn't do her photography; she wouldn't go out or see friends. Then she'd sent her sister a strange message saying: *'Ellen I'm not real – oh make me real – you are all of you real!'*"

Henry, who looked as if he'd seen her ghostly manifestation, jumped up and began pacing about as if dictating one of his gothic tales:

"They'd just returned to Washington . . . he'd built her a

new house there . . . he had gone out for a walk . . . when he returned . . .". On he went. We can hear her Henry calling out to her, "Clover . . . Clover are you there?"; feel his worried consternation at getting no reply; see him bursting into her 'studio' . . .

"Alice?" Katharine was addressing me: "Did you ever see the photographs she used to take of herself?"

I did, I said. There were, so I believed at the time, an unconscionable number of self-portraits. I'd thought her vain, but now I saw my mistake: they were all of a grainy, insubstantial nature.

"They were in no way flattering," said Katharine. "But I suppose they provided evidence."

"Evidence . . .?" inquired Henry propping himself up beside the mantelpiece.

"Of her being *real*." She spoke impatiently.

"Except," I added, "that she never really believed it; right up to the end, evidently."

"Killing herself, however," Henry opined, "that is, realizing that she could *be* killed, would have proved her 'reality'. A paradox," he concluded.

"No," Katharine said fiercely: "a tragedy".

"Bien sur." Pause; then: "Yet she was married."

Katharine's laughed bark-like. "And do you suppose gaining a husband is like acquiring a nursemaid or a healer? Besides," she went straight on, "everyone knew there were 'difficulties' in the marriage."

Silence.

Once again I recalled Thussis and the sensation of pleasure, the vibrating waves of heat the honeymooners had given off; the sense that the world, including all of us, had become a backdrop to their romance; and, most of all, how her betrothed, that other Henry, had kept touching her – the brush of a fingertip – as if having to check she was real, or truly his, or to make sure she had not disappeared.

"What would it be like, I wonder," I hear myself ask, "to

have someone cherish you to the point of terror?" My voice is too loud, the question a 'blurt'.

"Terror, Alice . . .?" Henry strides across the room to place a restraining hand upon mine.

I lower my voice: "I meant to say 'excess'." Then I add, more conversationally: "Aunt Kate once told me having a mate does not save you from anything except the indignity of having to call yourself an old maid."

"I guess marriage saves no one from despair," says Katharine reaching for my other hand.

It's at that point I remember something else from Thussis.

From my window I could see straight through the gray-blue portals of the Via Mala – that old-time *Evil Way* – with its melancholy rocky crags rising on either side red as the rust on an ancient sword. In the waning afternoon, dark shadows deepened against a background of sheer gray rock. Pine trees clung on for dear life. The next day we took the carriage-road winding into it, advancing like a group of simple, credulous readers into some darksome romance. Or a burial procession.

I did not say any of that of course. Instead I recalled how Clover's Henry had one day said of her: " 'Oh, my wife is a charming blue . . . she reads German, also Latin, also, I fear, a little Greek. So, as I tell her, any woman learning Greek must buy fashionable dresses.' "

"And how did she 'take it'?" asked Henry, claiming not to remember.

"Oh, *then* she could take it," I said.

"But not forever?"

"No, not forever. "You once called her a Voltaire in petticoats," I reminded him.

"Did I? I suppose I may have . . . yes . . . she seemed to have had her wit clipped a little; but then, at the time I mean, I suppposed she had expanded in the affections."

An unfortunate word to choose, I thought, that 'expanded'.

But practical Katharine was already thinking ahead: "Now we must look to Ellen," she counseled. "She will be feeling the strain of her sister's death – added to their father's." And with that she left the room.

Henry remained. Presently I recalled a visit I'd had from Clover back in '82. She'd just returned from Washington D.C., where she'd entertained Henry among other *de chic* guests in her drawing-room: 'He may in time get into the 'swim' over here,' she'd reported, 'but I doubt it. I think, Alice, that the real, live, vulgar, quick-paced world in America will continue to fret him. No, I believe your brother prefers a quiet corner with a pen where he can create men and women who say neat things and have refined tastes and are not nasal or eccentric.'

"You're smiling, Alice," observed Henry.

"It's nothing," I said. "I was remembering Clover . . . at her sharpest."

"Indeed." He consulted his pocket-watch. "I see I must go." Florence, and Fenimore, were calling to him. He bent to embrace me and, checking to see the coast was clear of Katharine, took his leave.

I found her at the back window of our bedroom. "Henry's gone," I told her: "you can come out now." Her reflected smile was lopsided. She was drawing circles in the glass: faces with dots for eyes and dashes for mouths; under each one she wrote a name: Sara, Fanny, Clover, Ellen . . . So then I reached out and put an 'X' over the circle that had been Clover. "Oh, Alice." But it was not meant cruelly. I'd already begun to imagine what it must have been like for her: mixing the chemicals with hand a-tremble . . . the cloudy fizzing cocktail . . . how her eyes would smart . . . but quick before it goes off . . . the tipping back of her head . . . throwing it down . . . .the unspeakable searing of her secret flesh and then a puff of light as if some giant camera had shot her gloriously alive before all the lights go out.

"Clover is dead," I said, thinking The Personage must

have suffered a muddled moment for sparing a rag-tag like me while sacrificing a substance-ful being like Clover.

Katharine nodded.

Now we must look to Ellen.

Before going to bed I wrote to Clover's sister: *My dear Ellen* . . . In due course I received an alarmingly crumpled scrawl:

'*Sorrysorrysorry* expect no more letters,' she'd written . . . 'I dread even to write my own name'. A soberer 'PS' followed: *But thank you, Alice, you are one of the few people who might have understood Clover's plight . . .*'

There was also a letter from Ellen's husband Whitman scrawled on Harvard letterhead *From the Dean's Office* saying Ellen was still showing the strain of Clover's death and did not feel up to writing letters. But he would be sure and tell her of my concern.

A letter from Aunt Kate repeated the 'horrible' news, also reporting – as if the same letter could properly contain them both – her own 'bad' cold and Rob's 'condition'.

"Poor Rob has gone off the rails again," I told Katharine, just returned from lecturing a group of educationists at The University of London. She put down her briefcase.

"Drinking?"

I nodded. "He's been diagnosed with 'progressive nervous degeneracy' and has had to be hospitalized."

"I'm sorry for his wife and children," she said tartly. Then: "Is there any good news, Alice?" She came up behind me, tapped the back of my head as if hoping to release a drop of sweetness.

"Oh yes," I said, "she says people are all over talking about Henry's new work, The Bostonians."

"So they would. And what are they saying?"

"Oh, Aunt Kate is no literary critic. She is proud of Henry regardless of what they or indeed common opinion says."

She did not inquire further, which was just as well.

167

Twenty-six

"So, you have had a relapse," observed the observant Dr Townsend. The pain had come on gradually, increasing and spreading like a scurrilous rumor. Katharine blamed Henry for taking me out in the rain, and for 'overdoing it'. "Overdoing *what*?" I asked. "Paintings . . . galleries . . . ," she named idiotically, as if Art itself were to blame for my illness. But I was in no condition to argue aesthetic's case, or Henry's. The rheumatic pains scissored through from my stomach to my hands, feet to hips, shoulders to neck. My head felt twice its normal size and weight. Some other devouring force pincered its way from muscle to muscle, organ to organ. Each time I was on the verge of falling asleep I was jolted awake as if by a double-dose of the Holtz Electrical Machine – except the current was inside me. "Sleep deprivation is a form of torture," I yodeled. It was horrible.

Katharine showed the natty little doctor into my bedroom then made to retreat herself; but no, no, he waved her forward. When his back was turned, she mimicked his glove-sucking expression, which made me titter even through my tears.

"So how is our patient?" he began: "has the salicene been of benefit?" I allowed as how I could not live without it, all the while rolling my head from side to side as if trying to loose it from the rest of my body. Townsend was amused by what he called my 'exaggeration'. "*Exaggeration*? How dare you . . ." I was about to kick him when Katharine caught my leg.

"Now now, Miss James," he waved, palpating my body

starting at the feet and working his way slowly and sadistically upwards. I winced and writhed as one on the rack. (Katharine later admitted having to restrain *her*self from kicking him as he 'worked me over'.) Yet in truth he could not be accused of having used any significant force at all.

The threnody of pain played on.

"I suppose," Katharine ventured from her chaperone's corner, "this weather does not help?" She disliked the dampness herself, how it crawled through the pavements up through the basements and floorboards and walls; how even the mice and cockroaches bore its message along with goodness knows what life-threatening diseases. On top of the dampness came layers of paperings and hangings and paintings and draperies which she found suffocating. She missed our New England countryside, its fresh air and open skies, its mountains, its trees, its . . .

Townsend flexed and unflexed my legs gymnastically rotating them at the hip, bending them at the knee, pointing them heavenwards. As he worked he referred to 'the legs' neurosis' as if they were a pair of deranged, slow-witted twins. "The legs cannot be hurried," he added. I pictured 'the legs' – Sally and Sue? Molly and Milly? – shuffling along like stubborn little girls and, in spite of the pain, began to giggle. At which Townsend and Katharine exchanged looks: *Could it be her mind rather than her body that is at fault?* Tears leaked from between my lids. He took hold of one hand, Katharine the other. My brief bout of hilarity – he called it 'hysteria' – soon gave way to a floppy exhaustion.

"*Bedridden women*," I croaked, quoting one of the doctors from back home, "*are such a trial to professional skill.*" Townsend ignored this. "Can you describe your sensations?" he tried. He really was a dogged little man. "It is as if," I managed, "some message from my brain is being intercepted so that by the time it reaches my knees it is distorted and indecipherable." Townsend hmm'd at appropriate intervals before delivering his verdict: a diagnosis of "gouty diathesis complicated by an abnormally sensitive nervous organization, brought about by anxiety and strain."

"And the non-functioning of my legs," I queried, "is produced by gout?"

"Oh! dear me yes," he responded gleefully. "I have seen people with their legs powerless for years from this cause!"

Katharine narrowed her eyes in the manner of a goat getting ready to head-butt. Truly, I feared she would do him a damage.

"However," I heard him conclude, "I believe time and medicines will do it." He wrote out another prescription for salicene plus an even stronger tonic. "What tonic?" she queried. "Hemp," he replied. She saw him out. Upon her return she related their conversation, acting both parts with consummate skill.

Townsend: "I firmly believe Miss James will improve when she is . . . how should I put it . . . when she . . . (He finally manages to spit it out) . . . when she reaches middle life."

Katharine: "I take it you're referring to the menopause."

Townsend (eyebrow in mid-hoik): "Indeed."

Katharine: "But that could be some way off: Alice is not yet forty. Is there nothing that can be done in the meantime?"

Townsend: "The womb is a mysterious organ about which we know little, alas."

Katharine: 'And who's fault is that?"

Townsend: No reply.

Katharine: "But is it possible that such symptoms could be caused by some abnormality?"

Townsend: "I should say if anything it's the womb's 'emptiness' that is the probable cause."

Katharine: "Please . . . not that ridiculous old theory. Something is wrong with Alice's womb that is depriving the organs and muscles of vital function, and causing her extreme pain. Her womb does not go wandering about her body like some sleepwalker in a nightcap any more than mine does – or yours for that matter. Good day, Doctor."

I applauded her little show calling *Bravo*. She bowed. I told her, "You, Kath, are my best medicine, dear." She scooped up one of my hands and pressed it to her bosom. "And you are mine," she replied: courtly, enigmatical. What could she possibly mean? I wondered. How could I be anything other than a trial to her? Or was she parodying herself now? But it was not the time for such questions. We shared the absurdity of a medical man who had been as intimate with me as my mother yet could not speak openly about an every-day gynecological event. "He appears to know very little about the female anatomy." She considered the good doctor frankly lazy, apt to take the easy way out by prescribing pills rather than trying to discover the root cause of the problem. "By my last count," Katharine reckoned, "you have had at least sixteen periods this year, each one lasting nearly two weeks, is that not so, dear?" It was so; moreover the blood flowed so heavily that the rag situation, according to Wardy, had become desperate. "'Tis not normal, in my experience," she'd opined. Which Katharine thought a far more intelligent response than Townsend's.

By the end of the week I'd received a whole stack of sympathy letters. "Oh, for heaven's sake," I protested to Katharine, "why do people write me such invalid pap? I feel like a goose being forced-fed on sugary meringues." I thrust out my tongue in the way of one about to be violently sick, *gagaghh*.

"Listen to this," I gasped. It was a letter from William: "'You poor child! . . . You are visited in a way that few are ever called to bear . . . stifling slowly in a quagmire of disgust and pain and impotence!'" I waved my arms, conducting as I read. Then Katharine joined in: "*Stifling in a*

quagmire of disgust," we yodelled, off-pitch, warbling operatically: *"and pain and im-po-tence!"*

Truly, it was the best medicine of all; for the moment, even
Clover was forgotten. But what could they know of the
reality of my condition? Of sharing one's body with an
internal torturer who varied both method, direction and
ferocity of torment according to his perverted pleasure:
today a skull-splitting headache, tomorrow a spinal mas-
sacre, etc etc etc. Yet – allow me a contrariety – I could not
bear to have it 'played up' by others. I was alive, Clover was
not; nor my brother Wilky; nor little Herman; nor the multi-
tudes slaughtered on battlefields; nor those who'd perished
in poverty and oppression.

But I must reply.

Katharine took her place at my desk and waited while I
gathered my drug-dispersed thoughts.

"Begin 'Dear Willy,'" I dictated: "Tell him that amidst the
horrors of which we read every day my woes seem of a very
pale tint indeed. Tell him, as for my so-called 'quagmire of
disgust, pain and impotence', I consider myself one of the
most potent creations of my time, and though I may not have
a group of Harvard students sitting at my feet drinking in
psychological, or indeed psychic truths, assure him I shall
not tremble at the last trump. There. Sign it: *'Always your
loving sister, Alice.'"* She looked up, unusually rosy. It must
have seemed to her an odd little speech, uncharacteristically
serious for one such as me. I was not always such a brave
little soldier, yet my words *had* been brave, so that once
having said them, I knew them to be true; and just to make
sure I wasn't talking tosh, I repeated them to myself: *I shall
not tremble at the last trump.* No tosh: I meant each word.

"Do you doubt their veracity?" I asked.

There was a pause. "No, dear, I do not."

The next morning she confessed to what I had already
guessed: she would soon be defecting (again) back to the
States to look after her ailing father.

Neither she nor Henry would be with me over the Christmas holidays.

Time nevertheless would pass. I saw a mangle spilling out the days like great wet sheets. Henry could make time pass of course so that it slid smoothly, lightly, drily by; no flapping and slapping, no clattering of mangles for Henry. Time would wrap me in its sticky envelope. Time entrapping yet emptied of significance, of connection. Time spitting out reams of Christmas twaddle. Time going off in a great puff leaving only a photograph behind: a gap where a breathing human body once was, a Voltaire in petticots. Time leaving me at the mercy of the living: my landlady, Mrs Dickson and Wardy, my nurse. Time chattering. Time creeping over me like one of Mr Darwin's Galapagos turtles.

Twenty-seven

Katharine returned in the new year. "It's absolutely shameful," she cried, flapping about like a ruddy duck in a rage. "Look to your nose, dear," I warned. It had begun to glow. That she ignored. "Everyone in London and Boston is talking about it. He has used us 'Bostonians'- as he refers to us *en masse* as if we were a school of fish – as his models, making us look foolish and . . . He has distorted, simplified and exaggerated: it is absolutely inexcusable."

She stopped churning about and faced me: "Tell me you deny it."

It was a challenge, but also a plea for me to join her, to rescue her from her own helpless rage. Well I could not. Perhaps I understood too well the process of separating oneself and others from one's characters. My brother had made it clear to me, as he had to all those who had challenged him on this same score, that his creations were the product of his imagination.

"Surely," she tried, "you must admit the portrait of Olive Chancellor is outrageous."

I would admit no such thing. The 'portrait' of Olive Chancellor (manipulative, hysterical, 'peculiar') was admittedly painful. But it did not follow that it was of Katharine. More likely it was based on a number of different women in the Boston 'movement' who behaved with Olive's stiffness of manner and dogged rigidity of purpose. *My* Katharine was nothing like that; *my* Katharine was flexible and adaptable, elastic to the point of . . . . Oh, she might be able to whistle through her teeth and do crowcalls, but she was nothing like that vulnerable wooden doll, Olive Chancellor.

"Poor Olive," I muttered.

"So you admit . . .?"

"I admit," I said, "only that he was writing what he perceived as a 'type' – not *you*."

"Oh, but how could he!?" Katharine burst out, rather chillingly Olive-like. She began reading aloud the description of Miss Birdseye, 'the poor little humanitarian hack'; followed by that of Dr Prance, the typical 'Yankee female: spare, dry, hard, without a curve, an inflection or a grace.'

"Really, it's too much!" She slammed the book closed. "A shameless parody of poor Elizabeth."

"But, Kath dear, " I objected, "those descriptions are from Basil Ransom's point of view, not Henry's."

"Oh, but . . .".

"But what?"

"Well, he's just so ignorant of the basic issues of our cause."

"My brother," I countered, "does not pretend to write political tracts."

Katharine pulled a comb out of her hair only to replace it.

"It's just so full of . . . vitriol against us." She began flipping through the pages stabbing at one passage after another.

I objected: "But you must admit it's also highly amusing." I referred to the description of the librarian, a Miss Catching. And the jibe that if Verena were to expose Basil as one of their 'traducers', she – the librarian that is – would not know how to treat such a revelation; in other words, would not know under what letter to file it.

I covered my mouth.

"You find that amusing?" She shut the book.

"I'm afraid I do."

"Very well. And how do you like the image of yourself?"

I started. "You think I am . . .?"

"Verena Tarrant of course, the little speechifier."

It was too absurd. The girl was far too lovely and openly loving, too generous and expressively 'natural' to be based, however loosely, upon *me*; though she had reminded me at one point of our poor dead cousin, Minnie Temple. Yet, I reasoned, she cannot 'be' Minnie Temple because only Verena can 'be' Verena: she is made of words, only words. That is what it means to create characters. Just so, the characters in The Bostonian, as in his other stories, had been created out of all of us, yet *were* profoundly none of us. I imagined how he would proceed: like a chef choosing ingredients from here and there, yet even as he reaches for this spice or that herb, he is not consciously aware that he is doing it. But in the end it all comes together. Only then do his characters – for they are his – take on 'lives' of their own. Still, it remains an illusion.

"I do not say the characters are direct copies" – she was intent on pursuing the matter – "Henry's much too clever for that. Nevertheless, is it not about the corruption of an innocent, about the subjection of one will upon another?"

"And which of us is the innocent and which the corrupter?" I was in a reckless, mocking mood.

"You may find it all . . . elevating," said Katharine, "but I do not."

"I can see that."

"Well, how would you like to be described as a snobbish, pathetic, hysterical . . . *grotesque*?" She proceeded to read out: 'morbid . . . grim . . . shy . . . rigid . . .', her voice trailing off ending in a sort of moan.

I had to admit the women in Henry's book were for the most part a 'faded and dingy human collection'; that only Verena Tarrant escaped the charges of grotesqueness, plainness and risibleness. But what, I asked myself, had impelled Henry to write such a 'below the belt' book? Had he consciously set out to expose 'women like us' to public ridicule? Was it his intention that we examine ourselves as if we *were* the characters in his book? Decidedly not. It would have been the tension of the situation that would have appealed to him: an older woman with financial and social clout 'taking over' an innocent, talented, beautiful girl who then sets about exploiting her for her own aims like a performing monkey. But it will have been an abstract relationship that Henry the writer had set about exploring.

"Why," I managed at last, "I wouldn't mind at all being described as 'passionate'. As for being the putative model for Verena Tarrant, unfortunately I do not fit the part. No one this side of the Adams Asylum would take it into their head to describe me as handsome. And," I went on in more serious vein, "as for Olive's worry about Verena marrying . . ." – I laughed: "Where is the likelihood of that for me?" But then I began to wonder if she could be right: that Henry might indeed have been writing about me by omission, as it were, revealing my tragedy through the fact that no Basil Ransom had come into my life to 'rescue' me as he had Verena Tarrant.

Katharine saw it quite differently. "In that case," she said, "you are well out of it." She accused me of 'refusing to see the obvious': how we'd fallen into another of Henry's traps, that it was his intention to cause just such a rift between us. And with that, she strode out of the room – returning almost at once: "Your brother," she added, "for all his cleverness, does not know he writes about himself."

My heart thumped. "Of course," I argued, "he writes about himself, including himself in the hodgepodge that is creation – which he knows very well, by the way; yet he remains Henry the author: himself only himself." Yet, having said that, I had to admit I'd thought of Basil Ransom as Henry, or rather the Henry Henry could never be, the one who acted rather than stood by watching. But that was evidently not what she meant. She hesitated before coming out with her 'bombshell':

"I believe Olive Chancellor is Henry himself."

I stared. *That again.* I did not like to think of it. But *was* it possible that Henry had loved, indeed did still love, *outside*? There was no question but that it was love as described in the book, however 'peculiar intense and interesting' between the two women. Could it be that Henry was able to write about their 'condition' precisely because he knew of it himself and therefore pitied; yet was all the more scathing because it frightened him that he could feel, indeed had felt, such a thing gripping his own heart? Could it be then that Katharine was right? Had he exposed, along with Olive and Verena's 'Boston' relationship, his own 'peculiar' proclivities? For how else, I now began to reason (coming dangerously close to Katharine's position), could he have thrown himself into such a character as Olive Chancellor with her 'pulsing passion'?

At last I managed to ask: "And how is that?"

She did not reply.

"You think he is jealous of you?" I supplied.

"That is correct."

"That you have taken me away from him?"

Katharine nodded.

"That he wished to be 'attached' to me himself?"

"I wouldn't phrase it like that myself. But look here," she gathered up the book, flung it open and pointed: "It says here that Basil Ransom thinks: '. . . *only if Olive Chancellor takes Verena away to Europe, only then would he not be able to follow her.*'" She looked up, triumphant. "And isn't that what *I* have done with you?" The question vibrated around us. I was, I'll admit, secretly gratified to think I might be beloved of both. But there was something wrong with her logic. "Oh," I pointed out, "but Henry was already here in London. You took me *to* him, not away from him. So that I could have both of you." I paused, unwilling to be torn between the two people I loved most in the world, before adding: "And I do, do I not . . . have you both?"

We went on arguing about The Bostonians until I began to think of it as Henry's delinquent creation, which it would become increasing hard to defend. Katharine held to the view that the novel was overdone and cartoonish. If it was harsh and overdone, I riposted, it was also true. Why, I could name several in the movement who were 'like that'.

"Like what?" Katharine's eyes narrowed.

"Types," I hissed.

But Katharine could not forgive its lack of understanding of, never mind sympathy for, the women's movement.

"But it is a literary work, a romantic drama, not a history," I insisted, choosing a passage for its musical quality, its depth of feeling, its humor. She listened impatiently as I read. It was for me like drinking my brother in, siphoning his consciousness directly into mine. "How," I entreated, "could you not be seduced by his words?"

"Easily," came her snappish reply.

The space between us had grown thick and distorted, almost as if we'd engaged in gymnastics or fisticuffs. Our breathing was labored, we perspired, our arms hung at our sides. Katharine's hair looked as if it was about to lift off her scalp. Eventually we agreed to let the matter rest but it would soon ignite again fueled by some remark or other.

Katharine was not alone in her condemnation. The public, it transpired, had largely turned against the book. Bostonians resented the one-sided critical portrait of their city. Aunt Kate scolded Henry for basing Miss Birdseye on Elizabeth Peabody, Hawthorne's sister-in-law. And it did not go unnoticed that the Brahmin Olive lived in a small elegant house on Charles Street as did Mrs James T. Fields and her 'Boston Marriage'.

William complained of the book's having too much 'descriptive psychology', by which he meant, poor prissy Willy, sex. As I told Katharine, "He refers to the relationship between the two women in the book as an 'inverted passion'." Well, she couldn't give a fig for that. I wrote telling him not to be such a bourgeois prude and an oaf. It was a work of genius. It eluded simple interpretation. It could not be pinned down. Like Henry himself.

The reviewers did not like it either. I called their criticism superficial but it began to sound feeble even in my own ears. The most cutting remark of all (*"Why, the figure of Olive Chancellor lives upon his very doorstep!"*) overheard at one of Katherine's Saturday Morning Club meetings – confirmed her suspicions.

Twenty-eight

Henry returned from the Continent bearing a screen decorated with brilliant prancing peacocks and intertwining lilies.

"Much too fine," I objected: "take it away."

"It will act as a barrier against the draft," he argued, asserting its practicality. Although its fineness was therefore beside the point, he added: "It might as well be fine."

He positioned the screen at the foot of my day-bed. Whereupon there came a wind. Or something like a wind. Together we watched the candle on the mantelpiece with its strong oval flame flicker and gutter before finally going out, plunging us into darkness.

Henry said nothing, but I guessed his thought: Not even the *fine* screen had the power to stop *it*. Everything existing in the visible world, my brother believed, was an imperfect mirror of some hidden reality or unseen world. Eventually he turned and there it was (he'd re-lit the candle) written on his face, not exactly a thing to 'believe' in, but a sensation, a force, an inspiration from which the imagination – call it the soul if you like – receives its most rarefied nourishment. Without 'it', I knew, he would not, could not write.

But I was beginning to feel queer. Such things were beyond our knowledge; we were bound after all to earth.

"How do you find London upon your return, Henry?"

"Ah, London," he began, "the indispensable place." He went on expansively, describing the great 'soup-pot' that was London from scruffy children and carpet beaters to riders and horses and walkers carrying portmanteaus holding tooth-brushes and sandwiches and . . . .

"Henry!" I shouted. My brother was not easy to interrupt in full-flow. "I can read your next London review for myself; what I want to know is how are you *taking it*?"

The novel in question lay on the table between us. Had it been there before? I did not think so; but perhaps we had been too distracted by the *fine* screen to notice it. But it could not now be avoided. Henry turned it face-down.

I said, "They have not been kind to you."

"It is not the job of the critic to be kind, my dear Alice. They are paid raptors."

"And you," I said, "have been their latest prey."

I watched as my brother, turning to gaze out the window, sucked in his cheeks. It was a response so familiar – his way of removing himself – and touching, that I had to look away myself. The pain of it. After that he rose and began polishing one of the lamps with his middle finger, as if to say: *They have savaged me enough, go no further.* I would not add to his hurt. I would not say I found The Bostonians in some way prosaic, or that I thought he was capable of a kind of writing that went beyond it. I would certainly not convey Katharine's diatribe, or her fury.

"The raptors be damned, Henry," I said at last.

His brow contracted. He reminded me that the novel (referred to as 'an account of contemporary Boston') had been called 'inadequate' by a certain influential critic. He'd tried to brush it off but the damage, I saw, had lodged within him. He had expected more. But he would not let them get the better of him. As if fearing paralysis, he had already moved on, the next book was already sketched out. Still, I understood, it would be there underneath: the fear of 'the beast' waiting to pounce.

"So," I said, moving us on: "How was it on the Continent?"

"Ah," he breathed, his whole countenance relaxing. "The terraces at Saint Germain," he began, "were luxuriantly residential, thickly inhabited, replete with prettiness." On he went to describe a visit to the Theatre Francais in which he'd sat 'in a sort of languid ecstasy of contemplation'. After that came a disquisition on the audience, beginning with "a number of old gents who looked as if they took snuff from boxes adorned with portraits of the fashionable beauty of 1820 . . ."

"Henry!" He was like a child at the back of a schoolroom lost in a dream. I rapped my knuckles on the book: "Enough lyrical gymnastics. How *was* it, I mean, with Constance?"

He feigned surprise, as if he'd forgotten he'd just spent three months in her company: "Ah, Fenimore."

"Constance . . . Fenimore . . . call her Ishmael for all I care." I was losing patience.

"Fenimore," he allowed, "is, as ever, a superb guide."

I took aim with the book but restrained myself from actually throwing it. "I guess you have been *gallivanting* together?"

He recoiled from my barbarism. My brother, as I should have known, hated vulgar innuendo.

"She is not typical of an American woman in search of a husband," he allowed with sudden directness.

"True; yet she is in search of a particular one," I pointed out.

His expression went vague again: "I believe she is made of many shades . . . several women at once. It is possible therefore that one of them desires a conventional ending."

His implication was perfectly clear: *he* would not provide it. He was prepared to admit to 'a mild excess'- whatever that might be – but that was his limit. I understood then what I had always known ever since witnessing an encounter between Henry and our mother in which she'd tried to persuade him *"towards a favorable attitude of heart towards . . . towards . . ."*

Henry: "What is it, Mother?"

Mother: (all in a whoosh): ". . . the divine institution of marriage."

Henry, who had listened politely to the well-meaning speech (while examining his fingernails), then answered with an almost unbearable glibness:

"If you will provide the wife, the fortune, *and the inclination*, Mother, I will take them all."

At this point I, who had been attending as if to a tennis match, interpreted my brother's remark to mean, 'I am not inclined to it *now*'. But there was my mother's expression – it had gone from hurt to puzzlement and finally to horror – so that I understood something momentous had occurred.

Now here it was again, the pulling back, the dis-inclination. So where did that leave Constance? Do you feel *anything* for her, Henry? I longed to fling at him. But that would have been unfair; besides, like my mother, I was reluctant to intrude further. Henry, having lit a cigar, was gazing at the glowing tip. I saw we must move on.

"Alice," he began in his drawing-room voice, "are you aware that there is in London an unquenchable fashion for Americans?" I made an impatient gesture. *Nor do I care to know.* But on he went about the Princess of Lorne and other royalish personages. It was as if we'd agreed to fashion a clay bowl between us but were then unable to agree on the desired outcome: 'Let us make a deep bowl,' say I. 'No,' says he, 'let us make it elegantly shallow'. Oh but Henry's private bowl – if such an image could attach itself to my brother – was deeper than any I could fathom. A better metaphor would have been the Charles iced over. The deeps were there, would always be there. He must be allowed to skate on whatever surface allowed him to go smoothly, brilliantly, on.

*

"My brother says it's a spirit put the candle out," I later told Wardy in a scare-mongering voice. But instead of quailing in terror the normally superstitious creature haw-hawed, saying it only proved that the Jameses were all 'off their rockers'. The surprising part of it was that in 'intellectual' matters she deferred to us while in trifles about arranging the room, or draughts, or what-not, she was as obstinate as an old mule. "Anyone with any sense in their head," added she, "would know it was the 'owling East wind." And just to prove it, she got down on all fours sniffing like a mongrel dog, lifting carpets and feeling between floorboards. She'd already stuffed an extra 'snake' under the hallway door. Eventually there came the "aha!" of enlightenment. The window on the landing had been left open an inch: "by you-know-who," said she, wagging a thumb in the direction of 'downstairs'.

At which the landlady, Mrs Dickson, appeared, having come up to deliver a bowl of tripe and potato soup which had, she swore, "ealing properties'. "'ealing for what?" asked Wardy suspiciously. "Whatever troubles you." "Humph," said Wardy, "nothing troubles me." "Well, bully for you." "Now now, ladies," I intervened. Wardy helped me to the table before huffing out. Mrs Dickson busied herself arranging the bowl and serviette. "There you are," she said, looking on admiringly, as if I and my meal were the subject of one of those dark, dull paintings of domestic interiors, *Invalid At Her Meagre Repast*, which Henry detests for its mundane furniture and lack of imagination. Then she stood, hands crossed over capacious apron-front, the very image of a proud maker of tripe and potato soup.

I raised my spoon, steeled to compliment her on her concoction, but she spoke first: "You seem quite comfortable, Miss James." I looked up. *Comfortable?* I supposed so, allowing for the fact that I'd been laid up with rheumatism in my head, unable to move or breathe for twelve hours. Then, even more remarkably, she observed, sighing mournfully: "You are always 'appy with yourself, Miss."

"*Happy* with myself?" I repeated incredulously. "Kind of you to say so, Mrs. Dickson, but it is not how most people view me. As you are no doubt aware, Wardy thinks me 'a miserable afflicted little thing'." "Ah well," pronounced Mrs. D, "each to his own. I shouldn't worry too much about that one. Anywhile the soup is chilling under your nose."

I raised my thumb causing the bowl-end to tip. *Happy*, came its judgment as it broke the starchy surface and began, very slowly, to sink. *Each to his own*. Was that how it would be: would I sit, or lie, here in this room while the world came in, so many perambulating spoons and ladles, declaring me well or ill, happy or miserable? *Such a brave little soul you are, Alice! . . . Poor wretched Alice, such a poisonous jellyfish!* And when the pronouncing spoons will have left? Will I see what they saw? But suddenly – the spoon had sunk to the very bottom of the bowl and the thick grey-white gluey mush had closed over it – suddenly it all seemed quite freeing, and funny, for it meant that I could be anything, anything at all. *Oh what a brave little jellyfish am I! What a poisonous little soul!* Or nothing at all.

After supper, I was helped back to the couch. Katharine had moved it so that I could see out, at the same time be within three feet of the fire. I wore two layers of knitted underclothing, a flannel lined wrapper, two wool shawls over my shoulders and a heavy tartan rug over my legs. An extra fur cloak in case of a sudden blizzard. I could easily be mistaken for an esquimo.

Thus I reclined in the smallish room, legs stretched out before me, midway between window and fire. To look out . . . or in, where the fire-demons would be having a knees-up? No . . . flames, I told myself, only flames. Wolf-howls? No, only the dry wind slicing round the chimney. I was safe; I was 'comfortable' and 'appy in myself'. I turned again towards the window observing how the frost-pointed lights stood out against the darkness, and how the city roared like an outraged frozen lion. And yet, what was going on out there? The newspapers shouted out more cases every day: old and young dying of influenza, freezing to death; millions without work malnourished and starving. What did I –

tucked up with my rugs and pictures and plants and books (more and more books) and reading chairs and reading lamps and fireplace and andirons and drapes and silver soup spoons &etc – what did I really know of that other outside world? Nothing. I would soon find out.

Twenty-nine

Wardy stood at the hall mirror adjusting her 'dressing-up' bonnet: green shirred stuff with pink frilly rose-blobs. "Going somewhere?" I asked, sweet as wormwood. It was Saturday, she reminded me, her day off. She and her hat were going to the the-ay-ter. She and her hat – nurse takes a day off – but why shouldn't she? – and where did I get the right to pronounce upon her hat and her accent even if they did make me cringe?

"What will you see?"

"The Pantomime, Miss, at Drury Lane, split your sides laughin', so they say. Pity you can't see it, tho' I daresay you'd be snooty about it. Nevermind, I'm away. I've arranged with Mrs Dickson to bring you your tea. Keep an eye on the fire, we don't want another conflagwhatsit." Only the other day she'd discovered smoke rising up from under the fender owing to the carpet and rug having been laid too close up to the grate.

"Con-flag-ration," I offered.

Three hours later she returned flapping like a hen on fire and never mind about the Pantomime. "Windows in the house on the corner are all busted up, Miss, and the shops are all shuttered and barricaded along Piccadilly."

"Henry!" I gasped, stumbling towards the window. His house was next to the corner. His windows would be smashed and he lying cut and bleeding.

"Calm yourself, Miss." She was sure he was safe and as it turned out she was right. He had gone on dictating through one of the worst hullaballoos, it having provided 'material' for a certain passage to do with 'radicals'.

During the next week Wardy would continue feeding me her lurid version of events: "A shower of eggs and tomatoes and worse went flying in all directions . . ."

"Worse . . .?"

Titter-titter, holding her nose: "You *know*, Miss . . ."

"Ah, I see."

On she went: ". . . and ladies dragged from their carriages and robbed of their jewels and frightened half to death . . . and the footmen running off with their cowardly tails between their legs!"

Well, hurrah, said I, it was the best news I'd heard in years and about time the fat and their flunkies were taken down a peg; so then she accused me of trying to provoke her; so then I snarled and ordered her out of my sight before I bit.

Next morning Katharine returned from Cambridge. She'd brought with her Mrs Montague Cookson, wife of the defeated Radical candidate: a small, dark, purposeful figure with no thought for formalities. Just having her there in the room – and Katharine of course – was enough to restore me to myself and my own sense of justice. Arguing with Wardy, I realized, was like using a fly-swatter against a bird of prey. But here was a true fighter for the cause; someone I could believe and believe *in*. Her version of events could not have diverged more from Wardy's:

"Children lying about on shavings, rags, anything; famine looking out of babies' faces, out of women's eyes, out of the tremulous hands of men." She spoke of destitution, the general frustration; things she knew of from her own experience. She'd performed good works under a clergyman in the East End, had seen more of the way the poor lived than any other woman of our class.

"Thousands of families, half-a-dozen children and their parents living in one room, having tasted no food all winter but 'sops' . . ."

"Sops?"

"Bread soaked in water."

I thought it might well be preferable to tripe soup but refrained from saying so.

The demonstrations, in her view, were a legitimate and honorable means of petitioning the government, conducted peacefully but corrupted by louts and fanned into violence by the police.

"And I am not talking about skivers but honest hard-working men crying out for work. But there is none: so how can you wonder!"

Wardy, who had been listening at the door, chose her moment to deliver the tea, cups jigging in their saucers. Katharine did the serving and pouring while Wardy stood by, arms crossed over chest. "That will be all, Wardy, thank you very much." No, she would not budge, she was sure she sniffed sedition in the sitting room. Unsheathing a duster from some pocket or other in the way of a scabbard, she aimed it at Henry's prancing peacocks.

"I daresay," she opined (swat-swat), "it has been dreadful for the poor tradesmen."

"Oh, the tradesmen," waved Mrs Cookson, more inclined at this point than I to treat the feather-head as human: "the tradesmen can look after themselves."

Enough. Before she could reply I ordered her to bring more hot water and some extra sandwiches. The three of us sat about trying to make sense of a world where we, the privileged, could engage with the plight of the unem-ployed while someone of their own class denounced them as 'rabble-rousers'. Mrs Cookson thought it might be our very privilege that allowed our sympathies to develop without the coarsening effect of having to work for a living and experience other hardships. Katharine dis-agreed. "Surely anyone with an imagination, a capacity for sympathy . . . connection . . . must feel the frustration . . . to be willing to work but be turned away time and again, to have to beg . . . to be so hungry you are ready to do anything, anything for a piece of bread . . . and your children starving and no room to breath . . . intolerable." She shivered.

We drank our tea, nibbled at our ridiculous crustless sandwiches.

"William, my brother," I offered, "believes we are not 'wholes' but divided like jigsaw puzzles, our brains like fields enclosed by walls. The phrenologists have proved it: the thing we call mind or consciousness is not a coherent entity but a myriad of possibilities."

"But how do we *act*, what do we *do*, faced with all those possibilities?" entreated Katharine.

"We do the right thing," I said. There was a pause. "We throw in that segment of our being, that capacious net of conscience, of identification, with the underdog."

Mrs Cookson rose. "Alice – may I call you Alice? – it's a pity you are so unwell; otherwise, your voice would reverberate from a soapbox in Trafalgar Square."

"Hear hear," said Katharine, regarding me with something akin to pride.

"What *would* you do," Mrs Cookson asked, "were you not . . .?"

"Do . . .?"

"I mean . . . ," she gestured out the window, towards the Square. They waited for me to speak, full of tea and sandwiches and sacrificial zeal. "You see, it matters very much," said Mrs Cookson, "what we do."

I had a sudden image of myself, or not of myself but of an Alice unafflicted, dressed in breeches and waving a placard (GIVE THE WORKERS WORK!). But they were waiting to hear what I would do in a real situation were I in good health. But I was not, and it was too easy to pretend.

At last Mrs Cookson spoke. "I am quite sure, Alice, if you were well, you would be out there lending your support one way or another."

At which Wardy charged back in with, "Then I say thank the good Lord she is *not* well!"

We managed to ignore her. I thanked Mrs C for her belief in me. Then, looking hard at Katharine, "I would certainly be proud of any woman who put such beliefs as ours into action."

*

Next morning Wardy was off, breakfast-less, "to partake of the Spirit of our Lord." I was about to ask, *How can you pass the time in mindless prayer when the stormclouds of revolt are gathering?* but I knew precisely how she would reply, her mouth all bunched up in disapproval: *Stormclouds of revolt? They should all be arrested!*

"Wardy," I tried, "please understand, it is not the working men who are to blame for the damage to property, but roughs and thieves. As for the police, they are behaving disgracefully."

"Well," taunted she, "and how would you know that, Miss?"

I could have snapped the little boobie's head off. But then I thought of how she'd been chosen out of all the girls in her orphanage to go to some pathetic ragged school to learn useful things like giving injections and pills and taking blood and giving sponge-baths and lifting invalids and so on but unfortunately *not how to think.*

"I should say it was very natural that the police did not want to get themselves hurt." It did not help her cause that every ignorant utterance came out with a *flounce.*

"How can you say that," I cried shrilly, "when they wear protective armour and helmets and carry shields, while the workers wear hardly enough to keep out the cold?"

"Quite right too," she replied, stomping off chin-ho.

I called after her, "Where is Miss Loring?"

She scuttled back, hands on hips. "Out," she snapped.

Later, she arrived breathless with news of further demonstrations. "I found myself in a great crowd round the Square . . . In the middle there were men haranguing and shouting and . . ."

"Were they workmen or roughs?"

"Oh," she replied, turning up her nose, "I would not for the world have looked at them!"

"Then why on earth tell me about it!" I shouted erupting with frustration.

"I thought, Miss," said that person with equal indignation, "that you would be more concerned for myself being jostled in the crowd than for a bunch of dirty men raising their fists to the sky. And next time I warrant it'll be your brother's windows they dash in with their bricks, mark my words."

"Let us hope not," I growled, "but if they do, it will not be a strike against literature but an eloquent cry for work."

"Humph," she went, "time for your pills."

I swallowed one, then another, aware that all I'd done by trying to 'educate' her was merely stupefy her with my own radical notions. Still, I tried once more to extract from her some sense of what was going on in the Square. Had the shops, for one, got their windows repaired yet? The nose went heavenward again: "Oh, I have never been to see them." And with that, she gave one of her girly yells and rucked up her petticoats – she'd spied another cockroach. "Oh, I've got my eye upon him, don' you worry, Miss!"

"I'm not," I muttered, my reality shrunk to the size of a black beetle. And two, three, helpless females staring at it; for by now Mrs Dickson had arrived waving a towel, "Whatever shall we do? How I wish Miss Loring was here to tell us!" But Miss Loring had gone out. Oh, but where? Wardy took her eye off the cockroach.

"What is it?"

"I believe I saw Miss Loring when I was out."

"Saw Miss Loring where, when?"

"I can't be sure, mind, since I wasn't looking, as I mentioned. But as I passed close to the Square, not very close but not far, I could have sworn I saw a policeman heading in her direction, if it was her that is or someone tall as her, she was raising her fist and shouting . . . I don't know what but it can't have been nice with her mouth opened wide like that. And I don't mind saying I said to myself, 'I don't care if it is Miss Loring, if he arrests her she will deserve it!"

I asked her, very calmly, why she hadn't told me before, to which she gave no rational reply, so then I ordered her out of my sight forever. Mrs Dickson followed. Where the cockroach went I knew not and cared less. Outside all I could make out was a dense black fog. I will go mad, I thought, living shut up with creatures of infinitesmal mind, with the vision of blinkered horses, in which only the 'nice' is acceptable, in which everything from a shoulder of mutton to a new frock is described as 'pretty and sweet'. Like running one's head into a feather-bed. As I would later tell Henry, "You're lucky with your Smiths. My own Wardy is as ignorant as a fish and as narrow as a hatband." Later still I would come across those same words in The Princess Cassimmissima.

Thirty

February, 1886

'Black Monday' they called it. Two marchers had been killed and over a hundred injured. And Katharine, my Katharine had been arrested during one of the demonstrations and thrown into a holding cell at Grantham Prison, along with nine other 'rabble-rousing' women.

My Katharine, a 'jail-bird'?

Their cell is at the far end of the women's wing. There are no beds or cots, just two long bare slatted benches ranged along opposite walls, as if meant for opposing teams of players. Katharine sits alone on one bench while the others crowd together on the other. The only sources of light are from a slit in a heavy wooden door dubbed 'the eye' and a small barred window far above eye level. In one corner of the cell is a 'nuisance bucket' with a lid that keeps sliding off. The scrap of curtain, made of torn, stained, flowery chintz, leaves a gap when closed. It would barely cover a potato," she thinks. But the women know what to do: when one of them enters to 'do her business' the rest of them look away, cough, stamp their feet and generally make a racket. "We may not have bread to eat, but we have our dignity . . . ." "Aye, that we have."

Katharine sits alone facing 'the nine' as if she were their teacher and they her pupils, divided from her not by age but class. "How did that arrangement happen?" I later asked. She shrugged. Just how it was. She'd tried to join them on their side of the cell but they'd closed ranks. It only takes one, she said, reflecting how easily a class could be led into a 'gang' mentality, with one 'weak' one being singled out for derision. So she sits across from them, odd 'man' out, determined to show she isn't afraid. A couple of the women screw up their faces in sympathy or apology while the rest shuffle their feet and avoid her gaze. They themselves are divided, she sees, not a solid thing. Some are 'for' their own leader but not necessarily against *her*.

The Warder opens the one-eyed door, throws in a pile of filthy rags and clunks down a bucket of putrid water. Looking from one bench to the other, she says, "You ladies planning a wrestling match? I wouldn't advise it." A wrestling match might be a relief, Katharine thinks. As she rests her head, the brick wall snaggles her hair.

The women tease her for a 'lady'; worse, an American. "We don't need your help, we can fight our own battles."

"I was not fighting *your* battle."

"So you weren't with us?"

"Support, yes . . . .but driven by my own ideals."

"I-*deals*, eh . . .?"

"Fairness . . . equality . . . the right to work . . . not to starve . . . responsibility of the state . . ." Her voice trails off.

Wag-wag, go their heads; bat-bat, go their eyelashes. "Spare us the speechifying."

But something is happening outside the prison. Katharine puts her finger to her lips then climbs up onto the stool placed below the window. She looks out, turns. "Snow," she mouths. She expects to be mocked but that is not what happens; instead, they are excited, wide-eyed. They take turns clambering up to peer out. Katharine imagines the grubby, rank air of their cell filling up, flakes leaping over and under one another, perishing but endlessly renewing themselves, undaunted blobs, until they're enclosed in a continually circulating whiteness, snowflakes without end, as if someone is turning their cell over and over like a glass paper-weight, with them floating about inside.

Yes, well. Prison is no place for snow, or fanciful visions. But if you check the papers for that date in February, '86, you will find a snowfall recorded in London of 3-1/4 inches.

Their food is brought in on carts: billy cans with greasy soup; hard bread; tin mugs with bitter tea.

No prayers are expected of them.

They listen for the prison bells to help them mark the hours.

They begin to feel like a class of dunces, envying the criminally-inclined 'regulars' in their flannel dresses and warm underskirts and stockings: the prostitutes, the thieves, the pick-pockets, the poisoners, the arsonists, the drunkards, the murderesses; in other words, the ordinary 'fallen' women, the simple-minded wicked and the villanous 'trash'. They – the rabble-rousers, the politically motivated mischief-makers – are kept to themselves, denied uniforms and exercise, lest they 'infect' and incite the 'real' prisoners, who may have been wicked in their ways but are now tamed, quiet and content. Any contact with 'the demonstrators', it is feared, might revive dissatisfaction, breed open revolution.

Katharine thinks they look like nuns in their grey and white uniforms.

Soon the cell is in total darkness except for the square of gauzy, luminous snow-light. At some point they are thrown a pile of dirty, damp mats. The nine women arrange themselves in a circle. Katharine drops to her knees. Someone pulls her in amongst them. Fair's fair.

"Where are your children, then?" a voice asks.

Katharine gazes up towards the light. "No, nothing like that," she replies. She blames the War. "So many of our young men were killed, many of my generation had to remain unmarried." It's a story she has told before, and in a way it's true. "A bloody shame," says one; "Well out of it, for my money," says another; while a third offers to 'fix her up' with her brother.

197

"Were you tempted?" I later asked.

"Only slightly."

"What did you do before marriage?" she asks the women.

"Farm worker . . . hat-maker . . . dressmaker," they count off. Three say domestic service; two nurses . . . two factory workers.

Katharine's 'vision' is by now taking shape. She will contact Lady Charlotte Guest who started a night school for young females. She will argue for the right of working-class women to learn at home; more radically, for bringing learning into women's prisons. Education, she rehearses, must be unbiased with free access to all, and must be spread as wide as possible. She thinks of asking the women if they would ever consider attending one of the new 'night schools', but she knows they will only scoff. But if you could learn in your own home, wouldn't that make all the difference?

Education, thinks Katharine, is the key. Education is her solution to the ills and inequalities of the world. (Did I also fit into her educational program: *Care for the Hopeless Housebound Hysteric*?) The Society for Study at Home. If the women trapped at home with tots, the elderly and infirm and otherwise housebound, could not come to the classroom, why, the classroom would come to them, with specially prepared lessons in history, literature, the sciences, which they would study and absorb; and in due course the knowledge they acquired would lift them out of ignorance and squalor and oppression; and they would learn – *learnlearnlearn*, the very word a lock-breaker – to stand up for themselves, to free them from their chains.

But they want to know more about her: where, for instance, did she come from? She tells them about her family home, a twenty-five-acre farm overlooking the sea on Boston's Gold Coast. Surprisingly they listen, rapt, as to a fairy tale. Someone imitates her accent, Beverly 'Faahms', like a sheep baaing. Their section of the town, she tells – white, wealthy, 'purebred' – was divided by the railroad tracks from the rest of Beverly, or 'beggerly'. "No blacks allowed except as servants: no riff-raff. Private, keep out . . ."

"What brought you over to this country?"

"My friend Alice."

"Your *friend*?"

She ignores the rude snooks, and soon they die away. Most of the women are asleep, variously snoring or whimpering or dreaming their impenetrable, protective dreams inside the cold. It is almost dawn before a new Warder throws them a pile of blankets.

*

Henry's first stop was to reassure me about the damage to his flat. "Two windows have been smashed; I, however, as you will have observed, remain unsmashed." He was looking jaunty and jowly. The bowtie a mistake.

"Katharine is in prison," I announced. I explained the circumstances.

He stood. "Is it possible?"

"Perfectly."

"Where is she? She must be bailed out immediately."

"I believe they've been denied bail – and visitors."

"Quite outrageous." Was this remark aimed at an unreasonable penal system, I wondered, or Katharine for her troublesome action?

Later – so we discovered – he contacted his friend Lord Rosebery, then Chairman of the London County Council, who 'pulled strings' to get her out. She refused, of course, but the prison authorities more or less ordered her release. She would leave, she insisted, only on condition that the other nine were also released. Against all expectation, they acceded to her demand. As Rosebery told Henry, they were relieved to be shot of the lot of them.

Thirty-one

Katharine had done up her briefcase and was drawing on her gloves. She would soon be meeting her cronies Josephine Butler and Charlotte Guest. I imagined them at *Lady* Guest's house in Chelsea perched on chairs with cabriole legs sipping ditchwater tea and tutting over the snow and the Education Bill and Home Rule – was it really such a wise thing? – and had any of them had a phrenological reading lately and wasn't it thrilling to discover what part related to which? . . . and what was one to do about a society that cared more for a dog with a broken leg than a starving underclass? But it was a flawed picture. The chairs would just as likely be capacious and of a good quality but threadbare with use by adults, children, dogs & cats . . . and the tea might well be strong and dark as coffee and be accompanied by slices of rich fruitcake. As for the talk, it would begin with themselves – wasn't that what was missing in male chambers? – a kind of introductory intimacy, a warming-up before they turned (oh must we? yes I guess we must) to the 'business' of the day; and while the men (liberals and radicals alike) might call it gossiping and sneer at it, these intellectually brave women who would also sip quite strong tea would defend it on the grounds that one's society and one's self were in an analogous relationship; that is to say, if you expected your society to have a heart, you yourself would have to demonstrate you were in possession of one.

But how was it in prison? they wanted to know . . . And how was her poor invalid companion Alice . . . and how was Lady Guest's husband's gout . . . and Josephine's boys; and then the weather (the snow had turned to slush outside but it was still raw and damp). And, finally, there would be work: education; plans for.

Katharine stood before the hall mirror. She had her spectacles with her; she would put them on later. But it was time to do up her tunic, the black-watch with the onyx buttons, *fifteen* from throat to hem, aligned right of center like an admiral's coat. Her hat, a bowler with a peony-like paper bloom erupting from its black velvet band, sat squarely upon her head. Reaching round to the back brim she gave it a small shove sideways so that it sat rakishly forward and cocked to one side, thus balancing the right-of-center tunic.

How *could* Henry think her pinched and plain?

"I don't suppose you can see much like that," I grumped.

"Well enough," she replied tersely, stiff with tension.

There she stood, unmoving, while I observed her standing and so it went on until something gave in her and "Oh, Alice," she unfroze and came and placed her cheek against mine: "It will be alright, everything will be alright." Then she straightened, that whole long spine of hers righting itself inside the tunic; and there was the hat filling her out with its roundness, and the blue-cupboard eyes in shadow; and at last she aimed herself at the door and swept out – off to talk 'plans' – leaving me to recall Dorothea Brooke's plans, and Harriett Martineau's plans, and Millicent Garrett Fawcett's plans, and The Ladies National Association's plans, and The Society For Promoting Employment for Women's (SPEW's) plans, and everyone else's plans but my own.

The wolves commiserated: a whole furry fanged pack joining me in a chorus of howls as I sat with my knees up writing useless letters to politicians who would pass them on to even lesser flunkies for reply, and newspaper editors who would not deign to print them.

"Your brother to see you, Miss James."

Henry hesitated, as if fearing a clawed-and-fanged Katharine might spring out at him from the skirting boards to attack him for daring to use his influence on her behalf.

I paused in my letter-writing: "It's alright," I said, "she knows you were trying to help."

"Lord Rosebery: ah, that . . . ought I to apologize?"

"I suppose you might if you ever meet face to face. Your avoidance of one another is becoming farcical, like something your friend Wilde might dramatize for the stage."

"I will mention it to him when next I see him. But speaking of writing, I'm interrupting your flow: shall I wait?"

"It's only a letter to the Prime Minister."

"Ah, and upon what grave issue are you lecturing him?"

"Don't mock, Henry. They voted to repeal the Contagious Diseases Act. An abomination, as I'm sure you realize."

He felt for his beard as a child for its cuddly toy. My brother, I thought, does not like laws or history 'in the raw'; to keep his attention I must make a scene of it. But how? The law as it stood blamed women for prostitution while their male clients were let off without a blemish to their record. Yet prostitutes, as Miss Butler had pointed out, were clearly victims of male lust.

"Henry," I tried, "*I* would be on the streets if not for . . ."

"Alice?"

"Henry. Please pay attention. Had I been born into poverty, had I not been the beneficiary, like you, of a protected, privileged upbringing, I might well have been forced into that awful gulf from which society has done its best to make escape hopeless."

"Is that what you have written to Mr Gladstone, Alice?"

I admitted I had written something along those lines. "I have also pointed out," I added, "what I and many others perceive to be the State's true concern: By arresting soliciting women – even tho' it is not illegal – and imprisoning them, it ensures that men can hire prostitutes without infection. Can that be fair, Henry?"

"Fair . . .?" His hair, which had been receding at an alarming rate, had been cut close to his scalp, producing the effect of a rather dirty egg. "My dear sister, it is not a word I hear much spoken nowadays."

"But surely you believe in upholding it?"

Henry stood before the peacock screen. I suppose he was thinking of one of his characters and whether or not they would concern themselves with the nature of 'fairness'.

"Tell me about the demonstrations," he said.

"You should ask Katharine. She was there: as you well know."

He nodded. "But you supported their cause?"

"Naturally."

"Indeed," he pursued, roused by the 'scent' of action: "I believe, were you not ill, Alice, you might have enjoyed a career as a dangerous little revolutionary."

"In that case," I asked, "do you suggest, like Wardy, that it is just as well I am ill?"

Henry sat, folding his hands humbly into his lap: "We are well out of it, are we not, Alice?"

"Are we?" I challenged, unsure of what it was we were well out of (marriage? liaisons? political action? employment?).

Silence.

My 'success' was making me reckless. I went on: "What, Henry, would you say about a tale that alluded to certain violent movements – socialism, anarchism, 'terrorism'- responses to the general *malheur* one is aware of in this strange country in which we find ourselves marooned?"

Henry unfolded himself.

I related my idea. The tale would be set in London in the year following Krakatoa. I 'painted' the opening scene as I imagined it, describing how every morning and night for two years after that event these London skies – thousands of miles away from the original blast – were still affected, turning blood-red followed by stainings, layered washes and glazes of carmine, cerise, orange and purple, one sliding into the other. I went on to explain my idea, how it was the explosion which had caught the attention of a certain character; the explosion as a symbol of what was needed to address the *malheur* of her society.

Henry ran an unlit cigar along his upper lip, taking in its aged tobacco scent.

"Go on," he encouraged. But suddenly, doubting my own capacity, I could not. I was no Henry: Henry who could, with a mere glimpse from a doorway or a window, suggest an atmosphere of tension, a premonition of imminent disruption. Henry, having strolled the wet streets of London, could describe the reflections of the lamps on the wet pavements, the way the winter fog blurred and suffused the whole place producing halos and radiations, trickles and evaporations, on the plates of glass. Henry could make them shine like pomegranite seeds; make you want to slurp them up so that the blood-red juice ran down your chin in the most unladylike fashion.

"Alice . . .?"

"Yes, Henry," I managed to reply. I was thinking, unfilially, how 'my' tale – if it was mine – would have little or no style, and therefore less 'rigmarole' (as William rudely called it) than Henry's; on the other hand, it would have more 'feeling,' as Aunt Kate required; added to that, its very own explosive quality. My Krakatoa would crackle and hiss and spit; my Krakatoa would rain down its sinister fallout over London; my Krakatoa would explode, again and again . . .

"But what," he was now demanding, "does your 'heroine' *do*; what is her *raison d'etre*?"

I hesitated. I had begun to regret having spoken; but it was too late for a retreat.

"Oh," I began, feverishly nonchalant – I'd burst into a sweat – "she is a rich, strong, vital American . . . During one of her tramps around London she becomes aware of herself as a hypocritical 'adventurer', a foreigner enjoying the freedom and ease of London thanks to her money and position.

But she begins to wonder, *feel*, what it would be like if every door of approach -into the light, the warmth and cheer, into good and charming relations – were to be slammed in her face."

"Ah," supplied Henry, "a revelation."

"Are you laughing at me, Henry?"

He denied it; once again, in spite of my obviously deteriorating condition, urging me on.

"Leonora . . ." – there, I'd named her – ". . . is in a state of exclusion, of weakness, having chosen to live in mean conditions among the lower manners and types, the general sordid struggle, bearing the burden of her *prostituting* position with its ignorance, misery, poverty, vice . . ." I broke off, for without first-hand knowledge of low-life London, of what precisely it would mean *to sell one's body*, not just once but repeatedly (numbingly, painfully), how could I, or for that matter Henry, describe such a thing?

"But why has she come to Europe?" Henry was needing to know: "what has brought her here?"

I explained how she'd been transplanted from America and promised marriage, then abandoned for some unaccountable reason.

"Yet she stays on?" he guessed.

I nodded. "She observes the seedy goings-on beneath the vast smug surface of the City."

"She prowls about," interjected Henry gazing intensely at the blank stretch of wall opposite as if he can see the bleak scene forming there: "turning her gaze on the vast, tragic, dark, menacing City . . ."

I was beginning to feel weak. Still, I managed to stress, it was her experience of the 'low' life, a life at the hands of men who would handle her roughly, that would radicalize her still further.

Henry leant forward. Such a character would only be of interest, he supplied, if she had the advantage, or disadvantage as the case may be, of an acute, indeed, a hungry sensibility. She would note as many things and vibrate to as many occasions as I might venture to make her. "Thus," he concluded, "it is necessary to give one's own fine feelings to the humbled young woman."

"*Humbled*, Henry?" I cried, sick with outrage, yet hobbled. I saw that I'd already lost my Leonora to Henry. But I must insist on my part in her reality, her *truthfulness*: "On the contrary," I managed. "Fine feelings she may have, but that alone would become tiresome; no, there is the question of what she will do: dream, risk, attempt . . ."

"Ah," he pursued excitedly, "an adventure!"

"No!" I shouted. I had never raised my voice to him before – but there it was. "Henry," I kept on, "how infuriating you are! An adventure indeed: you pompous, patronizing . . . *pig!*"

He rose, alarmed. "Alice . . ." Clearly he feared another 'attack'. But he could not stop me. Leonora's resolve, I told him, would harden. She would give away her money. She would rent a house in the poorest section of London. She would make contact with . . . the agents of change. She would do more than merely fume, like the others, against injustice . . . She would show all the flaneurs, the players, that this was no mere *adventure* . . . She would sacrifice her life for this. 'We're looking for a new order,' Leonora would rail, fuming, 'and what do they do but stopper our mouths with, with . . . *cheese*.'

"Her clarion call," I added, "is: '*I am Krakatoa: see if I am not*'!"

I felt the air crackle about us.

"Do you believe in her, in *it*, Henry?" I whispered. It no longer mattered to me *whose* tale it was, only that it should 'live'.

My brother stood once again before the peacock screen. Had I been an artist, I thought, that is where I would paint him, a black shape against the brilliant, stylish screen. "I believe," he replied nodding in its direction, "only in keeping out the draft." And with that he reclaimed his seat, hooking the thumb of one hand over the pocket of his vest, and the forefinger of the other through the fine, ear-shaped handle of his tea-cup. It only just fit. I wondered what William would have to say about 'keeping out the draft'. Did it express a need for keeping out certain unpleasant-nesses? But I was the sister and sisters, being creatures lacking mental 'stoppers', are free to say anything. And, peacock screen or no, there was still a draft howling about our feet.

Henry's eyes, I saw, had hooded over again. He would take his leave. But not before I'd thanked him for the Rigatello he'd brought me from Venice and given Mrs Dickson, (who'd forgotten to give it to me until that morn-ing).

"Thank you, Henry, I adore strong Italian cheeses."

*

After that – but what had happened?- had *I* erupted? – I was allowed no visitors. It was for my own benefit, as Katharine explained, acting as my protector-cum-jailor while writing up the results of her work: a comparative essay entitled, Home Studies Programs for Disadvantaged Women in Eng-land and America.

A knock at the door which I know to be my brother's. Mrs. Dickson gets there first. She smiles and ushers Henry in as usual, at which point Katharine, who has flown down the stairs, bars his way. "Alice isn't well at all – she cannot – will not – see you!" I hear. The exclamatory rise of her voice carries. It's a lie, of course; I am never too ill to see Henry. But I haven't the strength to run down and deny it.

What will Henry do?

Silence. My brother is, as he was when we were children, when I depended on him to defend me against William (*Leave her alone*, I imagined him telling William, quietly assertive, manly, while removing me gently from the fray) overwhelmed, reduced in the face of a superior force. Now, once again, he stands at the bottom of the stairs as if magnetized or watching a play at the theater.

The next day morning there is a peremptory knock – not Henry's. Henry has sent one of his doctors to call on me.

"Shall I let him in?" asks Katharine.

I nod.

"Shall I stay?" she asks.

I tell her I would rather face the butcher alone this time, if she doesn't mind.

"As you wish, Alice."

Dr Hooper is an energetic man with faded red hair. The contrast is most striking: I feel certain that if I poke one of his cheeks the flesh will bounce back with youthful vitality; while the hair can only announce itself as a senescent thatch. He produces a hand for me to shake. I extend mine but somehow it misses its target.

"Ah," he says, revealing a slug-like tongue upon his palate. Then, bizarrely: "Has the protuberance of your eye-balls increased lately?"

"Not that I am aware," I reply.

After an examination of my heart another portentous 'ah', so that I fear a diagnosis of heart-failure at the very least. But no, it is a 'vivacious' organ. He begins packing up his instruments then stops and straightens:

"I am inclined to tell you the truth, Miss James."

At least this one doesn't presume to call me Alice. "I expect nothing less."

"Do you wish to hear it?"

"I do."

Katharine, when I later report it to her, says in her thoughtful way, "Is the man, I wonder, a maniac, or a genius?"

Wardy, on the other hand, when told of the doctor's 'gruesome' prediction, cries out: "Mercy! He never! How

could he say such a vile thing – and then leave you his bill?"
When I laugh, she slaps her skirts, "You shock me, Miss. I
will never understand you, that is a fact. How you could be
cheered up by such is beyond me, truly it is!"

You will not die but you will suffer to the end.

Thirty-two

"Miss Woolson," announced Wardy – and there she was, Henry's 'friend' Constance Fenimore Woolson.

She is plain, small ,inclined to *embonpoint*.

She is overdressed.

She is delicate of health.

She is ages older than Henry (well, three years).

She is a she-novelist.

She is deaf.

She is a '*meticuleuse* old maid' (Henry).

She is . . .

What is she doing here?

Henry, having spent the winter months with Consance on the Continent, had deposited her back in Italy like a small but dangerous parcel before returning to England himself. Yet here she was again. Earlier I had received a letter saying she would be coming to Oxford 'to do research'.

She has come to sniff out Henry.

Constance – I could not bring myself to call her *Fenimore* – produced from her voluminous holdall an ear trumpet. It was not the usual 'horn' but a new-fangled telephonic device with a mouthpiece at one end, an ear-piece at the other, and connecting the two, a six-foot wire. "It is only old friends who will take the trouble to speak into it," she proclaimed, tossing the 'telephonic' end over to me. It slid to the floor like an eel. Constance, tutting, returned it to my lap. "There now," as if to a child: "try – and – keep – hold – of – it." I managed to do so. "Just speak naturally, not too loudly or you will blast my brains; and not too softly or I sha'n't hear a word. Now say something," she ordered. I uttered the first word that came into my head: _Henry_. "Too soft," she bellowed from the other end: "louder please". "_Drawers_," I boomed, which made her blink. "There is no need to be vulgar, Alice, as well as over-loud." We went on like that until we reached an agreeable compromise.

She settled herself in the square old oak, her elbows propped onto its high arms. I thought of a bull I'd once seen, huge and dignified and full of its own bullish gravitas but with a pile of straw sitting like a church lady's hat perched between its horns. The effect here – her torso was quite majestic but her feet failed to touch the ground – was similar. Yet one tittered at her (likewise the noble bull) at one's peril, for she was a woman of depth, insight, sensitivity, not to mention considerable writerly talent.

"How _are_ you, Alice?" she asked in her throaty way. Indeed, so encouraging to intimacy was that carefully-modulated voice, I was tempted to confide the doctor's hopeless diagnosis. But I caught myself up: death one could converse about, but not eternal suffering. At last I said, with some truth:

"I have been enjoying a period of relative good health and revelling in it. The doctors round about say I will either die or recover – which they have been saying ever since I was 19 years of age. And, as far as I can tell, I am neither dead, nor completely recovered. But what of your own health?" I asked. I already knew from Henry that, aside from her growing deafness, she suffered from bouts of depression which she dealt with by rattling round here there and everywhere.

"Baldwin," she replied, "has tried me on a pair of artificial eardrums, but unfortunately they became infected. The pain made me think I should be mad, or dead, before morning. Thus, _domage_," she added: "the trumpet."

"I'm sorry," I said.

"Are you?" she asked sharply, but before I could reply she

said, "Oh, of course you are, you know all about pain. I was forgetting. Insincerity is so common, and so trying. Forgive me, Alice."

She really is well-intentioned, I thought, but inclined to over-earnestness – and open-heartedness. It was unsettling. Her tiny foot tapped beneath her skirts. Tea was served. Wardy poked the fire while we munched on scones and sipped our tea.

"Have you heard about 'poor' Gladys Evelyn?" she inquired.

"Naturally," I replied. Who hadn't heard about the actress seduced by W. H. Hurlburt under the name 'Wilfrid Murray'?

"Marriage of course had been promised," she pursued, "but the slippery H-M pleaded that the promise, if any, had been conditional upon Evelyn being 'a chaste and modest woman'. Which – according to him – she 'obviously was not'."

"The verdict," I added, "was announced in his favor – a hypocritical 'no promise of marriage'."

"Did you ever doubt it?" she asked conspiritorially, and with a shade too much triumph in her voice. Doubt *what*? If I let her, I saw, she would go on poking and prodding until she drew blood, which she would then contrive to join intimately with hers. An assumption of defeat, of failure . . . women together. I recalled a passage Henry had written about her:

She is fond of irretrievable personal failures . . . She is interested in secret histories, in the "inner life" of the weak, the superfluous, the disappointed, the bereaved, the unmarried . . .

But had I, she wanted to know, never suffered a seduction, a betrayal, a disappointment?

Oh, I might have told her a tale . . . about me as a still-hopeful girl, about a visit to my friend Fanny Morse at Beverly, about being introduced to the *beautiful* Charles Jackson; I might have given her details of his loveliness

. . . how he had the *nicest* face and the *sweetest* smile you ever saw . . . how for a year after that I couldn't open a book or gaze out a window without seeing his face superimposed on print or glass or stupid blank doors . . . oh, but the tease of it, the melancholy hopelessness of it all. *You see*, I might have concluded with lip all a-tremble: *he was already engaged to Miss Fanny Appleton!* I might have gone on moreover to confess, how, as a young woman, I'd longed for him to look at me the way he looked at her: *Oh! but things are all wrong, aren't they?* I might have finished up crying. But I would not give her satisfaction, would not have her gloat over my own 'inner life'; indeed, would not add to her store of forlorn failure (besides, a 'crush' was hardly a grand passion). I would not allow her to put her arms around me in sisterly sympathy, in conjoined bitterness. *No!* I wanted to shout down her ridiculous tube. It was an insult; I did not want her 'worthiness'; I did not want *her*.

Stop. Her tube is no more ridiculous than is she.

You, Alice, are the risible one.

Our cups were empty, our side plates held only crumbs, a few hard raisins, a smear of butter.

"I read your story 'The Lady of Fishing Island'," is what I said at last.

Her small foot tapped beneath her skirts. *Now she is waiting upon my judgement.* The 'Lady' of the title, I recalled, is a nun-like creature who appears among a group of miners at their island camp in the middle of Lake Superior. Rough men. But 'The Lady', so long as she remains remote and spiritual, has the power to transform them, so that they become 'good' and clean'. But once she falls in love with one of the men, that is the end of her 'power'. Her love is unrequited, she becomes abject, the men revert and she dies. The object of her affection also suffers from unrequited love.

"Darkly disturbing," I managed.

"Ah," she smiled, waiting for me to say more.

Let her wait. "The message is quite clear, is it not," she

asserted: "Love makes us human, but is bound to be fatal."
She held out her hands hoping, I thought, to be contradicted.
But who was I to disabuse her?

I must have shivered then, for she got up and pulled the
rug closer round my body: "You must not get a chill." Her
touch was tender, almost motherly. She will soon be fishing
for news of Henry, I thought suspiciously.

There was a pause while Wardy, wearing her anxious-
devoted-servant expression, refreshed our cups.

"And how is your brother . . .?"

There was not the least doubt which brother she was
referring to. At last, I thought, the true reason for her visit
– and her solicitousness.

"Have you not seen him?" I asked ingenuously, knowing
full well that Henry had made himself unavailable to her.

"I have not – this time," she said.

"Henry," I offered, "has broken into a new novel and
must not be disturbed."

"Of course." She waited.

"But he is well. He sometimes finds the London dampness
to have a depressive effect. I believe Baldwin has prescribed
him strychnine. Have you tried it? I have, it's quite effective."

"Indeed," she said sulkily. "The best medicine for me is to
'up sticks', but failing that I opt for guarana."

"Oh, I prefer hemp; I swear by it."

We continued with our digression upon medical men and
medications until Connie, drawn like a moth to the fatal
object, said: "As you no doubt know, he recently suffered a
pain in his kidney – caused, I believe, by inflammation."

Henry? A pain in the kidney? I did not know of it.

She continued, "The pain led to an outrageous neuralgic
headache, which in turn made him feverish. And that in
turn caused him one night to throw off his blanket and fling
open the bedroom window. (*But how could she know such
a thing . . .?*) Which promptly caught him a chill. The 'cold'

214

lodged in his legs which ached rheumatically and in his gut –
which ached also – and in his lower back. So," she continued
proprietorially: "*we* rushed two urine samples to Baldwin in
Florence – *we* were in Venice at the time – but. . . ." She
paused dramatically.

We?

"By then his symptoms had begun to disappear," she
went on. "He began to feel better and better until, by the time
we returned to Florence – thank heavens – don't you know,
he was completely well."

She sat back, absurdly pleased with herself for knowing
such things about Henry. What she didn't know of course
was that Baldwin shared medical gossip *about her* with
Henry – which Henry then shared with *me.*

I flung off the rug and swung my legs around like clubs.
"So are you engaged yet?" I asked spitefully.

Connie flared, "Do not be satirical, Alice, we are the best of
friends. Anyway," she shook herself like a wet *dachs-hund*, "I
am far too superior for matrimony. My idea of love is,
unfortunately, so high that, like my idea of the office of
minister, nothing or nobody ever comes up to it."

Liar.

"And your Miss Loring . . .," she leant forward: "what
does Henry think of her?"

I longed to say: since she was privy to Henry's urine
samples, she no doubt knew of his feelings concerning
Katharine; instead I trotted out the conveniently ambiguous:
"Henry neither likes nor dislikes." I was fed up with being
interrogated. But she was not to be denied.

"Do you really believe him to be such a cold fish?" The
haughtiness had gone; she was appealing to me.

Henry, a cold fish? "On the contrary," I replied, "I think
him too sensitive a fish: one that cannot take too much heat."

She rose. "Alice, my dear, is there something you know
about . . .?"

"About . . .?" I knew of course what she was getting at.

"About Henry's . . . about Henry, that is."

About Henry.

Connie, *fishing* for a clue as to Henry's 'intentions', was now waiting – as one read in railway novels – with bated breath. She *wants* Henry, I thought. I pictured the small figure encased in its stylish Italian frock down on her knees (disturbingly, like the 'Lady' of her story) pleading with him. And Henry? He observes with interest and curiosity the parting in her hair: *a rather sad slice of scalp* . . . There he stands before her not out of deliberate cruelty but because he cannot help himself. What else can he do? If he moves in any direction he will be forced to act, and he cannot.

As for Connie, I reflected, her stories were shrewd and sophisticated but her simple heart bled. Her letters to Henry urged him to create a woman who loves 'even greatly'. 'If you will only care for her yourself,' she pleads . . . 'the thing is done.' But he will not – cannot – help her. My brother, I longed to tell her, is not one for 'intimacy'. Where does it lead? To the bed-chamber. And where does the bed-chamber lead? To death. My brother had learned too well from our parents' marriage: men may gain strength from the women they marry but in the end they are leached of that strength. *Led-bed-dead* – I tracked the logic: He will never respond as you wish. You will not *have* him. He may be tempted, but he will not jump in.

Pity left me. Did she not see it, as everyone else did, how Henry 'fell' for witty *old* bats whose memories went back to the time of Napoleon? "Old women are marrying young men all over the place," he had proclaimed: If you hear next that Mrs Kemble (73), or Mrs Procter (84), or Mrs Duncan Stewart (85) is to marry me, you may know we have simply conformed to the fashion." Fashion, I thought, was Henry's 'get-out', as was age. He could flirt with those old queens and battleaxes, those 'human largenesses' all he liked, and not get entrapped; whereas Constance (small, handle-able, eligible, possible, sensitive, intellectually *right*) would bind him to her. The poor thing would want to be good heavens *loved* – the greatest danger of all.

"I know nothing about Henry," I said at last, "that you would wish to know. Another cup of tea?"

She shook her head.

"Will you be returning to Florence?"

"Just as soon as I finish my research."

I did not ask what it was she was 'researching'.

She sniffed the air: "It will be spring in Florence," she mused, "while it is still cold as the grave here. I don't know how you and Henry put up with it." I said we had our compensations. She waited, I suppose, for me to elaborate but I did not. She shruggged, gave me a tearful hug and took her leave.

The next morning Wardy came into the bedroom earlier than usual. "Where is Miss Loring?" I asked. "She left early. There is a note for you." It was tucked neatly between the upside-down cup and its saucer. As soon as Wardy had gone I examined the envelope for clues, sniffing at it like an animal before tearing it open. Constance, it explained, had been too 'upset' to return to Cheltenham alone, so Katharine had gone with her. A fragment of the envelope had adhered to my lip; I spat it out. Outside the fog had come down, not a dirty dingy fog but a white, ectoplasmic haze. No edges, no definitions; the air itself thick as wet sheets; anything could be lurking within it. The envelope was soon covered, inside and out, with furious, half-legible scribbles.

Thirty-three

"Henry!" I cried, "what is going on?"

"Going . . .?"

"I mean *you* are wet – while your umbrella" – I pointed – "is perfectly dry."

He regarded his person and then the umbrella; was there a correspondence between the two? Evidently he'd been walking about in the downpour with his furled umbrella on his arm. Did the smash of rain upon his hat provide inspiration, or was it a simple case of absent-mindedness?

"You are quite right," he admitted, "I was rather dilatory in opening it."

"You will catch your death, Henry."

He smiled: "It is more likely that that gentleman will catch me – but not quite yet." He would soon dry off, he supposed, in the warm room.

I noticed a bright flash coming from his shirt-front and leant forward to view it. "Is that a new coin-pin, Henry?" I asked.

He peered down at himself. "Ah," he allowed: "a gift."

I waited.

"From Fenimore," he eked out.

"You don't say. But what is the image, my eyes don't stretch that far?"

"That you must guess," he said clapping a hand over the wretched thing.

"Must I, Henry?"

Apparently I must. Constance had given him, he explained, a choice of three mounted tie-pins: (1) an owl;

218

(2) the head of Bacchus; (3) the shield of Boeotia. Which had he chosen?

The game seduced me. My immediate guess – given Henry's own owlishness – might have been the owl. But Henry was never one for the obvious. No, it would not be the owl. Bacchus? He was, so far as I understood, a god different from all the other Olympian deities, a giver of joy and a soother of cares, experienced through intoxication and ecstasy and. . . . Noo, I decided, not Bacchus. I decided upon the shield; after all, Henry was nothing if not *protected*. As for their contribution to music and literature – Hesiod, Corinna, Pindar, Plutarch, I reeled off – were all Boetians.

"Number three?" I ventured.

Henry undid the pin and handed it to me, reminding me that by Roman times nothing remained of the Boeotian cities except their ruins and their names. No, it was not the Boetian shield. It was – *he* was – the rather effiminate youth with luxuriant hair reclining with a wine-cup in his hand.

Number 2: Bacchus.

Henry preened. I was furious with myself – I should have known of course. I recalled the myth in which worshippers would seize a wild animal and tear it apart in order to eat it raw – *sparagmos* – believing they were incorporating into themselves the god and his power. Having ingested Him, as it were, his worshippers became . . . other; intensified mentally, no longer mere mortals. The surrender of everyday identity. "Yes," I said at last, " I see."

I felt as if I'd been given a glimpse into the complicated workings of my brother's mind: that deep, wild place hidden beneath the coin-pin.

Bacchus. I looked up. Henry had reattached the coin-pin and appeared to be waiting. I imagined the pair of them in the jeweler's shop – Constance and Henry – in Venice? Florence? – *Constanza* offering him: *"One of those handsome coin-pins, Henry, any one you like . . ."*

"Henry," I said, fixing him with my sternest look: "That pin *advertises* her need of you, it . . .".

"A gift . . . generous" – oh, the feigned innocence! – "a mere nothing."

"It is *not* nothing, Henry; and for you to flaunt it like that is perfectly appalling. It is everything cruel, insensitive and heartless."

He sat quite still. Eventually he defined their relationship as 'a cautious intimacy', adding expansively: "I see her at discreet intervals."

I shook my head vehemently: "It's no good toying with her," I warned.

"Alice," he rejoined, "Constance is an intelligent woman. She understands when she is spoken to; a peculiarity I prize, as I find it more and more rare – except for you of course."

"Henry, I don't require flattery. Nor does she require your *discretion*."

He raised an eyebrow.

"Do not play dumb, Henry. You know perfectly well it's something else, something deeper, she longs for."

Everything in his attitude warned against pursuing the matter, but for once, I thought, I must speak out – on my own behalf as well as hers.

"Commitment, Henry: intimacy . . . *love*."

He held out his hands, but I was quite determined:

"There's danger in it", I said fiercely: "for Constance. Consider her desperation, her aloneness. What if there was to be some cataclysmic event, some . . . *drama*? How your own position would be affected. And as for poor, betrayed Constance . . . ." But I had gone too far already. He raised a hand as if to stop the earth turning. Proceed at our peril, it said – so I did not.

Thirty-four

"So," I charged – I and my low candle were waiting to pounce -"how was it with Constance, or is it *Fenimore* or *Constanza* with you too?"

She asked if she might not remove her hat first.

I said: "Go right ahead, be my guest."

She bobbed.

We were behaving absurdly due to being 'strung out': she with travelling, I with pain and worry. She removed her spectacles, her eyes smoky and red-rimmed.

"It's after midnight, dear," she blinked.

I said, "Tell me briefly and I will let you go."

"What is it you want to know precisely?"

"I want to know *precisely* about Constance . . . and you."

"Alice," she said evenly: "Connie was upset by your brother's behavior. She felt insulted and vulnerable, and was loathe to be alone. Surely you can understand that." She reached for my hand but I snatched it away.

"So you made sure she was not alone. And did you comfort her?" My voice smeared in the way of butter upon bread.

Now – here comes the surprise – my dear friend and companion laughed . . . and went on laughing, while I waited for the 'fit' to subside. "You ask what we did," she managed at last. "Well, I will tell you: *We exchanged recipes.*"

"Recipes," I snorted.

"Alice, Constance craved company," she explained: "ordinary, everyday women's talk. *That* is what she found comforting."

"So you talked about . . .?"

"Baked beans."

"Which recipes?"

"Please."

"*Which*?" I demanded.

She knelt facing me on the bed, her skirts spread around her. "Alice," she charged: "you haven't the slightest interest in cookery, so why ask and why should I tell you when I'm weary to the point of collapse?"

"Because I insist," I replied; merciless.

"Alright, then. On the subject of baked beans, the American versus the British. The traditional English preference is for a tomato-mustard sauce with only a pinch of treacle; which Connie, a Southerner, has adopted. I, on the other hand, a Northerner, favor lashings of blackstrap molasses, catsup and beer optional according to taste. Will that do?"

No, it would not do. "What happened then?"

"Happened?" she cried. "Why, I shovelled down heaps of her beans which I enjoyed immensely." She rubbed her stomach. My Kath was not above teasing.

"So you ate them together?"

"Yes, we . . . Oh, Alice, only you could turn the humble act of degustation into something filthy. However," she added, tittering rudely, "I admit to it."

"With no ill effects?"

"None whatever . . . now will that do?"

I pictured them together, Constance and Katharine, poring over recipe books and cookpots, heads together, Katharine's spectacles all steamed up, tasting from one another's spoons.

"You look well on them," I observed: "the beans, I mean."

She moued. "And you, I'm sorry to say, look like the mad Mrs Rochester."

"I have only been mad with jealousy," I rejoined.

That got to her, as I knew it would.

"Alice," she whispers: "come here . . . turn around, dear."

I go to her, turning so that I can feel her thigh pressing

against my back. Her fingers enter my hair; soon she is yanking my scalp this way and that. Then it's the hair-brush: short, purposeful strokes to get the tangles out, followed by longer strokes. I imagine the brush as a violin bow drawing its languid, lazy, nut-to-heel way across a string. Add the vibration of her lip against my ear, the humming of her breath. I cannot identify the tune, but no matter. More businesslike now – gathering up the ends – smoothing – returning to the crown – letting the brush's teeth sink into my skull and out again. Together we count – "1 2 3 4 5 6 7 8 9 10 . . ." – not stopping until we reach one hundred, my thin hair all flyaway and Katharine's arm about to fall off.

My turn now. Loosening the wiry frizz from its grips I work it until it makes a scribbly halo around her head. The brush's bristles are filled with hair from both our heads: my mousey ones and her coarse greying ones which join together to form a loose, prickly, fibrous ball. Katharine takes it up. "It's a wonder," she exclaims bouncing it lightly upon her palm, "we have any hair at all left upon our heads."

*

Wardy, against her principles, brought us breakfast in bed. I had taken some Godfrey's Cordial which controlled the palpitations but not the persistent cattiness.

"So how *was* Constance," I pursued, "aside from her baked beans? Is she still her worthy self?"

"I do not, as you know, 'buy' your brother's assessment of her. Connie is indeed *worthy*, Alice, and more. Aside from her writing, she is involved in the world, which makes her a lively and challenging companion."

"As I am not."

"I did not say that. You are always a challenge, Alice. Connie and I spoke a great deal about the education of women."

I yawned largely. "And does she suppose that learning

alongside men will widen their minds? In my opinion it will reduce them to the size of petit pois."

"You may mock, Alice, but it is a matter of serious debate. Indeed, there are those separatists who would agree with you, even to the point that the curriculum should be different, though not less rigorous."

"And where do you stand?"

"You know very well I do not think the feminine mind inferior to the masculine . . .".

"But . . .?"

"But it has been kept back for so long, and enfeebled and . . .". She broke off. "Oh, never mind all that, Alice, what I really wanted to tell you about were the female students. Constance took me to Cambridge, to see Newnham and Anne Clough and . . ."

"Who is Anne Clough?"

"Dean of Newnham. But her students . . . they were fantastical, quite wild in appearance."

I sat up.

"Oh, they were wearing all sorts of outlandish – flagrant – costumes: skirts over bloomers, bloomers over skirts, inside-out stomachers, men's bowlers . . ."

I cut her off. "I suppose they're convinced it's exciting to be shocking."

"The exciting thing, to my mind, is not apologizing for themselves." She paused, mid-toast, to stare at me. "I thought you'd be pleased, Alice; I mean, that such radical behavior would please you."

I wanted to be pleased, as much for her as for myself. But I kept seeing my younger self, all boresome insurrections trampled down. *I must not be rebellious. I must not punch the air with my fist or dance about shouting, or want to knock my pater's head off. I must become smooth and flat as if ironed out . . .*

I bit hard into my cold toast. I had a choice: to remain a bitter old miserablist denyer or – more snapping of toast – not let my own experience stop me from enjoying and celebrating their freedom. It was too late for me but not for them.

"Let us praise Cambridge's little band of radicals," I affirmed: "they are our hope for the future!"

"Hear, hear," cried Katharine, waving a buttery hand. And with that she began to 'dress' herself as a Newnham girl. Oh, she would go all skewed and topsy-turvy with her stays on the outside . . . and short pantaloons and low-slung belts and layers of coats like the Indians and Japanese, and float about like . . .

"And I shall have cropped hair and wear mannish shirts and ties and look neat and slim like a knife in its sheath and . . .," but I could not go on. My mouth was all trembly and be-crumbed. Katharine clutched my hand. "Be resolute, Alice, do not give in, dear." Do not, she meant, be tempted to feel sorry for myself. "No," I said, taking another sip – gulp – of the Cordial – "I will not."

Sometime later she returned to the subject of Constance. "Poor Connie is unhappy," she confided. "She feels all shut up, as she put it, in a British Promenade."

"Well," I replied, "for some women there is more to life than education. But," – a hard look here – "do you really not know why she's so unhappy?"

She paused. "I suppose she thinks of your brother. She says he has avoided her since their return. Is it so serious with her then?"

"Did she not confess it to you?"

"I suppose she did, in her way."

"It does not take much to see it."

"And what do you see, Alice?"

I closed my eyes. My brother stands before her. Now he sits, stands again, turns his back. Begins to move about like one of his own enervated characters. Goes to the nearest window and pretends to look out – anything to avoid her pleading gaze. He is seeing into the future – never mind the pleas of his own clamoring heart – how it will end. At last he turns to face her, eyes like the sky after rain at the farthest, palest horizon, blue fading to milk-white to . . .

"I see a terrible yearning," I say.

"And will it be satisfied?" she asks.

I shake my head. "Might as well pine for Michelangelo's David."

Thirty-five

"One step at a time, Alice." The rain that had fallen almost relentlessly during the summer had finally stopped, leaving a soggy matting under the Park's shrubs and trees; through it, here and there, a contorted Autumn crocus had succeeded in thrusting itself up. Katharine, stopping beneath one of the Irish yews, looked up: "Have you noticed, Alice, that while it is still relatively calm down here, there is an agitation in the higher branches?" I followed her gaze: yes, it was true. She undid one of her gloves as if to feel for the place where the air changed and the turbulence began; then she let it drop, the ungloved hand – a leaf, I thought at first – to settle upon mine.

"Shall we sit, dear?" she asked, and so we sat. The bench was green with bare patches and black wrought-iron curlicues at the side. Sitting on it suited me; the windlessness, the tameness, the *low*ness were after all my natural elements; but not Katharine's. Her back, I saw, was too straight, her hair too slicked, her face too scrubbed. She is altogether too *sober*, I thought: *something is coming.*

Above us the sky is a vast colorless emptiness with dissolving smoke-wisp patterns from the chimneys. But there are also the autumn colors to admire, the rose hips and rowan berries. Katharine points out a late flowering Viburnum; the delicacy of the birches; the plane trees tinged with orange.

"Of course they're not like our maples back Home." She says this quite factually. The word 'maples' acts like a switch igniting this tree and that recalled from Prides Crossing and

Beverly Farms, conjuring leaves so intense in color they almost hurt: not soft gold but brazen yellow; not burnt orange but blazing flame, and blood.

"True," I agreed, "but why yearn for a lost place, a lost past?" I was remembering a drive – ages ago – with William – somewhere around Tufts. He'd been enrolled there as a student and wanted to show me the 'distinguished' place. We'd just reached a railway crossing; when we'd gone over it, William said – as if jolted into noticing for the first time – "Our native landscape has a certain charm." How quaint, I'd thought; but then, seeing it through his eyes, I began to feel an excitement, an awareness of its broad, vast expanses, the suggestion of so many possibilities . . . and everything yet to be done. . . . But this England – with its traditions and its awful perfection – what was left to do? I rose up too quickly and became dizzy. The pretty, soft colors had become blurred and muddied forcing me to sit down again, bump, like a toddler who thought it had learned to walk but there it was falling again.

"It's all right," said Katharine cradling my head against her shoulder.

"No, it isn't," I blubbered: "Everything that might yet be done has already been done . . . was done centuries ago . . . there's nothing left."

"What mush!" she cried, shoving me away. "Have you forgotten the Newnham girls . . . and the workers' protests and the Irish cause and . . ." Things only *seemed* fixed and preserved, she went on, but so long as there were people prepared to *act* for change – there *would* be change.

The toddler must pick itself up and try again.

"Alice, dear" – a perceptible softening – "there's something I must tell you."

I already knew of course. It was not Katharine's way to pine for the past. Oh no, she would claim a thing or put it away forever.

"It won't be forever, Alice. It's just that . . ." She spoke urgently, passionately, until it was nearly dusk and a grey fawn glove held us. The problem was Europe . . . England, how it was all too . . . tight; how she could not find her true place here; how she did not know which direction to turn or how to use her energies and skills. Groups were clamoring for her participation since the demonstration, educationists wanted to 'pick her brains' about her Home Studies Program; indeed, she was wanted everywhere but felt she belonged . . . elsewhere.

I said we must go back before it gets dark but she remained fixed, intent on explaining: It was all too small, too confined; she needed to touch base again. "Alice," she was almost pleading, "do you never miss the sea back home, the mountains?" It was a question I'd once asked her, and now she was admitting, yes, that she missed our own dear rugged Eastern coastline. It was her medicine, how could I deny her? And there were her students she had abandoned, what would become of them? At which I longed to cry, 'So you choose instead to abandon *me*?' No, it was too late; she would go; I could not stop her. And there were her eyes to see to: they were getting worse and the Boston Eye Hospital was, after all, 'the very best'. But then she grabbed an arm – the other – quite roughly – urgently, saying, "You could, of course, return with me."

"Return . . .?"

"Home, Alice. Surely you have thought of it; surely it's what you intended back in '84?"

What could I say? do? *Home* at that moment was nothing more than the bench with Katharine upon it beside me. But she would go, I could not stop her. We had between us no engagement, no marriage, no children; only ourselves. Our lives, I saw, from now on would be more divided than joined. As for going back . . .

"You have a choice, Alice."

I denied it, recalling the Pavonia. I would never survive another such crossing.

"You would not have to swim back," she said drily.

"Oh, but I would, you see." The effort, I explained, would be at least as great, would leave me weak as a spawning salmon at the end of its run. "I am satisfied to be here," I concluded: "To *not* be here would take more than I possess."

"More of what, Alice?"

Henry's word 'inclination' came forth.

She sighed, "Louisa is ready to go home." Her voice scraped. "Apparently the Hospital Board of Governors are clamoring for her return."

Then there was her father who was not getting any younger; and Katharine herself with her own career to resume, students to nurture, a rambling property that needed urgent repairs, and an extended family to attend to. She was being drawn back. All her life, I saw, she'd had her occupations disrupted, had had to give up her real ambitions. As for looking after her father, her sister and me, that had been taken as a matter of course – *of course* she would do those things (even though it would not be 'of course' had she worn trousers). So *of course* she must please herself now before it was all too late. And I must let her go.

"I will bring you back some syrup," she declared.

You see, she was already thinking of home, of the fierceness of maples and their sweetness.

"So you will have Thanksgiving at home?" I asked . . . or accused?

"You know it's the one holiday I miss, Alice."

"That's because you're a great greedy pig." I stood, wobbled, righted myself. She felt for my elbow. "Henry will be returning to Florence," I said conversationally. I was trying for buoyancy. "He has offered me his rooms while he is away."

"Will you take him up on it?"

"Yes, why not?"

By this time we had made our way over to the duck pond. I suppose she was trying to distract me – *Look, Alice, look*, as in a primer – *See the boys and girls playing hide and seek in the great cedar.* There they were hanging from low branches, shimmying up and down with red cheeks creating their own warmth inside the cold wrapping of the day. In that moment I saw what she wanted me to see: what was alive and warm and vital and right there before me rather than some fantastical future of my own creating; so that later I would think, why did I go and squander those last few days before they had a right to be lost?

"And will you return?"

"Alice," she spoke deliberately even as I felt her tremble: "whether or not I am with you permanently, that is, *consistently,* I am hopelessly, *hopelessly*" – the repeated word fell from her lips – she was stumbling like a horse – fatal, you think – but then it manages to get to its feet again; and with it comes the conclusion of her sentence: "*constant.*" For a moment I thought she was referring to *Constance,* the 'constant' in Henry's life. But this was about us, about living as one even while apart with no need of proof because the certainty would be there, the way a fine scent permeated one's skin long after it had been applied.

Thus ended another chapter in our life together, and the start of it apart.

III. DE VERE GARDENS

Thirty-six

Wardy, sensing she was no longer needed what with the Smiths upstairs, had already announced her departure: A carriage was due within the hour.

"Do sit, Wardy. Now tell me, where will you go?".

"My Aunt Flo is always happy to have me."

"And will you be happy to be had?"

Wardy thought. "I don't mind, Miss. She is very decrepit but keeps a tidy home. I am highly appreciated, to be sure."

"As you are by me," I put in quickly – "only circumstances . . ."

"Too many servants," she broke in wittily, "spoil the brew."

"Indeed." I cleared my throat: "Of course it will all change when my brother returns. It won't be long. Then we will resume our original arrangement – assuming you are still agreeable?"

"I will let you know, Miss," she said pursing her lips in imitation of some practised crone or other. At which Smith announced her carriage. "Coming," she hooted. He had already taken her bag. She waved goodbye without looking back. She is really quite intelligent, I found myself thinking, in spite of being stultified by the Church and Toryism; and then: *I am quite fond of her.* As for me, she undoubtedly found me peculiar, un-Christian and half-dead. Would I ever see her again? I called after her: "Do take care, Wardy."

I'd objected at first to Henry's suggestion. His 'chaste and secluded Kensington *quatrieme*' was far too grand for me.

"Cockroach-infested lodgings," I'd told him, "are much more my style." But he'd insisted I would be doing him a service: "It will give The Smiths something to do." So I agreed.

The Smiths, I would soon discover, did not welcome the arrangement.

Now they were down in the pantry muttering over their employer's decision to give the flat over to his half-mad sister. "When the cat is away . . . ," Smith sing-songs as if the old saw had only just been invented, at which The Mrs chimes in with: "the mouse will play." For the mouse did indeed seem to be nosing into places she ought not to; indeed, the next you knew she would be prying into the master's private study . Oh yes, they would have to remain vigilant.

Upstairs, meanwhile, I-Alice-mouse was trying to decide which end of Henry's enormous dining table to occupy. Although two extra leaves had been removed it still stretched most of the length of the room between the long front windows.

How does he do it? I hear Katharine ask.

Do what?

Eat his dinner here, alone?

Henry alone, surrounded by candlelight and food, pale against the 'Pomegranate' frieze, the burgundy curtains on the long windows drawn against the dark; Smith appearing and disappearing noiselessly. Do they have conversations? Does Henry have a book beside his plate or a periodical propped against the cream jug? Is he planning a scene for a character not behaving as she was meant to behave? Or is he concentrating his attention on his food, deciding that the potato is too waxy, the chop gristly, oh but the broccoli, the broccoli is cooked to perfection? But the truth, as I knew it, was otherwise:

Henry rarely eats at home.

The room was full of Henry in dramatic mode: the olive-green paint playing against the blood-reds; the giant fern in its brass pot – did it tickle my neck as I ate? – that somehow contrived to appear delicate and predatory at the same time. It is like a stage set, I thought. And there was the table, a long pool in moonlight (I preferred the curtains un-drawn), lustrous with his secrets, faithfully awaiting his return. I traced a grain in the wood, black swirled with red.

"Rosewood," explained Smith serving the soup: "an exotic from the tropics, I believe." He waved a hand, as if to indicate some foreign country *out there*. He himself, he added, had never been out of London. Was he to be congratulated for that? I put my serviette to my lips. When I thought he'd gone I lowered my nose to the mirrored surface, and sniffed. "Is there an odor, Miss?" My neck snapped back. "Sorry . . . I thought you'd gone . . . I thought . . . rosewood . . . a scent . . .?" I could not go on. I wished for Katharine. Smith's expression read: *oh the woman is queer allright.*

You could not blame him. The master was away, and here was I behaving more like a child sneaking sniffs. Not respectful. Only the other day the Mrs had discovered me dangerously close to the primrose yellow walls of the drawing-room, close enough to lick (*but surely she would never do such a thing?*); and then fingering the tapestry in the hall, running a hand over the painted clockface, picking up the figure of the discus thrower, the master's favorite.

"It's all so . . ." *Henry*, I was thinking, but I made do with: "Not what I'm used to, you see." "Indeed," said Smith, "the master has excellent taste in all things."

Does that include servants, Smith?

I wandered about surveying the cool, clean lines of the drawing-room through the doorway and the way vertical lines of the tall-backed chairs echoed those of the mirrors and pictures, and the grandfather clock and the walking sticks in their sleeve. Yet – I reminded myself – consider the rosewood table, the porcelain bowl filled with rose petals, the

Turkey carpets, the stained glass, the hand-painted umbrella stand, and Italian lampshades. An interesting mish-mash, I decided, of fine, expensive things. But tasteful, always *tasteful*.

Katharine? are you there? what do you say to it?

"Insufferable . . . suffocating." She marches about scowling: *"Like living in a museum."*

As I thought. Katharine. I see her standing before the long window peering into the darkness beyond the gaslight's reflection towards the Gardens. And what does she see there but an admirable nobleman's park (more perfection, more protection); and to either side of us, row upon row of well-fed English, and Americans – they stay at The Thistle, a popular place with them, according to Henry. And Henry? Oh, she pronounces, he has surrounded himself with objects that exude a warmth which he himself lacks. *But you will not like to hear that, Alice, will you?* What can I say? I see Henry during boxing practice flinching from William's stabbing thrusts. He was good at bobbing and ducking even then; so he does not need me to defend him. And yet. As I point out: it does not become someone with her privilege in life to 'knock' another's indulgences. Oh, but – she protests – her Manchester house may be big and rambling but its 'things' are quite utilitarian.

If she were here, I think, I could go on arguing Henry's side. But however long I search behind this stand or that clock or that mirror – she is not.

Below me The Smiths, having retired for the evening, hear a door slam upstairs and wonder which door it is. The Mrs is of the opinion that her husband should go and check, but he declines.

"His own sister, he trusts her."

"More fool him."

Almost at once I have trouble breathing: something in the atmosphere – I'd lit one of the paraffin lamps – perhaps his reservoir pen – why has he left it behind? I wondered, did it leak? This place, the meticulous order, his 'luxuries', have everything yet nothing to do with Henry. Ghost objects. Yet they allow him to be. He requires their order: It is order out of which he must tease his complicated structures. Like this terrace, I think, these de Vere Gardens: ornate, pillared, balustraded; and the rows and rows of people within parading about, eating, sleeping, living, dying; as well as those that came before and before that – a palimpsest of possibilities. The furnishings, the 'warm' things, it was all critical for the production of his novels and stories. Everything had to have its rightful place or else the form would not hold – *he* would not hold. It is not coldness, I long to tell Katharine, but a fine terror. Over there, for instance, behind the screen . . . is it a hand-basin? I peer round it to a low bookcase; on the top shelf, something long and rectangular covered with a turkey rug. I must not look, he would not like it. But I do look and there it is, there they are, all lined up in a touching order: Roderick Hudson, The Lady, The European, The American, The Bostonians; finally, The Princess Cassimissima.

I drop the rug, terrified; of what? Surely Henry would not mind me observing his 'body' of work in its draped 'coffin'? But as I slip round the screen, I hear his voice, *In Strindberg's plays, you know, the screen becomes a symbol for death and dying.* Then a further strangeness, a vibration beneath the rug, as if the very words are stirring from their resting place – no, they will *not* die – as they knot round one another, chasing their own tails, until all the spaces are filled with Henry's *living words.* And when I look up, there he is, *Henry James* the author sitting in the corner chair, arms propped high like some religious personage, barely visible in the flickering, dim light, observing me, one leg crossed over the other, hands folded; watching to see what I will do. It cannot be, I tell myself, he is in Florence with Connie allowing himself to fall back upon her charity, assuming it is infinite. But Henry, I want to cry out, charitable is not the right word for what she feels for you. But he does not hear me. He is 'relaxing' after completing 'The Princess'. And why should he not? Another novel: page after page after page. A kind of miracle. Yet his study is as tidy and arranged as all the other rooms, though sparser. I reach towards one of the desk drawers. It would probably be locked; but what if it is not? There would be his letters: early ones from our mother and father, Aunt Kate, poor cousin Minny (but did he love her *enough*?); his friends, his . . . *Fenimore*. I take hold of the top knob . . . then withdraw my hand. I feel Henry watching me the way a child knows God is. His journals would be in there, all his secrets. No. I rise and blow out the light before looking back. In the darkness, there's Henry, his forehead thickly high-lighted in pale shiny oils, a painting of himself.

*

Later it came to me in a dream: a premonition of the disastrous thing that would almost certainly occur during Henry's stay at Bellosguardo.

My brother is holed up in Connie's apartment in the Villa Brichieri-Colombi, a rambling 14-room pile. She herself is correctly tucked up two or three minutes further along the steep road in the massive Villa Castellani. A heavy, convent-like grille offers a glimpse of its thick walls and noble quattrocento court, from which she commands a splendid view of the mountain terrain – and Henry of course. As for Henry himself, he enjoys a panaroma of Florentine domes and towers, with Fiesole and the Apennines beyond; on the Arno side, the soft valley in its green dress; and across the western end, the Carrara hills. But, alas, the season – this is summer – is freakishly wet and cold. He sits down to write a letter to his sister:

'Dear Alice . . . Constanza, my amiable and distinguished *padrona* has laid in a store of firewood and I have built myself roaring fires. I had planned to rest but have begun once

again to drive the pen at a steady but furious pace.'

He occupies a drawing-room and bedroom on the ground floor. He believes himself 'safe' from unnecessary intrusion. Connie he sees every day or two; indeed, often dines with her. But not tonight. Tonight he has been dining among some of the most artistic and delightful Florentine company – and now it is late and he is tired.

Costanza meanwhile is rather sleepless. Her windows are ajar . . . moonlight shines through . . . the garden wafts its heady, suggestive scents (jasmine, stephanoides, honeysuckle, gardenia). Her eyelids are heavy but she cannot sleep. She re-plays the day's conversation with Henry and is mostly pleased as he told her he thought she had done a brave thing in settling herself in the somewhat mouldy Tuscan mansion. She would profit from it *a la longue* as she would get quiet, sunny, spacious hours for work and have Florence in the hollow of her hand. She thanked him for his encouragement.

Yet she is left feeling dissatisfied; why? Something, she admits to herself, is missing between them. The word 'intimacy' occurs. We are not yet old, she dares to think, Henry and I. It is not too late for us. For years she has been sending him veiled and less veiled hints – but Henry, she realizes, will never act. Therefore, she thinks – concludes – decides: *I must.* Her heart does what timorous, terrified hearts do. So be it. *To act*, she thinks, *irrevocably, prodigiously.* Henry's words. Does Henry not champion greatness? she asks herself. Yes, he does. Therefore, she argues, surely he must allow himself, under cover of darkness, to surrender – *respond* even – to greatness. For what she feels – she is convinced of it – *is* great; and so (as she rises, dresses, closes the five minute gap between them) *he must feel it too.*

He does not. He lies – horribly aware of her footsteps approaching – rigid as a cathedral beam. *Oh no, do not . . .* his wish, almost a prayer, is fierce . . . she must not be hurt . . . but on she comes inexorably, appallingly closer. She is about to enact his worst nightmare, his *Albtraum* . . . His eyes are shut so tightly they fling out tears. But on she comes . . . the doorknob turns. *No!* he longs to bellow out; but he is frozen . . . silent. In his worst dream – nightmare – a dark wicked *alb* straddles his pale, draped body as he lies prone upon his bed – or is it a coffin? He is in a sleep paralysis and can do nothing to stop her leaning closer . . . closer . . .

"Henry?" Her voice is soft, warm, inviting; her form a phantasm . . .

Connie. She is dear to him . . . literary friend . . . companion . . . mother . . . confidant . . . but *domage* he cannot help her. He manages to whisper a strangled-sounding apology into the darkness. After an eternity – oh, it has all become a dreadful cliche! – he is aware of her crawling away hugging the stone-cold truth to her breast.

It is a scene I would do anything to erase. But I pray I am no sybil because if I am . . . I doubt that she would survive it.

But Henry must sleep, there is work to do.

In the morning he tells her, "However one loses one's way in the dark, it is best not to speak of it the following day – and it will soon be forgotten."

But he is wrong of course. She may not speak of it but she will never, ever forget it.

Thirty-seven

A knock on the bedroom door. I sit up arranging Henry's quilt carefully around me. The room itself, I observe, is quite austere, masculine, with its plain panelling and wash-stand and chair. I sense everything has been cleaned, yet I detect his French ink and cologne, his cigars. Him.

"Special delivery parcel for you, Miss."

I could not think where I was, and to whom the voice belonged, but I soon recollected: *Henry is away and I am staying in his apartment; Wardy is gone and I have inherited The Smiths.* Then I recalled my dream in which Connie creeps phanton-like into Henry's bedroom, and cringed: such melodramatic mush!

"Do come in, Smith." The door opened and in he came, clearing his throat.

"Don't tease me with it, Smith, bring it here."

"Very good, Miss." He stood beside the bed. "I did not wish to interrupt your breakfast, Miss. Mr James – your brother, I mean to say – does not like to be distracted from his morning egg and toast."

I pictured Henry decapitating his egg with one clean, masterful stroke. But Smith, I realized, was wary of me because he did not know my habits and that unsettled him. He must get things right, must be the perfect servant to the perfect master. Or even mistress.

"I am quite happy," I informed him, "to do two things at once. In this one respect only," I added, "I am perhaps more gifted than my brother."

The breakfast parcel contained two copies of Henry's new novel. 'The Princess' had already been published as a serial in three parts, but I'd chosen to wait for the complete edition, and here it was. A compliment slip fluttered to the floor with a note in Henry's crabbed handwriting:

'My dear Alice – Feel assured that anything you may read here, that may initially strike a note of unpleasant self-recognition (in a superficial way), you will not, upon reflection, take as a personal affront. I believe you understand better than anyone the process of 'making up' characters. They are never, in a word, real.
Yours, Henry.'

The book weighed in my arms. I opened the front cover, peeled away the onionskin leaf, brought the title page close and sniffed the ink: *Henry James. The Princess Cassimmissima. Published by Macmillan.* I read the list of other books written by the author, followed by the small print telling where the book was made and that it had been set in Monotype Times. Then came the usual disclaimer. At last, when it could not be put off any longer, I turned to chapter one and began to read, and did not stop until I had finished with it, or it with me.

I closed the book and waited. The story was familiar yet not familiar; mine yet not mine. Henry had used my idea as *une donnee* to paint a rather sprawling, seething, magnificently tragic picture; not to mention a cast of 'heroic' characters, all of whom pace about gesticulating and theorizing, and are inclined to 'act'. Except for one. Who is allowed to speak but does not, cannot, act. Her name is Rosy Muniment, the sister of Paul, the 'ring-leader' of the anarchists. She is a bed-ridden invalid. She is perhaps the most radical of them all.

'You musn't mind her being in bed – she's always in bed,' her brother went on. 'She's in bed just the same as a little trout is in the water.'

I felt myself going round and round *the same as a little trout*, and then *stuck up there like a kitten on a shelf*, and felt sick to retching. There had been other references in Henry's stories to odd, limited women, but nothing like this – there was no other word for it – *monster*. I re-read Henry's 'disclaimer', repeated the phrase *'You are not Rosy Muniment'*. But the denial would not hold.

> Rosy Muniment, the *cheerful little creature* dolled up like a monkey in a pink dressing gown
> Rosy Muniment, the *'strange bedizened little invalid'*
> Rosy Muniment, that *'strange sick creature (. . . too unnatural)'*
> Rosy Muniment, that *'shrunken countenance'*
> Rosy Muniment: as if she were some ridiculous, if precocious homunculus.
> *How could you, Henry?*

I forced myself to read on, ignoring Rosy and concentrating on the other characters. Rosy was, after all, the least significant in the entire book: 'a useless little mess', as she calls herself. But I could not ignore her, as I could not ignore myself. The more I tried the more *me* she became, *so miserable and yet so lively* . . . laughing *till her bed creaked again*.

I reached for a small mirror I'd found in the bedside drawer. The image reflected was neat and tidy, almost mask-like, the eyes a flat grey with pinpoints of howling black. "What a curiosity you are!" I told my reflection *with quaint self-possession*, "a fascinating freak of nature!" Whereupon it responded, 'I am a *hard, bright creature polished, as it were, by pain.*' I returned the smile (hard, bright, polished), marvelling at my own stoicism. There, I thought: you have become her; it is useless to deny it. Yet I must not, or else . . . what? I might not survive. *And my own brother would have been my murderer.*

My thoughts were getting out of control. I flung the little

245

mirror back in the drawer. I will get out of bed, I thought, swinging my legs to the side. But Henry's bed was miles off the floor. I wished Wardy was with me and not the smarmy Mrs Smith. No, I would dress myself and go for a walk in The Gardens. I would take myself to a coffee house and read the papers (had the Contagious Diseases Act been repealed yet?). I would . . . but the floor still seemed a long way down, and my legs unreliable. Besides, said a voice in my head (hard, bright, polished): you do not have to leave your bed to know what is going on.

> Paul Muniment: *'It's very wonderful: she can describe things she has never seen. And they are just like the reality.'*
> Rosy Muniment: *'There's nothing I've never seen . . . That's the advantage of lying here in such a manner. I see everything in the world.*

I sank back in bed mooing like an unmilked cow, marveling that The Smiths did not come running. But there was no one. Somehow I would have to get my legs back beneath quilt and blankets. Why did Henry have so many? The top one, the one I'd sniffed, had already slipped to the floor in the tussle. But it was a relief, the mess I had made of the bedclothes. Rosy's bed – it was important to distinguish – was never less than perfect; *she* is never less than perfect. She does not walk or sleep or cry or regret or long for anything or feel like howling like a hyena or . . . That is what is wrong with her, I thought: she is not human. A mind trapped in a husk of body.

Just like Rosy.

No: she is not me; I am not she.

Yes.

Rosy the know-it-all. Rosy, from her bed-throne, tells the little group of friends all about London: the crowd on the steamer, the drunken persons they will encounter, the view from Greenwich Hill, the history of Hampton Court. She has never been to these places or seen these things yet somehow she divines them. Is that what I do?

I dared myself to take up the book again; perhaps I had got it wrong, misunderstood. But there it was all over again: *Rosy's self-importance* . . . Patience, I told myself; but HaHah! it was *Rosy's patience* that was so irritating about her.

Dear Henry, Is that your true feeling? Do you wish that I, like Rosy, would explode, or dance a jig, or pull out my hair, or yours . . . rather than persist in my long-suffering, stupid, martyrish *patience*?

But our father had praised our mother for it.

And William had praised *me* for it.

I was trapped.

Or was it Henry who was trapped having to look after me?

'Paul Muniment 'had his sister to keep – she could do nothing for herself; and he paid a low rent because she had to have doctors, and doses, and all sorts of comforts. He spent a shilling a week for her on flowers.'

I was sick all over the place. I tried to get the image of Henry adding up what he'd spent on me out of my head, but could not. I loosened the collar of my nightdress and tried to slow my breathing. I could run away, I thought but where? And anyway *You, run?* Someone was pointing at me, laughing, gabbling more words from the book: *'You cannot go, you are ill. Who should know better than me? Besides, it's lucky you are ill; perhaps if you had your health you would be all over the place.'*

But if I were *not* ill, came the thought, would *I* have been 'all over the place'? What did that mean? The thing that rankled more than anything was having my own and Rosy's politics, or lack of it, conflated. Rosy Muniment was a wretched reactionary. Oh, she would like to make things better for the poor but was not for redistributive change and therefore would not pull anything down; whereas it was The Princess who saw the chance for hemmed-in humanity, who was the true radical, who was prepared to do . . . anything. But Henry had scrambled us up like a deck of cards: ears from this one, nose from that one, feet from the other. Indeed, the more I thought about it, I saw that there was more of *me*, plain as I was, in the Princess herself. Which made me wonder if, in creating The Princess, he'd actually imagined me, his own sister, and how it would have been had I been beautiful and powerful and rich. Was she an improved me? Or, rather, had he re-created me whole and well and therefore *'all over the place'*; that is, how I might have behaved had I not been plain and ill, etc., but with my radical ideas intact? In other words dangerously *incendiary*?

Re-reading Henry's note, I made a brave attempt to separate book from brother. The Princess was not me; nor was Rosy. The book is like a map, I told myself: it represents the land but it is not the land itself. But to be written about, even half or a quarter written about, was still distressing. Was I a radical, romantic Princess – or a repellent stick insect? Should I be flattered or appalled? It was too confusing.

'The little person in the corner had the air of having gone to bed in a picture gallery.'

There, I thought gratefully, he has allowed her to rest. I savored the image. I could see it quite clearly, the thick impasto, the room about her an enveloping, chocolatey darkness, only the figure's face a bright mask as she lies in bed, the eyes alarmed but the body quite still, almost stiff, the book she holds painted in a slash of red.

I drew the duvet over my chest, arranging my arms on top along two perfect parallel tracks, my face fixed in a smile of *fierce contentment*. There I remained, unmoving, until Mrs Smith found me. "Miss! Miss! Are you allright? Shall I call the doctor? Miss!"

*

There is light at the window and a commotion outside the room. A knock at the door. The Smiths, not knowing what to 'do' about me, have summoned Wardy.

"Poor Miss, you have suffered another relapse."

"So it seems."

"I came as quick as I could, only my Aunt wasn't well." She begins tidying the bedclothes, babbling. "But you aren't right yourself, are you? You have had a bad siege with your head. Never mind, Miss, we'll get you cleaned up and you'll be as right as rain."

Is rain right?

"Aunt thinks you have improved me very much, Miss. She says that I am much more *intellectual* than I was." She reaches under the bed, blushing. "Yes, Miss, I made several remarks about books the last time I was at home."

I dare not ask what books or remarks.

"Yesterday," she reports, "I visited my friend Becky, she nurses at Wandsworth Infirmary, and do you know what I saw there but a girl of twelve dying of consumption so thin and shriveled she looked five or six at most, and her mother's in a madhouse from drink and her father died the week before in a drunken fit, and there she lay trying to smile over some biscuits and . . . ."

On she goes babbling and sponging. Is that me mooing?

"That's right, Miss, just let yourself go."

She is *kind*, I think; but how can she fail to distinguish between worthless me and those brave, wasted children? How can she bear to touch me?

Because her job is to care and that is what she does.

She rubs my back with some strong-smelling stuff. "Eucalyptus oil," she explains, given to her by Becky.

"In my dream," I tell her, "Henry is dictating a passage to his secretary." I make my voice go deep and flat: "'*The poor creature is quite grotesque; in short, a pathetic female invalid.*' He is writing about me, of course."

"Mercy!" she cries: "Mr James would never say such a thing about you!"

Is that me mooing?

"Come," she encourages, "we'll get you a fresh nightdress on. The doctor should be here shortly." Another animal-like noise. What use another gladiatorial encounter with another great man, I think, and then the fierce struggle to recover one's self-respect? But he'd been called, was already on his way.

Thirty-eight

I was sitting propped up hugging a stone-cold ceramic hot-water bottle when there came a knock on the bedroom door: "Another package for you, Miss. It arrived yesterday, but you were in no fit state to receive it." She held the thing to my ear and shook: *rattle rattle. I pushed it away. Was I such an inconsolable child that I must be distracted with a rattling box?*

"Dare we open it?" Her voice quailed in the way of a distressed stage-actress.

"Oh, get on with it, Wardy."

I watched as she cut the string, lifted paper and sealing wax, parted the cardboard wings as if they were the flesh of a flayed horse, and dipped in her hand. A shriek followed. She flung up the sash and would have hurled the contents out if I hadn't ordered her to stop at once. "You'll bash someone's skull in, you silly pin – give it here." I took up the box, pointing to the return address:

"Look, it's from my sister-in-law Mrs James, who is no anarchist, I can assure you."

"Oh," she whispered, daring to peer further into the box: "but whatever can they be?"

I held one up for demonstration: "They be *sweet potatoes*. Have you never come across one before?" I offered it for examination but she hid her hand behind her back.

"Go on," I encouraged, "it won't (wishing it would) explode."

"I declare, I have never seen such a strange potato in my life. It's quite the wrong color."

"That," said I, "is because you have never been abroad."

251

"Foreign," she muttered, "I should have guessed."

"American to be precise," I corrected: "or does that count as foreign?"

"Humph," said she.

"By the way," I asked, "what is the date today?"

"Sunday, the 19th, Miss."

"Then on Thursday it will be our Thanksgiving." I gave her a potted history: "The white settlers stole land from the natives, then had the arrogance to invite them to a harvest meal the natives had taught them to grow. There was also Lincoln fancying a ritual to unify the country after civil war and . . ."

She cut me off (get to the denouement!): "But how do you celebrate, Miss?"

"Oh, by eating ourselves silly. Families get together to consume vast quantities of turkey along with stuffing, cranberry sauce and sweet potatoes – *and end up barely speaking to one another*, I managed not to add. Then came a brainstorm:

"Why not have our own celebration?"

I read her doubtful look: 'Surely you are not well enough and besides on your own you do not constitute a *family* and what have you got to be *thankful* for . . .'.

"Perhaps on this occasion you and the Smiths will join me as 'family'?"

That only seemed to mortify her further – she couldn't – they wouldn't . . . . She was on her way out when she stopped:

"How are they prepared, then, those strange potatoes?"

"Peeled and sliced," I explained, "layered into a baking dish, dotted with butter and bathed in maple syrup until it's 'candied'."

"*What* syrup, Miss?"

"Of course – I'm forgetting – no maple trees, no maple syrup." (But Katharine had promised to bring some back with her.) "Well then, corn syrup." Not that either. "You have treacle, I presume, golden syrup?"

"I suppose so . . . yes, Miss."

"And the turkey . . .?" But The Mrs, I knew, knew all about turkeys having grown up with them. The box also contained a sack of corn meal for making cornbread and muffins. "So," I said, "it looks as if we have all the ingredients for a real American Thanksgiving just like we had back home."

The James family is gathered: Father, Mother, Aunt Kate; William, Henry, Wilkie, Rob, and Alice. The two younger soldier brothers, Wilkie and Rob, are on leave from The War, for which the family will be giving Extra Thanks. But for Alice, who has recently turned thirteen, it is her recently married cousin Kitty who most interests her. Alice gazes across the table over the rising bone of the turkey's breast as if over the ridge of a glorious but impassable peak. *Married*, she whispers to herself, the very word gilded and garlanded.

"Pass the cranberry sauce, please, Alice."

There is something not right in the atmosphere, like a stagnant pool, she thinks, which looks sparklingly clear until you stir it up.

"Oh dear," says the Mother, "Cook has used too much maple syrup on the candied sweets."

It's true, bits of the hard 'candy' are sticking in Alice's teeth . . . *and* she has seen Wilkie poking between his with a toothpick. 'Henry would never do such a thing,' she thinks, turning to gaze at him beside her. He is looking extremely handsome with his hair parted and waved.

With all the people present there should be a great tumult, a babble of news and excitement, but there is only the sound of carving and serving, of knife sliding against fork, of Father's leg snapping and thunking, of jaws and teeth working more or less thankfully away. There is discomfort, Alice senses, among her brothers. Before the war she'd had four brothers, but now she has two brothers and two brothers. 'Two and two equals four,' she tells herself, but the truth of it will not hold.

William clears his throat. The chewing stops, the knives and forks pause in mid-air. 'He is going to tell us a story,' thinks Alice excitedly, listening hard, and she is right. The story is about a recent encounter in Cambridge with a lady reformer: "Her bonnet was all askew, her gray hair escaping in all directions, her spectacles slipping down a near non-existent nose . . . altogether a sort of drooping, dissolving effect . . .".

'Henry,' thinks Alice, 'could not have described her more vividly, though less cruel.'

"But what," entreats cousin Kitty, "did she want of you, William?"

"Oh, she was terribly wound up, insisting I attend some lecture or other, on Art Anatomy I believe it was, by a Dr William Rimmer . . .".

Here Father interrupts: "A f-f- fraud! Elizabeth P-P-P-Peabody," he spits out. His anger makes him stutter, breaking his words apart. "Do n-n-not go near her or any one of her circle, Willy-boy. Why, she's one of the most d-d-dissolute old biddies that ever walked the earth!" He points a finger at the turkey's scavenged carcass, as if it were the poor little woman herself about to rise up and pull at his own sleeve.

Now it's Mother's turn: "Calm yourself, my dear. Your sweets will be getting cold. They don't keep, you know."

The family goes on with its eating. But Alice is rattled. She cannot fit the word 'dissolute' to a little old lady reformer.

"Pardon me, Uncle," says cousin Kitty, as if reading Alice's thoughts, "but I have met her and found her to be quite, how shall I put it, endearing, and certainly well-meaning. She has a sweet radiant little . . ."

All eyes are on Father. He has begun to imitate the lady's mincing movements, her beseeching face and droopy garments; and while everyone except Kitty and Alice find amusement in it, he adds insult to injury by making her lack of stylishness in dress come to symbolize loose reasoning and a lack of discrimination.

Alice is longing for Henry to object but he does not. 'Yet he will be imagining her secretly,' she decides, 'and that is a kind of sympathy, is it not?'

Aunt Kate is impatient with the whole subject.

Alice and Kitty regard each other. That is the end of Elizabeth Peabody, they understand. The message is quite clear. Wearing spectacles, especially ones that slip down your nose, is to be avoided at all costs.

By now the servants are bringing in the dessert, a compote of fruits, and a Thanksgiving cake made from a recipe handed down by Catharine Barber James. Alice is helping Aunt Kate to clear away the dirty dishes which are smeared with a brown gravy and red cranberries, and cluttered with bits of orange 'candy'. William, Alice can't help noticing, is glaring across the table with one of his cross-eyed looks, like the one in the self-portrait he recently sent her signed with the inscription, *To my loveress, Alice*. But now it's Henry he's got in his sights:

"I have been reading some letters of yours recently published in The Nation," he announces. Henry, emerging out of his silence like a deep sea turtle from its shell, replies: "Indeed." "Yes . . . *indeed*," echoes William menacingly, "and I have to say, Henry, they show a disconcerting tendency to over-refinement and – he makes a rotating gesture with his wrist – *curliness*. If you ask me . . ."

'But he has not asked you,' thinks Alice.

". . . you should cultivate a more direct style."

"I see," says Henry. There is a pause; then: "And what of delicacy, subtlety and ingenuity?"

"Oh, to hell with them, and all that fencing you put in the dialogue. What you want to write is straightforward action with no twilight or mustiness in the plot. A good story, I'm sure you can do it." He sits back, the wise older brother giving the younger the gift of his wisdom. For his own good.

Henry mutters in French under his breath.

"Oh, and that's another thing, your constant use of French phrases – absolutely maddening!"

Wilkie and Rob are starting to titter and Aunt Kate and Mother are looking anxiously at each other. Then Father's leg begins vibrating under the table. "Come," Mother turns to Henry, "tell us how you are, dear." She is trying to distract him, thinks Alice, so he won't make Willy look a fool. "Have you quite recovered from your wound?" she now asks.

Uh-oh, thinks Alice.

"I am quite well, Mother," he replies tightly, regarding his plate as if noticing for the first time that it contains more pudding than he can possibly eat. The sound of tittering into napkins is heard from the other end of the table. Father raps at his glass. Henry, as they all know, does not like his 'wound' mentioned. It is not, like Wilkie's, a wound to be proud of; that is, a War Wound with capital letters. Their Mother has once again 'put her foot in it'. But their Father will rescue them with a speech on the occasion for which they are gathered. He is good at that. He rises. "Let us Give Thanks," he begins, "for all our brave boys, in this time of national crisis."

Cousin Kitty and Alice stare at each other. Aunt Kate and Mother are used to being left out, so they do not mind.

Father drones on about self-respect and good and evil and manly resistance, and duty and etcetera.

Alice knows that Bob has been homesick, and that their Father has had to send him rousing letters ('My darling Bobbins') about the Prodigal Son and the fatted calf, and so on, so that he will stay fighting like a man and not come home with his tail between his legs.

William and Henry are excused from The War. It must be, she thinks, because they are older and wiser.

"The crucial thing," their Father is coming to the end of his speechifying (while the custard is congealing on their plates), "Is not to do good for the sake of worldly success, but to hate evil, to feel disgust at it, and to turn from sinfulness to God's perfect love. Let us Give Thanks."

Chatterchatterhowlhowl, Alice hears. She bites her knuckles.

Henry has eaten the least of all of them. "Poor Henry," says Mother, "are you sure you're quite allright? Have you lost your appetite? Really you are too thin, dear."

William's eyeballs roll inexorably towards one another. "What can you mean, Mother, when he has all the world looking after him. Poor Henry, indeed! I should be so poor!"

Cousin Kitty has reported how all the young women of Boston have been clamoring to meet the young writer.

"Leave him alone," says Alice, coming to Henry's defence. "Anyone can see his mind is his battleground; and if any one of you can match it for wit and prescience, speak out now."

Silence. Aunt Kate whispers to her sister, "That child is too precocious for her own good."

But she stands her ground. "Henry will make the James name famous for all of us," she declares.

William is looking fierce, embattled, left out.

Alice hisses, "Unscrew your eyes, Willy, or they will stick like that!" But he ignores her; he is far too cross.

"And how," he asks, "does that compare with Wilkie and Bob giving their lives for our country?"

"But they have not," asserts Kitty: "Unless my eyes deceive me, they are both, thank heavens – even Wilkie with his wound – very much alive."

"And long may they continue," puts in Aunt Kate.

"Amen," adds Mother. "Would anyone like more pudding? cake?"

No one answers her.

"Anyway, Willy," Alice pursues, "you haven't either – given your life."

"Alice!" booms her Father. He has led them all to believe that William and Henry were meant for higher things than War (like Writing and Science).

"Please, dear," pleads Mother.

"But it's true," cries Alice.

William holds up his hand and smiles an odd sort of smile. "She is quite right, the little hyena."

Alice's lip trembles.

Mother turns to her: "Well, if you will sass your brothers!"

William goes on: "Our younger brothers are the best abolitionists you ever saw, and make common ones feel very small and shabby indeed. Unfit for a life of action as we are, I believe we are two of the very lightest of feather-weights."

Alice observing Henry notes how his lips, top and bottom, roll inwards until they nearly disappear. *No, William, I do not feel light as a feather, or in the least small and shabby.* But is he pretending? she wonders. However clever, he can never 'keep up with' William when it comes to 'manly' things; and he must know that Wilkie's 'wound' is ever so much more romantic than his own 'obscure hurt'. As for Rob leading black battalions into war – the thought of actually doing such a thing makes him feel quite peculiar, though he would like to have the *experience* of it. Oh, yes, she decides, *that* is what he envies.

But Father is furious. It does not matter what each is doing: brother should not turn against brother. It is a sin. And a sister should not take sides.

"My d-d-dear boy," he instructs William, "you must conquer this curse of self-doubt."

Cousin Kitty folds and unfolds her napkin.

"Don't be frightened," says Mother, "they won't stab each other. This is usual when the boys come home."

*

Next morning Alice and cousin Kitty go for a cliff walk under a low, grey Newport sky. "And what are *we* to be thankful for?" asks Kitty. Alice stops, shocked. "You have only recently been married, surely you must be thankful for *that*?" "It has been two years now," rejoins Kitty, as if that must make a difference. "But is it not wonderful," entreats Alice, "to be *married* – and to a *physician*?" She imagines being tended by an all-powerful being. Kitty smiles ruefully, "Some day, little Alice, you will find out."

Returning to the house, Alice goes up to the attic which Father has had built on so that they can gaze across the lawns to the sea; though mostly the great Austrian pine blocks their view. She tries to give thanks but all she can think of is Henry's hurt and William's poor eyes and stomach and feelings of shabbiness, and Wilkie's war wound that makes his ankle throb in the night, and the sore place on his back where shrapnel has lodged and that she has been allowed to touch; and Father's peg-leg, and Aunt Kate's 'frightful' mistake, and now poor cousin Kitty with her nerves and having to have 'rests' in insane asylums. Not to mention her marriage which has not saved her from anything and has itself become a hurt.

Alice, gazing out of the attic window, spies her two older brothers circling the garden below. As quietly as she can, she raises the sash, in time to hear Henry say he wished sooner to descend to a dishonoured grave than write the sort of book William has expressed admiration for. She does not hear William's reply. She wishes she had not heard any of it.

One by one the brothers 'peel off': Wilkie and Bob to their barracks; William to Harvard; Henry also to Cambridge (but they do not travel together), and Cousin Kitty back to her husband and to volunteer, along with her friend Miss Alcott, for nursing duty. Only Alice is left behind to roll bandages and assemble bullets. Alice, reading stories in Lady Godey's Book about wounded soldiers falling in love with their nurses, judges herself the most idle and useless, the most peripheral and irrelevant of them all.

Wardy was quite right about not having a family to make it a convincing Thanksgiving, especially as she and the Smiths had both found excuses not to join me. So there I sat alone at Henry's vast table gazing out across de Vere Gardens with its mostly bare trees and wrought-iron spikes. The sun was about to go down behind the pines. A band of cloud had formed but the sun shone through it lighting up the handsome rosewood dining table. Bandages and bullets . . . I recalled the feel of the bandages as I rolled them into bouncy bundles and lined them up, just so, neat as socks in a drawer, but quite useless really except for staunching blood and hiding the wounds made by the bullets which had made the bandages necessary in the first place; and now how absurdly cruel they both seemed, the hard *and* the soft, that Wilkie was dead (along with so many others, white and black), and Rob – well, had he ever recovered? The candied sweets had turned out far too sweet, the sprouts were overcooked and the turkey rather dry. We'd had little appetite, in any case.

"Will that be all, Miss?"

"Yes, thank you, Smith."

Beside my plate were notes from Aunt Kate, cousin Kitty, William and Henry, all wishing me a Happy Thanksgiving. Nothing from Katharine. I remained sitting staring out until the last light faded and the window dissolved into a huge dark shape floating in space. William and Henry, I thought, had anything changed between them? William had come to understand that Henry had little respect for his literary pronouncements, and Henry knew absolutely and conclusively that William had no love for his novels. Yet somehow it did not matter, or not much, I thought – a kind of comfort – so long as Henry acknowledged an innate superiority in William, and William was allowed to patronize his younger sibling. For they were brothers after all; and their small war was, if not winnable, at least containable. They would both survive it.

Smith threatened to light the lamps and candles but I refused, continuing to sit with my hands out before me like one of William's batty seance-attenders waiting for the table to speak. And then – so I imagined – it *did*. It told me I must *do* something with myself, *for* myself.

But what?

Gradually a plan took hold: I would leave de Vere Gardens and London. I would go to Leamington Spa where it wasn't so queer to be ill, and where I would be independent of Henry. I would book myself into The Regent – no, too self-important – The Temperance: yes, that would do while seeking a more permanent accommodation. But I would need help. I rang for Smith: "Where is Wardy?" I asked. "Hiding," came the reply accompanied by a rude snigger. Poor Wardy, I thought: she feels pushed aside by The Smiths. But that will stop now. "Please tell her I need her."

Thirty-nine

Wardy, chuffed to have been summoned and tickled to be going to live in the fashionably 'Royal' town of Leamington, was galvanized into action. *Chuffed* and *tickled* and *galvanized*: such words.

"That's right, Wardy, just like the Queen."

"Do not mock me, Miss," she warned fitting fists to hips like a threatening pitcher before snatching up a photograph of me taken in '73 with my hair up in braids, my whole life before me.

"Is that really you?" she asked.

(Was it my turn to be mocked?)

"Yes," I told her, "and it will need wrapping in newspaper."

"Huph," said she, which I translated: *as if I didn't know.*

We had returned to Bolton Row where we were surrounded by packing boxes and trunks. I'd written to Katharine just after Thanksgiving telling her we were moving, and had received a letter promising to 'take you in charge for the move'. But the move was upon us and she was not. At some point a rain-blurred postcard had arrived repeating the promise.

Wardy, meanwhile, had persuaded me to 'go through' my possessions. Go through? "If this is your artless way of trying to distract me," I warned her, "it will not work." But I was quite wrong, it did work. I became so caught up I was able to ignore the nerve pain that nipped me here, there and everywhere like some crazed crab.

I sat, or rather reclined, while Wardy held up various

garments for me to decide yea or nay: 'visiting' dresses, feathers and furs, hats and shoes, belts and other miscellaneous accessories. A 'thumbs up' went only to practical, comfortable, warm (Wardy: 'spinsterish') items; anything else she could take away for herself or her Aunt Flo, or cut down to give to her hospital children.

"No, too tight . . . too constricting . . . quite ridiculous . . . too *young*: I will never be seen in such a thing again.". Only the brown velvet dress could stay, and the green serge jacket with the velvet collar and plain black skirt."

"And the crinoline?" It stood by itself like a bird-less cage. I would not be its catch: "Away with it."

"But surely," she pointed out, "you will be needing it to go out in, even for a stroll around the Pump Room or Jephson Gardens." She had memorized Leamington's main attractions.

"I won't mind in the least," I reassured her. "I shan't be going out much, if at all, and if I do I'll droop my bedraggled, un-crinolined way about town."

She objected to my 'plainness': why if I could afford it?

Because, I replied, I objected to flounces and gewgaws.

"*Huph*," came again as she bent to retrieve a fur muff from the bottom of the trunk, dangled between her two fingers. I waved it away: "I will not be requiring the services of a skinned muskrat." She plunged back in: "Now what do you say to *that*, Miss?" she asked admiringly, flicking the fur bobbles as if they were bells. And there I was again, fourteen years old, in Paris, wearing my new white fur tippet. The family is on its way to the Louvre where I am about to witness the great paintings, and all the people gazing at them. Henry is to my left, William to my right; the smaller boys trail behind along with Father and Mother, arm in arm. I am so well, and therefore so rapturously happy, that every so often I rise up in a skip to make the bobbles tying the tippet bounce and hit me in the nose, to remind me that I am not dreaming it.

"Give it here," I ordered, wondering half to myself if it was possible that I'd ever worn such a thing.

"I'm sure I do not know, Miss," replied Wardy. "I expect you were young and foolish once."

"And now, you mean to say, I am merely old and foolish?"

"I did not say that, Miss; you are always putting words into my mouth." Words, I thought: perhaps I should cast those off too?

"Am I, Wardy?" I asked, serious now.

"Are you what, Miss?"

"Nothing, then, never mind."

We continued in silence, sifting through another box containing pictures and gadgets that I'd carted all the way from Boston. The photographs of my parents and brothers, oh, those must stay; but ice skates? hiking boots (worn traipsing after Katharine in the Adirondacks)? No, I would not be hiking or skating again. I had a vision of my discarded books and boots and muffs tumbling through the air like strange acrobatic birds.

"What catches you, Miss?"

"Nothing," I said, suddenly faced with the truth of it. Like shedding one's old skin after sunburn. Oh, one was tender and pink and raw but, if anything, more alive for the honesty of it. Nor would it end there. The 'stripping down' had only just begun. In Leamington it would go on: from skin to flesh to bone to . . .

"Wardy! I have just remembered something."

"Yes, Miss?"

"There's a lot more stuff that I left in the Boston store-rooms."

"What will you do with it? Do you wish it sent over?"

I shook my head, ordered her to bring me pen and paper upon which I scrawled:

Dearest William,

I have just remembered the stored things – a fair old mix –

mostly junk but a few good pieces. If there is anything you can use do help yourself . . .

I recalled a red rug which would do, I thought, for his study, and another rug for their parlour; the old kitchen traps would be useful in the country; and there were beds, blankets and linens. The keys to the trunks, I instructed, were with my lawyer. The pictures would do nicely on their walls. That left the crockery . . . barrels of the stuff. For some reason those felt harder to let go of. I saw myself setting my mother's favorite pieces out on a clean cloth for the boys and their wives and children, the gold rims repeating one another, the chink of cup against saucer . . . A fantasy of course. Still, I added a 'P.S.' saying perhaps the crockery could be kept aside for me. And the oak rocker with the carved back and upholstered seat? Oh, that, that I would like sent if he would be good enough to ship it across. The rocker would remind me of the sea, and my cottage at Manchester.

Weary now, I signed the letter and closed my eyes. Opened them. Before me, a familiar figure leaning in the doorway. An apparition, I suspected blinking hard.

"Gracious me," gasped Wardy, holding her heart.

"So, Queen Alice reigns from her bed," said the apparition.

I stared, rubbed my eyes. It was all too melodramatic, too absurd; like a scene out of Goldilocks and the Three Bears, and me about to yelp: *And there she is!* For there she was. Or perhaps I'd conjured her too. But no: "What's all the fuss, Alice? I told you I would get here in time to help you move." I opened and closed my mouth fishlike.

"Aren't you going to say anything?" she asked.

"You look well ventilated," was all I could think of.

She and Wardy set to work. In between each completed packing case Katharine would return to lay her hands on my shoulders and tell me of another adventure – she'd been hiking in the Adirondacks – or another success with her students; or cover my eyes with her open palms from behind as children do; or cradle my head loosening it from its fixed tilt; and then back to piling more books into a packing case.

That evening it began to rain. "The gutter must be blocked," she diagnosed, going to the window and looking up towards the roof. The blockage caused the rain to fall in drumbeats, in clots and clumps until we were enclosed in an almost solid curtain of rain separating us from the outside world. But meanwhile there we sat, warm and dry, enjoying the last fire in that place, with me reading from Henry's chilling tale 'De Grey', and Katharine interrupting with more stories about camping in wild weather and tramping vast distances and coming upon meadows filled with late wild flowers and, once, meeting a bear which she claimed to have chased away by bellowing boo at it.

The next day we boarded a train heading North. Wardy, no doubt feeling displaced, had decided to visit her Aunt for Christmas; she would return in the new year. I gave her her Christmas present (the fur tippet I'd managed to squirrel away, which pleased her inordinately), and bid her a happy holiday. So we risked travelling on our own; after all, I now had Katharine beside me, Katharine who was real and had turned up as promised, albeit rather late.

We were just pulling out of the station. Katharine threw off her hat and raised her arms to place it upon the high rack, swaying with the movement of the train yet keeping her balance. She moved so *loosely* while I sat like a toadstool, or a toad. Then she flopped back down and there were her ears which were quite enormous in relation to the size of her head. Really, I thought, she should comb her hair over them instead of behind. But what did my Katharine care for vanity?

"What are you staring at?" she asked over her spectacles.

"Nothing," I lied, reaching over to tuck a wayward strand behind one of said ears. At some point I tilted my head so it rested against the glass. "We can't have that," Katharine pronounced, "you'll wake with a headache and a jarred spine." Her arm went round me. If the other couple in the carriage thought it odd, they did not show it. In any case, what would they see? A tall thin woman, rather severe, considered by some to be 'masculine', with her arm around the smaller woman who appeared more fragile, perhaps ill. Whatever it was they were seeing, or told themselves they were seeing, let them see it, I thought. We would keep hold. A new year was upon us, and my Katharine was back, and we were on our way to Leamington.

IV. LEAMINGTON SPA
(1887–1889)

Forty

We'd crossed Newbold Terrace and were entering the underpass, dark and slippery with mud, its brick walls running with slime, when a shadowy shape loomed up ahead of us. "Do watch where you're going, dear," I warned. Katharine charged straight on. "Look *out!*" I yelped. The kissing couple – for that is what it was – leapt aside, flattening themselves up against the wall as we sailed past and out, straight through a pile of dog mess. "Damn," I cursed under my breath, "now Wardy will have to clean the wheels." Katharine threw up her hands, "Oh, don't take on so, Alice." We were like an old married couple sniping at one another to *slow down . . . speed up . . . wrong way. . . .* And what of the kissing couple? Had she intended to bash into them, thus forcing them apart? Or had she simply not seen them? The simple explanation was she was still sore about the move and behaving recklessly.

She had tried before we'd left London to talk me out of going to Leamington but my mind had already been made up. "The waters," I'd argued, "are known to help gout, rheumatism, lumbago, sciatica, liver and digestive problems." "In which case," she'd replied, "you should be a new woman in no time." The sarcasm barely covered the bitterness, and despair.

It was our first outing – the weather was cold but windless – and so she had asked, "Will you walk, Alice?" A simple question beneath which lurked the challenge: *Will you live Alice, or will you give up*?

I allowed her to raise me to my feet but promptly

crumpled. "Try again," she encouraged, "you're stiff with sitting." I obeyed but, as if over-drugged or wounded, lurched from table to chair-back to wall until it was clear that my legs, if not I, had indeed given up.

The bath chair it was then.

"Wardy is a soberer driver, by far," I grumped.

"Alice," she stopped short: "if you are trying to tell me I'm pushing too hard, you have only to say so."

We were approaching the Leam. Once there she man-oeuvred my chair close to the edge.

"Are you planning to do me in, dear?" I asked sweetly.

She braked the chair and came round to face me, her fine features all screwed up. "I do not want you *dead*, Alice – that is the whole point – I want you *alive*." She was willing me, that is, not to become another Leamington invalid, densely dull and lonely, the sands of my little hour-glass slowly but surely running out.

It is too late, I thought: I have already become one.

The lap-rug slipped to my feet. She bent to repair it.

"Don't fuss, I can do it myself."

"Alice, must you?"

Yes, I thought, I *must*. I was nervy with the new sensation that had begun to bloom in me: that of not being afraid. The prospect of becoming 'another Leamington invalid' not only failed to frighten me but – dare I say it? – pleased me. I would be free to submit to the thing that had already begun, and in that there was relief. *I am facing my freedom and my nakedness*, I thought, recalling William's prophecy. I was prepared to embrace it. Katharine was not. But why should she?

She propelled me along in her racy way. As we crossed the bridge a pretty, mild-faced shopgirl went by wagging her flouncy ducktail bustle. "Do you admire that one?" I asked teasingly. There was a pause, then Katharine leaned over and, whispering across the top of my head, hissed: "Not bad."

Not bad? Unaccountably – I knew she was teasing – it brought tears to my eyes. But she was unrepentant. "How did you expect me to reply?" She jolted my chair so I nearly tumbled out. "Must I comment upon the cheapness of the fabric and the overdone waddle, not to mention the unwiseness of going out in December without a cloak – and all in perfect French?"

By now we had arrived at a quiet spot near Mill Gardens overlooking the boathouse. Parking me beside it Katharine sat on the rustic bench along the path. Through the bare trees across the Gardens we could see the manor house, a romantically tumbledown farmhouse and a church in its graveyard.

"I suppose it's all quite picturesque," she said, holding her nose. Fresh sewage was being spread on the fields round about.

"You mean, I take it, a scene of deathliness, immobility and stagnation?"

She did not deny it. She was thinking of the troubles in London, the depression, the bands of unemployed men living rough in Trafalgar Square, the women supporting and demonstrating in their own right. She felt sure there would soon be an uprising, riots in the street . . . socialists . . . anarchists . . . people seeking alternative solutions. Was it right to withdraw, disengage from all that?

"And do you assume there are no such troubles here?"

She admitted the evidence of poverty; but not the scale of it, nor therefore the impulse towards rebellion and redress of grievance. She put her hand to her head. I saw that she was hurting; her eye condition had worsened, causing headaches. "I'm sorry," she said. "I don't know what got into me."

Oh, but I did. She'd been shocked to see me as I was, 'less' than the Alice she'd left at the end of last summer. Leamington was a place where people came to dip a toe in the waters and be cured or not; but, in any case, it was not a place to live; not a place to 'act'. Yet it was where I'd chosen.

"London, I confessed, "had begun to jangle my nerves."

"Well then," she pronounced unsteadily, "you will certainly find peace here." *Quietus*, she might have said. "But must you," she added more fervently, "join the march of Leamington invalids?"

"Invalids do not *march*, dear."

"Please, Alice, promise me you won't give up, not yet." How could I?

Oh, but I must: "Promise!" she shouted out, causing the cows, which were being driven in, to gaze our way. "See," she pointed: "they agree." Only resist, she seemed to be saying. Poor Kath, I thought. Her nose was red and chapped, her freaked hair escaping, her hat at a tilt. At last, to please her, I promised, and we tucked our chins in against the wind that had risen and made for Hamilton Terrace and my shining white stucco sanitorium.

She came to a halt. Would not these strange white facades, she wondered, work strangely upon the imagination, suggesting ghostly presences? I said I was determined not to be bothered by phantoms. "Let us hope not, Alice," she said.

That night I was awoken by a pain shooting up my right big toe, through my foot and up into my knee until the whole leg began to judder. "Hold tight," Katharine instructed as the shaking entered her also, leaving us finally in a tangled, disordered heap. But it was not the pain, finally, that reduced me to whimpering but the failure of words to express it.

"Katharine, dear," I asked when it had abated: "have you ever been in such extremis that you have feared for your life?" What I was really asking was, *Do you begin to know what it is like to be me?* Impossible question. She turned onto her back to consider it. The answer of course lay between us, in the near-unbridgeable divide between our two experiences, between her health and my ill-health, her doing and my not-doing. In the end, all she could think of was having nearly frozen to death during a hiking expedition in the Sierras. "My sleeping roll had become ice-glued to the ground. The cold . . . in the end," she remembered, "it went beyond pain until there was . . . nothing. Oh, it's hard to expain, but it was as if 'I' had disappeared."

"Were you afraid?" I asked.

She laughed. "No; I felt curiously free. I suppose I'd given up."

At which I turned to her in the dark with such ferocious fondness I feared I would burst. Katharine, suffering hypothermia, had touched a condition I recognized. There, in that leached cold place her pain had disappeared until there was nothing left: no ice, no grinning moon or granite cliff faces.

She'd been freed, as had I.

Towards morning Wardy came in muttering, "Another bad little attack, I shouldn't wonder with all the gadding about." *Gadding about*? The woman was mad or silly. She held out her hand for me to take the medicine – four grains of solid opium – but my hand shook so much they were swept clear off her palm.

"Now look what you've done." She scrabbled among the bedclothes until she retrieved them.

"Must she take so many?" asked Katharine mildly.

"Yes, she must," snapped The Ward. "Take my word for it, Miss, we have learned from bitter experience. Four grains and she's her own sweet self again." Snorting at her own joke.

The attack lasted three nights, leaving me limp as a leek. Yet I had survived; gradually I began to feel I could do anything, as if I'd been restored to my own fizzing self.

"Oh Wardy," I exclaimed, "don't you wish you were me?" (Hadn't Charmian imagined herself as Cleopatra?)

"You, Miss," she snorted, "when you have just had a sick headache for five days?"

That did it. So my glorious role was to be a sick headache. Was I to laugh uproariously or weep my heart out, or both? In the event, Katharine offered to take me out for a dose of the waters. "It may do you some good, you never know."

There was so much I did not know.

On our way we passed a number of poor, squalid creatures, scraps of old lace and ruffle: leftovers from the great human factory. How cruel, I thought, only wishing I could wrap the poor bewildered souls in my arms to cocoon them from the cold, from life on the streets.

Katharine steered round them.

At the Pump Room we stood in a queue listening to servants' complaints, winter apparently not being deemed safe for invalids to come out of their hidey-holes before ten a.m. The 'dame' filled our tumblers from the pump and handed them back to us, barking "Next!" We sniffed at our cups, bubbles exploding against our noses, rolled our eyes at the stench. "Must I?" I asked, while Katharine the Brave held her nose and made a dive for it – then spat, pronouncing it 'quite foul.' I hazarded a sip; swallowed. My stomach took one of its acrobatic turns. It tasted of dead birds and rotten eggs.

Forty-one

The next time I was well enough to be taken out Wardy pushed me to Lillington where I'd been with Katharine. We were crossing Kenilworth field when she braked, nearly flinging me out into a cowpat. "Should you like to be an artist, Miss," she asked: "I mean to be able to paint what you see?" I was too discombobulated to reply, though her question interested me.

"Miss?" "Yes, Wardy, I'm thinking about your question." I had seen so little during my shut-away life, yet some things I had kept fresh in my mind – certain scenes – foreign cities, paintings, people, mountains – childish impressions of light and color – a moment in a cafe or a museum. But to paint such a moment – would one be able to bring it back?

She tsked; all I need say was 'yes' or 'no'.

The brush with its smooth, warm handle is in my hand; now comes the squeezing out of color, the oily reek of it like life itself; then the mixing and moving about of said colors, the bounce of bristle against canvas; altogether the primitive pleasure of making one's mark. Yet when at last I stood back to admire what I had done, all I could feel was disappointment at the poor quality of the copy I'd made, how I'd failed to convey the drift and pull of the clouds, the peasant crossing the field like an ambulating scarecrow, and as for the cows . . .

Wardy had parked me in a meadow at Hawkes's farm. There I lay absorbing hay-ricks, hedges and trees, composing them into a multitude of pictures . . . the foreground grey with ghostly slants of sunshine, vanishing to reappear in the distance, so succulent, so smooth and so slow, so *from* all time and so *for* all time . . . and then coming within view the peasant in his field, as 'edgeless' as the landscape he appeared to merge into. But he was real and robust as anything and he came across and spoke to us about some allotments the landlord had taken to build on, worked for two years by poor men. "Why, that's criminal," I objected. But he just said with a shrug, "That be the nature of landlording."

The cuckoo imitates a clock to perfection.

When we got home there was a parcel waiting which turned out to be a sketch sent by a Mrs Sidgwick from Cambridge. The picture was of the The Cobb off which silly Louisa Musgrove had jumped.

"Do you credit it?" asked Wardy, peering over my shoulder.

How to reply? It was a perfectly *good copy*, I acknowledged, with its fussy clutter of people with their spindly or bracing bodies, but, oh, it was so very flimsy, failing to convey the feel of the scene, the *feel* of anything.

"Isn't it wrong, Miss, to have the sky cloudy," she went on, "because I've always been told that the sky in a picture should be perfectly clear, they say it is very 'ard to do. And" – there was more – "you should be able to see the stones and read the print on the notices."

What I saw was that her standard of excellence was in the number of recognizable objects. In which she was not alone. So that, in answer to her question – should I like to paint? – I understood that I would soon become frustrated with mere reproduction, would slash at the canvas with my brush in colors so fierce and thick that people would cry *What on earth is that? . . . why a child could do better than that!* Even Henry, I realized, would find it distasteful and vulgar. Best not try, I concluded.

Back home, I called for Wardy. Would she run an errand to the haberdashery shop, assuming there was such a thing?

"Oh yes, Miss Bond keeps a little shop with all sorts, we have already made acquaintance. She has an old mother of 84 on her hands, bad health and . . ."

"Does she sell yarns, Wardy?"

"Yarns? as in *wool*, Miss? You mean to knit?" she tittered, as in *You mean to fly?*

"Yes, Wardy, I do indeed mean to knit, unless you think me incapable of managing even that most rudimentary of female occupations."

"Of course not, Miss, only I did not think . . . after Miss Loring's shawl . . .".

"That will do." I waved William's letter in her face: "It's for my brother William's new baby, Margaret Mary. Go and choose a pattern: something pretty, a jacket perhaps, or cap; but not too complicated."

She returned all smiles from her errand bearing Mrs Stone's Treasury of Knitting Patterns ("The latest fashions, Miss") and a supply of white wool for *a plain little bonnet* which even I, she thought, could manage, assuming I could get my silly – *stiff* she meant to say – fingers to work.

Fine white Saxony on the thinnest wooden needles. Angel's wool. *Cast on twenty stitches* . . . But I'd already forgotten how to cast on . . . using one needle or two? Wardy stood by smirking as I tortured the tail of wool, wrapping my fingers this way and that to no purpose until she took pity on me, relieving me of the stuff.

"It's like this, Miss" – she demonstrated – "it will soon come back to you." *Knit plain for twelve ribs.* It was something to do with my hands . . . plain knitting back and forth . . . the clicking of the needles, their smoothness, sliding the tip into the loop of wool and pulling it through, the yarn light and soft as, yes, a child's hair . . . being tethered to it. I tried to picture her, my niece, Margaret Mary – a girl-child – a life created by William and Alice – the bobbing head wobbling on its stem – filling my hand – its warm, wet, milky, *baby*-smell. And the hair: was it blond, or had it already turned dark like William's . . . or mine (but mine was already turning grey)? Perhaps she was bald, like Henry? – they often were. I didn't know; I'd lost touch – the distance. *Touch.* How Mary Was Made: was there a pattern book for that? Godey's Lady's Book had not considered it a proper subject for young ladies to learn.

Knit one, purl one to the end of the row, then turn . . . count your rows.

"Are you all right, Miss?"

"I've lost several stitches, I'm afraid, Wardy."

"Well, I daresay you've been dreaming again. Never mind, give it here."

"How will it ever fit around the child's head, it's no bigger than a lemon?"

"Oh, you'll see when it's off the needles, that's the art of it."

Art? I thought, *art* in a baby's bonnet? But on I went increasing and picking up and slipping stitches and so on and so forth, all the time humming to myself, *'The spinsters and the knitters in the sun/ And the free maids that weave their thread with bones . . .'*

"Oh, Miss, what a sweet singing voice you have, I had no idea – only your stitches are too tight!"

Forty-two

Katharine and I, during our visit to the local art gallery, had been greatly taken by a painting entitled *Woman Reading*, by a French artist who's name is now lost to me. We had stood before it as if mesmerized, for the reading woman lay sprawled on a bed *stark naked*, the room in which she lay rendered in dark sepia. Then as we stood looking at it, or rather into it, the darkness began to take on a strange 'stirred' quality. As for the woman herself, she is on her front leaning her cheek on her elbow; her long red hair is parted in the middle. Her body is luminous, emerging as it does out of the shadows; yet at the same time her position seems quite natural.

"What d'you suppose she's reading?" I'd asked.

"Oh, I doubt she's reading at all," Katharine had replied tartly. "It is to my mind nothing but the artist's fantasy. She went on, "Can you imagine Henry being painted reading *with not so much as a stitch on?*"

To which I'd offered: "I guess Henry would be painted with his best bow-tie at least." Which ought to have made her chuckle but did not.

"Don't be ridiculous, Alice," she'd snapped. "You know very well he'd be sitting upright, fully clothed, in an arm-chair with his legs firmly crossed. Women," she then concluded, "do not read in the nude; or if they do, it is likely to be trash."

I said nothing only thought *Oh, how I would like to lie naked on my front reading trash while an artist paints me!*

But it was I who now, clothed in more layers of gown and

bed-jacket than a wedding cake, lay reading. As I did so – my bedroom faced pleasantly South – a parallelogram of light slithered slowly along the bed-clothes, allowing me to mark the sun's progress paragraph by paragraph. But, sun or no sun, I was aware of being 'kept warm' by Henry's new story ('The Lesson of the Master' recently published in the Universal Review), and moved by the story's own desire to be read.

But the wedge of sunlight was getting closer. Soon it would reach me – pleasurably, as I'd already anticipated; but instead it struck violently, shockingly.

"Shall I close the curtains, Miss?"

"Yes," I said, then changed my mind. "No, Wardy, leave them: the sun will shift soon enough."

"You can be sure of it, Miss," she said, handing me the day's newspaper along with a swinge at the town's radical mayor. I took aim with the newspaper accusing her of despising him precisely for being one of her own kind; while at the same time choosing to enthuse over a stodgy foxhunting squire – ignorant, idle and selfish – like a cringing dog ready to lick the hand that beats it.

"It fairly makes me vomit! Wardy," I concluded, "you are a shame and a disgrace to your class."

"And you . . . ," she begins threateningly.

"Yes?" I smile sweetly: "Go on."

"Nothing," mutters the little coward, fleeing. A minute later she returns with the post as if none of the above has taken place: "Who's the popular one today? There's a letter from your brother William . . . and another from a, let's see, Miss Jewett."

"Wardy, I can read the return inscriptions for myself."

"I was only trying to be helpful, Miss, so you know what to expect."

I glared at her, "I guess I prefer to be surprised."

The letter from William was all about my furniture and effects. Enclosed was a note from Alice with news of the children, particularly little Margaret Mary; with a 'PS' thanking me for the knitted 'object'.

But it was the letter from Miss Jewett that arrested my attention:

'My dear Katharine and Alice,

You may be surprised to hear from me after all this time, but I have been thinking of you *together* in the closest way, and how you think *together* and know each other's thoughts

as only those friends can who are very near and dear.'

She went on to speak of her own companion Annie Fields and their life *together*, ending with:

'I wish your 'reach' *together* is as firm and easy as ours . . .'.

Together and together and together. What a lot of 'togethers'! thought I, rather flippantly; yet there *was* a kind of comfort in it. I grabbed up a piece of writing paper. 'My dear Sarah,' I began. After thanking her warmly for her wish for our continued happiness *together*, I added, 'It gives us great pleasure to hear of the life you and Annie have created *together*. It is an accomplishment after all – your 'original' lives *together* – firm and easy – outside the usual bounds. Really, I think we are all to be congratulated . . .'. Katharine and I, I was pleased to add, were managing with our permanency, at least from time to time. I ended on a shamelessly self-congratulatory note saying with luck we would carry on and nothing I felt sure would threaten our 'reach' *together* until our bones fell asunder. Then for some unaccountable reason I added: *unless some magic transformation takes place in my state.* Then, astonishingly, it did. I met Bowles the Mesmerist.

Forty-three

We'd just passed the Pump Rooms when he came haring round the collonade as if on the run from an angry mob. Katharine held fast to my chair. "Thoughtless oaf!" she shouted after him but he'd already disappeared into the shrubbery. She checked my right shoulder for damage. I shook her off, saying it was nothing but she assured me, oh yes, 'an outrage' had most definitely occurred. That raised the question of how to respond. Should I be offended at an impropriety, insist on an 'insult' so that Katharine must then do something about it? But what? Having located the fellow – assuming she could find him again – would she be obliged to square up to him? *See here, my good man, my friend does not take kindly to being knocked about . . .?* But *had* I been 'knocked about'? I felt for my arm; did it harbor a grievance, or something quite other? The sense of smash faded and in its place came – unthinkable – that of having been *touched* by a man. (But had I?) For a man's touch, with the exception of my brothers and a series of doctors, was a rare and therefore unsettling experience.

Next day – it was Wardy's turn to take me out – there he was again: small and spare as a water biscuit, with the exception of a pair of shockingly red lips. Stripped of moustache and side-whiskers, and dressed accordingly, I saw that he would have made a pleasingly pert female. *'Beauty is enchanting, Alice, but apt to be weak,'* sounded Henry's warning voice in my head. But before Wardy could move me officiously on, the man had extended an ungloved hand: "Arthur Bowles, at your service." I refused it, of course. Some cock-and-bull story followed about having been in a tearing hurry, not that that could excuse such oafishness etcetc, to which I heartily agreed.

"Please allow me to apologize. If you will forgive my presumption," he went on presumptuously, "you look like a lady in need of some radical treatment."

The word 'radical' caught my attention; yet I was wary. "Is it your usual custom, Sir," I charged, "to accost women in public?"

Fixing me with a squinty look not unlike my brother William's, he half-shut his eyes and began intoning as if reading from a script tucked beneath the lids:

"You are in pain much of the time . . . pain, how it inhabits . . . inhibits you, forcing you attend to it, its seemingly random pattern . . . how in its grip you become less and less your known self . . . an animal . . . a wolf, I sense, yes, howling and keening and . . .

It went on

"I see you shut in a dark room invaded by [he searched for an image] pachyderms of pain . . . a desperate frustration to communicate what it must be like, to be taken seriously . . . for them to know . . ." His eyes shot open as he added:

". . . the never-endingness of it."

I was affected in spite of myself. How could he know of such things? His powers suddenly seemed formidable, even fearsome. I was tempted to tell him everything, beg his help, throw myself in his way. It was only Wardy touching my shoulder, saying, "Miss, are you allright?" that returned me to my senses.

"All that may be," I managed to inform him in a more-or-less rational voice, "but anyone seeing me as I am could guess as much."

He shrugged, gazing past me towards York Bridge and the River. "In that case" – a small, stiff bow – "I will not detain you further."

"No wait," I reached out, "how do you propose to put an end to my condition as you describe it?"

But he was gone.

Later I suffered a migraine which lasted three days and left me with a lingering fatigue.

"Perhaps," Wardy asked, "you should consult the gentleman we met at the Baths the other day, Miss?"

"I'm not sure 'gentleman' is a word I would apply to him."

"Why, Miss, they say he has healing powers."

"You mean like our former landlady's tripe and potato soup?"

"Mock me as you will, Miss, it's for your own good."

"And who are 'they' that have recommended him in your vast range of experience?"

She trotted out the names of some doughty invalids: Duchess This and Lady That.

"And what of Lord So&So?"

"Oh, well, they say the mesmerism does not work so well with the menfolk."

"Oh dear," I drawled out my sarcasm, "I can't image why."

"Perhaps it has something to do with their pipe smoking," said the clueless thing.

"Wardy."

"Yes, Miss?"

I could barely control my irritation. "If you used what you please to call your brain – you do have quite a good one – and if you spent less time talking to other intellectually starved servants you would guess as well as I why Bowles' fakery might not work with men."

She stopped bustling about and threw her arms in the air. "And who do you expect me to talk to, the Leamington swells and toffs?"

I had no answer for that. Later, she proposed a visit to the

Baths, adding: "if you are well enough." That would take my mind off Bowles.

"My mind is not *on* Bowles," I protested.

*

An assistant led us through the 'Hammam' or Turkish Bath, an octagonal area lit by a starburst dome and decorated with blue, red and black tiled panels. "This is where you will finish up," she said darkly. Beside four giant palms lay four women sprawled on slatted wooden recliners in various states of languid relaxation, or exhaustion. The echo of whispered voices.

We were directed to one of the side treatment rooms. Wardy helped me down the four steps and through a doorway into a saline bathroom where we were met by another white-coated assistant. "Welcome to the 'tepidar-ium'." I was assigned a cubicle and helped to undress, then laid on a slab where I was 'roughed up', the latest treatment apparently for rheumatism and fibrositis. At the end of the pummeling I was given an aeration bath.

After that came the 'Vichy Douche': warm water sprayed at ferociously high pressure to stimulate the skin and to my surprise, rather exciting. But then came 'The Needle Shower' enclosing me in its six brass arms like some malevolent Hindu god shooting me from his finger-ends with dart-like jets of hot and cold water. If I had not had the 'arms' to hold onto I would most certainly have collapsed. But the assistants were merciless and Wardy too respectful to stop them.

The torture proceeded. Since I could no longer stand on my own, the assistant placed me in a special contraption for paralytic patients. I was then wheeled down a ramp and dumped into a 'Zotofoam' bath where the temperature was slowly raised until I felt I'd been captured by a tribe of cannibals and would soon be boiled and eaten alive. "It is to cure obesity, it will help burn away fat," explained the assistant. "But I am not obese," I protested, "far from it." She pretended not to hear.

After that came the Bertholet Steam Cabinet, followed by the Hot Wax Bath in which my arms and legs were covered in layers of wax then wrapped in greaseproof paper and towels. I waved my arms like a giant tortoise in its last throes. "What purpose . . .?" I managed to gasp. "Pain relief," shouted the assistant.

Then there was the Electrical Treatment Room, where a lamp-like structure was turned on to 'stimulate' my paralyzed muscles, also my skin and blood. By this time I was the color of half-cooked pork. "I believe I am frying," I told Wardy, holding fast to the electrical bar. The smell and crackle of burning flesh.

After that I was slapped down onto a shallow stone trough as if I were a trout, and there massaged and sprayed with another high pressure hose. Then I was lifted off and placed on a stool inside a bubbling whirling 'Vortex'. Finally I was given cervical traction in which I was attached to a sort of chair-lift, my arms raised over my head and secured to a winding mechanism; as the chain wound I felt my bones come apart, cracking like nuts.

Eventually Wardy took receipt of my flaccid body, placing me back in the invalid's chair and wheeling me out the way we'd come. Oh, but it was not over yet. I was shown into the 'Frigidarium' where I was forced to spend at least ten minutes cooling down before being led into the 'Hammam' where, as promised, I was made to join the other women in various states of recovery, though I was too exhausted to speak or take in any of the gossip. Eventually, I was well enough to be dressed and led home.

The results were disastrous. The pain in my back was so bad I could not sit up. I had swollen neck glands and could not turn my head. I barely slept. Every time I was on the verge of falling asleep there would be another contraction of some nerve or other which was like being strangled, drowned and punched in the solar plexus simultaneously. The headaches were so severe I begged Wardy to be a dear and cut off my head. She declined, suggesting saucily: "Shall I bring Bowles to see you then?"

Forty-four

"Follow me," Wardy commanded him, only he slipped past her like the fox in Red Riding Hood, arriving first in the parlour. Catching him up she delivered a swift kick to his ankle sending his hat tipping into his hand. She hung it up along with his coat, throwing me one of her dark looks.

"Naturally my nurse will stay," I informed him, "and my companion, Miss Loring – "if you don't mind."

Katharine, playing her part, rose majestically from her corner.

Bowles suddenly pulled back as if he had misperceived something in his calculations. "Oh," he countered, his eyes travelling from me to her and back to me again: "But I do."

"Do . . .?"

"*Mind*. There is no need for two chaperones – or even one."

"In that case," I said, "we shall have to cancel the 'event'."

"It is a question of trust," he insisted.

"For me, Mr Bowles, it is a matter of propriety." I was as determined as he was, and he saw this.

"Well," he conceded, "I will allow it this once – but only one, if you please."

So it was agreed: Wardy would sit quietly in the corner and not interrupt under any circumstances. Katharine, who had work to do in any case, would leave us.

Bowles remained standing. He put me in mind of the little dancing master in Bleak House, albeit less humble than that literary personage. Indeed, once he rolled up his sleeves, which he'd taken the liberty of doing, I saw that his arms were roped with vein and muscle as if he'd been climbing up houses or cliffs, hanging there like one of Sara Darwin's pater's apes. And it was with those very arms that he now began arranging the 'set-up' for our encounter, placing a dining chair and Henry's nursing chair so that they were facing one another a pace or so apart.

"You will sit here." He stood gripping the back of the nursing chair, voice softly commanding. *Take your wretched hands off that chair at once!* I wanted to shout, but somehow did not. The chair – my only valuable piece of furniture – had cabriole legs and a high hoop-shaped mahogany frame, and had recently been covered in wine-dark velvet. Naturally low-slung, it suited small women such as myself and Constance Woolson, though not Katharine.

Since my ordeal at the Spa I had been bleeding heavily – 'flooding' Wardy called it, as if I were a river that had burst its banks. I'd also been having nightmares in which I haemorraged unstoppably: blood filling the the house, the street – until the River Leam ran red with it. Flooding indeed, I thought. My stomach was so swollen and hard I feared it would burst open with the pressure; yet I almost wished for it, for the relief. As for the pain, it went crawling about my body like some demonic infant with fanged canines and stilleto-sharp nails.

I managed to swing my legs off the sofa where I'd been comfortably stretched and hauled myself up. I assumed Bowles would help me but he did not, nor would he allow Wardy to do so. No, he preferred to watch me stagger across the room where I eventually contrived to fling myself into the nursing chair. Perhaps that is his secret, I thought: the deliberate arousal of resentment which feeds the muscles with a perverse kind of energy. Well, then, at least if I start 'flooding', it will soak into the clot-colored velvet, and not stain too disastrously.

"It is rather hard," I complained.

"All to the good," he replied, "it will keep you awake."

"But surely," I argued, "a somnolent state is required for your . . . procedure?"

Twitch went a string of muscle at his temple. "If you will take your seat, Alice, you will find out."

Alice? He dares to address me as Alice? Yes, he does. And I allow it.

Eventually we were settled: I in the nursing chair, he, straight-backed, facing me.

"Before we begin," I requested – reasonably, I thought: "may I know something of your procedure?"

"And why would that be necessary?" he inquired.

"Because . . ." – I hardly knew how to put it – "it would help to place you . . . as a mesmerist, a medical clairvoyant, a neuro-hypnotist, a . . .?"

"And how would it help, Alice?"

Sweat was pooling under my arms, blood bubbling out of me. It was hardly a question, barely polite, baldly accusatory. I wanted to cry out at its unfairness: *It would help to know because knowing is what I'm good at . . . all I'm good at . . . a useless body but a mind – at least that – that still burns on.* More rationally, I at last managed:

"Surely it is only natural that I should know something of what may be expected of me?"

He spread his legs then pulled them together again like a bird withdrawing from an insect's attack.

"Well," he drawled: "I prefer not to define myself one way or t'other as I find such definitions limiting. However, I have been known, for your information, to use magnetic passes when necessary, though I am more likely in your case to use hypnotic suggestion. But my advice to you now" – he leaned forward to cup my chin as if it were a rare flower – "is to put yourself into my hands."

I felt a tingling in my jaw as after eating a sour cherry that soon spread to other parts of my body. How easy it would be, I thought – now that I'd given him my chin – to allow my head and body to follow; indeed, for a moment I did let go, breathing in his nearness. (Good heavens, was he wearing *scent*?) But then I was frightened, shocked at myself, at the ease with which I was ready to surrender, causing my teeth to rattle in my head. After all, what did I know about him beyond Wardy's gossipy recommendation?

A spasm of pain. And still he held on, as if to receive the trembling into his own body, so that I nearly wept to have it shared. I am no longer alone, I thought, at which the spasm died down.

"Do you want to be well, Alice?" he asked, releasing me.

"Yes." It emerged, to my shame, as a sob.

"What has conventional medicine done for you, except to pump you full of drugs?"

My voice was barely audible, as if confessing to a crime, "Very little, it's true." Then I remembered. "Wait – it was worse than that." I managed to repeat Hooper's curse.

"Ah," said he sagely; unsurprised. "And did they by any chance have the temerity to impugne your sanity?"

I nodded in recognition. "Yes, they left me feeling less than human."

"So . . . ," he paused meaningfully: "will you now put your trust in *me*?"

Again I nodded. Already, without his touch, I felt lost.

"Good." He now approached Wardy and whispered something in her ear. She appealed to me; I gave her permission to carry out whatever he asked of her. She rolled her eyes like a frenzied horse but proceeded to my bedroom from which she emerged carrying a tray laden with my various medicaments. Bowles examined the substances, one by one: "Hemp pills . . . opium powders . . . Sloan's Ointment (Kills Pain) . . . Potter's Herbs . . . Universal Embrocation . . . Pinoleum inhalent spray . . .". On and on he went, pronouncing their names as if they were deadly poisons, before dumping the whole lot onto the floor. So ended our first 'consultation'.

Forty-five

His eyes were mesmerically attracted to one another. My brother William's eyes, as I recalled, also had a tendency to cross in moments of excitement, or distress, such as after having treated a nervous patient at the asylum where he was working. "What have you seen, Willy?" I asked. Appearing badly shaken he stared in my direction, only it was not me he was seeing. His eyes wavered, crossed, met, locked. I cradled his head while he described a black-haired youth with greenish skin. "He's entirely idiotic . . . sits all day with his knees drawn up against his chin, and a coarse gray undershirt drawn over them enclosing his entire figure." It was as if he'd seen a living mummy. But there was something else as yet unspoken, perhaps unspeakable. "What frightens you so, Willy?" I asked. He was hunched over like his patient; in time he whispered *"That shape am I."* Naturally I disabused him of the notion. But the apparition still visited him from time to time – it couldn't be helped – along with his self-mortifying identification with it. He would live with the dread of it, as our Father had of his demons, all his life.

Bowles snaps his fingers to bring me back. He'd replaced his dining chair with a foot-stool so that his eyes were now level with mine and happily returned to separateness. "What do you see, Alice?" *Alice* he persisted in calling me as if I were his servant. *"Miss James*, if you please," I manage to correct him; hypocrite that I am espousing egalitarian principles at the same time pulling rank. It won't do, I scold myself, I must not let England spoil me. He ignores me, in any case, leaving me with no option but to call him *Arthur*. "Tell me the first thing that comes into your head *Alice*," he commands, to which I hear myself reply: *"That shape am I."* *"What* shape is that?" he then pursues. The gentleness of his voice belies its authority. I reply: "The shape of pain."

It helped to picture William and his table-turners, and Henry's risible Bostonians; that is, to suspect him of fakery. Any minute now, I told myself, he would pull a cheap gold watch from his waistcoat pocket and begin swinging it to and fro before my eyes. *You are getting drowsy . . . your eyelids are growing heavy . . . soon you will be fast asleep . . .* But he did not. Instead, he drew his hands lightly over my face letting them pass over my breasts and belly. Never did he actually touch; yet their heat was scorchy. After that he began nosing between my legs with his legs. Could this be decent? As his knees urged against my skirts my thighs began to peel apart, a gap opening beneath my winter skirt like an unfolding scarf.

And still he continues to come forward . . . *Will he split me apart like a wishbone?*

"Are you prepared," he now pursues, "to let go of it?"

I know of course what he's talking about. There is nothing else to let go of. But suddenly I am frightened – so frightened I begin shaking all over. He does nothing. Watches. Like Henry. Mildly curious.

"Pain shapes my life," I hear myself whisper.

"Do you mean to say pain *is* your life, Alice?"

I laugh, though I do not find it in the least bit funny. Already, I think, he has betrayed me. Having lured me in by 'reading' my pain, pretending to understand and sympathize, he now speaks disparagingly of it. But I must try and explain:

"Strange as it seems," I say firmly, "I consider myself lucky. Pain has given me . . ."

"What has it given you, Alice?"

"It has given me . . . that is, it is my connection with the world. Even as I am removed, enclosed – hermit-like, nun-like, so to speak – I am open to the outer life around me. Through a glass darkly, perhaps – but that is the power of it – I may – sometimes, if I am lucky – see whole truths undistorted by the normal hustle and bustle inhabited by the healthy. And when it lets go, the world renews itself, like a fog clearing. So much so that I have almost wished for it with as much fervor as I have begged for its release."

"You admit, then, to a certain perverse enjoyment of it, perhaps even an attachment to it?"

You have misunderstood.

"It also contains my story, my history: the memories of my brothers, my Aunt, my parents, my childhood, New England; they are all connected with it and cannot be separated. It has been my lifelong companion. It is therefore not something to *get rid of* just like that." I snap my fingers in his face.

"You are married to your pain then?" he suggests mockingly.

Another laugh, fiercer this time, more like a bark. The way he puts it. Twisting my words. I lash out, only he is ready for me.

"Now now, Alice," says he, grabbing my wrists, "let us have no violence."

I am undone. Disarmed. My body like milk or heavy cream, slowly curdling in the muzzy heat of the room. Only my mind still floating free.

After that he looks me up and down as if assessing me for a fitting. "Next time," he informs me, "you will wear no corset or stays, or any other such female *contraptions*." He means, I suppose, my undergarments.

At this Katharine, who has on this occasion sat quietly in a corner pretending to read a book, is completely unmannered. Her face is livid as she looms over him. He rises to meet her, a hand guarding his own face. The left hand, it is.

Katharine stares at it. It is missing its fourth finger, she notices. By which time he has slipped away.

Later Katharine scolds me for a dupe. When I describe my 'hypnotic rapture' she throws up her hands: " Tosh! leave it alone!" Then she begins interrogating me with uncharacteristic suspicion, "Why must he stroke your arm? For what purpose must your bosom be bared?" To which I can only reply vaguely that it is all part of the 'hypnotic touch'.

"You trust him then?" she charges.

"Yes," I shout back, "yes I do, oh I do!"

Her face by this time is all blotchy. "Oh Alice, will you allow him to befool you?"

I laugh then, accuse her of jealousy.

She laughs back.

At which I see – feel – something else rising in her: *disgust*. Is that too strong a word? a lip-curling, toe-curling creeping thing attaching itself to me like a foul smell? No, it is not too strong. I am becoming less – there, I see it – in her eyes.

How could I believe in him? How could I allow myself to behave in such a common way?

"You admire him, Alice," she accuses: "deny it."

"His technique is effective," I admit."

"His technique," she snorts. "You mean his cheap seduction technique? It only makes *you* cheap, Alice."

"Jealousy!"

So it goes on. Our words grow harsher, more wounding. The force of our divergence is frightening. I'm aware of a loosening, a tottering . . . a succession of moments, each one wearing away . . . wearing down . . . a pumice stone on a calloused heel. The thing we have created between us – what to call it? – regard, loving forbearance – I hardly know – will it now – *go*? I see that she sees me, cruelly illuminated, as *vulgar*. What can I do about it?

"That is easy: refuse to see him again."

"Refuse?"

"Yes, refuse, ever again."

"Oh, but I cannot do that."

"Oh, but you *can*."

"No. I can*not*."

She grabs her briefcase and leaves the room.

"Where are you going . . . Katharine . . .?"

Forty-six

"No *corset*?" cried an incensed Wardy.

"It's alright," I told her, "you may close your mouth – and put the ungainly thing away." She was holding it around the waist as if it were a waltzing partner. "There's nothing sinister in it," I assured her, "It's merely so that I may breathe freely under the hypnotic influence."

She sniffed. "I don't like it, nor the way he makes free with his hands."

"Oh," said I provocatively, "but *I* do!"

When she'd finished flapping she asked, "But what does he expect you to wear? Must you go about naked under your garments, Miss?" Fuming like a fire she slapped her sides: "It ain't decent!"

"Do calm down, Wardy," I advised: "your grammar is slipping. I will wear the new knickers and the chemise with the shaped gussets." She herself had convinced me to buy such things as advertised in one of her women's magazines.

"And what will hold up your stockings?"

I rolled my eyes. "You have heard of garters, I presume?" And, truth to tell, it was a relief to be unboned and unmoulded, to not have my flesh pushed this way and that to create a false form. Besides, he was right: I *could* breathe more freely.

"Stand up," ordered Bowles making his lubricious way into the parlor. I stood. He looked me up and down as if he found my droopy person a disappointment; which I thought monstrously unfair as it was he who ordered the de-corseting in the first place.

Although it rankled to do so, I said – smoothing my skirt

over my non-existent hips – "I have done as you requested." Most women, as I well knew, wore the things to rein in their flesh whereas it was the opposite for me. Without the corset's false hourglass form I was flat and straight as a plank.

"Turn please."

Please? I turned, revolving slowly while he took in the disappointing sight of what he called my 'natural' shape: broad but flat, as if I'd been pressed and dried like a floral specimen, my dress a husk leached of color and moisture.

"Sideways please."

Again, I obeyed, seeing myself through his eyes as a thin and insubstantial stick figure. Well, so much for appearances! I thought (and what a good example of William's 'dissimulation', and Henry 'narrowness of vision'), for only on the surface was I such a dim, grey creature. I am like a carrot, I longed to tell him: a dim, dusky purple on the outside; but cut it open and its true nature will be revealed to you with its vibrant orange core.

But there was Wardy standing guard in the doorway.

He reached out – it was as if I'd been handed a galvanic ball – and guided me towards the nursing chair where he reached behind him and, without looking at her, gave the signal for Wardy to leave us. Which she did, making her displeasure quite clear by blowing like a whale from inside her own bony mouldings.

After she'd gone, Bowles sat with his hands folded in his lap and his head bowed as if in prayer, though it seemed unlikely that that was what he was actually doing. It is all part of the performance, I told myself, as his head began to loll to one side. Was he actually falling asleep, or had he put himself into a trance? At which his arms shot up forcing his clasped hands apart, and he reached out to me like a conductor to his orchestra. Or an ape to its mate.

So we begin. First he tells me my universal fluid has been blocked. How do you know? I ask. He does not look pleased, It is my business to know. What will you do? I ask. I will unblock it, he says. I say it sounds alarming and he says, Do you or don't you want to be well, Alice? I do, I say, I do, Arthur.

Good.

So we proceed. First, he needs to know what the pain is like. Which is disappointing as it reminds me of all the other doctors who have ever attended me. What is the pain like, Alice? Ho hum. So I tell him description comes best from a clear mind not a pain-wracked body, as my brother Henry well knows.

Bowles takes a deep breath, as if filling himself with patience: *Your brother is not my business.* Then:

Do you mean to say you are in pain as we speak, Alice? I am.

Very well. Now, Alice, tell me about your pain.

My pain, I begin . . . stop. I want to compare it to a wild animal, as I have done before, but the truth is that aside from my pater's stuffed animal collection and the Newport raccoons and foxes, and a white stoat that Katharine and I once saw scuttling along the Leam, I have little exerience of wild animals. So instead I say:

It is like a cat, a very large cat with jowls and a neck like a pig and fur thick as a polar bear's.

And what does the cat do, Alice?

He strikes with both paws, grabs on and refuses to let go.

Like a crab?

Well, I suppress a titter, a furry crab . . . should such a thing exist.

And where does he strike?

Today my spine.

Where on your spine?

Mostly the base but when he gets bored with that, he works his way up and begins sharpening his claws on my shoulder blades.

Ah – it is his turn for levity – the way my landlady's cat does on the frame of my sofa.

I am not a sofa, Arthur.

No, Alice, I realize that. So, he continues: he has got your shoulder blades in a sort of wrestler's lock, is that right? And will not let go causing the pain to vibrate up and down your body until you must scream or pass out?

I would not have described it so melodramatically myself, but that is not unlike how it is.

Good (deep breath). And what will persuade him to let go? Is there anything you can think of?

That's obvious: a plate of chicken livers, or roasted skin. Oh, and blood. He laps blood like milk; indeed, he prefers it.

Ve-ery good, Alice. Eyes closed, pleased. Now imagine the cat as he sniffs the offering; what does he do?

He lets go.

Yes! He retracts his claws, dropping off your spine, and makes for the skin and blood . . . And you experience the pleasure of release.

No, Arthur, you're wrong there, it is not pleasure. At first it is as if my bones do not know what to do with themselves and so they contract with an even worse pain. It feels as if the damage is done and cannot be undone.

But it can. Keep breathing, Alice. Remind yourself, the cat is not there, nothing is there. He has jumped off and has attacked the plate of food, gulping like the animal that he is.

That means he could jump back again – as soon as he has finished his meal, if he so chooses.

In which case you must learn to tame him, domesticate him . . .

Put him to sleep?

Why not, he has eaten heartily and is sure to be feeling drowsy. But first I suggest giving him a name.

What sort of name?

An emasculating sort of name.

A name for my cat-like pain that will render it flaccid, impotent, powerless?

As you say.

Alright, I tell him, thinking: *Dainty – Slight – Cloake – Mrs Parlour – Dovedale – Gyves – Tagus – Couch – Noad* . . .

But names are not just names, as my brother well knew. They are portraits-in-a-word, the summation of possibility, musical appelations, labels that determine, haunt, fix forever, transmute . . .

Alice?

I am right here, Arthur.

Potcher – Drabble – Perch – Pudney – Trendle – Gaye . . .

I do not have all day.

Okay, I have decided. He's called Cridge.

Excellent. A Cridge wouldn't be capable of hurting you. You are smiling, Alice?

That's because Cridge is purring, crossing his paws like a giant pink-nosed bunny in a shop window. But I know he's only acting, that he will strike again. Cridge is only pretending to look cute.

Never mind anticipating what he will do, how is it now, the pain?

There is an ache, a stiffness, a weariness, but the electrical current pain, the cutting nerve-blasting pain, the slicing of blade pain – has retreated.

Good. I'm pleased with you. You are over the worst.

But Cridge will strike again. His hunger for inflicting pain is insatiable.

But so is his hunger for food, Alice. At this point Bowles's mouth is close to my cheek, to my ear, his breath brushing my skin so all the tiny hairs are alerted.

Besides, he whispers, *Cridge does not exist.*

Panic'd, I reply, Do you mean to do something about him? For as strange as it may seem, the idea of destroying Cridge, now that I have created him, seems monstrous.

Don't you want him gone forever, Alice?

I . . . I don't know. By now I'm feeling confused, by Bowles's scent and the power, however absurdly employed, of my own imagination. In any case, I feel I must not betray

Cridge because Cridge – now I see it – is part of me, however damaged, not to mention damaging. Finally I manage to stammer:

If I got rid of him it would be like, like . . .

Like what, Alice?

Like destroying part of myself.

But he is your *attacker*, Alice, a creature who makes you *suffer*.

Yes yes, even so . . . . but even the most sadistic character – Gilbert Osmond, for instance – you have read it, I assume? – is not so easily disposed of. So it will take time to get rid of Cridge.

You are not writing a novel, Alice.

No, but this is an exercise of the imagination, is it not?

His eyes swivel loosely about as he slaps his thighs bringing our session to an abrupt end.

Forty-seven

"I'll warrant," Wardy accused, "he makes you stare into his eyes, crawl about like a babe, and moo like a cow."

"What do you take him for," I shot back, "a Svengali?"

"I daresay he does not have a Jewish nose," she allowed.

"Wardy," I scolded, "it is ignorant to believe that character can be read in terms of racial features any more than in bumps on the skull."

She shook her head, "Oh, but Miss," warned she: "I heard tell of one poor lady who was so possessed she made faces when *he (Bowles)* drank vinegar, started when *he* pricked himself with a pin, and no doubt would have given herself up for hanging when *he* committed murder!"

Had she forgotten it was her suggestion to consult him in the first place? Evidently. Well, had I wished to add fuel to her anti-mesmeric fire I could have told her about poor little Verena Tarant in The Bostonians who could do nothing without her father 'winding her up'; but I would not. Nor about Elizabeth Browning, who they say was 'creeped out' by the whole mesmeric exercise (it 'jangled her nerves' and 'curdled her blood'). Instead I told her about Harriet Martineau: "*She* was completely cured of her incurable cancer through mesmerism *and* taught her own servant how to do it." At which the melodramatically-inclined creature threw up her mitts and threatened to leave saying she would not be turned into no hocus-pocuser, and anyway Miss Martineau was no doubt a witch. And away she flounces.

At which Katharine took up the theme (I'd been bamboozled, hoodwinked, duped, etc.):

"Are you to be his *fish*?" she asked.

"It's you," I flung back, "who make me wriggle."

"I'm only trying to protect you."

"Trying to stop me . . ."

"Yes, stop you making a fool of yourself."

"Hwo-hm."

"Please, Alice."

Please? I sensed the suffering but cared nothing for it. My Kath had come to seem almost dull to me – her voice muffled, her face a smudge – compared to Bowles' scythe-like presence: how he cut through my resistance and how the light struck his blade-like edges. Was I mad? Oh, looking back – but that's too easy – it was like painting a clown's face over a priceless Della Robbia *rilievo*. But I'd become brazen, even a little reckless; that cruel, hard streak again: *heartless Alice*.

Finally she said:

"You must give him up or else."

"Or else what?" I knew of course what she meant.

"I am quite serious, Alice."

"I do not believe you," I lied.

"Then you do not know me at all."

The air had thickened between us until we were like two wooden spoons stuck in a cooking pot of hardball.

"Alright," I pronounced at last: "if you are going – then go."

"Are you quite sure, Alice?" She gave me this one last chance to change my mind but I was too far gone. At which – a triumph of timing – Bowles appeared. They slid past each other like eels in a too-narrow tank; Katharine departing with one last furious, sad, backward gaze.

What would she do, go where? I wondered, picturing her launching herself out into the world only to become hopelessly stuck in a blur of misery, having to hold to a railing to stop the trembling, biting her lip until it bled . . . To be so *cast out*. But she must *do* something, I saw, for people are beginning to stare, so she makes her purposeful way to the home of Charlotte Guest, or perhaps Mrs Cookson, or the famous Josephine Butler. Or will she go further and 'give herself up' to Constance Woolson on the Continent . . .?

"Alice," Bowles snaps his fingers. The mortifying scene I'd conjured, and the self-reproach – dear Kath, should I call her back? – instantly dissolves. *He* stands before me; is with me. I rise to greet him in all my natural glory; which is to say uncorseted, my vibrant orange essence shimmering before him.

You may sit, Alice.

I sit. He has done something to the seating arrangement, I perceive. Our chairs are closer than ever.

Are you ready, Alice?

I move my head; let him take it for a nod.

Then you will close your eyes, reach into your body to find a switch. There may be one central switch, say, at the base of your spine, or several linked switches. Take your time locating them, please.

Silence while I search about in the dark of my interior.

He takes my hands in his. At which all apprehension vanishes. A pleasant thrill runs from my fingers throughout my body . . . my heart pounds with joy . . . what he wishes for, I wish . . .

Now imagine turning off the switches, Alice.

But I have not found them yet, Arthur. Fortunately, I am still in charge enough of my faculties to decide for myself. I will let him be the caller, I will dance to his tune, but I will *not* fall under his 'spell'. And I will submit only so long as it takes to strengthen my nervous system, alleviate my female complaints and debilitating headaches, and tranquillize my mind. After that, he will be dismissed.

He is clearing his throat, flexing his nine fingers:

Alice, there are many different switchboxes, each clearly labelled: one for the right leg, one the left, and one for every other place in the body. Are you with me?

I am with you, Arthur.

You can see the wires to those switches, the nerves that carry sensation, pain, from one place to another and all passing through those switches. Are you still with me, Alice?

Oh yes.

Now all you need to do is reach up and turn off the switches.

And then?

Then you will feel nothing, no sensation will get through.

No pain?

The pain will be damped down because you have turned off the mechanism that controls that particular pain. You have used your mind to switch it off. It is in your hands, Alice. Now, shall we try it?

I nod again, which means I allow him into my body where I follow him down, down until I find the source of the pain which I suppose is my womb which is contracting and cramping and pumping blood again, and I push him out of the way and go flick to the switch which I locate somewhere deep and secret.

Well?

The pain is still there but somehow cannot get to me. No sensation can get through because *I* have turned off the switch – or rather *he* has used the power of *his* mind – or *my* mind directed by *his* mind to control *my own* body – so that it will obey *him* . . .

It's a start, he says. Now you will count to five before opening your eyes. By which time he has gone.

Forty-eight

He insinuates his hand, popping buttons one by one so they fly off, then peels back my skin until I am like one of those Vesalius illustrations in different shades of gory pink. He has opened me up and now he will step inside to assess me and then correct me: unkink my spine, massage my hardened womb, ease my thickened heart, unblock my pinhole of a digestive tract, revivify my slack stupid muscles.

He is a bee and I am his flower. Bowles the bee. See how he pokes his neck forward and back, forward, back, pulling and sucking at the pain, sucking it out of me until I am a clean hollow tube. Only I am mistaken, he is no bee and I am the buzzing foolish one. I know this because he keeps shaking his head, whipping it around so hard his hair is all flopped across his forehead and he has to throw it back again. Tell me, what have I misunderstood, Arthur? My voice is beseeching which I detest. He tells me to listen carefully. Which I am doing. So then he sets off again on one of his owlish drones which threatens to put me back to sleep:

Now you will make yourself go numb, Alice . . .

I want to cry out. But I have spent my life making myself go numb!

On he goes soporifically:

Your eyes are closed, Alice but your mind is awake because you want to learn to use your own hypnotic abilities . . .

I note he does not use the word 'mesmeric'. He admits the practice has long been discredited; although I am not sure I like 'hypnotic' any better.

that numb feeling

in your right arm, or your nose, or left ear
a tiny area of numbness
a comfortable tingling feeling
a heavy, thick numbness
that grows and spreads

His face is so solemn as he intones, his voice so owlish I am tempted to reach out and tickle him. Is this poetry or pap?

until it just seems to disappear
so you don't know how it feels
because it's as if it's not there
and if it's not there it cannot hurt.

Very logical, I hear myself mutter as on he goes encouraging me to pinch myself in one of the numb areas. So that is what I do, I reach up and seize my nose between thumb and forefinger as if to stop a sneeze, digging in with my nails until I feel . . .

Nothing.

Am I right, Alice? Do you see how it is? How you can make sensation disappear, learn how to allow your deeper mind to turn off those painful areas in your body until there is no discomfort at all, there is nothing . . .

But he is wrong. There is blood on my hand and my nose is already swelling like a turnip. Yet it's his next words that truly make me want to weep:

Only I cannot do it for you: you must do it for yourself.

Must I? I cry, already bereft. Must I always always do it for myself?

He nods. More flopping hair. That is what I have been trying to tell you, Alice.

Oh damn.

Forty-nine

His two tricks having failed he now proposes a more 'radical' approach involving a deal of heavy breathing interspersed with rude snorting noises.

Are you ready, Alice?

I say I am.

Now, Alice, your body is becoming heavy and limp . . .

Like a sack of potatoes?

Alice . . .

If I go on like this he will walk out of the room and not come back and I will have lost him. I apologize. Please. Proceed. Which he does, rising and coming towards me so that I feel the heat of his body closing in. The next thing I know he is taking my hand and, placing it lightly upon his upturned one, rising me from my chair. Eyes closed, Alice, he reminds me and then *Trust me* as he leads me across the room with the easeful assurance of a dancing master. My usual stumbly gait is gone. I am light as light itself and able to dance any dance so long as he is holding me in his arms and moving me about.

I am about to bump my nose into the wall.

I reach out with my free hand to stop myself.

Good, he coos, though I have no idea what it is I have done or not done that merits his praise. Yet it pleases me. Except I must not let it, I am not that silly. Now he releases the other hand and places it alongside the other so that both hands are flat against the wall as if searching for a secret panel.

What do you feel? he asks, and I reply: *a wall* and begin describing the texture of the paper and so on, but he is not interested in *all that*. Then what? There is a long silence in which he is filling himself up, with what I do not know, but whatever it is it will soon be transferred to me, so *I await it with anticipation*.

The heat of his body.

His fingers hover along my spine, never actually meeting fabric yet having already plunged in and scoured me out –

Now, Alice, I want you to go on feeling the wall with your
fingers

until something happens
something begins to give way
soften
until you are no longer aware of the wall's solidity,
until it really is no longer a solid barrier
until it has dissolved and you are
moving through into another dimension
a new reality, Alice, deeper . . . further . . .
into the real world

The real world? I echo.

yes the real world
where you feel more alive, more clear-headed
than you have felt for a long while
without pain or paralysis
where the world is like a painting come alive
where . . .

Are you with me, Alice?

My mouth opens but nothing emerges. He tells me I am capable of more. I want to believe him; but what more? Before I learned to cork myself up I felt charged with possibility (did not William call me a 'spurting fountain' and 'bottled lighting'?). But here he is inviting me to touch the source of life, its flow, its connections, its *dissolving walls*. *There are no barriers if you allow yourself to expand*, to touch *the source*. It is all hocus-pocus, I want to shout, but something stops me. What? I think of my brother Henry and his stories of the 'strange' . . . and William's *unseen world* from which, so he believed, the soul received its best nourishment. Was William's *ghayh* the same as Arthur's?

My head is starting to bang.

He leads me back to my place where he tells me I am now *pregnant with possibility*, and I believe him (a miracle!), and he says I am now infused with vital influence (bottled lightning!) and will soon have the power to sensitize my own body so that next time, next time, *you will be able to control the pain within your own body* – and even this I believe. Even so, it is all too much and I slump forward in a heap with blood gushing down my legs. Wardy comes running, "What is it, Miss, has Bowles done you a damage?" We look around, but he is no longer present to be chastised.

Fifty

"What d'you mean, he's not there?"

"I *mean*," she explained ponderously, "he no longer lodges in his rooms in Spencer Street, body and soul swept out, shingle removed. His landlady said he made off during the night, though he'd paid her more than enough to cover the rent. 'He was generous that way,' says she. 'Generous with Miss James's money, you mean', says I."

I interrupted her saga. "Surely he left a forwarding card?"

Her look said: *Which of us is the clever mistress and which the stupid servant?*

So that was the end of Bowles. And Katharine. Could anything be more deliciously cruel? It put me in mind of Henry and his art, the fierce purity of it, like bathing in ice water. I turned to my dressing table mirror: *What has Bowles done to me?* I asked of it. The answer came: *Nothing. He never intruded like a doctor with his disagreeable questions; nor took your pulse nor examined your tongue nor used some horrid percussor or stethoscope to listen for your heart.* So there.

All true, I acknowledged. And another thing, I confided: His ear once approached my bosom as if it were a pillow made of a thousand gosling feathers, but just as I was preparing myself to receive the weight and warmth of him he 'came to' and pulled away, more's the pity.

The mirror was mum, as if it had decided I was no longer worth speaking to.

What was I to conclude, then: that I'd been 'taken for a ride'? Should I admit to degradation? Or deny it was anything at all; that Bowles had come and gone having proved himself a fake, leaving the surface of my life as unruffled and tranquil as glass? My mind was a walnut – one that had been split open – while I kept trying to restore it to what it had been – my hands shaking – desperate to fit myself back together again. But, look, it's impossible: *I cannot make it fit.*

It was not merely my mind that had split apart but my whole *self*.

Alice: how to match her with she who had been before?

From time to time Bowles returned to me: *You alone have the right to decide what is wrong with you.*

I can make him last forever, I thought, wrapping his words around me like a greatcoat. Then, employing his *method of suggestion*, I 'tuned into' the pain – visualized 'Cridge' letting go with his claws – turned off switches – went numb – refused – the pain. *Bowles' Gift*: a fine title for a story, I thought, though I was too busy controlling switches and numbing myself to think of writing. Then, by the end of the week it happened as he'd predicted: I was able to walk without Wardy's help. I ordered a breakfast of scrambled eggs accompanied by toast and coffee; afterwards went to the toilet without having to strain and bleed. The other bleeding had stopped along with the cramping. And my spine seemed to have stacked itself into its rightful position with my head, migraine free, balanced just-so upon my neck.

"Well," I announced brightly to Wardy, "it appears that I have been cured by Mr Bowles after all."

"You have not been *cured*, Miss," she snorted: "you have been *seduced* – if you'll forgive me saying so."

"No, I will *not* forgive you" – I banged my fist for emphasis, adding: "how can you be so vulgar?" No, it would not do: such a trite, predictable, morally unserious outcome must not attach itself to me. Henry had written about such things in relation to 'feminine' fiction but *I* could never be so susceptible, or silly. No, it tremendously would not do. I picked up the nearest missile, my hairbrush, and flung it at her with enough force to crack a mirror. She ducked. Then on she went, *goose*, ignoring all my protestations and denials, to describe in gruesome detail (but how did she know?) the symptoms of the *commonest* of 'conditions': a fast-beating heart, bright, glassy eyes, an excess of energy. Which must be denied, strenuously. Though later, after she had gone to bed, I shocked myself by crying out, "Damn, am I never to be allowed to do the common thing?"

The answer returned: *No*.

Fifty-one

Bowles spoiled things.

Wrong. *I* spoiled things. I allowed myself to be hypnotized.

Before Bowles, I recalled, there had been a steadiness to my days: a sweet sameness, moments anticipated, repeated, relished. Daily excitements. The small things I cared about: a piece of finely-wrought prose – letters from home – newspapers – the taste of coffee – watching clouds – rain – *pain*. Even (or do I mean especially?) getting into bed, the realization of it – mattress, sheets, pillow, quilt – a relief so intense I'd lie there thinking *I am no more*. The kindest kind of death.

Then came Bowles.

After Bowles all that was lost to me: the steadiness, the pleasurable sufficiency. In Bowles' wake I was left feeling empty, implausible. I saw that I had been living – as Henry might have put it – on the wrong side of the tapestry. How could that faded, fatiguing daily grind have been enough? What did any of it matter? And why should I care? All was one: another marriage, another death, another doctor; a slice of toast to nibble one's way through with the industry of a gerbil . . . a nonsensical letter from Aunt Kate about sailing on a piano round the garden . . . another of William's annoyingly facile prescriptions ("Learn to do a fast crawl, Alice . . . good for the heart!")

Katharine. Must I 'rate' her beside the warm drinks and the watching of clouds? Yet how else to assess the damage? Our 'connection' was – had been – neither a marriage nor a commonplace companionship. We'd struggled to create something new yet as real, as intimate, as that enshrined institution. A way of being together that was original. Let us be different, we'd said, claiming something we knew to be profound without falling into a pattern. A female friendship? Oh let us simply *be* together. *Simply*? It was as if a sliver of bone had got stuck crossways in my gullet. A permanency, we'd called it. Which included the time we were not actively together, having agreed that the fine, invisible filaments uniting us – infinitely stretchable, would hold *no matter what*.

Did that mean, I dared to anticipate, it was reclaimable?

But I am getting ahead of myself. My thoughts at that stage still revolved obsessively around Bowles. His image in the washing bowl, in the face of a flower, superimposed on Katharine's photograph. The shame of it. Conscience, it is true, forced me to consider her; but my hypocritical body still yearned for him.

I made excuses for his defection. I'd offended him by failing to respond to his 'procedures' – so I reasoned – employing the warped logic of heartache. I was a hopeless case, he'd have concluded, deciding to move on; in which event, I told myself – poor ninny – I may be able to track him down. Doubt arose like an itch yet I would not scratch. Have faith, Alice, I told myself in the way of the fatally deluded. I got Wardy to bring me copies of all the spiritualist and clairvoyant journals. I searched the small advertisements for Bowles the Mesmerist. But the thing went on and he failed to appear, magically or otherwise. Disappointment coated me like wax.

The feelings, where would they go? There was an irrepressible aliveness about them, like fibrous, dense bulbs ready to swell and proliferate. Yet no implantation must take place, no watering, no encouragement whatsoever. Their tendrils – to continue the metaphor – must be forced to dry out, curl up, their 'heart' lose its vital substance.

That was not the end of the matter however. Presently

some other force took hold of me. Much of the physical pain and lethargy had already drained away, but this other thing – a lovelorn fury? – left me awake and *fizzing* – such a word – to my toes. Never mind William's 'spurting fountain', this was more like Old Faithful, a previously repressed spume 'letting rip'.

For a time I amused myself with watching the clouds as they billowed up, coupled, separated again, dashed about behind the jumble of stepped gables, chimneys and – craning my neck – the clocktower with its widows' walk. Then the curlicues of my own wrought-iron balcony came into focus, with the shrubby flowers Katharine had planted. *I must ask her to repot them*, I found myself thinking before remembering that she had gone. Finally I watched the raindrops: the classic occupation of solitary spinsters, celibates, *poets*.

Soon I was trading the hot heavy comfort of hemp and opium for the fresh stimulus of the early morning air. I barely recognized my newly functioning body as it trotted along the lanes of Leamington, and had me shoveling food into its maw until it was bloated as a bladder. What was I to do with it? One had to look after it like a horse or it would fall into a decline: feed it, exercise it, water it.

Why was this happening to me? Was I being tested like Job? punished for not appreciating Katharine enough? Or was it the old old story which all of us James children knew by heart: *Know this: there is only so much of life's gifts (genius, good health, etc.) to go around.*

Picture a scales: on one side is balanced rude health, on the other love.

You cannot have both, Alice.

But I did not mean to choose.

Ah but you did.

But I did not reckon on the price.

Tant pis.

So that was that. The only durable meaning I could

squeeze from the encounter with Bowles was this strange condition of mine, this cruel joke called 'being well.' Yet what good was it to me now that I was alone? I thwacked my walking stick along the railings and lampposts with such force that people shied away.

Fifty-two

"So," I observed, "the prodigal daughter returns." She shied away like a large, bone-shy animal. I reached out for her. "Please . . ." Still she hesitated. It saddened me to see her so nervous of me, as if I might attack her with my claws. "I am not a tiger," I said. The tabloid headlines that week had blared the news of a circus tiger turning on its beloved master and biting off his leg. I dared to take her hand. The skin was dry and sere, one of her fingers swollen. "It's nothing," she said, covering it with her other hand, as if it too was a mark of her shame. But surely it was I who should be beating my breast crying mea culpa.

"It was nothing but a *huff*," she declared, shaking herself as if to dislodge any remaining vestiges of huffiness.

I denied it as a 'mere huff'; rather a dramatic response. To which I added: "actually quite reasonable . . . under the circumstances."

She drew herself up. "That is why I should not have claimed it for myself."

"Oh," I went on, "but Henry believes in it implicitly . . .".

"Precisely. Louisa and Henry are the dramatic ones."

"Yet we respond to them . . . to *it*," I pointed out.

"It is impossible not to: that is the problem. It is coercive and cynical. It uses its influence, charm, power, whatever might be adventitious to one's cause. I cannot condone it. Insofar as my action was 'a drama', I repudiate it."

I did not blame her for it, I said.

"Oh but I blame myself."

"Do not . . ."

She cut me off: "I'm sorry, Alice." Her very unreproach-fulness reproached me.

"No," I shook my head: "it is I who drove you away . . ."

She covered my mouth with the swollen hand. "The important thing," she declared, "the thing I realized while away, was what a mistake it was – so cowardly – to leave you when I did . . . in the position you were in. It was, is, my place to stay with you, see you through the Bowles" – she waved a hand not knowing what to call it – "*affair*." She scanned my face for clues:

"I assume he is still . . . around."

I did not reply and she did not press me.

"I have returned, Alice," she continued, removing her spectacles, "because my conscience told me I must. I will vouch for you. I am your friend, your helpmeet, Alice, in wisdom as well as folly. I do not deny that it hurts, but I am determined to support you through it."

I could not but help but smile at her speechifying tone. "And if I do not 'get through it'?" I asked.

Turning to face me – to consider the possibility – a point of light struck her eye: the eye a cold body, the light a hot, needle-like shaft causing the cold body to melt at its touch, the eye to brim over.

"Oh, I really don't know," she admitted, once again shrinking from me. The pain of having been shut out, of being unfavored, of having had to witness an attraction she could not match, remained.

Did she fear contamination from Bowles? I wondered. So far as she knew I was still 'attached' to him and his course of treatments. Nor did I disabuse her of the notion. I confess it; I deliberately withheld the truth, prolonging her suffering. Heartless Alice? Yes and no. The truth as ever was compli-cated. My original 'romantic susceptibility' to Bowles shamed me of course, but having been abandoned by him somehow shamed me even more; as if that would make her think less of me. But so it was. She had returned to stand by

322

me – and would soon discover there was nothing to stand by – no intruder against whom I required protection. I was tempted to tell her that I'd dismissed him – thrown him out for an adventurer – if only I had! – but I could not bring myself to lie to her.

Did I still want her? she asked simply. It was her bravery that touched me then, her capacity for self-reproach, for correction for . . . I recalled her saying of herself she was hopelessly constant. On the contrary, I told her, that constancy *is* the hopeful thing.

Of course I want you . . . goose.

So to the ravelling, the moment by moment re-connecting. But of what had those invisible filaments been made; and had enough of them survived?

For the first two nights after her return, we slept together in the way of strangers, keeping a 'safe' distance. But by the third night I could bear it no longer. I must do something, I vowed, to reclaim her, re-learn her; replace 'she-who-was-not-Bowles' – and therefore a disappointment, a second-best – with she who was irreplaceably best.

But first I had to make sense of her, be *convinced* of her; and so I set out to 'read' her, yes, like a book; oh, not some potboiler full of mesmeric magicians and swooning damsels, but a rugged yet gentle New England story such as Sarah Orne Jewett might write.

It took place, to begin with, in the dark., and lasted most of the night, for nothing must be missed out, head to toe, front to back. There the story of her revealed itself word by word, image by image. No page was turned too quickly. Its underlying structure was exposed as my thumbs met bone. Once or twice she moaned but mostly she slept through it. In the morning there were bruises (kindly, unintentional).

"Do they hurt?" I asked.

She replied, "I thought you'd given me up."

"No."

"Well then," she asked, "when is he coming again?" Her

fingers tightened in anticipation around mine. Still, I made her wait. When it couldn't be avoided any longer I confessed:

"He is not – will not – come again." I told her of his defection.

"Alice!" For a moment I thought she would slap me. "You little tease!"

How could I deny it? I could not. But her flutter of fury was quickly overwhelmed by relief. Bowles was gone for-ever. She pressed me to her until we were scored back into each other's being, until we 'fit' again'; the restoration of what you might dare to call, along with sorrow, love.

Do not be fooled, Reader, we were not – could not be – as before. I was yet prone to conjuring him up kneeling at my feet, kissing my hand &etc. Katharine, observing what she called one of my dreamy 'sluttish' expressions, would refrain from asking where I'd been. Which was wise of her. Yet even as I allowed myself to wallow in the language and imagery of romance, I knew it for tripe. I blame it on Charlotte Yonge and her ilk. All those years of romance imbibed. Lovers constant and inconstant, present and absent, real and con-cocted – love would correct everything. 'My saviour!' cries our heroine. Shame on her – and me. Imagine nearing forty before learning to distinguish between attraction – or 'in-clination' as Henry had put it – and 'constancy'. Still, it took time, time not just to see that Bowles had been a kind of fiction – like a book you devour in one sitting then forget for the rest of your life – but to feel it. Yet it happened, the morning on which I woke up and saw not Bowles the mesmerist but my friend Katharine. She who would *endure*. As she never tired of reminding me, the whole beauty of our relationship was in its 'balance'. There must be no 'victor' and hence no 'victim' ('saving' or even hypnotic 'healing' would therefore not come into it). Neither would dominate the other. "That is the whole point," argued my dear returned Katharine. "We are, as it were, collateral: no super-ior, no inferior." It was all terrifically sensible.

Fifty-three

My brief flurry of health did not alas continue. The doctor blamed an overstimulated nervous system, as if that nest of nerves had the capacity to plot its revenge against me for a mere fillip. Wardy snorted behind her hand. In her own way, she was relieved to have me back 'as I was'. "You mean you wish me helpless and dilapidated again?" I charged. "I mean," she insisted, " I prefer you with your feet on the ground." "But my feet are not on the ground," as I pointed out, they were raised up on the sofa-bed with extra cushions beneath.

"Oh, Miss . . ."

That I should be so pitied by my nurse!

Later there was a rap at the door, and my brother was announced.

Katharine, who had resented me 'summoning' Henry, now stood by, one hand draped possessively about my shoulders. Perhaps, I considered, she does not trust me with a man; not even – or especially – my own brother.

She asked politely after his stay at the Royal. He allowed it was sufficiently comfortable allowing for an 'overdressed room' and 'an underdressed chop'. He then returned the compliment – if such it was – by asking politely after herself and her family. She summarized the situation by a coolly uninformative: "They are as well as can be expected." Then: "I'm off for a restorative swim if you'll excuse me."

We sat silently together. It was not Henry's intention to 'clear the air' of Katharine but to redefine the room's influence, claiming it for ourselves alone; as if we'd been enveloped together inside a capacious fur wrap.

"How are you, Alice?" Henry asked warmly. It was his first visit since my move to Leamington.

"In your presence," I reported, "I feel entirely restored."

He made a mock-prayerful gesture. "But generally . . .?"

"Oh, generally I am committed to the intricate work of being sick."

"Ah, *the intricate work of being sick*," he repeated, enjoying the sound of it if not its implication. "Yet it is a solution, I suppose?" he went on.

"A solution to . . .".

"Oh the practical problem," he leant forward: ". . . of life."

In spite of my dilapidated *state*, I rose to embrace my brother: how could I not? For only Henry could come up with such a solution . . . to *the practical problem of life*.

"But in answer to your question," I resumed, "I am instantly better for not being asked how *we* are today: for that I thank you, Henry."

"Ah" – he understood my meaning at once – "the medical assumption of plurality."

"They are cowards, Henry."

"But how do you find Leamington?" I asked.

"It is not Paris."

"*Evidement.*"

" 'It is almost as flat as a table'," he began. Recognizing the quote at once, I joined him word for word: " 'and The Parade is obviously much appreciated by the many plump and pleasing and perhaps a little over-dressed dowagers'."

We finished together flushed and panting as if we'd run a race.

"One cannot do better," my brother offered, "than quote Hawthorne." The wink of a dimple suggested itself before retreating back into the crease in his right cheek. But how did I find the neighborhood of Leamington? he wanted to know.

I told him briefly about the Bachelers, on one side, with their five children. And Miss Percy on the other side, how she bustled about cheery-in-the-morning so you wanted to bash her over the head with a stiff broom, yet since she was altogether good natured you didn't. "She looks upon me as a pitiable object. 'Don't you get awfully tired of reading?' she asks; she who spends her hours strumming on her rattle-trap of a piano and is in and out all over the place twenty times a day. "Even so," I reflected, "I guess I'd rather have Miss Percy for interest than many of your great men." "Oh," said Henry, "but that is because you are the exception: you have remained unspoiled and . . ."

". . . virginal?"

"Entirely yourself, Alice."

But he was reminded of Bowles. William, to whom I'd written, had doubtless told Henry all about him.

"And the mesmeric exercise," – he approached the subject in his sidling way – "do you 'rate' it?"

"Oh, I do not *rate* it at all," I told him. "As for its effects, like its practitioner, it did not last." Correct, insofar as it went. But the truth – I was being unfair – Bowles *had* offered me something: a technique which I would be able to use on certain occasions and *would* perhaps afford relief.

"Alas," said Henry letting his fingers spread. Between them dropped paragraph after paragraph of our mingled, unspoken thoughts. We'd both been born, so it might seem, with a foreknowledge of loss, of giving up; a propensity – talent? – for living with less human nourishment in the way that others had to make do with inadequate food. The result in both cases, a kind of hunger.

"But Katharine, I gather" – his timing was impeccable – we were not after all the same in this – "has been returned to you?"

"Yes, yes she has." I was not – the point was made – I felt it keenly – *starving*.

"And yet," he sighed, "you are not entirely well."

What could I say? "I feel sure I will begin to improve."

Henry looked anxiously towards the door.

I reassured him as to her continued absence as she would

327

still be doing invigorating 'lengths' at the ladies' pool. We agreed William would heartily approve.

Then he said this. "You will get well, or you won't," he paused, "but either way it lies between yourselves." He gave a little bob or bow of his head as if inscribing a punctuation mark in space. In the silence that followed it occurred to me that my brother would have sneered at Katharine's idea of 'equality' just as he had sneered at her favorite female historians. Yet he held her equally responsible for my well-being.

Fifty-four

The letter had come from Aunt Kate. *"Dear Alice,"* I read out: *"I hope you are not suffering unduly, and that Katharine is with you, and Henry when he can."* Henry, in the flesh, presented himself. "And how is our admirable Aunt?" he inquired. "She is," I told him – "in her own words – 'as well as can be expected' . . . But there's bad news, Henry." His body strained forward like a leashed hound's; not, I fear, entirely to his credit. The scent of blood did not excite me, it made me feel sick.

"Yes, bad," I repeated. "It's Winny Howells." Winny was the daughter of Henry's friend and publisher Dean Howells. "Not dead – yet," I reported – "but continuing to weaken and lose flesh. Aunt Kate says she can barely stand without support. Weir Mitchell is still force-feeding her like a goose."

"Yes," said Henry recalling how her father had once nicknamed her 'the lunch fiend'. "A rather tasteless attempt," he added, "- one sees it in retrospect – to make light of the matter."

I glared at him. "There was nothing light," said I, "about Winny's condition, now or then."

Henry was silent. Our family had once spent a summer up in Maine visited by Winny and her father, and Lizzie Boott and her father. Even then Winny was 'not well' with her pale cheeks, sunken, glittering eyes ringed with black like a sick raccoon's. We were all gathered on the terrace, I remember, overlooking the ocean, enjoying the cooling breeze while Dean Howells read from one of his stories. I have only a dim memory of the story myself. What I do recall was how halfway through the first installment Winny put her hand to her stomach and asked to be excused, how she stumbled her way into the house.

"Of course she's too thin," our mother had observed, clearing away the remains of the meal, "but she will not touch a morsel. I have tried everything from clam chowder to strawberry ice-cream, but the child will not be tempted."

"She is delicate, certainly," Mr Boott had remarked.

"Well, it *is* the latest fashion," said Lizzie, who knew about such things.

And then William had said he found it romantic, even glamorous.

"She is too young for glamor," Aunt Kate snapped.

Her father, trying to be philosophical, muttered: "I suppose she's going through a phase."

Now I gripped the arms of my chair. "Seventeen years," I said, reflecting back, "is a long time to be 'going through a phase'." No, she was not being stylish, she was *ill*. What were the doctors doing, still calling her hysterical, force-feeding her until her eyes popped and her throat turned into a hen's craw and she could not speak for weeks?

But Henry, for all his exquisite sensibility, was not 'with me' at all; nor, more importantly, 'with' poor Winny as she was. "It was certainly a becoming frailty," he said, persisting in the fiction. "Slight, erect, thin, almost transparent" he went on dreamily – for me, unbearably. Was it that very transparency – as if she were already an apparition – he found so 'becoming'? Henry then – compounding his error – added the words 'ethereal' and 'interesting'- the same ones he'd once used to describe our cousin Minny Temple, now long dead.

Is it 'interesting' to be dead?

Is it easier to love the dead than the living?

I could barely speak for picturing Winny, her legs like arms, her arms reduced to driftwood sticks. I see her holding to the newel posts like some ancient with creaking bones while the rest of us listen to her father reading from his wonderful story. Is it wonderful? Are we 'all ears'? I cannot remember. Oh, but Henry can:

"It was called 'The Wedding Journey'," he says. "I seem to remember it was currently being serialized in the Atlantic . . . terribly good . . . too good to miss."

What can I say? Words, I think, do not merely fail, they betray. I suspect I am producing rather ugly noises, like a train approaching slowly but dangerously out of the dark. Wardy thinks it wise – she is right – to show my brother out. "For your own protection, Mister James," she says darkly. Later Wardy says, "You haven't touched a morsel of your food, Miss." "No," I agree, "I have not."

*

Henry returned the next day to see if I was 'restored'. "I am not a chest of drawers," I sniped, which clearly amused him. Since my sharp tongue was returned to me – so went his thinking – that must mean I was 'myself' again, and the danger passed. I would not maul him.

He examined the chair and finding it up to his exacting standards of dust-freeness, he sat. He had shaved his beard, I observed, so that his jowls were now exposed as well as the deep lines around his mouth like a pair of parentheses. My brother, I saw, was in some distress. He had not slept well, I also observed, judging by the shadowy craters under his eyes. He would soon, he explained – adding "reluctantly, of course" – be leaving Leamington. It could not be helped: London beckoned. But before he went he wished to consult me about a new idea. I lay back and listened.

"There is a young person," he began: "beautiful perhaps, with a great capacity for life . . ."

I tried picturing this emerging character of his – young, female, thirsty for experience.

"I take it, Henry, we are speaking not of a love-match, but of one of your female protagonists?"

He allowed that it was so. "The problem is . . . her life is" – he chose his words carefully: ". . . doomed; that is, compromised by illness."

"I see." Only I lied; I did not. Why, I wanted to shout, make her of all things *sick*? The subject – which I knew only too well – I found repellent; or at any rate, too close to my own experience. But then I recalled a conversation William, Henry and I had once had:

"But Willy, if the self is simply a stream of thoughts, who or what is it then?"

"*They* are," he'd replied. "It's the thoughts that are thinking them . . . they are thinking each other . . . each pulse replaced by another."

"And our tales?" Henry had asked.

"Our tales are spun but we don't spin them," had been William's response: "they spin us."

At the time I'd felt quite indignant, as had Henry (vibrating dewlaps, I noted), but now it began to make sense. Henry, I saw, had no choice: the subject would continue to be the thing – prodigious . . . disturbing . . . impossible – that would – must – claim him.

"She is early stricken," he continued, ". . . disintegrating . . . condemned to die while still enamored of the world."

"And is she also 'enamored' of a worldly being?" I asked. "Do you encourage it?"

"Oh, absolutely."

He regarded me with his keen, appealing eyes. "Yet how is one to write about such things, about illness and infirmity, with good taste?"

I laughed then, a real howler. Which made him rise from his chair and Wardy come running so that I had to reassure them both I was still in my right mind. Well, I could not help myself. For hadn't he already written about an invalid *in good taste*? Indeed, wasn't that was the whole problem with

Rosy Muniment: that hideous, barely disguised parody of me? That it was precisely in 'good taste' was in my view what made it so wretched. I barely knew what to say, how to speak, torn as I was between wanting to help him – enter his fictional imaginings – and fly at him like a taloned harpy and scratch out his eyes crying, *To hell with good taste!* But I'd already caused him enough worry.

"What precisely," I asked, not unkindly, "is the problem, Henry?"

His reply, when it came, involved an admission. "It is not," he hesitated, "a frank subject after the fashion, with its elements well in view and its whole character in its face."

"No," I agreed, "it is not." *You will never succeed, dear Henry, in writing 'after the fashion'.* I was tempted to shout, *Oh, for pity's sake, give it up, Henry – it isn't you!* Truly I could not see why he should be so *bothered* about it – but he was. For however much he was championed as an author appealing to a 'superior literary taste', it was his own secret – deep – desire to write *after the fashion*. Poor Henry, I thought, how he longs to write a novel that will fill the new display cases at WH Smith's; that everyone, even Wardy, will read and gossip about. But he will never do it, I knew, nor must he try. I had some responsibility in the matter: I must convince him to continue doing what he did best.

But I found myself distracted at this point by Henry's tie. He'd forgotten, I noted, to attach Connnie's coin-pin so that said tie flapped loose from his vest. I reached over and tucked it back in.

"There," I patted his ever-expanding bosom before going on with my advice, aware that I was contradicting my earlier, negative, response to the subject.

"But that is precisely why 'the subject' will suit you," I argued. "There will be secrets and compartments, treacheries and traps. Besides," I continued my encouragement, "granted the situation of a sick young woman, menaced with death and danger, is it not the very shortest of all cuts to the most interesting state of all?"

"*The most interesting state of all*," echoed Henry, his lazy lids lifting, pleased with the phrase and its import. "The writer, you mean," he pursued almost excitedly, "*can't* be concerned with the act of dying!" At this, he looked so relieved at finding his way to an 'understanding' that his 'half-dog' face lifted, tightened, and glowed before continuing with more confidence: "Let him deal with the sickest of the sick . . . it is still by the act of *living* that they appeal to him . . . the process of life gives way fighting, to the soul of drama that is . . ."

"Yes, Henry . . ." I waited patiently and was soon rewarded for it. He concluded, quietly triumphant:

". . . the battle against death."

"Precisely," said I, adding a phrase that had come to me, "Live as she could but love as she would."

*

After he left, a story began 'to spin me' (one of William's lovely phrases, that). It was made up of bits and strands, a patchwork of memory, supposition and threadbare fantasy. As for the 'characters' – if I may so dignify them – 'she' is called neither Winny nor Minny but . . . Ginny. The gentleman is called Paul.

The house is quiet when Paul calls to say good-bye. Ginny enters the spacious parlor '*with her swift sliding step and her old free laugh*'. Even as she approaches – the swishing of skirts – a light, attractive scent . . . something else medicinal beneath – it is the observing words which fill him with bursts of pleasure; but they also – he is aware of this – distract him, cut him off. She is even thinner, he observes, paler, more compromised by the bouts of haemorraging which she has been known to suffer and he has heard about. As her icy hand with its bird-bones fills his, the thought enters his mind

She is failing, and at once he is stricken with shame. But he must not allow it or he will be become indecisive. The world is different for Ginny – as it is for the ant or the ancient – she who must steel herself for the cataclysm of what is about to occur: her own abandonment.

"Is it not detestable," she manages to quip (*quip!*), "that you should be going and leaving me behind?"

"Wholly," he agrees, failing utterly to offer the obvious.

But she must sit down, the asking has cost her. "Well, my dear Paul, tell me," she encourages bravely. So he does. He tells her his plans and she pretends to be pleased for him. Her voice manages to be light and tripping. "The doctors talk to me of a warmer climate" – she has not yet given up hope – "perhaps we will meet next winter in Rome?" He notes a barely perceptible tremble at the side of her mouth, a pulsing vein beneath a layer of transparent skin. He is tempted to extend a finger – to 'read' the vein – is there a message for him? – to make the trembling stop . . . He recalls his older brother advising him to be 'more active' in the relationship, more masculine. But he must *not* act or something terrible will happen: she will – they will both – *vanish*. Whereas if he resists, the scene will continue to spin itself forever and she will remain interesting forever, while he will remain . . . free, forever.

He says he will write, and he does. He tells her he has been to see *Frou-Frou* at the Gymnase and has spent hours at the Louvre. He has not been extravagant; he has dined modestly. On the other hand, he has managed to live at the best hotels and done trips in the most comfortable way.

Later Ginny writes to Paul's sister Charlotte saying, 'I am very glad that he has gone, although I don't expect to see him again in a good many years.' She does not see him at all because she will, within the year, be dead of another lung haemorrhage.

Fifty-five

"Henry, Willy is concerned about Aunt Kate." I shook William's letter by one of its corners. "He says she has been found wandering about Quincy Street quite lost."

"Lost . . .?" he echoed. It was Henry's last day in Leamington and he was not concentrating.

"Yes, Henry, *lost*: like a lamb."

The 'subject' of Aunt Kate was an impossible one of course since we had both turned our backs on her. But while the 'subject' of Aunt Kate could be avoided, 'she' could not.

"Henry," I admitted: "I tell myself a dozen times a day I'll write such and such to her, but then I do not. But I will pull myself up and do it today."

My brother produced one of his faux-agonized expressions: yes – certainly – alas – he too had 'neglected' her. But had I, he wanted to know, felt her to be in some way 'prodigious'?

"*Prodigious*?" I scoffed: "*Aunt Kate*?" I was gripped with a sense of her *pliability*, her over-eagerness, her too-willing care of us. But then I caught myself. How must it have been for Henry, a boy, delicate, made much of? Surely it had left him with a softer spot for her in his heart. He looked away. If so, he was unwilling to indulge in 'feelings'. Oh, but her 'secret', *that* he could entertain.

"Her secret, I mean to say," he clarified, "was what made her 'prodigious'." There was no denying it: we cared more for *that* than all her years of looking after us. It was not to our credit.

"*It* could be made much of, certainly," I agreed. "While *she*" – exquisite cruelty – "could not."

He added: "And the infamous Captain Marshall . . .?"

"He was – is – the interesting – *repulsive* – thing."

"And the secret . . .?"

"The violence," I submitted, "was all in his meanness and coldness."

Together, we saw that that would be enough to 'break' anyone; thus, the violent disruption of the marriage.

"I suppose we must not abandon her?" he asked at last.

"Not with impunity."

But the question remained for him: "Did we"- Henry's unpardonable sin – "make use of her?"

"Of course we did," I said: "we allowed her to take care of us; but being children we were by nature ungrateful. And committed, above all, to a good mystery."

We lived through a long, ripening silence. The truth, if such it was, could not be undone.

"What else does Willy have to say?" Henry asked at last.

"He says they are all thriving . . . Alice is run about by their new little Margaret Mary . . . Oh, and they claim she takes after you."

My brother, obviously relieved to be released from the 'subject' of Aunt Kate, said: "I shall send a telegram at once commiserating."

"He tells *me*, silly Willy, to read as much comic literature as I can."

Henry grinned.

"There is, I'm afraid, a 'PS': another death."

"Who . . .?"

"Ellen Hooper's husband." I pronounced his full name: "Ephraim *Whitman* Gurney." As I did so I recalled Ellen's own whistling tone, the breathy adoration with which she'd spoken of him (*Oh, Whitman!*) during that first year of her marriage.

"Of what did he die?" asked Henry.

I scanned the letter again but found no cause of death. "He was," I pointed out, "dean of an entire Harvard faculty." Henry avowed he should not like to carry such responsibility himself; it would not be conducive to one's health. Then he announced, alas, London beckoned; he had "a good deal to do, and besides,"- he gave one of his auctioneer's nods first towards me and then towards the empty rocker where Katharine liked to sit – "a third person is rather a superfluous appendage." I did not disabuse him of the notion.

Later that evening Katharine and I turned to one another. Dean Gurney's death was of course regrettable but it was Ellen, we agreed, who was now at risk. First her father, then her sister Clover, and now her husband: *What would become of Ellen Hooper Gurney?*

Fifty-six

We were right to worry about Ellen: she'd confessed to William she was longing "to join Clover and Whitman". And how had he responded? we queried. By telling her, of course, that she must *live*. Silly Willy. I tossed his letter into the fire.

"Why *must* she live?" I asked Katharine.

"You know perfectly well why," she replied.

"Do I?" I scowled at the curling letter. "So we must spout the usual thing merely because it's expected of us, whip up fortitude and forbearance like a batch of stiff meringues? Oh, live, live, by all means *live*!" One fist reamed the other: "But *why*? why *must* she?"

Katharine removed her spectacles. "What would you advise her instead, Alice: *'Oh, die, die, by all means die . . .'*?"

I refused to be bullied. "Only imagine, Kath," I pleaded my case: "first her father, then her sister, then her husband. How could anyone be so cruel as to wish her to live after so much loss? *That* is why I say nothing would rejoice me more than to hear that she was gone."

"I see," said presiding Judge Katharine. She stuck her glasses back on: "May I take it then that her death would give you no pleasure?"

"You know perfectly well it would not," I replied. "I am not cruel. My heart is wrung for poor Ellen, but I would rejoice *for her sake*, to know that she was out of pain. And after all," I added, "does it not take great courage to discontinue oneself?"

Wordlessly, Katharine reached into a pocket of her skirt and handed me the telegram:

Boston, Nov 1888
I regret to have to inform you of the tragic death
of Ellen Hooper Gurney.

The telegram lay in my lap like a discarded railway serviette. Ellen – so I see her – stands beside the track outside Cambridge near a cluster of sad, old warehouse buildings. A strange place to wait, I think: a straight stretch where the train – the Chicago, Burlington and Quincy line – is known to speed up rather than slow down. And there stands Ellen, dressed for the occasion in her best coat with the fur collar; and as she waits the *parfum* she has dabbed behind one ear and then the other – but what about her wrists? – rises strong, furred and slightly rank- into her own nostrils; and for the first time she thinks of how she will smell later. Will the *parfum* outlast the smell of decay? She is amused to think of it as she swivels her feet in the gravel, jumps on and off the sleepers like a child playing a game of catch-me-if-you-can. Sensibly, instinctively, at the sound of the train's warning hooter off she leaps. That's right, Ellen, *shoo*. Another warning whistle. *Get back, you're standing too close.* By now the wolves are howling like train whistles. As for the birds of night, they're pulling her by her hair with their tiny fangs, up up and away. But their grip cannot hold; here comes the train – *express*; there goes Ellen springing forward as if to an order from our old schoolmistress Miss Hunter:

Jettez, Ellen, jettez.

Katharine went about in a respectful, sad stupor while I reclined with my unforgiving conscience. Rejoice? After the fact, I could not. That someone of Ellen's delicacy should have had such a violence done to it – and that I had somehow wished for it – was not easy to be reconciled with. "Don't be ridiculous, Alice," said Katharine: "You never

340

imagined such an end for her, but only a gentle release from her unhappiness." She was right, of course; yet how to rid myself of the ghastly *impact* of the moment, the collision of iron against flesh and bone?

"All our ripe and mellow are vanishing," I whispered. And with that my own thoughts of 'discontinuance' were set in motion.

*

Ellen's suicide was the second of an accumulation of deaths during that year and into the next. Does their order matter? Katharine would insist 'yes', but I would say 'no'. What matters is that they happened at all, as if some sinister infection in the air around Boston had wormed its way into the brains and hearts of its victims causing them to reach for a vial of poison or make for the nearest cliff or stretch of railway track or . . . .

After Ellen – but before her had come Clover – came Lizzie Boott; then came William's friend Edmund (another of the Gurneys); then our old schoolmistress, Rebecca Hunter.

Came did I say? I mean of course *went*.

Lizzie Boott. She and her husband had been spending the winter in Paris with their infant son when her sudden death was reported. "Pneumonia, they call it," I reported sneeringly.

"You do not credit it?" asked Katharine.

I admitted I did not. It seemed obvious to me that she simply could not cope with the roles of wife and daughter and now mother. "Think," I said, "how she'd clung to her father, and he to her; how they'd seemed more connected, more extreme – dare one say *married* – than any unblooded pair; so that the insertion of a husband, however pleasurable, would come to seem a violent act, the axe with its wedge dividing plant from parent – just not to be endured."

Katharine was silenced. But was it right to acknowledge

341

one's impossible position in so irrevocable, so damaging – for others – a way?

"Not everyone," she added, "is on such familiar terms with suicide as are you."

"Why how dare you, Katharine Loring Peabody." I hated the acts, the bad endings – surely she knew that?

"Yes," she acknowledged, "but by such an act are we not forced into their secret miseries more than we might want to be taken?"

It was undeniably true, I conceded, and undeniably important to the picture. "Still, I say bravo, for though it is, yes, painful for us, is it not brave to suppress one's vanity, to be able to confess that the game is simply too hard for it to continue?"

Only the sound of her rocking, to and fro.

William's friend – the next 'victim' – had used chloroform, altogether a 'sloppy suicide' – so I gathered from William's letter. Gurney had written the definitive analysis of apparitions and ghosts. Now, I thought, he is of their number, untidily bespattered.

And last – oh, but surely not least – on the suicide list, our old teacher herself, Miss Rebecca Hunter. According to a local newspaper report she'd died

'by venturing too near the sea while taking the sea air
along the cliffs where the waves run high
and irregularly, and she was drowned.'

I see Miss Rebecca Hunter. I see her smoothing her skirt as she slides in behind a small table looking freshly scrubbed, hair smooth and shiny, teeth white as baby wool. In her careful and precise way she listens while I or Katharine or the others stumble through our recitations. After that she announces we will go out for a 'blow' leading us in a gaggle along the cliffs.

"Blatant lie!" I cried, throwing the clipping from me.

"Why, what are you impugning, Alice?"

"What am *I* impugning? I yelped. "It is *they* who impugn, who cover up the truth. Think, Katharine, about those cliffs. Did she not tramp them every day of her life? Could she not walk them with her eyes closed?"

Katharine, retrieving the crumpled-up newspaper clipping, smoothed it out and re-read it. A *source*, I muttered, watching her. She takes her clues from written sources, that is what she does, thought I. But not newspapers, for heaven's sake, not newspapers. She put the cutting aside.

"I'm afraid," she admitted, "you're probably right, Alice."

That at least was a relief. "Oh, but why be afraid?" I went on. "Surely it is better that she took control of her own demise than slipped off the edge like some stupid ewe."

"Ewe?" she laughed. "I believe you once called her a moose in skirts."

"Did I? I don't remember. But if she was a moose," I thrust out my jaw, "what were we?"

"Oh, Alice."

That night we entertained Miss Hunter. Miss Rebecca Hunter, her fingers busy with bright worsteds: *star-stitch, sontags, block patterns, loopy borders* . . . Becky Hunter does her knitting while we read from Godey's Lady's Book. What do we read? A passage by Samuel Johnson? An article on the formation of dew? A receipt for apple dumplings? 'How to make a wedding breakfast for 40 . . .?'

"Tell us, Miss Hunter, how to become a mother – how to make a baby . . . Tell us about the *war*, Miss Hunter . . .".

Miss Hunter smiles imperturbably. *Now, girls.* White teeth, smooth hair, star-stitch, block pattern, loop border, knit one, purl one . . .

"O tell us about the poor old maid who threw herself off the cliffs she knew like the back of her hand, down the forty steps and into the sea."

Now, girls, let us all draw the backs of our hands.

343

"Miss Hunter, tell us about your mother. What will she make of her daughter *venturing too near the sea*?"

Silence. She has come and gone in a slow arc and then a commotionish splash. There is no such word as *commotionish*. Never mind. The waves go blipping over her as if she were just another bit of seaweed then close neatly over her like a seam doubly sewn from the reverse of the garment, as Miss Rebecca Hunter taught us, leaving no evidence at all. A tragic accident, tut-tut.

Fifty-seven

I signed the Christmas money orders I'd made out for William and Alice's boys: $3.00 for little Harry and $2.00 for Billy, envelopes enclosed.

"Is it enough, given the rate of exchange?"

"Don't fuss, dear," Katharine grumbled: "It will do perfectly well."

I ran my tongue along the envelope flap, stuck it down and left it for Wardy to post in the morning. Then I took up my usual place on the daybed, with Katharine occupying the rocker. The window out of which we gazed, high and wide and south-facing, let in warmth during the day, but as it got dark it loomed like one of Mr. Whistler's solid black portrait backgrounds.

"The shortest day of the year," noted Katharine.

As we watched, the lights of Leamington began to come on: one across the way in the basement where the soup was being made, one in the attic where a servant was arranging her cap, one on the main floor where the lamps and candles were being lit for a supper party. So it went on until the solid black rectangle had been splashed all over with yellow bursts and flares.

People killed themselves all the time, Katharine reasoned. Rarely a week went by when a body failed to be fished out of the Leam. There was nothing special about 'our' dead. Four? a drop in the . . . yes, ocean.

Was that supposed to make me feel better?

"Let's face it," Katharine said – pitiless, rational – "they were lost to you the day you left for England."

"Lost?" I repeated, flinching. But she was right of course: friendships did not easily survive an ocean's separation.

We returned to our separate books and thoughts. After a time Katharine began to yawn, and then – yawns being catching – so did I. Still we sat. The fire was dying down. Katharine rocked. An adventure in patience, I thought to myself, in persistence. The courage to resist temptation, to not act selfishly. To not act. To be bored. To have the courage to be happy. To settle down with our living, and our dead.

In due course all the lights across the way went out, Leamingtonians tending after all to turn in early. So the pattern was reversed and the Whistler loomed again. Wordlessly, Katharine rose and blew out our own lamps before feeling her way back to the rocker.

Darkness. Unframed, unpictorial; no edges; no inside or outside; no ending and no beginning. A sensation of floating, weightless, freed from gravity. (Would we go tumbling about like lumps of coal?) The darkness felt kind then, almost motherly. Had we become *enwombed? encrusted* like pies? Still we sat, until it seemed not just that we would not move, but that we *could* not. Presently, I felt sure, we would be absorbed until there was nothing left of us.

Is this what Henry means when he calls the darkness *palpable*?

Beastlike, it swallowed time.

A tiger-pounce of panic. I felt the hairs on the back of my neck stand on end.

"*Horripilant*," I hissed, absurdly pleased at being able to use such a word.

"What, dear?" Katharine's voice emerged as if from far away.

"Nothing."

The darkness, quite sated, yawned.

It was getting cold. We knew there was a window because it let in a draft. At some point Katharine came and, piling on

346

another blanket, curled herself around me. My hearth companion.

"There now, stay close. It wouldn't do for one of us to happen to vanish."

Stars. Flung out across their black bed.

"Clover – Ellen – Lizzie – Becky" – one for each, we counted. A fine spangling. Thus we totted up the loss. Then we slept, squashed together, groaning at the discomfort. Blinking, we woke to first light.

"Come along, dear," said Katharine, at last, hoiking me up quite roughly.

"It cannot get worse," I said. But with the morning post, it did: Winny Howells' name was added to the list. That made five.

What did the light care?

Fifty-eight

"Do you realize," I said, "that all along Winny had had some terrible wasting disease?" The news had come from Aunt Kate. Katharine, that prosaic plant, asked to know its name. "She didn't say," I replied impatiently: "besides, *what does it matter?*" The point was, I explained, that in the end Winny did not die, *as accused*, of thinness or nerves: she was *ill* – only the medical men were too blind, ignorant and incompetent to know it.

"The funeral is next Friday," I added savagely.

Having signed my condolence letter I turned to a clean page and drew a circle, adding names at the ends of spokes around its perimeter, beginning with Minny Temple and ending with Winny Howells. "We have come full circle in our year of deaths." I held out the page for Katharine to see: "From Minny," I pointed out, "to Winny." Snickering squeezing out of me like sourish cream.

"Enough," warned Katharine, "or you'll make yourself ill again." Sometime later – we'd had our supper, the fire was lit – "Shall we have a Nuremberg Christmas Tree, Alice?" It was the latest 'thing', made of goose feathers to save fir trees. She believed it to be preferable.

"What of the poor geese?" I asked.

"I believe they do not necessarily kill the geese for their feathers."

"No," I pointed out, "they do for our dinner."

"Oh, Alice."

I held up my hand, "Alright . . . I give in."

Earlier she had proposed a trip to London.

"And what will we do there?" I had asked.

"We will *live*, dear."

Was I, were we, not already living? I asked. Did we require the *grande monde*, the red gleams and blurs of Christmas illuminations, the dazzle of shops and cafes, the vulgar encrustations of theaters, the flashing lamps of elegant houses and carriages, the whole uproar of pleasure and prosperity, the richness and clatter and calamity of it all to convince us we *lived*? Must I be jostled about by the crowds in Trafalgar Square only to drool over Nelson's hams?

"This is *my life*," I argued defensively: "steady and unadventurous perhaps but not small; no, minute by minute, a grand, fat, billowing, all-encompassing life. For a woman," I went on, "might have an amount of experience out of any proportion to her adventures. It is for the imagination to supply them, with the help of literature and reports of friends and the clarity – if such it be – of one's own eyes."

"Bed!" I went on, making her jump in alarm; then lowering my voice: "or a piece of finely-wrought prose (here I quoted from The American, words enfolding me like an embrace: '*He lived over again the happiest hours he had known – that silver chain of numbered days in which his afternoon visits, tending sensibly to the ideal result, had subtilised his good humour to a sort of spiritual intoxication.*') Altogether a lived life, a peopled life, an experienced life: including friends . . . and pain, yes even that. As for the 'wider' world, I may be a poor paralytic on my daybed, but I can still imagine Stanley slaughtering the savages or Parnell's standing ovation, led by Gladstone, as he entered the Commons chamber. In other words, the world and its wars, struggles, suffering, joys & etc is mine. As it happens, Kath, I relish much and miss very little from my invalid's perch."

Breathless, I stopped.

She was staring as if she'd never seen me before.

"Besides," I added, "I am not well enough. I cannot gorge on London like Henry."

That did it. London was abandoned and the Nuremberg tree was installed. It was 'dressed' – lightly, as the feathers would not tolerate weight – by Wardy and Katharine, with directorial 'tips' from me: *too high . . . bare spot just there . . . a crooked angel*. Splendid, it was too.

On the Monday before Christmas Mrs Bacheler from 'next door' brought me a 'giftlet' with effusive wishes from the whole family. They are people who, refreshingly, send 'love' rather than 'duty'. "Mister Bacheler said to bring it today," she reported reprovingly. "I told him we must wait until Wednesday, Christmas proper, but he says give it over now as the world could end on Tuesday. God-forbid, says I."

"Does he wish me to open it now?"

"So he does."

A little brass tray for pins, costing three pence. How do I know the price? Because Wardy took a week to choose it for them, and I had to advance the money. Not that that could diminish its effect. In return, I handed over a basket of provisions including a pineapple, which object she claimed never to have laid eyes on before.

"Oh, Miss James!" she exclaimed, rather overcome.

Katharine nevertheless remained restless clearly wishing to go, if not to London, then somewhere else. I shook my head. *Where* we went, I argued, was not the point. *This* was our destination; we had arrived, were already taking part in 'the act of living'. "Here, in Leamington?" she asked doubt-fully. Was it possible to *plunge* into Leamington? It was, I insisted. And so – but was I 'up to it'? yes, I was – we went for a Boxing Day outing.

"Will you walk, Alice?"

"I will."

Katharine held my elbow as we made our way into Jephson Gardens. The lanes were crowded with families taking the air and the waters. It was a fine winter's day, the Gardens filled like a great tankful of feather-tailed fish, the sky above watching with its cold, clear, mordant expression. Even Katharine was mollified. We had managed a compromise; she had not inflicted London on me; she had satisfied all my miserablist complaints and negations; surely nothing else could go wrong.

"What do they take us for, d'you suppose?" I asked meaning how would we be 'classed'? Not English and not 'rawly' American, for we'd lived here too long for that. No, they would have difficulty placing us: perhaps German? No, too darkly colored. Spanish perhaps? No, too plainly attired. Well, then, French, yes, French. Blue stockings, that would be it! We began chattering in French but soon gave it up. We were after all *Americans*, so why not play up to it? "Why not indeed?" we agreed, tut-tutting and drawling out, "Why, would you look at that!" and giggling in the way of Daisy Miller and her ilk.

I'd begun to feel elated at being out and about among other living beings. But special; different; *American*. Katharine was looking sceptical – was I suggesting a *superior*ity? I denied it. "Yet we *are* our own creations," I began gesticulating, "our own 'artworks': we can make ourselves up as we go along." Speechifying; full of myself. "While *they*" – nodding at our English counterparts – "in their established European mold can't be like us. *They* are a bundle of other people's histories, creatures of circumstance – *they* can never be newborn, poor things." Katharine pulled my elbow closer against the stares and titters.

"Here we are," she posed in her teacherly way, "brilliant and refreshing and all that, but living in King Arthur's Court."

And what was the effect of *that*? she wondered.

"I guess," I ventured, "as Henry would have it, "we Americans are apt to be rather innocent and so liable to being spoiled."

Katharine stopped so abruptly we were bumped into on all sides.

"Does that make us Little Red Riding Hoods?" she challenged, hands on hips; "while *they* are all wicked wolves with 'fangs' of corruption?" Her eyes were tearing with cold but behind that there steamed a hot fury:

"Alice," she said tightly, "it sometimes surprises me that your dear brother, who is ever the one for complexifying all manner of quite straight-forward situations, chooses to simplify this matter of the comparative British and Yankee characters."

I pointed out the inconsistency in her argument: previously she'd accused Henry and me of being prone to crash under the weight of our internal contradictions, and wouldn't it be better to be more focused and less paradoxical and always going all about the houses?

"And anyway," I finished up with *my* hands on *my* hips: "what saves us is our ability to see our 'paradoxes and complexifyings' as hilariously funny – so there!" She opened her mouth fishlike but nothing emerged.

*

It was New Year's eve. "Did I ever tell you," I said conversationally, "I once asked my father for permission to commit suicide." Katharine looked as if she might be sick.

"And how did he reply?"

"He granted it of course – shrewdly."

"Explain yourself."

"He understood that in the granting of it I would be discouraged. The child who is told to 'go ahead and jump off a cliff' knows perfectly well it must, therefore will not."

"Oh," she cried: "but it would take an iron nerve to test the child so."

I agreed. "Yet he went further still."

"What more could there be?" she asked incredulously.

"He asked me to do it in 'a perfectly gentle way' in order *'not to distress my friends'*."

She gasped.

Was it not absolutely brilliant of him? I asked.

Before leaving at the end of the week she knelt before me as I sat in the rocker. "Do you plan to propose?" I inquired.

She shook her head. "This is serious, Alice. Promise me," she whispered.

"What?"

"You know."

Did I know? Of course I did.

"Why?" I asked.

"Because your remains will be hung in a tree where the harpies will peck at your flesh and you will stand no chance of an after-life. There will be nothing gentle in it."

I snorted; such threats, as she knew perfectly well, mattered not a fig to me. But would I promise?

"I cannot," I said at last, proclaiming "Any one who spends her life as an appendage to five cushions and three shawls is justified in committing the sloppiest kind of suicide at a moment's notice."

"In that case I cannot go," she declared, adding: "And I must."

"Why must you?"

"Because if I don't, I shall be forced to discontinue you myself." She stood, reached for the paperweight on my desk and waved it over me. She was nothing if not clear of purpose, my Katharine. So, grudgingly, I promised.

Wardy tries to cheer me up with feeble bits of holly she has purloined from the Park; while Mrs Hussey the landlady tries to fatten me up with a pudding which immures me in such squalid indigestion I can only hope that I may fizzle out before next daylight. Which sets me thinking once again: is it not my right to dispose of my body when life – the pain of it – becomes intolerable?

But you promised, Alice.

Katharine, my straight-talking, straight-playing Katharine.

I took out the commonplace book she'd given me for a Christmas present. (I'd given her a new-fangled haversack Wardy had found with a belt that went around the waist.) Holding the small, leather-bound thing, soft as a glove, in my lap I slid a hand inside. The paper felt smooth as skin, inviting, reassuring. Once you've written something, anything – so it seemed to say – the name of a washerwoman, the address of a new spa therapist, a new diet – the latest dead – it will cease to be daunting: only begin. Marks upon a page. Diary writing: a female occupation:

> *'I think if I get into the habit of writing a bit about what happens or rather doesn't happen, I might lose a little of the sense of loneliness and desolation which abides with me . . .'*

But was it possible to commit myself to something other than mere silly scraps? I could, I supposed, begin by using the 'scribbler' to try and fathom why the 'act of living' had become too much for Clover and Ellen et al. And why, paradoxically, that same 'act of living' continued to be for me – a wretched, reverberating volcanic mouse with a jangling fluttering body enclosed between four walls – still (in spite of my threat) the most interesting state of all. Before long I began to imagine stories and settings: characters speaking, plotting, prevaricating, forming attachments and unforming them; hopeful, beautiful, kind, scathing, sardonic, disappointed: sentence piled upon sentence, clause within clause, language woven like fabric, light yet warm and so shimmering with suggestion they made you gasp. What twaddle, I then thought. Better to expect nothing, I counselled myself wisely. It is only a bundle of sewn-in pages: a book you can make a mess of, a book in which you can write anything at all, even your own dimwitted thoughts, since no one will bother to look at it, a book to be thrown away at the end. So I open the cover, slowly, and place my chip of lead-pencil upon the clean, fleshlike first page . . .

V. LONDON (Again)

(1891–1892)

Fifty-nine

And then she died. But not just yet. First she must undergo (must she?) further pressings and pummellings and palpatings. She has grown quite thin, her face more like something found on the desert floor picked over by wolves and illuminated from within. Her eyes, those flat orbs the dusty grey of cats' fur, appear by some process to have become clarified, like gin.

"Decorative at last in death," say I.

"Please . . .," entreats Katharine, who has rushed over from America.

Henry, not to be undone, has scurried back from the Continent.

She should have considered it inhuman to have remained away, I hear her tell him, adding rather unnecessarily: "Alice is, really, too ill to be left."

The trio are awaiting the 'great' Sir Andrew Clark, FRCS, eminent London physician, surgeon and doctor to *the Prime Minister* William Gladstone, *the Author* Henry James and now *the Sister* Alice who has gone into pie and appears to be flaking away. He is already an hour late – but hark! here he comes, the door flies open and in he steps, a veritable bouquet on legs, "The *late* Sir Andrew Clark!" he booms – a joke he has used too many times before. "How he adores an entrance," whispers Henry. Perhaps, I think, he will cast him in his next play.

But to the point. He has 'endowed' me with cardiac complications, a spinal neurosis affecting my legs, a delicate embroidery of the most distressing case of nervous hyperesthesia, and rheumatic gout of the stomach. "Well," I manage to drawl, "there's a panoply of miseries that ought to satisfy the most inflated pathologic vanity. However," I add, "there is nothing new in it, they have been with me for years." He smiles thinly, pulls up a chair and arranges himself in it so that his florid face is on a level with mine. *Now,* I think, with not a little excitement.

"The breast," he intones.

My hand flies to it: instinctive, protective. The left breast , it transpires, contains a lump, a very lumpen lump which has been there for the past three months.

"The breast," he repeats; stops.

"Doctor Clark, I should like to hear of it sooner rather than later."

"Ah, yes, the pill without the sugar: a true austere and masculine Calvinist."

Masculine? What is the fool on about? I may have grown dry and sexless before my time but I have not actually changed *sides.* As for austerity, I much prefer the feminine science of life – intelligent and succulent – to any dry sapless husks of masculine reason. But sugar I can do without.

"What news, Doctor?"

He folds his hands high up over his chest, as if to protect himself from a blow, and twiddles his thumbs.

"Miss James, the breast contains a lump."

"I am aware of it. And the nature of the lump?"

"Tumorous."

"Are they not synonymous?"

He moues.

"And malignant?" I inquire.

"Oh, I wouldn't jump to conclusions."

"And I, doctor, wouldn't dream of jumping anywhere at present."

"Ah ha."

The first order of business, they agreed – whatever the tumour's fate (and mine) – was to get me away from

Leamington. *They* agreed; yes, Katharine and Henry actually put their heads together: one pale and clean of outline as a new-laid egg, the other more like the nest of a sluttish bird. Was I pleased? I nearly wept. But what was to be done about William? Henry wanted to know.

"Done?" I asked.

"Shall he be told, Alice?" Katharine interpreted helpfully.

Having considered the matter I said: "Oh no – not poor Willy – he'll fuss so – only tell him I have developed heart disease."

So having said my goodbyes to Leamington and a party of waving, tearing Bachelers, I was put in an invalid carriage on the Great Western Railway, along with Wardy and Louisa, the slavey from Leamington, and taken, by Katharine, to rooms at the South Kensington Hotel in Queen's Gate Terrace, where we were neighbors with 15 pianos, 23 uproarious children, and an anxious Henry close by. "I'm sure my brother would considere it unaesthetic to die in an hotel," I complained to Katharine. "In that case," she reassured me, "we'll have you carried down the back stairs while he's at lunch or dinner." Nevertheless, off she went to find us a house. Eventually a suitable one was found at 41 Argyll Road on Kensington's Camden Hill, built in the '60s in revival style, with four floors, arched bay windows, balustrades, a scraplet of garden in back; and with the lease came a Mrs Thompson, cook.

Sixty

Henry, allowing himself a brief respite from me, had gone to Paris for a week. The 'prodigy' of his visit had not been the devoted Fenimore, however, but the young John Sargent: "tall, athletic, dark-haired, dark-bearded with vivid grey-blue eyes . . ."

Katharine interrupted him to inquire: "Aside from being a remarkable physical specimen, what does he *do*?"

"Sargent? My dear Katharine," he informed her, "aside from an agreeable penchant for society and the *beau-monde*, he does with colors what I attempt to do with words."

"I see," she translated: "you mean he paints."

Henry nodded.

I was more interested in knowing about the young American woman who'd disgraced herself by posing for Sargent.

"Ah," he cocked a devilish eyebrow: "the Gautreau scandal." He went on to describe the painting as "etiolated as a plant starved of light, its colors mainly of peat and mud." Against this background shone the figure's unclothed flesh.

"Surely you exaggerate," said Katharine.

He denied it. "On the contrary, Mme Gautreau is half-stripped. The dress she wears is entirely sleeveless, of black satin, plunging to beyond the depths of decency, and held up by a single delicate gold-link strap"- he was clearly enjoying himself – "the other having slipped off her shoulder."

"Or been pushed?" suggested Katharine.

Henry grinned, a rare event; and then it spread – an even rarer one.

"But what of the young woman herself?" I inquired. "Tell us about the model, Henry."

"Indeed," Katharine pounced, "Why would a young American girl put herself into such a compromising position?"

Henry turned from Katharine to me, me to Katharine. Was he feeling embattled? Impossible to tell. He told us what he knew about Amelie Gautreau or 'Madame X' as she was known: that she hailed from some backwater in Georgia, had been dragged over to the Continent by her battleaxe of a mother and had succeeded in snagging a rich Frenchman.

"That is all very well, Henry," I said, "but it doesn't explain her motive in modelling for Sargent."

He shrugged. I pictured the girl arriving at the painter's studio holding her arms clear of the brown afternoon dress she was wearing. 'Will this do for my pose?' she asks. Sargent does not reply, merely holds out what looks to Amelie like a long black drape or shroud. She laughs; he cannot be serious. Oh but he is, perfectly. Amelie makes a snorting noise through her nose as she disappears behind the partition. She is nineteen years old. A crude little Southerner, he thinks, smiling to himself.

"I am concerned," interrupted Katharine, "by the gap of privilege between them in terms of age and situation, not to mention sex."

Henry winced.

Back behind the curtain I see Amelie reach into her bag and begin applying a coating of lavender powder to her face, throat, arms, décolleté. Then there is rouge which, contrary to custom, she does not apply to her nose or cheekbones but to her *ears*. No jewelry, she decides, only her wedding ring. Here she pauses picturing her husband with his fists balled up and his face going puce forbidding her ever to pose again. *Stuff him*. Smiling defiantly, she raises a small tiara in the shape of a peacock to sit atop her piled-up hair. She is ready: half-naked but noble and proud.

Which pleases me. But perhaps I have been dreaming, or writing.

"Alice? Are you awake? Are you in pain?" Katharine had rushed to one side, Henry the other.

"Yes," I said, and "No", in that order, both being half-truths.

"Shall I go now?" Henry asked, straightening. His features seemed to shift about as if made of soft clay so that I could imagine a sculptor pressing, stretching, pulling together. Katharine, I sensed, was about to agree it might be a good idea, but I shot her a 'look'.

"No, Henry," I told him: "do not go."

But there was Amelie stepping out from behind the partition. She is slender, full-bosomed, with white skin, auburn hair, dark eyes and *a ridiculously long tip-tilted nose*. Sargent, in spite of himself, catches his breath. She appears even more statuesque in the dress. A column of darkness, he thinks. Turning this way and that before the mirror she says, "Mother will have a fit." And then she declares: "It will be the end of me. I cannot wear this."

"Oh, but you will," says Sargent.

"Paris was scandalized," Henry was telling us – "it was all quite delicious."

"Delicious . . .?" charged Katharine.

"But what of poor Amelie?" I demanded.

She was right, Henry acknowledged, on both counts. Her mother did have a fit, and it was the end of her reputation; though it would not stop her modelling, or the artist painting.

Amelie takes her pose. At some stage she allows her 'carriage' to droop. "I'm plum tuckered out," she whines, using an expression she has learned not to use in polite society. Sargent wishes she wouldn't open her mouth as it spoils the effect. Just then one of her straps slips off her shoulder and dangles along her arm. She reaches to replace it but Sargent orders her to stop: "Leave it as it is." It is just the touch he needs, and to hell with the consequences. But it is her luminous flesh that is most astonishing; also, how her head is turned away offering up the whole wide, naked expanse of her bosom to the viewer. Take me, she seems to be saying: *Do with me what you will.* As for the dress, its very simplicity, its sleek blackness draws attention to her hourglass figure and an absence of petticoats. Her thighs and belly are clearly traceable just beneath the fabric. No breathing space between dress and body. As if it has been painted on.

"Art or no art, he took an unconscionable advantage," tutted Katharine. Henry would neither agree, nor disagree. "The mother," he told us, "apparently stormed into Sargy's studio declaring her daughter ruined and ordering him to remove the painting."

"And did he?" we chorused.

"Certainly not. He did however agree to correct the errant strap." Henry's expression softened, "Of course the girl's reputation will never recover. People trace the implication of things . . . guess the 'unseen' from the 'seen'." He paused, adding: "alas."

Katharine muttered something unrepeatable.

I suggested he write a tale called, 'The Errant Strap'. But even as I said it, I perceived there was something horrible about the poor girl's flesh as it had been rendered, a bluish tinge corrupting the ruddy glow of youthful sensuality turning it to a deathly pallor, as if she were already a corpse, her head lolling in death.

"Henry?" There was no reply. I saw only his retreating back, as Katharine hustled him out of the room.

Sixty-one

Dissatisfied with Sir Andrew's uncertain diagnosis – and at the prodding of Constance Woolson – Henry had arranged for his own preferred physician and friend, William Wilberforce Baldwin, to 'have a look at me'. Henry himself was away in Ireland working on another play and recuperating from jaw-bashing dental work, but had written to inform us of the arrangement: 'As Baldwin is passing through London, it is to be hoped he might provide some suggestion of more than British ingenuity as to the alleviation of pain'. Which amused Katharine, to think that at the last trump it could only be an *American* doctor Henry would insist on for his sister.

I waited for the usual interrogation but it did not come; nor the usual examination. Had he, literally, only come to *have a look*? If so, I thought, he would be mighty disappointed. But what he did next was this: He fixed me with his penetrating gaze before touching me, astonishingly, front and back with various parts of his own body: an ear to my chest, a brush of knuckles to my cheek, a trail of fingertips 'mapping' my shoulder blades. Nor was there anything unnatural in these actions: no repugnance or judgment; no dissociation between us, no yawning divide between the well and the unwell. Stethoscoping? All it did, in his non-majestic opinion, was to place another icy barrier between doctor and patient:

"We are losing connection the more instruments we invent."

I offered an instance of eating ice-cream with a spoon instead of one's tongue. My nurse, as I explained, had recently seen a girl child buying 'a ha'porth of ice cream' which was dabbed on a bit of newspaper. "For an extra half penny you get a spoon, apparently; but the girl went without and used her tongue."

Baldwin was delighted with the analogy. "I see you are touched with your brother's narrative gift."

"If I am, it is only with the lightest of feathers."

"And modest with it." But speaking of Henry, had I read his recent article on Guy de Maupassant in the *Fortnightly Review*? Yes, I had. And what was my view? "Well," I told him, "I do not like to blow the fraternal trumpet – but I think it brilliant." "Indeed," Baldwin agreed, "I wish he did more of that kind of thing." "Oh," I told him, "but he thinks it unworthy, you see."

We sat in companionable silence after that, as if we'd known one another for years – which I suppose in a sense we had through Henry – until I felt myself drifting off. At which he began telling *me* about *his* own ailments – which of course woke me up: Graves Disease, gout, heart arrythmia, pneumonia, influenza and – the cruelest of all – a black depression.

Who the doctor and who the patient?

For a moment he allowed his large hands to dangle pawlike between his legs, weighted with hopelessness; while I found myself at once desirous of 'improving' *him*.

"But you, my dear Alice" – he finally managed to rouse himself – "I may, may I, call you Alice?" (At last, a medical man asking if he may call me Alice.)

"Of course," I replied. At which he broke into an irresistible smile.

Dr Baldwin (polite, urbane) was a striking-looking man with fine features, intelligent eyes, and a wildly sensuous mouth. Highly articulate of course; knowledgeable yet modest about all sorts of things, and possessed of very winning manners. But all that alone would have made him merely superior. There is something else, I thought, taking one of his hands in both of mine, wanting more than anything else *to comfort him.* This was no hearty, yawping Sir Clark, you see, no caricature with a professional beside manner. I was tempted to call him 'divine Baldwin', but no, this was a man – entirely human – open, exquisitively sensitive – vulnerable himself – I knew it of course from Henry but this was *palpable.* Because he had experienced unwellness in himself, he could divine it in others. How did he know? Oh, not because he had to ask or do elaborate researches and testings; but by absorbing through his own pores, literally, the true essence of the matter. And by grasping one as a whole, instead of merely as a stomach or a dislocated elbow.

"It is all here," he explained gently, "the body tells its own story, Alice." He lay me back against the bank of pillows as you would a wounded bird on a bed of leaf litter. His gaze was direct, his eyes fiercely clear yet gentle. I nodded, too moved to speak. *If only there had been a man such as he in my life.* But I could not afford the extra pain of such a thought.

I am being found out, I thought.

"Do you mind very much?" he asked.

"Mind?" I closed my eyes smiling like a cat. Not only did I not dislike this 'being found out', it was what I'd been waiting for for much of my life. To be given something firm to stand on; to put an end to my fatal imaginings.

"Will you know then?" he asked.

I would I said. In that case, it was his opinion that the cancer of the breast had metastasized from an original malignancy in my liver.

"Breast cancer?"

Yes, he concluded from the pain in my shoulder blade.

"And the liver . . .?"

That he detected from the 'earthy' hue of my complexion – bilious, I guess he meant; or what Henry might describe as 'gamboge and luteous'.

"I see." He took my hand. I held on.

"There is a surgeon," he began, "William Halsted, Johns Hopkins. I have observed his work – ground-breaking –

mastectomy as a treatment for breast cancer. But in this instance . . ."

The thought of the ocean crossing, the surgical ordeal, was not to be borne.

"I mean, in your particular case," he continued, "it would not be indicated as an option; that is – the truth – there would be no point, Alice, in surgically removing your breast, given the state of your liver."

"Then there is nothing to be done."

"Not done, no."

"You mean I will die?"

"That is all," he said. "How long it will take I cannot predict: months, a year or two at the very most."

He fixed me with a beam of the Florentine sun he seemed to carry within him.

"That's too good," I told him, almost dissolving with relief. "But shall I suffer?"

"Oh, no, not a bit."

"Then shall I live?"

"My dear Alice," said he, " 'to live' is exactly what you must take the trouble to do." And with that he prescribed various 'palliatives' such as a higher pillow (he'd also recommended it to William for his sleeplessness; it worked); as many glasses of Chateau Lafitte Rothschild '70 as we could afford; daily massages; and managed doses of strychnine as a stimulant should I become depressed.

Aha, so that is where Constance gets her taste for strychnine.

Morphine as needed of course, tho' preferably not taken *with* the strychnine.

I raised my arms – or they raised themselves – it could not be helped – and encircled his neck.

"Thank you, doctor: thank you very much."

April 26: *I am absurdly happy.*

*

369

Katharine, who had been present all along, bent moistly over me hanging there like some bony, clattering thing shot from the sky.

"Get off, you great albatross: you're hurting me."

"And you . . ." She laughed, dashing at her eyes.

"Never mind me," I said; and then – it was time – long overdue – my own illnesses having always obscured hers; my own self-preoccupation stopping me from noticing; my need for her to be invulnerable so she could look after me (selfish selfish Alice). But now I would, must know:

"Katharine, dear, *will you be blind?*"

"In time," she stated, "yes". The frankness catching.

"Is there nothing to be done?"

"Apparently not."

"You have seen a specialist?"

"The best, according to Louisa."

"In that case," I sniped, "he can be depended upon. But what will you do?"

"Do, Alice?" It was her turn to mock. "I will read in braille; learn to knit; find my way in the dark. In short, I will live." She gazed – two blue, hazy orbs – in my general direction. "After all," she confessed, "it has been coming on so gradually – sneaking up on me, as it were – I daresay I will hardly notice. And you are not to think of it."

Years of darkness and only the wretched Louisa to lead her by the hand, tell her what obstacles she was about to collide with . . . How could I not think of it?

Later I instructed her to pen a note to William. At once she took up her writing pad. "It is time," I said, "he knew about the tumor."

She raised an eyebrow. "Are you sure, dear?"

"Yes. But say nothing of a malignancy or anything of that nature. Let us go gradually so as not to alarm him."

She wrote in her precise hand with the paper held close and at an angle to catch as much of the light as possible.

When she had finished she offered it to me to check over. "I cannot distinguish your e's from your o's," I pretended to complain, "but it will do." Then I asked her to add a PS, as follows:

'What you said about Baldwin, Willy, that he had 'social genius and gallant personal pluck, but no more exact science than a fox-terrier' – my eye! Oh, you may be right about the science bit – but it matters not. His is an entirely alternative – that is, original – medical approach; more of a partnership or collaboration.

'He is also" – I could not resist – 'quite delicious in looks and manners.'

Katharine lay down her pen. "So," she charged, removing her spectacles, "you have found a man at last who meets with your approval." What could I do but agree?

Sixty-two

"How can you be so chirpy, Miss?" Wardy's nose was red as an early Queen Anne cherry. "Anyone would think you were happy about what he told you."

"So I am," I replied. Previously I'd thought myself courageous for daring to be *un*happy; now I understood that it might take more of that quality to be *happy*: "Why, it is easily the most supremely interesting moment in life."

Katharine understood at once. "At last," she said: "something to get hold of."

Having something *actually wrong with me:* the relief of it left me giddy. Something with a name; something that would explain the pain; something all the queen's horses and all the queen's medical men in England would acknowledge actually existed: palpable, lumpen, real.

Henry, newly returned from Ireland, cast about for an understanding:

"It is, I take it, a certainty?"

"If you mean is the diagnosis definite: yes it is."

"Then there is no hope," he ventured.

"Oh hope," I laughed, "that's something else entirely."

"You have . . . faith?"

I laughed. "Good heavens, no. No hocus-pocus at all."

"Yet you are hopeful?" he ventured.

"Yes" – here I surprised myself – "yes I am. What I *hope* for is to reverse Hooper's curse." At which Wardy piped up with: " *'You will not die but you will suffer to the end'*. I remember it very well, Miss. What a horrible man, how dare he!"

"Quite right, Wardy."

To Henry I explained my *hope* was in reversing it. "I shall submit and resist at the same time."

"Submit and resist . . . ," echoed Henry.

"I believe," said Katharine, "she means she has ceded her body to the 'feminine' principle of frailty and submission, while cultivating with her mind a 'masculine' strength and indifference to pain."

Henry thanked her for the explanation.

"I shall be known henceforth," I intervened, "as 'the stoical hysteric'."

Katharine however would not have it so.

"Am I not to be stoical, then?"

"Oh stoical, by all means." It was the label 'hysteric', medieval and damaging, that must be abjured.

But there was Henry, getting up to go, suggesting – did I not think – after all – he understood my reluctance of course but – was it not time to tell William?

"What shall I tell him?" asked Katharine, later that evening.

"Tell poor dear William," I instructed, "only that there is evidence of 'a tumor'."

"No more?"

"No more."

His response, by return post, was no less than *five* pages long, and offered much chivvying and philosophizing and 'bright notes' and 'look on the little good in each day' and to being 'relieved from the post' and 'the doom of nervous weakness' &etcetcetc . . . . 'Above all things' finishes up Brother Polonius – *if* it should turn out to be cancerous 'take all the morphia (or other forms of opium if that disagrees) you want and don't be afraid of becoming an opium drunkard. What was opium created for except for such times as this?'

Oh Willy.

*

373

June 17th. I am drunk with the infinite gradations of light and shade. I shall soon become a Yankee yelper, a spouter of Walt Whitmanish wonder, a singer-outer of rhymes, Twinkle Twinkle, an aged crabbed child under the stars . . . born new and in danger of becoming absurd. The gift is that I am forced to witness and not participate. Until pain invades me again and I go down again into its holding well . . .

And what a deep well it is. The walls are slimy – shades of the Leamington underpass, rich in moss and liverworts and such. Frogs lurking in the cracks. The smell? What you would expect: dank, medicinal, the suspicion of urine.

The main problem: how to rise up and out of it?

But there is a lift. I am saved. It's one of those contraptions made of ironwork mesh of which the French are so fond. In I step. But as we ascend I become aware of a change, a gradual unravelling. The lift is no longer made of metal at all but words. Henry's words; his metaphors, his figures of speech like tapestry yarns spooling all around me – knotting – netting – entrapping. But another dose of something-or-other and I am free and on the rise once again. Above me not a black Whistlerish rectangle but a square of hopeful baby-ribbon blue in its frame – with the lift's message writ large. Alice, you must not let yourself become *wrapped up* in Henry's words, however seductive, but must find your own voice.

Sixty-three

"I'm in a muddle," I confessed. "Cross that last bit out."

"Which bit?" Katharine asked, pen poised for a slash. She'd begun, in spite of only barely tolerating fiction, faithfully taking dictation. Did she think my tale the ravings of a dying mind? If so, she did not let on. Or not much.

"Where I describe my 'heroine'," I replied. I had been picturing Connie Woolson. But this was fiction, I told myself. My character must be herself and only herself.

"What is the problem, Alice?"

"Phrenology," I replied.

She pursed her lips.

"Do not be satirical," I countered. "The question is not just *how* to describe one's characters in their physicality, but whether it is defensible to do so."

"But surely your 'characters' need to be fully realized, Alice. Your readers will like to think – illusory as it may be – that they can see them 'in the round', as it were. It surely follows, therefore, that you must describe them?"

Oh my logic-bound amanuensis!

"The question is," I argued, "can 'character' be described in terms of facial and/or bodily features?"

"It is assumed to be possible," she supposed. "But you doubt its desirability?"

"I doubt its moral assumption."

"And that is . . .?"

"An analogy between the outer and the inner man." I waved the pocket Lavater which William had sent me

375

(Willy, how could you?). "Zoological Physiognomy . . . revolting stuff . . . face of a brute = heart of a criminal; receding forehead = brain of a chimp; stooped gait = cannibal; big nose = Jew . . . Even Henry," I cried, "falls for it. I mean, there's Newman with his 'noble bumps and high forehead &etc'." What can it mean? That the body is 'readable', of course, but what does it tell us, and is it at all accurate or indeed meaningful?"

She agreed such comparisons were likely to be based more on ignorance and prejudice than any kind of science.

"However," she pursued the matter: "portraiting or describing has always been done, even in some of the accounts of historical personages." She paused. "If you deny it, what is left?"

I raised a half-balled fist, "To refuse easy assumptions!"

Oh she could support that. "But will your heroine have no face or figure then? will she go about stark naked?"

I aimed the Lavater at her but it did a belly-flop onto the floor. Bending to retrieve it she held her back with her other hand. I saw that she had aged: the coarsening and whitening of her hair, the dried-pruning of her weathered, New England skin – it had never been English, after all.

"Well, it would be amusing, don't you agree, to have her go about starkers?"

"Hush, now, Alice," she entreated.

"Katharine," I growled: "I am not a dog to be pat to sleep."

She removed her spectacles and pinched the bridge of her nose; but I was not impressed.

"I cannot create like this," I declared: "*in tandem*. It's not like riding a bicycle. Oh, it is all too . . . *lumpen*." I flung the word out carelessly, without a thought as to where it landed or what damage it might do.

"Then write it yourself!" she cried, stomping off to her garden.

Two minutes later she returned. "By the way, what will you call her?"

"Her?"

"Your . . . protagonist."

"Ah."

I am silent, fearful of saying 'her' name out loud. If I do, I think, 'she' will dissolve before she has been wholly concocted. Also, I am afraid not only of exposing her, and making her risible, but of 'fixing' her with a name that is just as false – as incriminating – as a dark stubble on a jutting chin.

"Her name, Alice?" asks a persistent Katharine.

"Hectoria," I whisper.

Silence. She looks to the ceiling. Bites her lip. Slowly – very slowly – begins shaking her head.

"It will not do, Alice."

That put me in a porcupine rage. "It is the name I have given her; how dare you laugh!" But she was equally 'hot' and warned me against 'acting up' – it was not good for my health.

"*Health*?" I cried, "what health? I am dying."

"Oh fine, then, die," she declared sans frill or fluff. But if it went on, she threatened, she would have me shipped back to Boston. Boston? 3,000 miles of sea-sickness and my righteous indignation turns to pulp, and I flop back into my tangle of shawls swindled into savorless amiability.

Katharine. She vowed to stay with me to the end. She would not return to her sister Louisa or her aged father or her students or her beloved American landscape. And would I allow her to do this, to give up everything for me? Yes – selfish Alice – I would. I would allow myself to absorb her as a sponge sucks up life-giving moisture, make use of her as my right to an excellent death.

You will not die but you will suffer to the end.

I will not.

My bones were being ground into knobbly pebbles before being dumped into a tumbler, like agates, for smoothing and shining.

Pain but not suffering. I would not call it suffering.

Refuse all curses, Alice.

Katharine, below me, works the earth. I watch from the window – a glimpse of sky, the sound of rooks in Lord Holland's Park, and many a feathery bit of green – as she digs and hoes. We have been sent seeds by Fanny Morse. Our poppies are blooming. Before long I imagine myself being carried by my slaves through the tangled bloom at midsummer among sweet peas, mignonette, cornflowers, pyrethrum, pansies, carnations, daisies, musk and nasturtiums . . .

Slaves?

What in the world has Baldwin given me?

Sixty-four

1891

He came towards me, solid as a house. But houses, as I reminded myself, are *not* solid. "Do sit, Henry." He sagged rather than sat, as if hoping to disappear down the side of the chair like a sticky mintball wrapper.

"You are lopsided, dearest, like one of Aunt Kate's cakes."

He shifted about in an attempt to right himself. I could not help comparing his demeanor with that of the previous January. The American had just opened at Southport to great acclaim, and Henry had returned to rehearse his triumph first with Constance in Cheltenham, and then me, re-performing the simpering bows he had taken and re-living his triumph.

"And how did you take it?" I had prompted.

"Ah, my zeal was only matched by my indifference."

"Henry," I'd snorted: "I do not buy it for a moment."

"Well you may not," he'd rejoined archly, "but I find the form opens out before me as if it were a kingdom to conquer."

"Henry! – only beware" – it had slid out of me – "you are no Bismarck!"

Still, I had been pleased for him. But a debut opening at the Opera Comique, I sensed, was a different kettle of fish-faced critics and grinning gainsayers from the cosy provincials who had filled the Winter Gardens in Southport back in January.

"How is it progressing, Henry?"

He confessed he'd already had to do a great deal of what he called 'play-carpentry'. A scene did not sound as it should; actors balked at their lines; speeches needed to be made less 'speechifying'. "Naturally," he finished, "I have had to compromise . . . make further revisions . . ."

"Towards its improvement, I take it?"

"Oh, the cast could not be bettered: Elizabeth Robin as Claire Cintre, Compton as Newman . . ."

"There is certainly dramatic tension in the story" – I took up the banner – "even melodrama in the machinations of the Countess's family."

He had no doubt that *that* aspect of it would claim an audience's attention; on the other hand . . .

"You are uncertain" – I guessed – did I not share his writing concerns as fully and sympathetically as he shared my physical ills? – "as to how the more internal, psychological interactions described in the novel will come across."

He did not deny it.

"Henry," I waved towards the table, "kindly fetch my copy." He did so. I then asked him to read out the scene in which Mme de Cintre receives Newman for the first time. He crossed his legs and began: *"'Mrs Tristram has spoken to me a great deal of you," said Mme de Cintre gently . . .'."*

Here Newman – the American of the title – after seating himself, gradually becomes aware of his own discomfort. There is a sense of being wrong-footed, of not quite knowing how to behave with the Countess, in that foreign world of hers: *'He felt as one does in missing a step, in an ascent, where one expected to find it. This strange, pretty woman . . .'*

There is not a line of dialog. Only after an unconscionable length of time does Newman 'do' something. Having survived a moment of panic (he feels himself 'drowning'), he 'saves the day' (and himself) by performing an act – so characteristic of him – which represents in the novel the restoration of his self-possession.

" 'He *extended his legs*,' " read Henry, closing the book.

"It is a magnificent passage."

But was it – indeed was the novel as a whole – *enough like a play*? No, I thought, it was too *literary*. Even Newman's interest in Mme Cintre is expressed in bookish terms:

'. . . *he had opened a book and the first lines held his attention.*'

How to dramatize *that*? No, the more I thought about it, the less I believed it to be advisable. But was I to voice my doubts and thereby risk hurting Henry? Yes, I decided, I must; because he will be further tempted after this to make an 'assault' on the stage. It will be too exciting, too enticing to resist. The siren-song of money and fame . . . And it will be – I see this as clearly as I see Constance giving up – *a disaster*. Better to hurt his pride now than allow him to fling himself into the fray, only to become publicly damaged – exposed – humiliated . . .

If I do not tell him the truth, who will?

"But Henry," I spoke gently, "will there ever be actors good enough to convey all that goes on under the surface; will they be able to be *still* enough? After all," I pursued, "what actually happens? The settling of a dress, the turning of a face, the meeting of eyes and the looking away . . . finally, the extending of a leg . . . These 'actions', as you have written them, attain enormous significance. But on the stage, Henry? People will hardly notice such delicacies, such *smallnesses*. They will become bored; they will shuffle about; the reviewers will be scathing, the money will not warrant . . . You are in danger, Henry," I concluded, shocking even myself.

He held up his hand, as he had done once before. "Do not be hard on me, Alice. Stevenson has already put in a cruel 'dig' . . . do not add to it." Steadying his voice he went on: "Necessity has laid its brutal hand on me. My books don't sell, and it looks as if my plays might."

"Will you slum it then?"

A 'blow' had clearly been registered but he rallied. "It will amuse me," he managed, "while offering financial rewards."

"And if it does not?" I persisted.

"An exciting gamble it yet remains. Therefore I am going with a brazen front to write half a dozen more."

"And will they be filled with dates and currants? Please, Henry," I entreated, "do not become a baker of edible little dramas."

"Pray for me," he whispered in a squeezed-out voice. He then rose and set off but abruptly stopped, turned:

"Alice, I almost forgot . . ." He stood there looking pale and loose-fleshed. .

"What is it Henry?"

"Our *chef de la famille* is in England, indeed, here in London."

"William . . .?"

"He has come for the opening and . . ."

". . . to say goodbye to me. It's alright, Henry, we needn't pretend. So where is he and when may I see him?"

"He has been lunching at The Reform Club and is presently waiting – he sidled over to the window – for the news to be broken to you; and if you survive it, I'm to tie my handkerchief to the balcony as a sign . . . ."

"A sign of *what*, Henry?" His anxious 'handling' of me was getting on my nerves; his assumption that some kind of attack would 'come on' and that I would 'go off' upon seeing William for the first time in, what was it? *seven years*. I assured him that, with the help of 200 grains of bromides, that I was not a cannonball, and that I looked forward hugely to seeing Willy.

"But how has he managed it?" I asked.

"Only thanks to Aunt Kate's legacy: he, as her male heir, received $10,000."

"And you, Henry?" "I was given hardly a mention," he said meditatively, "but surely she has done well by *you*?"

"Oh," I drawled, "she left me a life interest in a shawl."

He pursed his lips: his solution, I suppose, to 'the problem' of expressing amusement. As to the shawl, we agreed it was her 'revenge' for my failing her.

"But the letters, Henry, do not forget the letters – Mt Vernon Street – or had you gone by then?"

He waited for more.

"It was after our parents' deaths. I was ill in bed. Aunt Kate had found a drawerful of letters which she proceeded to burn. Katharine, alerted by the smell, caught her in the act but was too late to save them. She remonstrated but Kate told her they were family papers and she thought it better that 'the children' should not see them."

"I suppose she was trying to protect us . . .?"

"Or deprive us of vital information."

He said nothing. The burning of letters . . . it was a long time ago . . . he hadn't been there to feel the full force of it. But as for the money – Kate's legacy – we agreed that William, with his large family, needed it more than we did.

It was time to summon the watcher at the gate. "He will be freezing out there," I said. But Katharine 'put down her foot'. I had had enough for one day, could he not see it? The two brothers, she instructed, were to come tomorrow, assuming I was 'up to it'. Henry, consenting, took his leave.

Sixty-five

My big brothers, my book-ends. William and Henry: the one hairy and grizzled as a bear, the other bald and fleshy as an infant. What did it say about them? That one was more hidden while the other proclaimed himself more open – unsheathed, unwrapped – to the world? William . . . Henry? But surely it was the other way around. "Really Henry," I heard myself say, "Willy should lend you his beard and what remains of his head-piece."

Wardy brought chairs from the parlor placing them close by. "Do sit," she invited in her politest company voice. They did so, flanking my sickbed, one each side, marking its perimeter with their substantial bodies. "Have an invalid mint," I offered, holding out the bowl of 'medicinal' sweets. Henry, simpering, took one. William, with his lantern eyes and a tendency to self-denial, declined. I'd already taken one. Unless I sucked on peppermints, I explained, my mouth tended to dry out. "It's the drugs, you see, according to Miss Ward who learned about such things at her orphan school – isn't that right, Wardy? (the poor booby actually curtsied) – "as well as" – I *moued* – "the laying out of the dead." William pretended not to hear while Henry pulled on his invalid mint as if it were a cigar that had gone out. I kept on sucking.

Henry. At first glance, this brother appears rather a dull, opaque fellow, easily passed over. He is a banker, you think, or a politician perhaps. Look closer. See how his thumb is hooked in his waistcoat pocket – where it likes to live and swing – not quite knowing how to declare itself. On the other hand, there is the fantastical bow-tie. Then the eyes, see how they move about; they are never still and miss not a thing, real or imagined.

William: my older, highly inquisitive brother: this one wears his personality in his face. *He* will never be passed over. Sweet, charismatic, twinkly of eye, hirsute and handsome; yet those eyes, for all their crinkly curiosity and courage – they gaze unflinchingly at me – do not see as far into the unknown or the impossible, or indeed the unsalubrious, as his younger brother's.

Do I appear to reveal a preference here? Then let me take their hands – one each – in mine. By the evidence of those – both fleshly, firm, warm and male – they are entirely equal and barely distinguishable. My brothers. I see them as young men in tall hats and black gloves – we are in the Louvre stepping as quietly as we can among the busts (which, it seems to me, are observing us with not a little alarm). Once we have 'gorged' on the 'significant' paintings, Henry leads us to a cafe where he orders a baba au rhum. William, saving his dollars and his waistline, watches him with his leanest, hungriest look as he devours the melting baba. "You will spoil your appetite – and get fat," he bursts out. Henry orders another.

"Willy, it is a draught of champagne to see you again," I tell him.

"And you, my little grey-eyed doe."

But where to begin? I feared he would jump straight in to the subject of me but was soon reassured he would not (painful subjects were never, I recalled, his forte).

"How is London?" he began.

"Ah London," I replied, "we are over our heads in scandals."

"So I see, so I see." William, keen for such tittle-tattle, was all a-twitter about Cleveland Street, a house containing a whole platoon of male prostitutes . . . Lord Somerset . . . others . . . the shock . . . could I imagine such a thing?

Could I? I laughed: well of course I could:

"Everyone knows the social elite are regular clients and as for Prince Eddy . . ." I said the only thing that shocked me was the audicity of the cover-up. William rubbed his hands together like an insect, vibrating with the thrill of it, while Henry stared at us both. But here his voice changed, his whole body drooped. Oh dear, I thought: here it comes.

"Alice . . . how are you?"

I opened my eyes, which had shut with the mint-sucking. The danger of opiates is that after an initial period of stimulation and euphoria one is in danger of falling asleep.

"I am my brothers' sister," I replied. "At any rate," I explained: "that is how my visitors address me. Quite humiliating," I added, "to a free-born American woman, don't you think?"

Henry looked bemused, as well he might.

"Ah," said William, drumming upon his chair-arms: "still my little lionness."

But his question, he delicately reminded me, was *how* was I, not *who*.

The invalid mint which I'd sucked to a sliver went forth inadvertently from my mouth, dropping onto the front of my bed-jacket, where it stuck. Henry froze; William jumped up and began fussing with his handkerchief. I waved him away: Wardy would take care of it later. It was merely one of many unavoidable accidents. "One is no longer in absolute control of one's bodily functions," I explained, "given a dissolute diet consisting of opium, morphia and strychnine, interspersed with Baldwin's red wine, and the occasional sip of thin gruel or soup."

"Mn," said William.

Henry avoided my gaze.

"It seems only a moment ago," I said turning to Willliam, "that you were getting married and, come to think of it, I was horizontal then as I am now." The crows around his eyes lifted their wings.

"Alice is not with you?" I asked.

"Alas, she doesn't travel well."

Like a cheese.

"And the children?"

"Thriving."

"And your work?"

"Ah, that." He was much taken up with what he called 'stream of thought' or 'the more elusive elements of meaning' overlooked by other psychologists. "Like a bird's life," he continued more animatedly, "with its flights and perchings."

I smiled at the image. "And the specific project?"

"Well, I mean – hope – to show how language expresses this in its sentences as they flow . . . in its full stops and periods and pauses . . . with their sensorial imaginings . . . places of flight filled with thoughts of relations and . . . rest and . . . uncertainties."

"Ah," I observed with a nod from one brother to the other: "first comes the practice, then the theory." I heard my mistake at once, of course, only it was too late to take it back. Silence. Another round of invalid mints. This time William took one, sucking furiously. At last I said:

"I guess we should thank our Aunt for your being here, Willy."

"She has made it financially possibly, certainly."

"How was it, I mean with Aunt Kate?"

She'd been living in New York, he explained – West 44th Street – in the thick of it, but with each visit she was becoming more forgetful. Then a sharp decline.

"She was once," I recalled, "Father's intellectual equal. He depended on her," I added, struck with the realization. And the fact of her life – looking back on it with the new distinctness which the completion of it gave – now seemed sadly wasted. Had she not been meant for independence, for a position? Yet she'd given herself instead to *us*. "And what did we give her?" I asked.

Henry turned marmoreal; William did not flinch – but then he had nothing to be ashamed of. The fact of abandonment rested with Henry and me alone.

"You," said Henry to William, "were 'with' her to the end."

William, misperceiving it as a slight, scowled. I saw us lining up – William and Aunt Kate on one side of the Atlantic (dutiful, self-sacrificing), Henry and I on the other (cowardly, shame-facedly); both images absurdly simplistic (impossible; inaccurate; inevitable).

"I'm so glad," I told him, "she had you."

Even as I said it, I knew it to be an illusion. The idea of 'having' anyone was silly. But then I was in a position to begin to know it, and my brothers, however clever, were not.

"Yes," he smiled, "and you," – he fixed me with one of his cross-eyed looks – "have Katharine."

The thought of 'having' Katharine set me coughing. When I'd recovered I added: "And Henry of course has been with me all along."

William reached for the Bible beside my bed. "You have been reading . . .?"

"The Old Testament . . ."

"And its effect?"

"Oh, shocking," I told him. "A work more calculated to destroy all religious belief never was writ, I fancy. As for that all-seeing-dancing-singing Being, He is really quite . . . repulsive."

"And our father's rather more benign divinity?" asked Henry.

"Especially not."

"You do not believe at all, then?" William asked.

"Only Henry's use of the semi-colon," I replied, "is enough to make me see God."

Poor Willy, shaking himself like a sack of potatoes, began explaining about other forms of religious and spiritual experience. But Katharine cut him off – could he not see that I was in pain?

"Time for another dose of morphine," she said, having consulted Wardy.

"An inestimable blessing," muttered Henry.

"Indeed," agreed Katharine, "but it's also a treacherous fiend that keeps her from sleeping and opens the door to hideous nervous distresses."

"Ah," intoned William, "the return of the demons. I recommend hypnotism – have I mentioned that I saw the great Charcot use it at Salpetriere?"

"Yes, Willy," I managed. "Come again, please, after you've been to the opening night . . . tell me all about it."

"Opening?" He looked for a brief moment nonplussed; then: "Oh, yes, The American."

Was that a *wink* from Henry?

Sixty-six

"I guess you'd have to call it a social success," William grudged, referring to the 'intimate' supper Henry had given afterwards at a 'cozy' restaurant in the Strand. He began ticking off the other guests: the Comptons and Miss Robins (the show's stars), William Heinemann the publisher, and Henry's theatrical agent Wolcott Balestier. "A select group," he supposed, oozing indifference.

"But not really your 'cup of tea', eh Willy?"

"Well, I fear my provincialism may have embarrassed Henry, though I was able to mention a performance I'd been to in Boston with Miss Robins as Hedda Gabler."

"Well done, Willy," said I, in a reversal of the usual fraternal condescension. "But the play itself – how did you find it?"

My 'psychological' brother, normally unrestrained when it came to speaking his mind about almost anything, was at a loss for words. He spoke of it as 'an occasion'. "The theater," he recalled, "was packed to the top" – he began sprinkling names like confetti – "with the American minister, Robert Lincoln, in a box to his left . . . another American millionaire to the right . . . a famous tycoon . . .," and so on and so forth.

"And with whom did you sit, Willy?"

"Oh, Grace Norton and I," he was pleased to say, "made up the Cambridge, Mass, contingent." Henry's Southern 'friend' Constance Woolson, he added, had sat nearby, thus expanding their little group into a thoroughly inclusive American one.

"But the production, Willy?" I pursued. I was determined to have some idea of the opening through his eyes.

"Oh," he managed, "it was obviously a success judging by the applause, really quite a roar."

"But the *play*, Willy" – here I had him – "do you rate it?"

"Whe-ell," he drawled, "I guess the heroine – meant for a French noble-woman, I guess" – he was doing an awful lot of guessing – "fidgeted about too much, as if still stuck on playing a neurotically morbid Norwegian. As for Newman – the American – well, I guess he was American alright."

"You mean he had the accent."

"Oh, the accent was there and then some."

"I take it you thought him . . . caricatured?"

"Oh," he burst out, "a stage American with the local color laid on with a trowel. And," he added, "a great deal of ugly overcoat." This latter item he went on to describe as having "sky-blue velvet lapels and buttons big as cheese-plates."

I held out my arms. "Oh Willy, how could you?" I cried. And although I laughed more than I had in ages, it did nothing to calm my fears for Henry and his entanglement in the world of theatricals. But – he consulted his fob-watch – he was all out of kilter – it was time for him to go.

"Calm yourself, Willy or I will accuse *you* of hysteria."

"Alice" – abruptly he assumed the 'role' of doctor – the pain, how is it?"

"Oh, the pain is very well, thank you."

He entreated me to be serious for once in my life.

Ah, my life. "Well, Willy, I guess there are times it feels as if an animal were gnawing away at my breast. Once," I confessed, "I managed to faint away. But not to worry, dear, so long as Wardy pours enough of the right 'cocktail' of stuff down my gullet – that kills it off – the animal, I mean." My best smile, I gave him.

"And you do not feel . . . hemmed in?" His hand, I noted, had begun creeping towards mine, as if it had nothing to do with Henry himself. Soon it began tapping and stroking, tapping and stroking. Was he trying to send an SOS? If so, I could not read his message, only that his touch was comforting.

But did I feel hemmed in? I replied: "I could be bounded in a nutshell and count myself a queen of infinite space."

"Do I detect a quote?" he growled (tap tap, stroke).

"Hamlet, only slightly adjusted. Of course," I admitted, "there are sometimes unfortunate . . . side effects." I did not elaborate, preferring to spare him the horrors that had begun visiting me – vivid, photographic, hideous – printed as it were on my eyelids – making sleep – the nights – an all too familiar – nightmare. Beasts – the return of the wolves – howling – the chattering birds . . .

"Alice?"

"Yes, Willy?"

"If you are having nervous trouble – it is not uncommon in such cases – I recommend mesmerism – or hypnosis, as it's now called. As it happens, there's a reputable fellow here in London, a Charles Tuckey – I've read his book actually on the therapeutic effects."

I laughed – not without pain – at the suggestion, reminding him that I had already tried it with, uh, 'mixed' results.

He waved it away. "That was mesmerism – quackery – this is medically creditable. Give it a try, Alice . . ."

He came closer, looming like a fog, the tremor visible, violent. "Dearest Alice . . .," he whispered. The tremor entering my bones, percussing through all the hollows of me. "Willy, you're crushing me," I protested. Then I hissed into his ear: "You once promised to marry me." "Did I?" he croaked, whispering in return that in twelve years of marriage he had never once talked with his wife about "the innumerable things that are of the most importance" as he had with me. Finally – as if torn from him – all ragged about the edges – "How Henry will miss your conversation!"

I was tempted to remind him I was not (yet) the dying Pegetty, and he was not David Copperfield.

I pushed him away as roughly as I could though I had the strength of a flea. "Farewell, Willy-boy. Be well. Don't give up on Henry. Let Rob know when you think he can take it. Oh, there's a Will – Katharine will see it through – I'll be there before long – place me beside the parents. Off you go, dearest." And off he went.

Sixty-seven

"I should like to turn into a peak when I die," declared Constance Woolson. Since word had got round of my 'condition', my old friends – Annie Richards, Fanny Morse, etc – those that remained alive – were queuing up to 'see me off', as if I were going on a long journey. A kind of honeymoon, albeit tinged with a certain mortuary flavor. Only Connie was prepared to give death its rightful name.

"And you, Alice?" She'd been fitted with a new kind of ear-trumpet hidden in her sleeve, so that mercifully we no longer had to shout.

"Oh," I replied, "I anticipate a pile of neat, unassuming grey ash, the sooner the better."

She frowned but did not look away. Her skin seemed thinner, more transparent – beneath the buxom shape you could sense a wren's bones – as if suffering had caused a physical reduction. Henry again. That heroic docility, that acceptance of his committed indifference. Yet her own 'inclination' remained, the need to reach him in any way she could. Did she 'care' for me beyond the fact of my being Henry's sister? I thought not; yet if the sight of me brought him to mind, caused a quickening in her already hopping heart, well, was it not a compliment, a kind of 'caring'?

"You were at the Opening?" I began.

"Yes," she smiled to herself, "and several other performances, as Henry's guest."

Henry's guest. I waited. "And?"

"He was dreadfully nervous at the Opening. At about four o'clock his knees began to knock together. Having refused

394

dinner he then went off to the theatre and walked about the stage dusting the mantel-piece and turning down the corners of the rugs."

"As he does with mine."

She paused. "But then," she went on, "an extraordinary transformation took place. As soon as the curtain went up he became calm as a clock."

"Tick tock," said I.

"Do you mock the occasion, Alice?"

"Never. But come," I encouraged, "tell me about the play."

"It has had an 'honorable run'."

"So I gather from the reviews," I said. We both understood the implications of 'honorable'.

"You think . . .?" she began.

"It is not for him," I said straight out.

"You are convinced of it?"

I nodded.

"Of course," she pointed out, "you have not actually seen it."

I admitted it was so. "But I know my brother, and his . . . capacities." I went on, "I can only hope he'll stop at this 'honorable run'. But I suspect he will go on until . . ."

I feared her eyes would pop.

"Is there nothing you can do to stop him?" I entreated.

She shook her head. "He has complained about being straight-jacketed by the stage, it is true, yet he is quite determined to see it through . . . to the bitter end."

Tea saved us.

"What will you do now, Alice?" "I will live," I replied simply.

"Will you write?" She'd spoken of her own new novel – stories 'rolling' out at an alarming rate.

"Is that not living?" I shot back.

"Indeed."

But I was not convinced of it. Writing for Connie, I saw,

was not life; it was a retreat, a place she went to observe others living; and it had tired her out to do so, leaving her depleted. She needed 'filling up'.

"For some time now," she explained, "we have been planning – perhaps Henry has spoken of it? – a theatrical collaboration."

This last – her true meaning neatly embedded – a 'collaboration' of the affections. And there beside it, in all its terrible enormity, the truth: *She is living for Henry.* That 'flame' – you felt it beneath the feathery surface – burned – had never been quenched – more intensely than ever. Her situation was as bad, if not worse, than any she or I – or Henry – could ever dream up. This, I saw, was what she would think – it was only natural:

Now that his precious Alice is gone, should he not be more attentive to me?

"And Florence?" I asked.

"Oh, Florence." She began confessing that Florence without Lizzie and her little family, and Mr Boott, would be a sad place and perhaps she could move permanently to Oxford.

To be near Henry, I thought. What could I to say to that? I considered extending a sisterly wish. *Oh, I do hope that you and Henry will – what? – marry? live happily ever after . . .?* My other option I saw was to warn her to be sensible, to give up any unrealistic expectations.

"There has been a letter."

"From Henry?"

"From Henry. He has been over to Italy for a reviving break." I did not say when the letter was dated.

She waited.

"He has seen the Pope. He describes him as 'a flaccid old woman'."

She waited. Was this how a surgeon felt preparing to cut off a limb? "He describes the men as" – I quoted – " 'bare-chested, bare-legged, magnificently tanned & muscular'."

"And the women?" she asked.

I waited. "He fails to mention them."

She rose up like a dignified spectre, her near-burst of Southern temper, like one of that region's flash floods, having quickly evaporated.

"We shall see," she said tightly, revealing – still – a remaining sliver of hope like one of those near-invisible ice needles known to fall from Boston roofs and implant themselves fatally in people's skulls. She would risk all – bravely or foolishly? – she would give him – after I was dead and buried – a seemly interval of course – one last chance. After that – why, he would assure her of his undying friendship – even a possible play together – and then what? Why, she would return to Italy where she would give up trying to be near him.

She left me with the manuscript of a recent story entitled, 'Dorothy'. In it, 'Dorothy', decides it is better to be dead than leave her villa, so there she lives slowly wasting away. Was it a hopeful sign? wondered Katharine. Could they not take it that Connie, like her 'Dorothy', would live for a good long while in her Tuscan villa?

Sixty-eight

"So it's you."

Bowles the mesmerist – alias Dr Tuckey the hypnotist – bowed shallowly – it would not do to scrape the floor with his nose – presenting in his re-incarnated form as conservative, respectable, *scientific*. Yet how to take him seriously; indeed, how to 'take him' at all? Bowles the Jack-in-the box, a respectable physician with the edges knocked off and a moonbeam personality, was having trouble meeting my gaze.

As for Katharine, was she not heroic to have traced him to his Park Lane 'practice' and brought him to me? I mean, what if I 'succumbed' again? Did she not risk all? "If he can be of help . . . ," said the Selfless One in a cracked voice. What matter, was the implication, if I should succumb *at this late stage*?

But would I? Would a repeat rapture come and lift me out of myself? Would I – at the mere sight of his whiskers – roll my eyes heavenward and part my bow-lips in a moan of pleasure a la Bellini's Theresa *en orgasme*? It remained for me, for us both, to find out. As for whether I would 'give him away' professionally – that also remained, as it were, to be seen.

"So," I observed, "you have risen in the world."

And you have sunk, he was big enough not to say. Instead: "And you still have a good while to live." Naturally he'd assumed such reassurance of lastingness would please me. It did not.

398

"That is not what I want to hear, you idiot!" I yawped. Nothing could warm my spinsterish heart, I explained, but to be told the end was nigh.

Seeing the havoc he'd wrought, he then tried to patch it up: "Oh, but you won't be uncomfortable."

"Uncomfortable? What can you know about it?"

Poor Bowles-Tuckey, looking as if he might burst into tears, began mopping his brow with a tiny pink handkerchief. I burst out laughing: *Was I once infatuated with this pert little Lazarus?*

"Perhaps," Katharine interjected, "You could give us a demonstration so that we might learn the trick of it?" After all, had she not already learned how to administer morphine by the hypodermic method, and hadn't Harriet Martineau's niece been taught how to hypnotize her aunt to soothing effect? His gaze travelled slowly from one of us to the other and seeing that we were not to be separated and that it was something we would manage or not together, he nodded, reaching into the depths of his travelling bag out of which arose a bulky object wrapped in black fabric which he unwrapped ceremoniously flap by flap staring down at it as it lay in his lap like a man in love, or as if he himself had been hypnotized. The object – indeed striking to the eye – was an ornately carved silver gilt lancet case.

"Mr Bowles . . . Tuckey . . . whatever your name is," she held up her hand as he began lifting the thing from its case, "I hope you do not intend to perform a bloodletting."

His smile was a crooked one.

He denied it.

I wished he was less handsome.

"In that case," Katharine permitted: "please proceed."

Here Bowles-Tuckey flipped open the lid to reveal two 'thumb' lancets made of mother-of-pearl with gold rivet indentations like huge golden moons or eyes for the comfortable placing of the thumb while performing a phlebotomy. Oh, but *these* would not be used for such a violent, bloody purpose – quite the reverse, he reassured us.

"Indeed, you will feel relaxed, refreshed and pain free."

"Do you guarantee it?" asked Katharine.

"I am merely your source," came his narrow-eyed reply: "It is for you to reap the benefit." So saying, he brought the open lancet case close to my face, at first level with my eyes but then raised it to a position above my forehead which Katharine complained could he not see was causing a strain to the eyes and eyelids; which in turn caused him to lose his temper and shout at her *did he not know precisely what he was doing and there must be no talking whatsoever during the session, was that perfectly clear?*

She raised a hand as if to order him out of the house or strike him but I entreated her to desist.

"Continue, Arthur," said I.

So he did, instructing me to keep my eyes steadily fixed on the lancets within their case, my mind riveted on the idea of them. What 'idea' could a pair of lancets possibly have? I thought, ready to dismiss the thing for a farce. But as I stared at them the gold moon-like indentations seemed to stare back at me so that I could not take my own eyes away if I had tried (though I was vaguely aware that my neck had begun to ache). At some point he moved the case downwards which for some reason caused my eyes to close. Then darkness. I felt one of my arms being floated up towards the ceiling where it remained for some time before floating back to earth.

At this point he instructed me in a wispy voice to imagine myself in 'a happy place'. I was about to shout, There is no such place! when a vivid memory-picture arose of the Falls at Niagara where I had been taken by Aunt Kate. I am eighteen years old standing before the Falls unable to move or be moved, hypnotized by its apparent mass like a flowing sheet of curved solid glass as it slides continually over the ridge followed at last by a cataclysmic separation into individual droplets in which I feel myself falling falling falling. . . .

"Alice!" came the snap of his fingers. Or perhaps it was the lid of the lancet case shutting, I do not know, but all at once I was wide awake.

"How are you feeling, Alice?"

I admitted to a sensation of warmth in my back and breast.

"And the pain?"

I smiled, "What pain?"

Sixty-nine

"Confine yourself to the vernacular," advised Katharine: "no decorative bequeaths."

So I began, "I, Alice James, Spinster of the Town of Manchester in the County of Essex and Commonwealth of Massachusetts, in the United States of America, now living at 41 Argyll Road, Kensington, England, make this my will and testament as follows . . .".

My property (I still owned the Manchester (US) cottage) and stocks, which amounted to an estate worth about $80,000, I left to William, Henry and Katharine, to be divided equally. To Rob and his family – he had a rich father-in-law – I left $10,000. The remaining I divided among various female friends and relatives; and to my namesake, Wilky's daughter, I left a gold watch and $2500. Rob's daughter, Mary, and William's daughter, Peggy, were to get $2500 a piece.

Katharine began adding the figures. A sum remained.

"Yes, another $1000 is for your cousin Alice Gray." She had earned my admiration by struggling for years without money to pursue a career in art.

"That leaves $150."

"Yes, that's for Wardy – Miss Ward."

For the rest, all my Boston furniture, including the portrait of Henry, was to go to William and Alice; and my pictures, china, and English furniture also to Henry.

To Katharine, all my remaining personal effects: silver, jewelry &etc.

The American Consul at Birmingham had been contacted by Katharine and wangled into coming to witness it. How good to get a Boston witness, I thought. Yet when the time came I lay in a semi-faint, draped in as many frills as could be found for the occasion, with Wardy at my head wearing the thickest layer of her anxious-devoted-nurse-expression. The Consul kept threatening to read the Will out loud, but Katharine restrained him with difficulty – causing him great frustration – arresting the flood of his eloquence.

Finally – it was like a scene in a novel – the document was placed before me. Through a mist I vaguely saw five black figures – others had been called upon as witnesses, including Annie Richards and a Miss Blanche Leppington – and so I signed, barely recognizing my own wayward signature. Eventually they all trooped off to Henry's for an elegant tea served by The Smiths, where the Consul, according to Henry, entertained them with his whole history and the digestive processes of his domestic circle. "You were well out of it."

At the end of it all Miss Leppington had confided to Katharine, "Alice's face will remain in my thoughts as the most pathetic I ever saw and in my imagination as the most picturesque and American."

When Henry heard of it, he told me, "Well, you can't say you've done nothing for your Race since you've brought that about – the picturesque and the American – in your own person."

Picturesque at last, I thought: *and* American!

Seventy

"What is it, Alice?"

"Nothing."

"You have at least three stories inside you, Alice. Choose one." Tea or coffee, simple. She'd bought me the fattest scribbler she could find. Places; people; things people say . . . but a *story*? It was, I began to see, a quite different kind of writing from the scraps, the letters, the diary entries . . .

"I will never manage," I said miserably. "I will surely peg out before the end."

"Never mind, do as much as you can."

Katharine is my obedient scribe. When I hesitate, she hesitates. When I stumble, it is if her hand has been snagged. On good days we swoop and pounce together kestrel-like, and then there is progress. On bad days however when I have trouble concentrating I must steer through it in the way of a child on a bicycle wobbling her way between two converging carriages.

There are too many images in my head at once, too many possibilities all clamoring for attention like needy children. There is the 'real' Constance and the 'idea' of Constance. But she must be transformed into Hectoria. And in spite of her absurd name she must not be absurd.

"Did you know she was the grand-niece of James Fenimore Cooper?" I informed Katharine. Yes, of course she did. But there she was obediently taking down my words, my drug-fueled imaginings spooling and spiralling from who-knew-where; while her hand – riding along – loop-de-loop – steered by invisible filaments – formed the words, sentences, paragraphs on the page. Such gentle obedience, such *mansuetude*. The word pleased me; its literal meaning: 'accustomed to the hand'.

But the story so far?

What story?

It comes as in a dream. Or perhaps it is a dream. Hectoria has gone to Venice. She has taken rooms in the Casa Semitecolo. It is winter and there is freezing fog which enters her chest with every breath like so many ectoplasmic goblins. She has had a bad bout of influenza. Her nose streams unromantically and she is feverish. Will he come? she thinks, gazing out into the fog, and then fears it, aware of looking as unattractive as she does. But that is absurd: if he comes, everything will be all right, she will be restored.

"Can she be that naïve?" challenges Katharine.

"Naïve?" Oh, I see the problem. I have not done her justice. She must tell her own story, how it feels to pace back and forth on that cold Italian floor, to wait for someone who may never come, to shiver and sweat with fever, to feel her life as a writer has come to an end, that all her ideas have fizzled out while up on the roof a cat yowls . . .

I ran a finger along the still-wet needle trail on my arm. I brought the finger to my lips. My decision, writ in blood on my forearm, was made. I would claim the 'I' for myself; or rather, for my character, Hectoria. She who will demand, and get attention from the reader, even if she cannot get it from the lover she desires; will get it when she chooses; seduce when it pleases her. The taste of blood, even if it is only her own. Writer and reader, fated to become lovers.

"Alice?"

The taste of drugs, sharp, sweet, bitter, like a Sicilian orange, the kind, according to Henry, which grow only in the shadow of a volcano.

"Of course Henry will hate it," I pronounced. He will call it *cheap and easy*. "In fiction," I mimicked Henry at his most constipated, "there must be distance, observation, space, in which to expose the impediments to understanding a character and his feelings. The novelist, that is to say, should abhor the terrible fluidity (oh, how it comes pouring out!) of self-revelation."

I'm afraid we burst out laughing. Poor Henry, as if such 'revelation' were akin to disembowelling. But where was I? Where was Hectoria? Still pacing her cold rooms feeling . . . what? No narrator on earth, however fine of perception, could ever be as intimate with the truth of how she felt about what happened, or failed to happen, as she. It is too easy to hide behind the so-called 'objective' voice ('she imagined', 'she wished', 'she remembered', 'she succumbed', etc.). But I am too exhausted to continue. I must wait for her voice to speak to me. For her to come to me.

"But must she be so pathetic?" asks Katharine gently.

"No, only truthful."

"And what is to happen?"

"Happen?"

"In the end?"

Ah. I closed my eyes. One of the muscles in my cheek began to twitch and then, to my horror, came a most inappropriate snigger as I imagined Hectoria's dumpy little body floating down from her hotel balcony like an unfurled umbrella, eventually landing like a pile of funeral garb on the cobbles of that picturesque little street. At the same time my tears flew out incontinently, unstoppably as I heard her singing out Henry's name (but I must change that absent character's name, of course): operatically, absurdly, hilariously. Katharine attempted to staunch the flow with her hankie but I pushed her hand away. What I had to convey was her desperation to be cherished, her simple, human longing for love. She must come across not as naïve but brave, imbued with a kind of foolish hopeful American trust . . .

"The problem with the 'picturesque', I complained, "is that it cannot tolerate the real thing."

"The real thing?"

"Her body must be removed from the cobbles of that *picturesque* street, the Consul must close the area. Gossip must be avoided at all costs."

"I'm afraid there is another problem, dear, closer to hand," declares Katharine, the pedant; to wit: "How can she narrate her own suicide?"

I open my eyes. I do not know. But I can do no more. I must rest and so must Katharine. Her eyes are slitty and red-rimmed behind her spectacles as if she has not slept in a week or been silently sobbing her heart out.

*

A week later, unaccountably, she brings a photographer in to 'shoot' me. Wardy forces my arms into a satin bed jacket and ties a necktie rakishly around what is left of my scrawny neck. I think of a sentence out of Portrait of a Lady: 'Her poor winged spirit had always had a great desire to do its best, and it had not as yet been seriously discouraged.' But the resulting photograph showed nothing so much as a dried moth pinned to a page.

Seventy-one

William had claimed that cremation was fussy and expensive but my Kath, not one to be discouraged, wrote to the Cremation people at Woking outside London for their circular and lo! it turned out to be as simple and inexpensive as toasting marshmallows, and only six guineas and one extra for a parson. So my body is to be carried in a hearse to the Waterloo Station and from there by train to Woking where an anonymous clergyman will read a short, no-fuss service; then I will be well charred on both sides and my ashes scraped into a little wooden box.

"Where d'you want it placed?" asks Katharine.

I look up to find her removing streaks of grime from the wall-paper with a bit of india rubber.

It? I had not extended my imagination that far. "*It* really is the mind-twistingest of all conundrums."

"Is it, Alice?" *Rub-rub-rub.*

"How am I to decide on where I want to 'be' when I won't 'be' at all?"

She calls it 'a simple choice'.

"As in coffee or tea?"

No reply.

"Well, then," I hear myself say, "I should not like my bones buried in this damp, black alien English earth."

"There will be no bones as such" – brushing her hands into a pan – "only grit and ash."

"Ah."

Then: "I could carry it – the remains – back with me," she offers, magnanimous to a fault.

Me, she means; and 'back' to the States.

"Oh," say I, "I couldn't endure the journey again."

"You won't have to," grins the imp: "While I'm tucked up in my top berth convulsed with seasickness, you may be assured of a peaceful journey."

"You have thought of everything, haven't you?"

"If I do not," she replies, tossing the india rubber to me: "who will?"

Really, it is the most bizarre conversation I have ever had in my life, or rather *death*.

Dearest Willy,

It has been decided. I-as-ash in my eventual marble urn (to be designed by you, I gather) am not to be used as a parlor ornament for your new house but to be buried beside Father and Mother in the cemetery at Cam. Otherwise, as Henry warned, we shall become myths. I presume he meant 'we' exiles here in the Old World. I hope that meets with your approval.

Yours ever, Alice

Were those my bones rattling as I signed?

It was time for my sponge bath. Wardy removed my night-dress revealing the folds of flesh which had begun to drape themselves about my bones. The tumor was doing its best to outgrow the breast itself. I tried to hide the horror from Wardy but she would not be denied: she had seen worse, she assured me, in her short time. "What worse?" I asked ghoulishly. To which she maddeningly replied, "Wouldn't you like to know?" So then I countered with: "Well, did *you* know" – in my scare-mongeryest voice – "that witches are known to have three breasts?" At which she drew back as before a revenant making desperate grab for the crucifix she insisted on wearing outside her apron.

But the silly had already guessed I was 'one of those'.

But here comes a surprise. She is sponging my back when suddenly, in mid-sponge – quite astonishingly – she asks: "Should you have liked to decorate your own home, Miss?"

The question affects me more than I can say. However I manage to hide it by having one of my retching fits. As for an eventually answer, my tongue is tied, my vocal cords could be sold for old shroud lashing. The truth? I cannot fib; not while dying.

"Yes," I manage at last, all quivery-quavery: "yes, I should."

She cocks her head to one side. "You surprise me, Miss."

"Do I? I see no reason" – a rush of breath returns – "why a taste for pretty wallpaper should not co-exist with a taste for the vote."

But my little speech exhausts me and I fall into a reverie in which I am busy papering an entire wall in my bedroom at Quincy Street, the one that overlooks Harvard Yard. What do I choose? Why, black-edged 'In Memoriam' cards.

"There, there," soothes the Pious One with her long narrow Fra Angelica face, assuring me my unshriven soul will enter Paradise.

I have no interest in Paradise, I tell her, and ban her from wearing the cross. But then I think wonderingly about how while I'd been an invalid in my Quincy Street bedroom Miss Eustacia Ward had been toddling about a Gloucestershire village. And here she was now looking after me. Was that not a more fantastic thing than Paradise? I thought as a blessed peace fell upon me. How I got from the bath to my bed I cannot say.

Another note to William:

'It is as simple as any fact of nature, the fall of a leaf or the blooming of a rose, and I have a delicious consciousness, ever present, of wide spaces close at hand, and whisperings of release in the air.

Your always loving and grateful sister,
Alice'

Seventy-two

"Do show Henry my story," I instructed Katharine. I meant of course after my demise. Her reaction was unaccountable. She screwed up her eyes and swivelled her mouth to one side:

"I believe that may be unwise."

"Unwise? Is it after all such a poor thing?"

"No," she insisted, "it is not to do with the writing so much as his reaction to it." She looked about as if to make certain he hadn't manifested out of thin air. 'I mean," she attempted to clarify, "it may frighten him . . . threaten him." She was being unusually dramatic. "I feel that he may do something irretrievable."

Her words shocked me, forcing me to consider the story from Henry's point of view. Of course he would hate it for being *cheap and easy*, but more than that, he would assume, and would he not be right? that it was *about him*.

But I have no strength left. "Do what you think best with it," I tell her.

A finger of light streams through the thin curtain. Henry is fresh and sad, drooping of eyelid and pallid of face, yet resonant with excitement. He presses my cheek with the back of his hand. His new play, he tells me, is called 'Mrs Vibert'.

Has he already forgotten my warning? Apparently so.

"What amuses you, Alice?"

"Curtains," I murmur. *Curtains going up, curtains going down*. "Is it not a droll coincidence?"

A rueful smile. As ever, he is able to read my thoughts –

but only in part. *My* curtain may be about to fall for the last time; *his*, he apparently feels sure, will continue to rise for years to come, and to rapturous applause. How can he be so sure? But the future, I tell myself, is no longer my worry. (Though I believe – I am determined – Irish Home Rule, like Emancipation, is one of the immutable moralities sure of triumph in spite of all set-backs.)

He asks after Katharine. "She has been watching over me all night," I tell him, adding: "I am working away as hard as I can to get dead so as to release her to the outside world – as well as you of course." He demurs, says it is not a release that he anticipates with much enthusiasm.

"What more, Henry?"

He describes his new young acolyte: handsome, bearded . . . a sculptor.

"I am thinking of commissioning a bust of you."

"Will it include *all* my busts?" I ask impishly, touching my left breast. Oh dear, I have embarrassed him. But, come, he knows very well that there is no time for a bust, with or without the extra lump; unless it be a death mask – for which I have given my permission.

There is still the 'problem' of Constance. I am determined not to let him forget. "Her story 'Dorothy'," I ask him: "have you read it?"

He gives one of his auctioneer's nods.

"In that case, you know there is a message in it for you."

He turns his head away, as if to avoid an unpleasant smell or a tastelessly decorated room. He has moved on, I understand, taken up with new friends, reinvented himself: Henry James, the playwright. In the drama gesture is all.

Another mistake.

"Please, dear . . .," I murmur, but I sense him already rising to go and Katharine preparing to take his place. Has so much time passed? Unsurprisingly, they do not keep watch together; though I hear him report to her that I have been "making sentences." *Making sentences*, the phrase makes me smile. Have I been telling Henry about Hectoria in a quavering chirp? I have no recollection.

I know now what will happen. Katharine, who has had the intention to 'deal with' Hectoria herself, and knowing better than anyone my intention, will attempt to complete it to the best of her prosaic ability. But before she has gotten very far she begins to ask herself: Am I really doing it the justice it deserves? Her doubts having crept in now grow great. She begins to suspect she was wrong and that I was right after all:

It must go to Henry.

She understands it calls for someone with a writerly flair to fill in the gaps, to realize its author's intention of *orchestrating* it so it will live. As Alice well knows, she thinks, knowing herself to have no ear.

She has begun sorting through my correspondence – another necessary chore – when she comes upon a letter from William that especially catches her attention. It is dated August, 1890 and it says, 'I am entirely certain that *you've got a book inside of you* . . . which will come out yet. Perhaps it's the source of all your recent trouble.' Carrying on with the sorting, she will find another badgering letter from William: 'I do hope that you will leave some notes on life and English life which Harry can work in hereafter, so as to make the best book he ever wrote.'

Which Harry can work in hereafter.

In her thoughtful way she will reflect on the matter. But the final 'act' – it makes me chuckle to myself to think of it – will come upon her suddenly – an impulse of the moment. She is tired and let us say grief-stricken, and so one day she knocks peremptorily on Henry's door; Smith opens; she thrusts a package into his hands. It contains my story along with the manila envelope full of scraps of unfinished bits. There is a covering letter explaining my wish that the story at least be made public in some form or other. "Please make sure Mr James gets this," and she dashes off before she changes her mind.

Katharine waits to get word from Henry but alas none comes. She puts off travelling home for a month – there are things left to do concerning my affairs – but still nothing. At some point she confronts Henry and asks him about my novel. He tells her he has no knowledge of such a thing.

And the stories? fragments in the envelope?

He sucks in his cheeks. As far as he is aware, there is only a diary containing a few precious *telles-quelles*.

The only thing I regret is the pain which this will cause Katharine. She will blame herself for a bad decision. But that is foolish, the responsibility is all mine. She has merely obeyed my instructions. It is I who failed to consider the consequences.

Henry is reading my story. He reads it rather hurriedly, I see, turning each page tremblingly. It makes him almost sick with horror at the thought of it coming to light, of the publicity, of his implied role in the story. Then there's the prediction of 'Hectoria's suicide. How would poor Constance like to read that? Impossible. It is, he decides, the sad, violently misjudged product of a morphine-soaked brain. It is not a beautiful story. He considers reshaping it, turning it into something less incriminating, something approaching a story *en temps et lieu*, but there is no time. Besides, its publication in any form would be a disaster.

Flames nip at me, eager to conclude. Early spring, I guess people are poking at their bonfires. The smell of burning hangs in the air. The feel of her open palm on my forehead, slipping down to cup my cheek then pulling itself lazily across my mouth so I can kiss it goodbye. Katharine, my beautiful counterpart.

Seventy-three

If the aim of life is the accretion of fat, the consumption of food unattended by digestive disorganization followed by a succession of pleasurable sensations – then I am one of life's great failures. A sack of whippety bones; enormous eyes; a nose worthy of a Christmas reindeer.

We have finished 'Dorothy' and gone on to the memoirs of the Electress Sophia of Hanover. I guess it's Katharine's last-ditch attempt to bring me into the fold of true history. It is a story about Sophia's sister Elizabeth, Abbess of Herford. That excellent woman knew every language and science under the sun, corresponded with Descartes, was also very handsome, &etc. But – and here is the rub – her nose was apt to grow red and 'all her philosophy could not save her from vexation'. So when this misfortune overtook her 'she used to hide herself from the world'.

Poor Liz, think I, for which of us has not a red nose at the core of her being which defies all her philosophy and courage? So it is with me.

"Dear Kath," I entreat, "will you powder it?"

Vanity plays her hand to the end. The puffing powder makes me gag – and Kath herself – and Wardy – but it is worth it. Anything not to die with a red nose!

*

Pain falls away. Never mind that I am addicted, as the medical men say, as one of the 'weaker sex enfeebled by illness but selfishly fond of pleasure'. Yet I am perfectly clear

415

and humorous and would talk if doing so did not bring on revolting spasms of coughing. I can still manage a whisper, however, so into Henry's ear I dictate a final message to be cabled to Willy: TENDEREST LOVE TO ALL FAREWELL AM GOING SOON ALICE.

This year has been rich beyond compare, the heart all aglow with the affections of friend and brother, the mind deeply stirred by the human comedy with its flow of succulent juices, the spirit broadened and strengthened even as the carcass withers. But there is something I have left out, tidied away. The folding of history in the manner of a hope chest.

Once upon a time there were two brilliant, successful brothers . . . oh, and I almost forgot, two other brothers called Wilkinson and Robertson; otherwise known as Wilky and Rob. What hope did these brothers have? Lamentably little. They were not brilliant; not what you would call 'successful': quite the reverse. But oh, I want to cry out – if only I could – failure is . . . *necessary* . . . *essential*. Was it not what the pater taught us all those years ago? For without it there was nothing to the eventual accomplishment? But what, dear pater – what if the afflictions, the trials, outdid one? Outdid your boys?

There was a war. A Civil War. So it had been called. Wilky and Rob enlisted. Rob, our youngest brother: Rob or Bob, *BobBobBob* like a little cocksparrow. The odd thing – was it odd? – was that they had both led regiments of free black men. That in itself was a triumph, was it not? That in itself should be remembered. And then Wilky was wounded at Fort Wagner. Here are the facts: A canister ball entered his ankle and shattered the bone. Was not removed for eight days. And when he returned, a shell fragment hit him in the back, settling into a neat little pocket under the skin near his spine. When he came home afterwards I was afraid to go near him fearing – as if his body had been peppered with assorted exploding devices – he was in danger of 'going off'. A girl's fantasy. Whereas the truth, of his having to live with constant pain, was too awful, too ordinary, too familiar. Wilky 'adipose and affectionate' – so Father had once described him – was afflicted with hysterical blindness, heart trouble, Bright's Disease.

And little Bob? He was 'awful homesick'. The pater scolded him for effiminacy, told him to *force yourself like a man and do your whole duty*. But no forcing could overcome the truth as he saw it. "Our side has won," wrote little Bob at the end, "but I feel I have lost."

After that? The two brothers bought a plantation down in Florida with money borrowed from our father. People called it a 'mad venture'. Unsurprisingly it didn't work out. But I say the following adjectives shall, must, be added: brave, brave and true, and decent. Yes, but hardly a success, alas.

Wilky died of heart failure.

Rob is still alive but drinks alcohol and has to be hospitalized from time to time.

Enough. I dropped them into the story and now I propose to abandon them once again, repeating the whole disastrous thing.

As for me, tucked up in my invalid's bed? Oh I was protected by my sex. I did not have to earn a living or 'act the man.' And as I did not have to fight I received no wounds to the body. But according to Henry, our 'upbringing' – such as it was – had consequences for us all. *Funesti*, he called it. Fatal.

Then there was that other notion put about by our father which we absorbed right from the beginning, which asserted that in any one family there is a limited (i.e., finite) fund of health and pleasure. Imagine a sort of bank account of well-being and accomplishment; so that, for example, if one of us took sick, it would be in order that the others could remain healthy. This theory he also applied to success, intelligence, genius. Unfortunately, by the time these attributes got to Rob and Wilky, their store was sorely depleted, having been 'used up' by William and Henry.

And little Alice? Where will she 'stand' between the 'successes' and the 'failures'? Will she distinguish herself or be blown away, another sooty flake like Rob and Wilky?

Last night I had a dream in which Lizzie Boott appeared along with Clover and Ellen Hooper. They are standing up in a boat, just putting out to sea. The sea is tumbled like bedclothes. They pass from under a cloud into bright sunlight but still look back at me standing at the edge of the shore as if beckoning to me in their mute way to join them.

That scene now fades and father appears, his beard curling jocosely among the clouds. I tell him the latest news. "In the last year Henry has published *The Tragic Muse*, and also brought *The American* to the stage, *and* is planning further theatricals. Then there's William's many volumes of *Psychology* and something about varieties of religious experience. Not a bad show for one family – especially if I get myself dead, the hardest job of all." And there is something else besides: a serious, private thing not to do with accomplishments, or not as such.

Dear Pater – guess what? Those creatures you called 'chattering birds of night' turn out to be plain old bats with delicate connecting draperies, tiny pointed ears and teeth, and bead-eyes; precious and perfect as persian miniatures or tapestries done with the finest needles.

The howling wolves? *Puppydogs.*

So much for your demons, dear.

And your curse.

Seventy-four

I am at the theater, or so it appears. I have been given a seat in the front row, reserved for me by Henry. The curtain twitches but doesn't open quite yet. It is the moment before, to be distinguished from other later moments. Let it soon be filled, I think, *pray*, with the applause Henry wishes for. Let it be marked like a book. Let it extend and stretch like the night sky or a story with no *fin*.

The curtain opens on Act One. A well-appointed drawing-room. A fire in the hearth. Two chairs face one another and in them sit my brother Henry and his doctor and friend, William Wilberforce Baldwin, who has been staying with him.

It is evening and they are relaxing after dinner, paunches-ho, beside Henry's fire. His dainty lyre chairs barely contain them, especially after the partridge and pudding. Port and cigars will now be drunk and puffed respectively according to male ritual. Baldwin looks about the room, for the moment avoiding Henry's troubled expression. The room, he notes approvingly, glows with the evidence of Henry's success. He is naturally aware of its extreme orderliness, somewhat unusual, he considers, in someone of artistic sensibility admiring particularly the Persian rug (not to be compared with my own cheap Turkey rug) and an inlaid display cabinet with a serpentine front and swan-neck pediments.

Now Baldwin, with Henry's permission, rises, goes towards it, makes free to turn the key, the better to examine the romping stags, simpering geishas and laughing buddhas.

Concerning this piece of furniture, by the way, I was told of it by Henry with not a little pride; alternatively by William with not a little ill-concealed glee. 'Monstrous', he called it, predicting it would give its owner nightmares'. In the same letter he wrote saying Henry had 'covered himself, like some marine crustacean, with all sorts of material growth, rich seaweeds and rigid barnacles and things, and lives hidden in the midst of his strange heavy alien manners and customs.' To his credit, however, he added this: 'Beneath all the accretions, he is still the same dear innocent old Harry of our youth.' In my reply to William I pointed out there was no accounting for Henry's tastes. Katharine put it down to his 'change of life'.

But to return to our little drama.

"Katharine Loring . . .?" begins Baldwin. Henry frowns, he does not like thinking about her, especially in relation to me. Baldwin however admits to something of a fascination for 'the friend'. The word 'unwholesome' crosses Henry's mind. "No, no, nothing like that," says Baldwin, reading him. "I mean only that I have long been puzzled – may I be frank? – about Miss Loring's motive for tending to Alice so . . . faithfully."

Silence. "You suspect . . .?" insinuates Henry.

Again Baldwin is forced to clear the air with a doctorly wave. He is not expressing himself well. It is not an easy matter. If he is not careful he will insult poor Alice and, by extension, Henry. How to put it delicately? What he really longs to say is *Why on earth, man, would a healthy, vibrant, dynamic, productive, free spinster (but with family responsibilities of her own) choose to give it all up to live with a wretched invalid, albeit the sister of Henry James?*

"I suspect nothing," comes the reply: "merely the medical man's prerogative; and the writer's, I presume?" he adds interrogatively. Henry nods but there is tension, Baldwin observes, in the chords of his friend's neck. Baldwin, who has assumed an infinite curiosity on his friend's part, realizes his mistake. Henry has two 'blind spots', and this is one of them. Tread softly, he counsels himself. The question of an 'intimacy' is clearly beyond discussion; though how to account for it in general may, he assumes, be broached without danger.

"An attraction of opposites . . .?" he chances.

Henry appears not to react one way or the other.

"But about Miss Loring herself," he carries on: "I have been considering the possibility of a way out."

"A way out . . .?" echoes Henry.

Baldwin is pleased. He has engaged his friend's attention, diverting it from the source of anxiety. Best not to mention the sister at this stage.

"A way out of doing all the things she might have done had she – Miss Loring – Katharine, that is – been entirely free."

"I see," says Henry.

Baldwin groans. He is not sparing Henry any pain. What he sees – what they both understand is that if Katharine had not attached herself to Alice, she would have accomplished a great deal more. And yet he's now daring to suggest that that in fact may have been one of her motives. A way out, that is, an easing of her own burdens; so that she and Alice, in the end, there is a kind of parity, they become co-equals in the 'game' of invalid and carer.

Henry is thinking quite the opposite, of all those who have said to him, *What would she do without Katharine?* No, there has not been 'an equality'. "She has no doubt enjoyed the 'role' of saviour," says Henry, not without venom.

"Do you really think so?" asks Baldwin.

"Do you not?" Henry queries, feeling miserably exposed.

"If you mean she has proved indispensable, it cannot be denied; but not as a motive – to save – no I do not."

"Then what is left?" asks Henry, who has to blink hard to rid himself of a vision of a monstrous Katharine looming up before him barring his way, stopping him from saying

421

goodbye to Alice. Suddenly he is struck with another possibility. "Perhaps she has devoted herself to 'saving' Alice from me?" The smile is a painful one. Baldwin, who is a musical man, thinks of an analogy in sound, the scraping of a violin bow, and winces in sympathy. In the end there is only one thing to do: to ease Henry's mind, and his own.

"Of course your sister is extraordinary."

Henry agrees, daring to add: "An extraordinary failure."

Baldwin is both shocked and impressed. "Of course she naturally attracts . . . in her situation . . .".

"Yes, we have all . . . had to attend to her."

Baldwin smiles to himself. He believes that Katharine has done more than 'attend'. She has entered Alice's pain with unconditional love and sympathy and – unlike William with his 'tragic' view of her and Henry's too-close identification – adopted Alice's own stoical attitude. Which has, it might be said, saved them both.

"But surely," he ventures, "one must allow for an extreme devotion?"

Henry cannot deny it.

A knock is heard from Stage left. Good timing. Here comes Smith with a nightcap. Pause while he pours their brandies. Baldwin, sniffing his tumbler, congratulates Henry on his choice. Henry accepts the compliment. They both know it can't be put off forever. At last Henry takes courage and questions Baldwin about me. He has seen enough to know there is no hope; rather, the only true hope is that I may fizzle out sooner rather than later. I hear him tell Baldwin that although I am a receptacle of recurrent, renewable, inexhaustible forms of disease, my lucidity and moral command of the situation & etc, allowing for Baldwin's belladonna and William's morphine, are unimpaired.

But how is Henry to formulate his question? An idea comes to him for a tale about an invalid. He is not concerned with the squalid details of her illness but in the consequences of it, and its eventual outcome. Now, let us see what happens if . . . He is the tale's designer, its arranger; he is a scientist making an experiment: Will she be happy? Will she suffer? Has she made use of others (the unpardonable sin)? Will she be redeemed in the end? I see that he will gradually turn my death from a hard fact into a soft idea; which is not to say he will forget me. Finally, Henry is able to pose his question to Baldwin:

"*Can she die?*"

Baldwin gives a rueful smile. He does not want to pain his friend any more than is necessary; at the same time he must be truthful. At last he gives his consoling reply:

"They sometimes do."

The scene ends with Miss Ward ordering Louisa the housemaid to shut all the windows and doors as the corpse will turn black if exposed to the air.

Notes

As this is a work of fiction I have taken certain liberties with the facts (such as we know them) and shape of Alice's life, such as:

- Henry didn't actually attend William's wedding.
- I have simplified the Jameses' house moves in and around the Boston area; also Alice's moves back and forth in and around London and between London and Leamington.
- Katharine Loring's comings and goings are radically pruned and simplified, as is her own life/work story.
- I have simplified the 'servant question' by reducing Alice's help to one nurse-servant called Wardy. She actually had several different nurses along the way.
- Alice would not have witnessed her father's famous 'vastation'. According to Edel this occurred in 1844 in London four years before Alice's birth.
- Alice refers here to the repealing of the Contagious Diseases Act in 1885 though it didn't occur until '86.
- Henry, William and Alice discuss the Cleveland Street scandal in 1891 when it actually 'broke' in 1889.
- Henry's many trips abroad, including his times spent with Constance Woolson at Bellosguardo, have been telescoped and simplified. The Gautreau scandal he refers to actually took place in '86 but here it occurs later.
- The contents of Alice's Will are all correct except for the last $150 – she did not leave it to Miss Ward but divided it between her Cambridge US dressmaker and gardener.

- There was no Arthur Bowles in Alice's life though she was hypnotized at the end.
- The publication dates of Henry's novels are approximately correct; as are the 'Black' Monday demonstrations, also the deaths of childhood friends Clover & Ellen Adams.
- For those who know the life well, there will no doubt be many more 'errors'. I stand behind Emily Dickinson for protection ('Tell all the truth, but tell it slant.')
- I have used certain expressions and turns of phrase taken from Alice's letters and others' of the James family, but all conversations are invented.
- The question of Alice's health, or lack of it, is an intriguing one from a 21st century perspective. It would be all too easy to assign her a diagnosis of ME, irritable bowel syndrome, hypochondria and/or mental illness of one sort or another. However, the symptoms of endometriosis as variously described on the Internet suggest she might well have suffered from, among others, this hugely painful condition – not clinically recognized during her lifetime. (It was 'discovered' with the use of laparoscopy.)

According to Strouse, Alice's cancer diagnosis should have been that the breast cancer had probably metastasized to the liver, and not vice versa. In modern practice therefore she might well have been advised to undergo surgery, though it's still unlikely that she would have agreed to make the journey back to the States.

Acknowledgements

My warmest thanks to readers Alison Easton and Elizabeth Burns for their time and invaluable feedback; and to the writing group for their patient and supportive listening to Alice as she went through her many drafts.

A special thanks to Richard Barnes for his meticulous and thoughtful editing.

My appreciation also goes to:
Alan Greenwell for his IT wizardry
Amanda Bingley for her book on opium and also computer support
Willem Hackmann for details about the Holtz Electrical Machine
Shanti Cole for hypnotherapy materials
Adrian Cunningham for his book about The Vale of Heath
Jo Alberti for advice about Josephine Butler

A special thanks to Eric, who provided the feline inspiration for Cridge.

Bibliographical Sources

I have drawn heavily on Alice James: A Biography, by Jean Strouse (Houghton Mifflin Co., Boston, 1980); Alice James: her life in letters, edited by Linda Anderson (Thoemmes Press, Bristol, 1996); The Diary of Alice James, edited by Leon Edel (Penguin American Library, 1982); and Henry James: A Life, by Leon Edel (Flamingo, 1996).

Colm Toibin's masterly novel The Master inspired this one – with no pretension to comparison.